What You Do to Me

"Sometimes a book gets everything exactly right—the ultimate love story and a heart-pumping mystery all wrapped up in a *Daisy Jones and the Six* vibe. *What You Do to Me* is storytelling perfection."
—Annabel Monaghan, author of *Nora Goes Off Script* and
Same Time Next Summer

When We Let Go

"An emotional tale of mothers and daughters, loss and acceptance . . . A fully entertaining and at times thought-provoking read from first page to last."
—Midwest Book Review

"*When We Let Go* is chock-full of warmth, heartache, and hope. This moving story explores the bond between a mother and daughter joined by circumstance rather than DNA and is perfect for anyone who's ever had to start over. The story is simply beautiful in its unfolding."
—Tracey Garvis Graves, *New York Times* bestselling author of
Heard It in a Love Song

"With the strong voice and insightful prose for which she has become known, Weinstein builds a powerful and memorable story of homecoming, first love, second chances, the truths that set us free, and the families we find for ourselves."
—Pam Jenoff, *New York Times* bestselling author of
The Woman with the Blue Star

"Every one of Rochelle Weinstein's novels is compulsively readable—but *When We Let Go* takes her enviable talent to the next level. Insightful, exacting, and brimming with empathy, this story of second chances is Weinstein at her very best."
—Camille Pagán, bestselling author of *Everything Must Go*

"Poignant and heartfelt, this one truly shines."
—Allison Winn Scotch, *New York Times* bestselling author of *Cleo McDougal Regrets Nothing*

"Rochelle Weinstein creates compelling, authentic characters I didn't want to let go of in this deeply heartfelt novel about love, loss, and the family ties that can break us—and make us whole. I absolutely loved it."
—Colleen Oakley, *USA Today* bestselling author

"With vivid characters, perfect pacing, and unexpected twists, this story grabbed me from the first page and held my heart until the very end. Rochelle Weinstein has proven herself as a master storyteller."
—Kristy Woodson Harvey, *New York Times* bestselling author of *The Wedding Veil*

This Is Not How It Ends

"Readers who enjoy watching a protagonist's journey to emotional truths will appreciate this story of a woman struggling to determine how hers ends."
—*Booklist*

"The journey to the inevitable ending still manages to take some fascinating turns along the way."
—*Library Journal*

"An immediately and exceptionally engaging novel by a writer with an impressive knack for the kind of narrative storytelling style that rewards the reader with a story that will linger in the mind and memory long after the book is finished."

—Midwest Book Review

"In Rochelle B. Weinstein's latest, *This Is Not How It Ends*, Charlotte Myers is caught between two love stories—neither of which she expected, both of which come with great loss. Poignant and evocative, Weinstein has crafted a story that draws you in and won't let go. Keep the tissues nearby, especially for the heartbreaking yet gratifying conclusion. A wonderfully moving read!"

—Karma Brown, bestselling author of *The Life Lucy Knew*

"A beautifully written tale about love and the unexpected choices we are forced to make. Full of rich description and soulful characters, Weinstein's original story will have you turning pages quickly."

—Elyssa Friedland, author of *The Floating Feldmans*

"Set against the backdrop of the vibrant Florida Keys, *This Is Not How It Ends* beautifully highlights how two single random encounters can influence the trajectory of our lives. This poignant, character-driven tale about love and the choices we make will make you laugh and cry. A thoroughly captivating read."

—Tracey Garvis Graves, *New York Times* bestselling author of
On the Island and *The Girl He Used to Know*

Somebody's Daughter

"Weinstein has found her latest novel debuting at precisely the perfect cultural moment. *Somebody's Daughter* explores the disturbing rise in cyberbullying—and how women (and mothers) cope with unmerited guilt and shame."

—*Entertainment Weekly*

"[A] summer reading must."

—*Aventura Magazine*

"A deftly crafted and thoroughly engaging read from cover to cover, *Somebody's Daughter* showcases author Rochelle B. Weinstein's genuine flair as a novelist for narrative storytelling."

—Midwest Book Review

Where We Fall

"Weinstein has given us a wonderful tale of life and its distractions. She gives us characters that are flawed and yet lovable . . . You will find yourself affected to the very core by the depth of her work."

—*Blogcritics*

The Mourning After

"A heart-wrenching tale of loss, loyalty, and the will to overcome . . . Weinstein explores the difficult facets of grief that are often too painful to recognize, the solipsism of mourning, the selfishness of regret, and the guilt of moving on . . . Ultimately, this novel full of mourning has a large, aching heart full of sympathy and potential, and will keep the reader listening for signs of restored life."

—*Kirkus Reviews*

"Weinstein hooked me with her first novel, and *The Mourning After* has made me a fan for life. She has that rare ability to hook you from chapter one, keep you turning the pages and then continuing to think about the characters long after you have put the book down."

—James Grippando, *New York Times* bestselling author

What We Leave Behind

"Compelling . . . *What We Leave Behind*'s twists and turns generate real tension, and Weinstein renders Jessica's feelings with enough complexity that her ultimate decision carries emotional weight."

—*Kirkus Reviews*

"Each word of *What We Leave Behind* invokes raw emotion as we are brought deeper into the soul of a woman that can be any of us. This moving story will echo strongly with any woman who has had to face love and loss, life and death, and everything in between."

—*Long Island Woman*

WHAT YOU DO TO ME

ALSO BY ROCHELLE B. WEINSTEIN

When We Let Go

This Is Not How It Ends

Somebody's Daughter

Where We Fall

The Mourning After

What We Leave Behind

WHAT YOU DO TO ME

— a Novel —

ROCHELLE B. WEINSTEIN

LAKE UNION

PUBLISHING

Published by Lake Union Publishing, Seattle

www.apub.com

Amazon, the Amazon logo, and Lake Union Publishing are trademarks of Amazon.com, Inc., or its affiliates.

ISBN-13: 9781662508271 (paperback)
ISBN-13: 9781662508264 (digital)

Cover design by Shasti O'Leary-Soudant
Cover image: © Gabriela Alejandra Rosell / ArcAngel; © B. Godart / Shutterstock; © Yvonne Röder / plainpicture

Printed in the United States of America

For Steven, Brandon, and Jordan
My music, my stars, my world
and
For Doug Cohn

Where words fail, music speaks.

—*Hans Christian Andersen*

FOREWORD

When I first wrote "Hey There Delilah," I had no way of knowing the impact it would have and the many fans and listeners it would touch around the world, so it's amazing to see that after all these years it still resonates.

A few years back, we had toyed with the idea of basing a TV series or film around the song, thinking it would be fun to give the fans the fairy-tale ending they were looking for, so when Rochelle approached me with her idea for recreating the players and story, I loved it. One of the biggest compliments you can get as an artist is when someone tells you that the art you made has inspired them to create something beautiful. It's so fun for me to see this reimagining, with "Hey There Delilah" being the inspiration for this love story. What a crazy, incredible, and humbling feeling it is to just watch as the song continues to find new ways of getting into people's hearts.

If you love the song, I think you're really going to love this book.

—Tom Higgenson, Plain White T's

PROLOGUE

Miami Orange Bowl
September 28, 1991

September in Miami was blistery hot, but Sara shivered at the first notes of the familiar song. The crowd around her stilled in near reverence, quieting for what they all came to hear. Though the song had played countless times on the radio, it was magic when performed live in a stadium crammed with adoring fans. Sara knew that every girl imagined the famous lyrics were written for her. They imagined being loved like that. By him.

She watched as he cradled the microphone, remembering his hands on her face. Remembering her name on his lips. "I'm right here if you get lonely." He had once whispered those words in her ear. "Close your eyes. Listen to my voice." Watching him perform, she felt the overwhelming feelings return. She imagined surprising him. Telling him she couldn't live without him, that it didn't matter that they were from different worlds or what she'd have to give up. She loved him. And the way he sang their song, she knew he still loved her too.

As he sang the last words, "what you do to me," he looked her way. And though she knew he couldn't see past the bright lights of the stadium, she thought she saw a look of recognition flicker across his face.

She smiled back.

Until she heard screams. And everything went black.

CHAPTER 1

"LEVON" BY ELTON JOHN

New York
2023

Cecilia James takes her seat in the crowded ballroom, already thinking about the next big story. Tonight's about the past, but she's always been steps ahead. As the magazine's founder introduces her, highlighting Cecilia's notable career at *Rolling Stone*—making her feel a lot older than fifty-three—she replays the conversation she had in the elevator with Chris Martin about his yet-to-be-released single "Lily of My Dreams." Lily is not Dakota Johnson, Martin's girlfriend, and Cecilia's intrigued, making a mental note to contact his people.

This inquisitiveness, the inherent need to understand every song, every story, has made Cecilia *Rolling Stone*'s darling. Decades ago, at twenty-six, she discovered a career gold mine when a chance encounter sent her on a quest to find the woman who inspired "What You Do to Me," the hugely popular love song by the band High Tide. The song topped music charts and broke records, but it was also personal for Cecilia. Desperate to unearth the truth and prove herself, Cecilia broke the story behind the hypnotic track, resulting in one of the magazine's most popular columns, Backstory. And tonight, she's being honored with an award. Not the Lifetime Achievement, something less "your career is nearly over" and more "we're ready for even greater things from you." Tonight, Cecilia will receive the *Rolling Stone* Spotlight Award.

For two decades, Cecilia's Backstory column has revealed the secrets behind songs, brought muses and lovers and strangers together—and at times, pulled them apart. Although "What You Do to Me" didn't have a specific name in its title, it was written for someone, and the magazine ran with the concept. She smiles when some of her favorites are mentioned, glancing at her former boss, Joan. There was the most romantic love triangle of all time, Clapton's "Layla"; the one with the bold twist, the Kinks' "Lola"; and the more obscure but provocative "Rhiannon."

Guests and industry insiders chant Cecilia's name, and the applause carries her toward the stage, where she takes her place behind the podium.

Wearing the sapphire dress she carefully chose for the occasion, she trained her eyes on the teleprompter, narrowing in on a story of passion and purpose. Her story.

Music has occupied Cecilia's life from the day she was born. It has been a salve, providing comfort and the right words when her own fell short. And while her columns entertain readers, they leave her with the most important lessons of all—recognizing the many sides to a single story and how relationships, in their countless forms, are about letting others in, letting go, and trust.

The room is dark except for the spotlight on her face, and though it should warm her, she feels cool and charged. Her words drown out the faint tinkling of silverware, and when the ballroom door opens and closes, the sharp latching sound stops her heart.

He's here. She knows it's him. He always knows when to make his presence felt. He stands, listening, and a calm seeps through Cecilia's skin. She takes her eyes off the teleprompter and glances in his direction. "Who knew the impact that song would have on any of us?" She raises the glass of water hidden in the podium to her lips. "Pardon me. Even I get choked up by my stories." The man doesn't move. He simply waits in the back of the room, a shadowy figure she can't see clearly, but she knows every line on his face, the glint in his eyes. He's the reason she's on this stage. He's the reason she stumbled across that first story, the one that launched her career. She had to lose him to find herself. And now here he is.

She's giving her speech, the audience rapt, but Cecilia is somewhere else. Somewhere with him. Remembering the day when everything changed.

CHAPTER 2

"AMANDA" BY BOSTON

Los Angeles
September 1996

Cecilia James sat in her cubicle in *Rolling Stone*'s Century City office, scrutinizing a column on Tupac Shakur for inaccuracies and grammatical errors. The piece, slated to run on Halloween—more than a month since Shakur had been shot in a drive-by shooting in Las Vegas—was already causing a stir, as the industry grappled with his tragic death.

"My office. Two o'clock," Cecilia's boss and managing editor, Joan, had said when she arrived that morning, tossing Cecilia the crisp pages. The writer, a seasoned professional, didn't need Cecilia's amateurish mark-up, but read-throughs were part of the job. Cecilia didn't mind, not when she worked for the legendary magazine, one that once had allowed only men on its masthead. Granted, she wasn't on the masthead, but she knew that would come.

Cecilia lived obsessively in the orbit of *Rolling Stone*. It was the only magazine her parents had ever subscribed to, and she fixated on the glossy images and mysterious faces. While other children read *Green Eggs and Ham* and *Curious George*, Cecilia flipped through the magazine's pages, sinking into its allure. As soon as she learned to read, she lost herself in the tales of war and politics and rock and roll, and what she couldn't yet understand, her father explained. The quote taped to her desk from an article featuring the Clash's Mick Jones served as a reminder of the magazine's vital influence. Jones said that people needed less fighting and more dancing. If there was ever a time Cecilia understood the power of music, it was then. Music had the ability to change the world.

Cecilia relished the magazine's synergy. Each issue captured the essence and evolution of music and pop culture, a bible of trivia and facts that spoke to generations. The business was known at times for its scandalous reputation, wild parties in glamorous settings that induced celebrity bad behavior. It was easy for anyone to get caught up. Cecilia had snorted a line of cocaine with members of a squeaky-clean boy band, who remained unnamed, and resisted the temptation to fall into bed with a man twice her age—and his sexy girlfriend—because she loved Pete, would never betray Pete. She knew better than to let reck-lessness derail her. Cecilia planned to be a star. Not like her idol Stevie Nicks, but she'd find a way to inhabit Stevie's world. And then she'd write about it.

Cecilia's lucky break came after serving as the magazine's lowly intern—fetching coffee, picking up dry cleaning for photo shoots, booking reservations at Matsuhisa or the Ivy when VIPs swept through town. At the time, she'd been in the office, thumbing through the hot-off-the-presses August 25, 1994, issue with the Rolling Stones on the cover. A. J. Ferrell, a highbrow writer from the New York office, was visiting at the time, and she had landed on one of his articles. She calmly pointed out to A. J. that he had used the phrase "*kick* a gift horse in the mouth" rather than "*look*." A. J. immediately pounced. "That's a misprint. I never said that." The two had a heated exchange, with A. J. so angry his head practically spun off his body, spitting out, "You're a fucking intern, Cecilia. You don't know a thing about writing."

"I know it's *look* a gift horse in the mouth, not *kick*," Cecilia said.

By then, the entire office had paused to take in the scene. No one had ever dared to argue with A. J.—this was a first.

Not only did A. J. back down, but A. J. also never visited the LA office again.

After that, Cecilia was promoted from minimum-wage intern to able-to-quit-her-waitressing-job editorial assistant.

∾

Hunched over her desk, Cecilia finished editing the Shakur article, pitch-perfect with an unbiased take on a complicated life. She admired the writer's skill, how he managed to juxtapose the imperfect man plagued by arrests and gang violence against a gifted musical legend, and she wondered if she would ever capture a story so eloquently. Setting the pages aside, she appraised the mounting stacks on her desk, wondering if she'd ever get through them all. Her Filofax lay open to the date her father had last called. Aunt Denise had died, and Don wanted to talk.

Cecilia had refused to respond, hardly saddened by her aunt's passing. She was Cecilia's last guardian, nothing more than an uninterested babysitter, but Cecilia knew she'd have to face this, face him.

Cecilia whispered the words "let it go," reminding herself she worked for one of the greatest magazines in the world. Over the course of a few years, she'd done shots with Steven Tyler, sang karaoke with the cast of *Friends*, and brought Anthony Kiedis a roll of toilet paper in the company bathroom. She worked at *Rolling* Fucking *Stone*. So why did Don James make her doubt herself?

Cecilia would always remember her first day at the magazine. She had stepped off the bus on Century City's Avenue of the Stars, fresh out of CSU Northridge, with a stack of *Daily Sundial*s in her leather portfolio from when she'd been editor, and she marched toward the sleek building. Dressed in the brand-new Doc Martens she'd saved up for weeks to buy, she'd paired the shoes with a flowery baby-doll dress and black leather jacket, a nod to Courtney Love. It was *Rolling Stone* magazine; she couldn't show up in a boring suit and loafers.

When she neared the building's entrance, she studied her reflection in the exterior glass. Brushing her blond hair off her face, she slipped a wispy strand behind her ear and smeared another coat of MAC Vamp on her lips. The image whispered confidence, though her brown-and-gold-flecked eyes hinted at her youth, a dash of self-doubt. But after she stepped through the lobby and entered the thirty-first-floor reception, Cecilia whispered to herself, "You're Cecilia Fucking James. You were born for great things."

$\sim$

Cecilia Caroline James had entered the world a week past her due date on May 30, 1970, the same week Ray Stevens's "Everything Is Beautiful" captured the number-one spot on the Billboard Hot 100. Cecilia's parents were music aficionados, and they named their screaming infant after the Simon & Garfunkel song—and Neil Diamond's "Sweet Caroline"—stamping her early on with musical greatness.

Theirs was a rhythmic family with tuneful sounds running through their Hollywood Hills home like another child. Music was everywhere at once, scurrying around corners, impossible to evade, playful and seductive. Rock and roll albums crammed the shelves—Joplin, Dylan—and Cecilia and her parents would jam to the words, holding their pretend microphones. Friends packed their incense-filled living room, and it was always Cecilia's parents dancing in the very center, swaying in each other's arms. It was no wonder that Cecilia had equated music with happy endings.

Cecilia's mother, Gloria, was a free spirit, a golden-haired hippie who glided into a room smelling of Charlie in hip-hugging bell-bottom jeans and striped half tops that revealed her flat stomach. She was a kaleidoscope of color. Fleeting. Ethereal. Cecilia would cringe when Gloria and Don reminisced about how she'd been conceived at Woodstock when they were just teenagers, but deep down, she loved the story. Gloria, when she wasn't flitting around their house like a luminous spirit, sometimes gave piano lessons to the neighborhood children while Cecilia's father taught voice, guitar, and music theory and composition at a local university.

Don James was larger than life. Tall and handsome with thick, wavy blond hair. He and Cecilia had a secret language, speaking in verse, sharing their favorite lyrics. And in lieu of bedtime stories, he'd tuck Cecilia into bed strumming songs by James Taylor, Carole King, and Fleetwood Mac. And when she couldn't sleep, they'd stare into the night sky and count the stars.

To Cecilia, music was not just meant to be heard; it was meant to be *felt*. She felt it like a whispery breeze. Tender and carnal, melodies were hands, caressing her skin, tapping on deep-seated emotions. And when her parents went out, she'd invent stories behind the songs, detailing them in her diary, real-life interpretations with imaginary characters. That way, she never felt alone.

Cecilia had once believed her father's voice had magical power. She thought its tenor could chase away evil, that the rhythm could save her from life's curveballs. He was the trusted harmony, able to steady them or coax them out of any moody funk, so when Don left Gloria for Tori, the girl who worked behind the counter at Tower Records on Sunset Boulevard, Cecilia's world turned upside down. From that day forward, music became the paradox in her life. It brought joy, and along with that, a hell of a lot of pain.

~

Slamming the Filofax shut, Cecilia leaned back in her chair. This was what memories did to her. They snuck in, menacing and distracting. She shook off the anger and turned her attention toward the stacks of unfinished work, but all she could think about was whether to call Don back. Cecilia had saved his message on her office voice mail. She didn't need to play it again. She could recite it verbatim. "Cecilia, honey, it's your dad here. Don." Because she needed clarification. "You're twenty-five. Not a child anymore. Which is actually hard for me to believe. Anyway, we should be able to talk like civilized adults . . . about your aunt Denise . . . about . . . well, a lot of things. Please call me. We really need to talk."

Yes, she thought. *We should talk. About the fact that you don't know I'm twenty-fucking-six.*

Don was nothing if not a sore spot in Cecilia's life. One day he was serenading them with "Dream Weaver," and the next he was weaving dreams around Tower Records Tori. Cecilia was thirteen at the time, and Don starting a new family and a new job across town was catastrophic for an already awkward teenager. Their visits were pre-arranged and scheduled, and eventually, the calls dwindled, the cancellations became more and more frequent. Gloria hated Don with a venomous passion that sent vinyl records through the air, cracking them in two. So when Daphne, Cecilia's babysitter, agreed to move in, her presence smoothed out the wrinkles, organized some of the chaos. Cecilia loved Daphne, and the nights when Gloria crashed early or stayed out late, Cecilia would crawl under Daphne's covers and the two would watch TV until Cecilia fell asleep.

And then her mother died. Sixteen-year-old Cecilia was devastated. And furious. All she could think to herself was *How could she? How could Gloria leave me with Don? And that woman?*

Music, once Cecilia's refuge, became a betrayal. In those harrowing weeks following her mother's death, when songs reminded her of happier times, she flung the notes through the air, forbade them from getting close. Music was the reason her family was torn apart, and she shuffled through the days in stubborn silence. Until one of her teachers asked the class the origins of their names. And Cecilia remembered the rock stars who had inspired hers and the musical mark her parents had bestowed upon her.

After her mother died, Cecilia's aunt Denise moved in and Daphne moved out. Aunt Denise was a cold, angry woman who spoke in endless streams of consciousness. Cecilia began turning up the volume of KIIS-FM to drown out Aunt Denise's voice. And the music snuck back in. Soon she returned to writing, spinning words around so they danced like glitter across the page. She wrote of the songs she heard, dreaming up stories behind the lyrics, edgy and hopeful. And slowly, very slowly, music crept into the jagged pieces of her heart. And when she began to soften, welcoming her old friend, she forgave. She forgave the sounds for reminding her of what she'd lost, and she forgave the way music made her feel something others could not. Cecilia James gave herself over to music. Again. And though she missed her mother's laughter and her father's devotion, the hopefulness showed her a way to go on. She couldn't replace Gloria, but with music, she could replace Don—just as he'd replaced her.

Cecilia let out a faint sigh. She had long ago resigned herself to the fact that Don James wasn't the man she had thought him to be. He was not some knight in shining armor. Their relationship hung by a flimsy thread, so delicate it was nearly imperceptible. So Cecilia had invested her energy in her career, planting seeds, developing roots, and learning everything she could about the industry. Managers and publicists described her as an "old musical soul," an "encyclopedia of musical trivia." She was invited to all the best parties, received stacks of promotional CDs and concert tickets to any show she desired, but Don James always had a way of stealing a piece of her sunshine.

Reaching for the framed photo on her desk, she gazed at her mother, who was laughing into the camera, one arm draped around Cecilia's thin shoulder. If her mother were still alive, she would be thrilled for Cecilia. Gloria James celebrated every life event, every milestone. Birthdays were grand occasions involving dancing on tables and glimmery disco balls, but so were rainy days and trips to the mall. She would have shown up at Cecilia's office unannounced in her giant sunglasses, carrying a bouquet of colorful daisies. She would have passed around a joint, talked to anyone within earshot about Woodstock and how Cecilia had been conceived there. Today, that story seemed less cringeworthy. God, how she missed her.

As though sensing the ache, Cecilia's desk phone lit up, the ringing bringing her back to life. She picked up to hear her best friend, April, talking a mile a minute about her son and his bodily functions and wondering if Cecilia had called Don back yet.

"You and my sperm donor of a father should think about joint mommy-and-me classes," Cecilia said, attempting to revive the dying orchid on her desk with a can of day-old Cherry Coke.

"Your sisters are eleven and nine, CeCe."

"Half sisters," she reminded April.

A sound behind Cecilia prompted her to turn, and Dean from office services appeared. She cupped her hand over the phone. "Not now, Dean."

"Special delivery!" He waved the interdepartmental envelope excitedly. "We need your John Hancock."

His emphasis on a certain part of the male anatomy was impossible to miss. "Hold on, April," Cecilia said as Dean sashayed into her crowded space, stopping to greet the wilting orchid. "Poor guy," he whispered loud enough for Cecilia to hear. "She has no heart."

Dropping the delivery on her desk, he pointed, as though she hadn't seen the line waiting for her signature. Scribbling her name, she apologized to April while Dean hovered.

"What do you want? A tip? Scoot."

Dean shuffled away, but not before shaking his butt and blowing a kiss in her direction.

Cecilia tossed the envelope on her ever-growing pile and returned to her friend. That was when the anger burst through. "Why now?" she said. "He had years to make this right." The only response she heard was the sound of a baby suckling. "Sometimes I think I imagined it. Don being Super Dad. Don't you remember—"

"I remember everything," April said, baby Arthur burping in the background. She sighed as she asked the nanny, who surely had a higher salary than Cecilia, to take Arthur upstairs for his nap. "You can't have it both ways, Cecilia. You can't hate the man, blame him for everything that's gone wrong for you, and then expect him to be this upstanding father."

April wasn't wrong, but if Cecilia had a kid, she never would have let the relationship unravel. She would have fought vigorously. No matter the circumstances.

"Talk to him, Cecilia. See what he has to say. Find out the big Aunt Denise news. Maybe he'll surprise you." It was the patronizing tone she used whenever Cecilia ventured down the rabbit hole of father fault. "Aren't you tired of blaming your dad for everything?"

"You can't call him a dad. That's an insult to every decent father."

April ignored her. "Listening to you is exhausting. Nothing changes. You're acting like your mother."

"Don't you dare," Cecilia said.

"You know it's true. All that anger killed her."

Gloria James had died of an aneurysm. Because Don James made her crazy.

"She held on to all that *stuff*, Cecilia, and you know it made her sick."

Cecilia shook her head.

"Pete says—"

Cecilia stopped her. "No, April. Pete's off-limits."

"He's a good one. And you're going to lose him," April said. "You should talk to someone."

April's idea of help was a high-priced therapist Cecilia couldn't afford. Hating Don James was so much more effective. And satisfying.

"You've been together six years." April said it like it was a curse. "I met and married Will in less than that. And had a kid." Then she threw in the doozy. "You're not getting any younger."

Cecilia spit up the metallic-flavored soda she had been sharing with a dying orchid. Flashes of her mother appeared, along with the last thing she'd said to Cecilia that fateful night. She would've preferred Gloria's final words to have been extraordinary, something valuable to one day pass down to her imaginary children, but the words were remarkably unexceptional. They'd been lounging in Gloria's bed, wrapped casually in each other's arms, Gloria yammering about some Joan Collins drama on *Dynasty*, which somehow turned into a memory of Don and Woodstock. Gloria was tired that night. She began reminiscing, fingers stroking Cecilia's hair, going on and on about her ex-husband.

Her eyelids fluttered, and her words began to slur. "We were so in love, CeCe. Best sex I ever had was in Woodstock with your daddy. Then you came along. I was twenty, baby girl. Make babies while you're young." And that was that. Gloria nodded off to sleep. Cecilia covered her with a blanket and kissed her on the forehead, retreating to her room and her music. And sometime during the night, the aneurysm hit, and thirty-six-year-old Gloria never woke up. In the days following her death, Cecilia racked her brain for those final words, and here was April, plucking them out, reminding her that she hadn't granted her mother her dying wish.

April carried on her monologue about how Cecilia would never find someone else like Pete, someone so willing and loyal, warning her that if she missed their upcoming trip, if she pulled some "work-related stunt," if she didn't stop being so *hostile*, he would leave too. When Cecilia didn't respond, April stopped. "Are you listening to me?"

She was not. She'd just torn open the envelope Dean had left her, and she stared at a plane ticket. In her name. To Miami. At the same time, her computer announced, "You've got mail," and she saw Pete's name.

Passports. Today. 3 PM.

"I have to go," she said to April, quickly ending the call.

The ticket could mean only one thing, and she felt a tingling in her chest. It was finally happening. *Rolling Stone* was sending Cecilia Caroline James on her first official assignment. This was why Joan had called today's meeting. Cecilia bristled with excitement. But then another email appeared.

This is really happening.

The passport agency. *Shit.* She glanced at the time; her meeting with Joan was at two. On a normal day, she could cancel the appointment or postpone, but not today, not now. Pete would be apoplectic. Their trip was fast approaching, and skipping the renewal of their passports was not an option.

The image of Pete's worried face prompted a response, and she typed on the keyboard:

I'll be there.

She wasn't entirely sure how. But she would try.

CHAPTER 3

"FANNY (BE TENDER WITH MY LOVE)" BY THE BEE GEES

Los Angeles
September 1996

On the desk next to the photo of Cecilia and her mother sat a framed black-and-white shot of Cecilia with Pete. It was taken in 1992, a year or so after they'd officially begun dating, when Pete had been photographing the riots in Downtown LA for *LIFE* magazine. Cecilia insisted on joining—she could be pigheaded—and when they encountered a violent uprising of looters and protesters, Pete cradled Cecilia in his arms, dropping his treasured Nikon as he led her to safety. A photographer from the Associated Press snapped the chaos, capturing Pete and Cecilia in this intimate, vulnerable moment, and the photo appeared everywhere, eventually landing in *LIFE* magazine.

Cecilia lifted the frame off her desk, studying Pete's eyes, the way they homed in on her face. She remembered how tightly he held her, how safe she felt in his arms. In the background, violence inched closer, blurry, but their figures were clear and sharp.

That night he told her for the first time that he loved her.

Well, something like that.

Theirs wasn't a conventional relationship. Sometimes they went weeks without seeing one another. He'd be across the globe, away on assignment, while she darted around Los Angeles or traveled with Joan to the magazine's New York office. They had figured out a rhythm, modifying schedules for stories and spreads, working around deadlines, and carving out time when their bodies craved the connection. They understood each other's commitments, how her work meant crazy hours and how he might miss one of her events when he needed to shoot a story in some remote location.

But the night of the riots, their love rippled beneath their skin, their earlier fear so palpable, there was nothing left for them to say but that. She'd said it first. So unlike her. They'd just showered together, washing off the remnants of the afternoon. He'd slipped inside her while kissing the back of her neck. They were nothing if not an interesting match. His language was pictures and hers was lyrics and song. When he later poured her a glass of wine that she gulped down too fast, she switched on the stereo, and he powered up the television. And their worlds collided.

There, spread across the KTLA screen, was their picture, and coming from the stereo speakers was High Tide crooning "What You Do to Me," their famous song.

Cecilia gazed at their moment captured in time, reliving the feel of his arms around her on the street earlier that afternoon. And for one millisecond she gave in to the emotion, gave in to being comforted and sustained. Wholly complete. "I think I love you," she blurted out.

He laughed.

"I'm serious."

He moved in closer, his face unreadable. "You're serious?"

"Yes."

"You're never serious."

She took another step so they stared into each other's eyes. "Pete . . . I love you."

And he didn't wait long to say it back. "Good. I love you too."

He whispered in her ear, the words playing in the background, "Do you see what you do to me?" It was the first time she'd heard Pete use lyrics to express how he felt. That and his breath against her neck sent a trail of tiny bumps down her skin, and she collapsed against him, letting him wrap around her like he had in the picture.

After this tender rite of passage, Cecilia terminated the lease on her apartment, and they officially moved in together. She thought she was being pragmatic. She had never learned to drive, and because Pete's Brentwood apartment was closer to the office than her place in Santa Monica, the move saved her money on public transportation. It would be okay. He'd shoot pictures and she'd write articles, and together they'd synthesize a masterpiece. She told herself the relationship didn't have to change, despite being framed by a verse from a song. And a photo. Though it nagged at her whether they could live up to the feeling captured in both.

Cecilia loved thinking back to those first nights when she'd moved into his apartment and they'd lain on their sides, staring into each other's eyes after hot, urgent sex. And how much better Chinese food tasted when he was back from a shoot and feeding her dumplings with chopsticks. They played heated games of backgammon and always did the *New York Times* crossword puzzle together. And when they'd experienced their first earthquake in the middle of the night, they'd huddled in the doorframe of their bedroom, riding out the tremors together.

Lately, though, she had felt a different shift, nothing seismic, but as her job responsibilities grew, she wasn't as accessible. Last week, she had missed a planned dinner at their favorite restaurant, and when she got home, he tried telling her about his day and she fell asleep midstream, exhausted. She felt the subtle aftershocks. Pete, typically understanding, seemed agitated, just enough for her to notice. Pete wanted more. And this tiny red flag conflated with her reluctance to get in touch with Don. Her father was trying, but at times she thought it might be easier if she didn't hear from him at all.

So yes, maybe she had been a little hostile.

≈

At precisely two o'clock Cecilia logged out of her AOL account and barreled through Joan Kadushin's door. "You're supposed to knock," Joan shrieked. Which explained finding Ken, a certain someone's manager, and Cecilia's boss on the cranberry-colored couch in the throes of something that required him to button his jeans and Joan to zip up the back of her dress.

"You said you'd start locking the door," Cecilia reminded them, unflustered by the proclivities of the two.

"Hey, Cecilia." Ken waved, gathering what was left of their lunch and tossing it in the nearby trash. "Your timing's always impeccable." This wasn't the first time she'd caught her boss and Ken in the act. The last time was so graphic, she was certain she'd have to take Joan to the ER, an image of the woman she'd never unsee.

"Always great to see you, Ken," Cecilia said. "Did you get that wart on your ass removed?"

The bald man's cheeks flushed. "It's a tattoo, Cecilia."

"I know a wart on a hairy ass when I see one." A laugh escaped. "Though it did resemble Tarzan peeking through bushes."

Joan slid her feet into her four-inch heels. Her dress was the color of marigolds, a sharp contrast to her dark hair and skin. "Don't bother responding, Ken. She hasn't gotten laid in weeks."

Cecilia couldn't imagine how Joan knew this, but she wasn't wrong. Three weeks. That had been the night Pete surprised her with tickets for the Caribbean getaway. Since then, their schedules had been off, both of them working long, grueling hours after which they collapsed into bed, barely able to speak.

Ken grabbed Joan by the waist and planted a kiss on her mouth. And as he slid past Cecilia, he reminded Joan of their dinner plans that evening before disappearing.

"Why do you always start with him?" Joan asked, lighting a cigarette and taking a seat in her bright-orange leather chair.

When Cecilia had first interviewed with Joan, she was rendered speechless by the office high above Century City with its sweeping views of the snow-capped mountains to the north spanning east to Downtown LA. Platinum albums crowded the walls. She took in the signed art gifted by George Harrison and Eddie Van Halen, the antique phonograph Joan still used from time to time, and the dozens of photographs of a younger, kinder Joan with label heads Clive Davis and Ahmet Ertegun.

"Because he's married," Cecilia said, dropping the unmarked Tupac piece on Joan's desk. "Four kids, Joan. And grandkids. You think they'd appreciate your presence in their lives?"

Her boss inhaled the smoke, which accentuated the fine lines around her mouth, before tapping the ash into the gold-plated ashtray with Interscope Records' logo. "Your father really did a number on you," she said. Cecilia didn't argue, and she liked that her boss knew where she'd come from.

Cecilia had long ago established herself as the assistant to all, the darling with the intrinsic connections to rock and roll and a willingness to learn. There were only a handful of staff in the West Coast office, writers and advertising sales execs mostly, while New York City housed the executive offices, operations, and production. She was the first to show up in the mornings and the last to leave. Her brain burst with music-related facts, and she had her finger on the pulse of all the industry gossip.

"David Lee Roth's about to announce he's leaving Van Halen," Cecilia relayed to Joan.

"Anyone watching the VMAs saw their very public disagreement," her boss replied, unimpressed.

"I know who they're replacing him with."

Joan sat upright.

"Gary Cherone."

"Interesting." Joan exhaled, the smoke hitting Cecilia's face.

Fanning the air, Cecilia counted on the next tidbit to hook her.

"My friend at Epic said Eddie Vedder's ready to take interviews again. If we move quickly, we can get to him first."

Joan didn't respond. Cigarette ash landed on her desk, and it looked like she was thinking about who she would assign the piece to. When she thanked Cecilia for bringing it to her attention, Cecilia couldn't mask her disappointment.

"Don't with the sad eyes," Joan said. "I'm watching you, and just because I may make poor relationship decisions doesn't mean my professional instincts aren't intact. The artists like having you around, and so do their handlers. After the Alanis piece, you've got your first assignment. All yours. Congratulations."

Cecilia would have liked to jump out of her chair and squeeze Joan, but she restrained herself, swallowing the affection. She sat there beaming instead.

"Dean dropped off the ticket?"

"He did."

Joan shifted her glasses to the tip of her long nose and rifled through a folder. "When I heard you were going to be in Miami for your sexy getaway, this piece came down the pipe. You don't mind meeting Pete at the port? You'll fly in a day earlier?"

Cecilia hadn't noticed the date on the ticket, and she tensed. Pete would think this was some ploy, some "work-related stunt" as April had called it. She swallowed and told herself it would be okay. She'd figure it out. He'd understand, he had to, this was a huge career move.

"There's a band playing down there," Joan said. "The Hails. You remember my friend Lisa, the CBS entertainment reporter? Her son's in the band. I promised her a spread. Moreover, they're talented."

"I've heard of them," Cecilia said. "They've been likened to Radiohead."

"They're performing Saturday night at the Orange Bowl." Joan took another puff of the cigarette. "Opening for Oasis. The second opener, but still an opener. You'll have plenty of time to do the interview, get a few shots, and make it to the ship to meet Pete on Sunday."

Cecilia nodded, excited to tell Pete the news. Not as excited for his reaction to flying separately.

"You've really proven yourself, Cecilia." Was that emotion in her boss's normally icy tone? Joan rarely succumbed to warm displays. "I see a lot of myself in you. And while concerning, it's satisfying as all hell that I hired you and not Carly What's-Her-Name."

They collectively laughed. Carly was the niece of someone high up on the masthead.

"So you're going to go to Florida and do what you do best."

Cecilia nodded in agreement. "Capture the story."

And Joan responded, "Capture the magic."

Joan cleared her throat, catching the display of rare affection toward her protégé. "That's all settled, yes?"

Cecilia had little time to let it sink in. Checking the display on the Moonman clock from last year's MTV Video Music Awards, she saw she had thirty minutes to be at the passport agency.

Joan snuffed out the cigarette and clasped her fingers on the desk, signaling the conversation was over.

CHAPTER 4

"MELISSA" BY THE ALLMAN BROTHERS BAND

Los Angeles
September 1996

Cecilia would have raced down the hallway toward her desk, but she walked casually, head held high, holding the pleasure back. These were the times when she ached for Gloria while bitterly resenting her father. Gloria should have been there to share the news with. Gloria would have burst with pride, organized a celebration with champagne and confetti. That Don was alive and Gloria wasn't was like salt in an old wound. The man didn't deserve to share in her success.

Theirs wasn't always a fraught relationship. Before Tori, Don was a loving, doting father, and Cecilia was the apple of his eye. Their closeness was bound by song and nurtured in melody. But when Don left, taking Cecilia's faith and trust with him, her loyalty remained with her broken mother. Gone was the man who had lavished his daughter with love and attention, the creator of sunshine and stars. The way Gloria described it, he was none of those things, just a selfish, narcissistic prick. Gloria's stories painted over Cecilia's happy memories and highlighted

Don's absence. Cecilia had only her mother's word to go by. She worshipped Gloria and hated seeing her so stricken and distressed. On the rare occasions Don came around to take her for the night or the weekend, Cecilia feigned a stomachache, a headache, anything to avoid upsetting her mother.

And then Gloria died.

And just as Cecilia was preparing to move in with Don and his new family, Don accepted a three-year contract to teach in San Diego, expecting Cecilia to join them. At sixteen, Cecilia had opinions—strong, dramatic opinions about being uprooted from her home, her school, and her best friend, April. She considered being forced to live with Don and Tori and the siblings she barely knew a form of child abuse. She begged to stay in her house with Daphne. Battles ensued.

Eventually they reached a compromise, an arrangement that provided security and familial continuity. And that's how Gloria's sister, Cecilia's aunt Denise, came to live with her. By the time Cecilia graduated from high school two years later and moved into the dorms at CSU Northridge, Don had fulfilled his contract and returned to Los Angeles and a prestigious position at USC. Aunt Denise went back to her cave.

Back at her desk, collecting her things, Cecilia stole another glance at the picture of her mother. She slung her bag over her shoulder and headed toward the elevator, wishing she could call her, wondering what crazy exploit Gloria would take her on. Instead, she pressed the button for the lobby, remembering how she had called Don's office when she'd been promoted.

"Cecilia! It's great to hear from you." Then he had shouted, "Girls, quiet. It's your sister Cecilia," adding unapologetically, "It's bring-your-daughter-to-work day. Everything okay?"

The girls squealed in the background. That's how it had been since he'd left, Cecilia vying for her father's attention, having to remind him he had three daughters, not two.

"Yeah." And then she had stopped herself. It was a stupid idea to call him. She should've definitely hung up. But she didn't. "I got promoted." And she held on to the delight she'd heard in his voice when he said, "I'm proud of you, kid."

"I'm just an assistant," she'd said, keeping it to herself that she still hadn't made it onto the masthead.

"You were meant for great things, Cecilia James," he reminded her.

She was. And she let in a small sliver of pride.

"Maybe we can see you. Get together and celebrate?"

And when she didn't answer right away, he said, "Shoot. I've gotta go, sweetheart. Class starts in a minute." The girls chattered cheerfully in the background, "Daddy . . . Daddy," reminding her of what she'd lost. She had set the phone down, stomach turning, the earlier praise all but vanished in the air.

～

A short taxi ride later, Cecilia stood in front of the passport building, waiting for Pete. Shaking off the memories of Don, she stared down at her T-shirt with "Blondie" emblazoned across the front, wondering if the band's name would make it onto her passport photo. When she looked up, she spotted her boyfriend crossing Wilshire in her direction. She liked watching him. At thirty-two, he was fit and youthful, dressed in cargo shorts and a black T-shirt, and she admired the way he smiled at strangers on the street as though they were his friends. When he spotted her, his smile widened, and as he neared, he reached out to pull her close.

"Some hot girl was just checking me out, and I was wondering how I was going to explain to my girlfriend that I had to miss our date at the passport agency."

"Ironic," she said, offering him her cheek. "The same thing just happened to me with some hot guy."

They walked hand in hand through the glass doors.

"You have everything?" he asked.

She heard him, but her mind was elsewhere, swirling around the new story she'd been assigned. The gears in her brain had been activated, rotating and turning, and she couldn't make them stop.

His face slackened. "We talked about this, CeCe. Old passport. Application. You had to fill it out. You did that, right?"

Her brain came to a screeching halt. She was pretty sure she packed the documents in her bag.

"Please tell me I didn't just rearrange my whole day for you to mess this up."

His cheeks paled, and his arms dropped down by his sides. She dug inside her bag, praying for a glimpse of the file, and when she found it, she handed him the requisite paperwork. The color returned to his face.

"I told you I was in," she said. "All in."

He told her that wasn't funny, even though that hadn't been her intention.

"You're cute when you get all worried," she said. And to make up for it, she made a mental note to initiate sex later that night.

∼

After a wait that seemed endless, the woman behind the counter called their names, and soon she read their applications and marked up their forms.

"Grand Cayman. Cozumel. Ocho Rios." Her eyebrows raised with interest. "Newlyweds?"

"Not yet," Pete replied.

The awkward silence that followed was louder than the clicking of the woman's pen. The word *marriage* appeared like a neon sign. It wasn't the first time. The subject had come up—indirectly—as Pete had recently cut back on *LIFE* assignments, opting to be closer to home. To her. As an intern, and then an assistant, Cecilia didn't have that kind of flexibility, and they'd had a few delicate conversations about commitment and the lingering effects of her father's abandonment. But as they renewed their passports to travel to some of the most romantic islands in the Caribbean, Cecilia wondered if he planned to propose. And as she let this idea simmer, her chest began to tighten.

In the elevator he asked, "You okay?"

"I'm fine."

He needed to get back to work, and she smiled up at him, brushed his cheek with her hand. "I really love you, Pete."

"Why does that sound like an apology?"

She wanted to tell him her news. She'd thought of nothing else the last hour—that and now a proposal—because he'd be happy for her. Her name on her first article. Cecilia Caroline James. She'd already decided she'd include her middle name. *Sweet Caroline.* And even though the change in plans might cause a tiny hiccup in their travel schedule, she'd be on the ship, in the ocean view suite they'd upgraded to. But something held her back, and they both returned to their offices, and later, he was inside her, and they moved in rhythm, and it felt good, really good, and she wished they could stay that way forever.

He settled beside her, and she coiled around him.

"I have to meet you in Miami," she finally said.

He had been holding her close, one hand draped along her shoulder, the other playing with her hair, but then his fingers froze.

She untangled herself from his stiff arm, propping herself up so she could look at him. "Joan promoted me today, Pete. My first feature story." Well, technically Joan hadn't mentioned a promotion, but it was assumed. "It's just a day earlier, but this is huge news!"

She smiled brightly, but his expression was mixed.

"That's terrific!" he finally said.

"Right?! I've been waiting for this for three years. Three years of tagging along on everyone else's interviews, three years of fact-checking and proofing pieces that weren't mine. I've been waiting for this my entire life."

He listened, his eyes following her lips. "I'm proud of you, C. And I'm not surprised."

And then he kissed her.

"That didn't feel very sexy," she said.

"I'm actually unbelievably happy for you."

"You seem unbelievably quiet."

Their legs touched, though the rest of them felt far apart. "This trip," she began, "it's important." And she wiped the hair that fell in his eyes, thinking she could wipe away his fear. "I'll be there!"

"Are you sure? Because lately it feels like you're off somewhere." He waited. "And you've been, how do I put this . . . ?"

"Hostile." She sat up, cross-legged on the bed, her sleep shirt draped across her lap.

"I would've called it aloof. Distant."

"Aunt Denise died."

"You couldn't stand her."

"Fine. But this thing with my dad. You don't know how it is." She didn't want to rehash it with him. She started chipping at the black polish on her toenails instead.

When she gazed up, his beautiful eyes held on to hers. They sucked her in and made her weak. "I'll meet you at the port, Pete. It's not a big deal. Other than this is my first byline!"

He smiled, and she could tell it was sincere. He was thinking. His nose twitched when he was in thought. Her finger reached for the tip, and he brushed it away, the smile slowly fading.

"You know I'm happy for you. But you can't blame me for being a tiny bit worried."

"Don't be."

"Nobody knows you like I do, Cecilia. It's all over your face. These stories . . . I know what they mean to you, what they do to you, how you get caught up, lose track of time . . ."

"I'm not going to mess this up. I promise."

A question filled his eyes and his voice lowered. "Sounds like you're trying to convince yourself."

She turned toward the wall, studying the pale gray, wondering if what he was saying was true.

"You know I love this about you," he said, coming up behind her, his breath on her neck. "I love how you chase the heart of a story, how it grabs hold of you."

Now it was *her* actual story.

She turned to face him, the pull unmistakable, the love all there.

Neither of them brought it up, but their last attempt at a trip sat between them. They were supposed to meet friends at Big Bear Lake, which happened to coincide with music's biggest night of the year, the Grammys. It wasn't Cecilia's fault that two of her coworkers fell sick and they needed all hands on deck. Cecilia promised Pete she'd meet up with him, hitch a ride north as soon as she could, but the Grammys lasted for days—parties and interviews and brunches and hangovers. She never did make it to Big Bear Lake, but it was a week she would never forget. And it took him almost as long to forgive her.

He pulled her toward him. "Having you on that plane with me means no escape hatch. No award show. No artist in need of a diaper."

"Fly down earlier with me. We can have hotel sex on *Rolling Stone*'s dime."

"Can't. I have a big meeting that day. I would. If I could."

And she pulled him back on top of her. "And I'd fly out with you. If I could."

"I love you, Cecilia."

The way he said it, her stomach did a flip.

"I told you I'll be there." She took his face in her hands. "You have nothing to worry about except margaritas and tan lines."

The visual momentarily broke the tension.

Staring into his eyes, she saw forever, and it excited and terrified her. What if he left her the way Don had left Gloria?

"I love you too," she said. And she pointed at the freckle under his eye. "And I love him." And then she pointed at his chest. "And I love what's under there." And before he could respond, she slipped her hand under the covers, feeling his excitement. "And this cute guy."

His hand found hers and squeezed. "Tell me why you're here."

She pulled back. "Like here? Right now?"

"In this relationship." And when she sat there, wondering if this was a rhetorical question, he pressed. "With me."

She had never been very good at layered conversations. She scooted toward the stack of CDs, knowing exactly the song she was looking for. Music answered questions, solved riddles, but he stopped her, forcing her to look at him. "Not a song, Cecilia. You. Tell me in your words why you're here."

She fumbled with the answer and drew a blank. It hadn't been a choice. They had a familiar rhythm. They met at a bar. They clicked. Effortless. Wasn't that the way relationships were supposed to be? After a few minutes of awkward silence, when she was certain she could hear the faint beating of his heart, she formed a response. "Maybe I just don't know who I am without you."

This seemed to appease him. His dark eyes softened. She could fall inside their warm brown.

"I know you didn't come up with that yourself."

She smiled at him coyly.

"That's that George Harris song you've been singing all week."

"Harrison," she corrected him, pushing him down on the bed and climbing on top of him, paraphrasing the words. "What is life without you, Peter Shepard? It's nothing."

CHAPTER 5

"JACK & DIANE" BY JOHN MELLENCAMP

Miami
September 1996

Cecilia touched down in Miami after a near-sleepless flight, giving credence to the term *red-eye*. Her long legs were twisted miserably in the tiny space they called legroom, babies cried, and the passenger behind her kept knocking into her headrest. She woke with a terrible kink in her neck from using the window as a pillow, and she couldn't find her Walkman.

The flight attendant welcomed them to Miami. "The local time is 5:48 a.m. and the temperature is 77 degrees."

She thought back to Pete dropping her off at the airport. He had kissed her on the forehead, whispering, "TTM."

"To the moon," she replied.

And when she was just about to slip through the automatic doors, he snuck up beside her to remind her just how happy he was for her, how his earlier concern had waned, and how she was going to nail this piece and all the ones that followed. They held each other a little longer, and Cecilia felt their shared excitement guide her through the airport doors.

That happiness quickly faded away as one of the wheels on her oversized suitcase fell off, and then she was wedged between two people at the gate who were arguing over her head in a language she couldn't decipher. It reminded her of the call she'd received from her stepmother just minutes before leaving the apartment.

Cecilia and Tori seldomly spoke. Most communication went through Don, and even those conversations were at a minimum. Cecilia never needed a *stepmother*. Even though Tori entered their lives when Cecilia was young, she had Gloria back then, a fully capable parent, and when Gloria died, Cecilia didn't need a new *mommy*, especially one closer to her age than her father's. Not that Tori had ever really tried. And Cecilia understood Tori's lack of interest in her. It trickled down from the top, and since her father had turned into a limited, absent dad, Tori followed suit. After Don, Cecilia blamed Tori for everything.

Cecilia and Pete were just about to leave the apartment for the airport when the home phone rang, the caller ID flashing *Don & Tori James*. Because her father rarely called, Cecilia imagined some dreadful scenario. But it was Tori. And she was calling about Don's birthday. "He's turning forty-six, CeCe." Cecilia hated when Tori called her that. "I'm planning a surprise party that night."

The only surprise worth witnessing would be watching Tori disappear, and Cecilia could barely contain the expletives burning her tongue. "I can't talk right now," she said, biting the bitterness back and explaining that she was on her way to the airport, throwing in a shameless brag about the story she was working on.

"Just write down the date," Tori said. "We're celebrating at his favorite restaurant."

"I don't need to write it down, Tori. I know his birthday."

Cecilia's annoyance felt combustible as she remembered all the birthdays she had spent without Don. The hypocrisy of these two.

Tori's voice became flat and whispery. "It would really mean a lot to him if you were there."

Cecilia knew she had to hang up or she would say something she would regret, and she had promised herself she would practice self-control, *not engage.* "Noted, Tori." And she hung up.

After the plane landed in Miami, as Cecilia ran her fingers along the dirty carpet in search of her Walkman, she kicked herself for letting the phone call dampen her spirits. This should be the most exciting time in her life, and all she felt was irritation. She thought about calling April—the woman never slept—but April wouldn't appreciate another diatribe on Tori and Don's faults. Besides, he'd managed to reach out on this year's birthday. And the year before. But was that enough to offset the years he'd forgotten? The birthdays she hadn't heard from him at all? She wished she could let it go. She wished she were wired differently, that she could just let things roll off her back like Pete did. But she couldn't. Not when it came to Don James.

~

With her belongings deposited at a nearby hotel, Cecilia, refreshed and recharged, made her way to the iconic Miami Orange Bowl stadium. Upon her arrival, she was introduced to the Hails, five twenty-somethings whose career was not-so-quietly taking off. Cecilia had already done her homework. She knew that Franco, Zach, and Andre formed the Miami band when they were twelve, playing together through high school. When they entered the University of Florida, they expanded the group to include Robbie and Dylan. Five young personalities meant creative differences and honing a musical identity, so those first few years, the band experimented with different sounds and cross-blending genres. What emerged was a rock band with a fresh alternative voice and a newly inked deal with Island Records. *Billboard* magazine called the band "edgy, a riveting blend of up-tempo, bouncy tracks with soulful, raw acoustics."

Friendly and outspoken, the guys talked over one another. Cecilia snapped candids, capturing them in their natural element with a camera she'd borrowed from Pete. Andre started flirting with her immediately, while Robbie told the story of how the band came to be. But Cecilia wanted something original for the feature, something only she could unearth. Pausing for sound checks and rehearsals, she observed their interactions, the way they communicated with their guitars, bantered through the clanging of drums. The synergy reflected the camaraderie of the most cohesive bands.

While they were rehearsing a song titled "Broken Vows," Cecilia heard a commotion behind her. All eyes trained on a beautiful blond, hobbling barefoot, heels in hand. Abruptly, the music stopped. Dylan jumped off the stage, motioning for the girl to follow. They made their way to a row of seats, where Cecilia could make out their silhouettes. They stood close together, their faces almost touching.

Andre popped up by Cecilia's side. "She's the impetus behind 'Broken Vows.'"

Cecilia added that to her notes. She loved deep diving into what made a song a story. The words always had some hidden meaning. "What happened between them?"

"What hasn't happened? We could write six albums on their drama."

"Sounds complicated," she said.

Andre had olive skin, a goatee, and friendly brown eyes. When he asked her if she wanted to grab a drink after the show, she was caught off guard and laughed.

"Ouch," he said.

"You think being a dreamy musician means women fall at your feet?"

"Actually, yes." He smiled, revealing pearly white teeth. "Tomorrow?" he asked. "We have a sneak peek of some not-yet-released material. It's an exclusive gig at Tobacco Road. No other press. You should come."

Flattered, she replied to this guy who was probably a few years younger than her, "I'm leaving tomorrow on a cruise. With my boyfriend."

He winked. "Subtle. Nice. You're cute, Cecilia James. Especially those freckles. Don't think I can't see them."

This Andre suddenly seemed a lot older.

"We're starting at twelve thirty. Bring what's-his-name." And then he paused. "We're going to be superstars, Miss James. Tomorrow just might change your life."

~

Hours later, goosebumps speckled Cecilia's arms as she stood in the audience. A packed crowd roared after the Hails completed their opening set. The stadium vibrated as the guests stomped their feet against the fiberglass bleachers, the echoes spreading toward the Atlantic beaches. Lighters flared in the air as fans hollered into the night sky. The Hails captured their hometown crowd and fans begged for more. Cecilia knew she had just witnessed musical greatness, and she began calculating in her mind how she could get to Tobacco Road tomorrow and still make it to the port on time. If she nabbed the exclusive for their new single, she'd have something substantive none of the other trades had.

Back at the hotel later that night, Cecilia showered off the sweat and cigarette stench and located her cruise documents. According to the itinerary, the ship departed at four. With the showcase beginning at twelve thirty, she had ample time before boarding, and just to be sure, she called down to the front desk to ask them how much time she should give herself. She also enquired about a reliable taxi service.

Pete called the hotel before leaving for LAX, and she curled in bed with her cell phone nestled to her ear. "I'm glad we're doing this," he said.

"Me too."

"A week alone with you is going to be pure bliss."

"Us and a couple thousand other people."

"We'll make it our own."

"We will, won't we?"

"I love you, CeCe."

She told him she loved him too, slipping in that she had one more meeting tomorrow and then she'd be there.

"As long as you're on that ship, that's all that matters," he said.

And she promised she would be.

CHAPTER 6

"TOM SAWYER" BY RUSH

Miami
September 1996

In the morning, Cecilia looked over her list. She had crafted a timeline specifying when to leave for Tobacco Road and when to call for the cab to take her to the port. She'd accounted for traffic conditions and any other unforeseen circumstances with enough wiggle room to make it to the ship by four. She couldn't wait to share this bonus exclusive with Joan.

Cecilia exuded confidence as she got in the cab. The heat and humidity didn't bother her, not when there were gorgeous palm trees waving in the breeze. As they made their way through the heavily trafficked streets of Miami, she applauded her ability to multitask. She heard Joan's voice flit through her ear: *Everything good about Miami is better in LA, and everything bad about Miami is worse in LA.* So far, Miami had been shiny and welcoming. And in a few short hours she'd be floating on the ocean with Pete. She couldn't wait.

Tobacco Road sat in Downtown Miami off Brickell Avenue, a quaint neighborhood where canopies of thick trees surrounded some of Miami's tallest buildings. A green awning adorned the unremarkable turquoise building, its bold red-and-black letters spelling out the name of the iconic bar. Considered the oldest in the city, the watering hole opened in 1912 and had a history of scandal and boozy corruption, but it was its second-floor private den that made it a local hot spot for live music.

The elderly driver who wore a fedora and spoke to her in Spanish helped her with her bag. When she shook her head, not comprehending, he tried again. "I come to many show. Meet my first wife." Then he smiled. *"Me metí en muchos problemas aquí."* When she shook her head again, he pointed at the building with a glint in his eyes. "Trouble." That, she understood.

Cecilia had heard that a bakery was the front for the speakeasy during Prohibition and that gambling had gone on behind the doors with access to drugs and private after-hours parties. The history fascinated her, much as the history of the Whisky a Go Go or the Roxy in LA did. Every musical venue had its secrets, and after she thanked the man, she stepped through the entryway and let the mystery envelop her.

As promised, the Hails performed at twelve thirty. Cecilia mingled with a handful of guests—family, managers, and collaborators—and even joined them in downing shots of tequila. She felt jittery, maybe a wee bit drunk, but it could have been the music. The new track was something special, a culmination of the band's evolution, their maturing range and vocals. The Hails had come into their own, and they were remarkably talented. Cecilia predicted the song would go big, maybe even hit the Billboard Top 10. Andre smiled at her with those perfect white teeth, teasing her about how he knew she'd show up. "Now to get you to stay longer."

"Impossible," she answered with a smile as the tequila flooded her bloodstream, and she lobbed a few more questions before calling a cab:

CJ: How does it feel knowing you nailed this song?

Robbie: Gratifying.

Franco: It feels good. Like I want to get this thing out yesterday.

CJ: What made this track different for you guys?

Dylan: I think being back in Miami together, our hometown, our roots. College had a lot of distractions. Now we're older, more focused.

Andre: I'm ready to pay off my student loans.

Zach: Sometimes you just feel it, you know. All the parts just work. We're in sync. And this song has a lot of personal meaning for us.

Robbie: Yeah. This was a tough one.

Dylan: We made it a little more upbeat than our usual tempo.

Andre: It's called "Summer" because Summer sang with us in college. (Pauses.) We lost her. The song's for her.

CJ: I'm sorry.

Andre: Yeah, she passed away. She was like the sun. She rose . . . and then she fell.

CJ: I would've never guessed it was about a person, but the song has such soul. You've captured her essence.

Dylan: Sometimes the success of a song is just that, you know, the right tune, the right lyrics, the right muse. You feel it inside. It writes itself. Like, there's no other way to explain it.

~

It was close to two o'clock when Cecilia ordered a taxi. She was humming along to "Summer," the catchy tune stuck in her head, watching the guys horse around at the bar. Wishing to record the moment, the boys, and the pure satisfaction brightening their smiles, she reached inside her bag for her camera. She fumbled around, but it wasn't there. The alcohol heightened her anxiety as she tried to backtrack and recall the last time she had it. She headed in the direction of her suitcase, Andre following behind her. She was sure she hadn't put the camera there, but she unzipped it anyway. Folded at the top was her red silk camisole. Its black lace trim caught Andre's eye. He picked it up, but she snagged it out of his hand. "Have you seen my camera?"

He shook his head, eyes on the silky fabric.

She remembered having it at the stadium the day before and setting it down. She didn't remember putting it in her bag.

"Shit."

She checked her watch. *Breathe, Cecilia. This is why you padded your timeline.* But any detour would eat into her schedule. She swatted away the ominous premonition. *It's going to be okay,* she repeated to herself. She'd done the calculations. She would make it on time.

She checked her bag a second and third time, the anxiety creeping in. The camera wasn't in there. Andre eyed her, eyed her lingerie. "Damn, that dude is one lucky guy."

His compliment was nice, but she didn't have time for senseless flirting.

Someone shouted, "Anyone call for a taxi?" and she grabbed her things, waved to the guys, and raced outside.

Cecilia checked her watch again, as though she'd see something different, as though time wouldn't be moving forward. Traffic was at a standstill, and she explained to the driver, who spoke less English than the last driver, that she needed to make a stop at the Orange Bowl.

"Naranja," she said, dipping into her limited cache of the language. *"Bola.* Bowl." And she gestured with her hands, a makeshift bowl, but he misunderstood and took her to a nearby sporting goods shop, where an Alonzo Mourning mannequin held an orange basketball in the window. Cecilia spotted a woman in the parking lot speaking to her young daughter, and Cecilia rolled down her window, asking for help. The woman translated to the driver, and soon Cecilia was on her way to the port by way of the Orange Bowl.

Upon arriving at the stadium, Cecilia used her best broken Spanish to ask the driver to wait for her. *"Uno minuto,"* she said, holding up her pointer finger as she exited the cab and ran toward the stadium. But one minute turned into five, and then longer, when the security personnel refused her clearance because she couldn't find her press badge. Only after she pleaded and handed them a twenty did they let her through, and then she had another lengthy wait as the anemic staff scattered to locate the camera before finally handing it over.

By then, Cecilia had sweat through her thin T-shirt and denim skirt. She was sure the woman behind the counter smelled the tequila oozing from her pores. A swirl of nausea mingled with dehydration and an impending dread. She grappled with whether she should try to call Pete, but she decided it was best to keep moving and get to the port.

When she exited the stadium, she did a double take. The taxi was gone. Certain this was where he had let her off, she spotted her suitcase propped against the fence with a receipt attached and directions on how to pay. Worry crept in with each breath, sending her into full-blown panic. She eyed the line of traffic, searching for another taxi before dialing the cab company. After a seemingly endless wait, they advised her the next available driver would arrive in ten to twelve minutes. She clamped down on her lip so she wouldn't shout at the dispatcher and scanned her surroundings for a place to sit. She refused to look at her watch, refused to think about her timeline and how by now it was drastically off.

Now the temperature felt unbearably hot, and rolling the broken suitcase through the uneven gravel parking lot was an exercise in futility. Cecilia noticed a shady area a few yards away where a woman was seated on a bench, and she headed in that direction. As she got closer, she saw that she had stumbled upon a small park with a modest memorial. The woman on the bench ignored her, hiding her eyes behind a pair of sunglasses. A dog sat by her side, panting in the heat.

Cecilia inched closer to the memorial, a bronze dragonfly with wings dipped in colorful stained glass. Though she was sweating profusely, the inscription sent an immediate chill down her spine. She remembered the accident, the High Tide concert at the stadium that had ended in senseless tragedy, five killed and hundreds injured. Everyone in her world had worshipped the infamous band that took home every music award year after year. Had their career not ended abruptly, they might have captured more number-one hits than any band in the history of pop. Cecilia hadn't been working at the magazine when "What You Do to Me" hit triple platinum, but the band's impact lived on through its pages. And she would never forget the night she and Pete confessed their love, how he sang the words to her.

As she waited, she tried to think not about her race against the clock but about the victims from that horrible day. She held on to the song's familiar melody and hummed it to herself. There was a sultriness to the lyrics, a stark vulnerability that reminded her that true love exists. She believed that there wasn't a woman in the world who didn't wish the words were written for her. Rumors had circulated about the identity of the song's subject—a famous actress, a politician's daughter, any number of intriguing celebrities. No one had figured it out.

Dispelling Cecilia's thoughts, a car honked—blaring and insistent— and the woman seated on the bench raised a hand, signaling for the driver to wait. Cecilia turned back to the plaque, surprised to discover today was the anniversary of the accident. Five years had passed. September 28. The band that had once been larger than life had since broken up, their string of hits and Grammy wins now tied to a somber statue.

Cecilia studied the woman's wavy brown hair and tanned skin. She guessed her to be in her early thirties. When she saw a tear slide from beneath the woman's glasses, Cecilia reached inside her bag and held out a napkin she'd swiped from Tobacco Road, but the woman didn't make a move for it, so Cecilia stuffed it back in her purse. Maybe Joan was wrong, and the people in Miami were ruder.

Cecilia took the nearby seat, cursing silently to herself. Her buzz had begun to wear off and she couldn't shake a growing uneasiness. The combination had her babbling out loud, mostly about the song. "I've always wondered what it would be like to be the object of such affection. A photo of my boyfriend and me was featured in *LIFE* magazine. That attention really affects a relationship." The alcohol and the sun had clearly clogged her brain. "Now he's going to dump me if I don't get to the Port of Miami in the next thirty minutes."

It occurred to Cecilia that the woman could very well be in mourning—seated at a memorial, today—and blathering on about her own troubles felt terribly insensitive. "I'm sorry," she said. "Ignore me."

The woman did just that, her lips pressed together, when a petite, busty woman got out of the car and made her way in their direction. With a head full of braids and a warm, cheerful expression, she smiled at Cecilia as she approached. "You ready?" she said to the woman, though it didn't sound like she was actually asking.

The woman on the bench simply stood up, and her dog stood too. Her friend came closer, and they threaded their arms through each other's affectionately. Before they walked away, the woman from the bench turned around. "The answer . . . to your question . . . is it breaks you into a million pieces." And she walked away.

Struck by the pain in the woman's voice, Cecilia watched the pair stroll side by side toward the car.

"You need to let this go," she heard the friend say. "You need to let him go."

"What if I can't?"

And just as Cecilia saw a cab drive past the entrance to the lot, she heard the woman say, "I'll never let him go. He wrote those words for *me*."

The woman's ache clung to Cecilia as she watched them get into the car. She took her words apart. Knowing there was something this woman couldn't let go of reminded Cecilia of her mother's death, her father's abandonment, and the half siblings living out the childhood that should have been hers. The clamoring of emotions made her head swirl, and she thought about marriage, this trip with Pete and their plans to dive in the ocean, and the crushing weight made it difficult to breathe.

Dropping her head in her hands, she tried to shake away the mounting fear racing through her body. If she didn't make it to the port on time, Pete would see it as her turning her back on him. Tears filled her eyes, betraying old emotions that she kept tightly hidden, and she tried to hold them back. The effort almost made her miss the crinkled white envelope on the ground. Bending to pick it up, she saw the words *For Sarita* scrawled across it in black ink.

A yellow cab finally entered the parking lot, and Cecilia popped up, carelessly stuffing the envelope in her bag and racing to greet the driver, who by the grace of God spoke English. She explained her dilemma, how she had to be at the Port of Miami by four, which didn't appear to alarm him. He loaded her suitcase into the trunk and assured her with a fist in the air. "I get you there. I am Willy. Willy Wonka."

Cecilia vacillated between laughing and crying and then quickly returned to worrying. She studied the cars around her, glancing at her watch every thirty seconds. Willy sensed her apprehension and handed her a lollipop while he weaved in and out of traffic at an alarming speed and Cecilia swallowed back bile.

As Willy had promised, traffic opened up, and the Port of Miami sign appeared. Ships came into view in the narrow harbor with waters of dark blue, and hope snuck up on Cecilia. She had thought all was lost. Willy beamed with pride, quoting Willy Wonka, something about never having doubts. She glanced at her watch. It wasn't quite four, and she rested her neck back on the vinyl seat and smiled giddily. She made it. Taking in a deep breath, she could smell the coconut oil she would soon lather on her skin, the lime she'd squeeze in her tequila. It wasn't a mirage. That was her ship. Enormous and looming and bursting with people. With Pete.

Willy parked the car beside an "Unloading" sign and she hopped out, grabbed her bag, and handed him a bill she had been saving for the casino. Racing toward the embarkation area, she didn't even care that no one had offered to help. She was invigorated, sheepishly happy she'd pulled this off.

As she made her way to the entrance, a man in a Port of Miami uniform stopped her. "Can I help you, miss?"

A loud horn sounded, and Cecilia jumped.

She handed the man her embarkation documents and pointed at the *Carnival Inspiration* with a smile. "That's my ship. I'm meeting my boyfriend."

The man stared at her strangely. "Yes, I see that—"

"It's all there. Made it here at four, just like the paper said."

"Miss . . ." His eyes narrowed, and he hesitated briefly. "I'm not sure how to tell you this, so I'm just going to give it a go. Passengers must be checked in and on board by three. The ship sails at four."

For a split second, Cecilia thought she'd misunderstood. But then the man thrust the document in her face, her document, and pointed to the line that Cecilia had clearly missed. One glance at her watch and the queasiness returned, and she let go of her bag. Nearby, tugboats surrounded the ship, preparing to ease the floating city away from the dock. She had collapsed onto the suitcase when her cell phone rang. It was Pete.

She answered, calling his name, but there was nobody on the line. A notification appeared that she had a message, and she pressed the envelope icon.

"Cecilia."

He waited a few seconds, but by the quiver in his voice, she knew it was bad.

"Cecilia," he said again. "I can't do this anymore." He waited a beat before delivering the final blow. "It's over."

It was like watching a film in slow motion. The ship pulled away from the dock, throngs of guests hung over the balconies, sipping their piña coladas, *her* piña colada, and the song "Don't Worry Be Happy" carried on the breeze. Cecilia stared in shock, biting back the tears. The man from the Port of Miami slid away, and she dropped her head in her hands, reminding herself to breathe, reminding herself of who she was. But it was useless. Who she was was Don James's daughter. And if there was one thing the man had taught her, it was that it was only a matter of time before this relationship, like all others, would end in heartbreak.

CHAPTER 7

"ROSALITA (COME OUT TONIGHT)" BY
BRUCE SPRINGSTEEN

Miami
September 1996

"Isn't there something you can do?" Cecilia begged a silver-haired woman behind the counter. "Isn't there some tugboat I can hop on? A gondola that transports guests?"

"We're not in Venice, miss."

"People are never late? Two thousand of them managed to make it here on time?"

"Actually, they did." The woman didn't mince words. And perhaps sensing Cecilia's desperation, she suggested Cecilia check the airlines. "You might be able to meet him at one of the ports."

A glimmer of hope surfaced, and Cecilia called the airlines, only to be told that the flights were sold out. *This can't be happening.*

She called Pete again. And again and again. But the calls went directly to voice mail.

Cecilia sat over her oversized suitcase in the now vacant port as she contemplated her next move. Her head throbbed with the sinking realization that there wouldn't be sunset drinks on the deck. No spontaneous games of shuffleboard. No Pete. The ship edged out of the harbor, thin strips of smoke twirling from the smokestacks, the music and laughter a big tease. She punched in his number again, not even sure what she could possibly say, but this time the phone refused to power up. The battery was dead.

Though she didn't want to admit defeat, Cecilia knew there was nothing more she could do. Pete was furious. No apology could repair the damage. This was what he had predicted, and she had proven him right. For seven days he'd be reminded of her failure—when he took the scuba excursion alone, when he sat at their cozy table for two each night. And then it dawned on her that this handsome, newly single guy was on a ship with scores of half-naked women, and the gravity of what she'd done sank in.

Spotting a pay phone nearby, she searched inside her bag for her emergency calling card and dialed Pete's number, but the phone didn't even ring. The call, again, went directly to voice mail. Cecilia tried a few more times before slamming the phone against the receiver, her bag falling to the floor, its contents scattering across the concrete. She had to get out of there, but where would she go?

Gathering her wallet and keys from the pavement, her hand stopped on the envelope, the one she'd swiped off the ground at the memorial. It stared at her, unsealed, and when she picked it up, she felt the familiar tug that made her good at her job—nosiness—and with shaky hands, she removed the folded papers. The pages were worn and crumpled, but Cecilia recognized a lead sheet when she saw one, and this one was complete with melody, chords, and lyrics. There was no song title, only a date scrawled across the top in faded blue ink: June 28, 1979.

Collapsing on her suitcase, Cecilia studied the pages. Don had taught her how to read music, so she hummed the tune, trying her best to bury the mess she had made. The melody was familiar. She didn't need the paper. She could recite the words to "What You Do to Me," like most every fan.

When she skipped to the last page, she saw a handwritten message scrawled at the bottom: *I love you, Sarita.* It was signed *Eddie.*

Though the afternoon sun warmed Cecilia's skin, she felt a cool prickle on her arms. The wheels in her brain began to spin. Eddie Vee was the lead singer of High Tide, the band that wrote "What You Do to Me." The band responsible for the accident memorialized by the plaque at the stadium. Was this authentic? Could Eddie Vee have written this? Cecilia shook her head. It was impossible. But her mind latched on to all kinds of outrageous scenarios. When the woman at the memorial said, "He wrote those words for me," was she referring to the lyrics? Cecilia took a mental snapshot of the woman so she wouldn't forget.

Doubtful such a coincidence was possible—doubtful of anything at the moment—Cecilia questioned the likelihood that she had just encountered the woman who had inspired the song that captivated so many. The mysterious muse people had speculated about for years. Even with *Rolling Stone*'s resources, not a single reporter had uncovered the truth—and many had tried. The band never breathed a word; they remained elusive and tight-lipped. But knowing this didn't hush the feeling in her gut, the idea that beat loudly, pulsing through her with possibility. Could her unlikely meeting with the woman at the stadium have provided a clue to solving a giant mystery?

In the ship's absence, the terminal felt hopeless and barren, emphasizing Cecilia's misery. When she felt adrift and uncertain, she'd often look for signs from her mother. She believed Gloria communicated with her when Simon & Garfunkel was played on the radio or when life took her on unexplained detours. She refused to believe her mother would have wanted her to lose a guy like Pete, but what was her mother trying to tell her?

More questions than answers ran through Cecilia's mind. An unexpected opportunity had landed in her lap, though it didn't alleviate the helplessness of watching Pete sail out to sea without her. Now she needed to figure out how to get back to LA or *if* she'd go back to LA. She had to tell Joan what she found. It could turn out to be nothing, but what if it was something big? Maybe she was meant to stay the week in Miami investigating.

Finding her calling card again, Cecilia keyed in the numbers on the pay phone and dialed Joan, guessing she was probably at Sunday brunch. Relief flooded her when Joan picked up after the first ring, a noisy restaurant in the background.

"Joan." She cleared her throat. "It's Cecilia."

"I thought you'd be well into the deep blue by now. Is everything all right?"

"Yes." But then she changed her mind. "No. Maybe."

"Pick one, Cecilia."

"Yeah, I'm not very good . . . I tried. I did. Everything was on schedule . . ." Her voice was tight, the words squeaking out. "I nailed the piece . . . got us an exclusive you're going to be happy with . . . but then I left my camera at the stadium and there was a woman . . . and I think she dropped this envelope—"

"Get to the point, Cecilia."

"Okay. Right." Everything with Joan was a writing lesson. "I found an envelope with the lead music for 'What You Do to Me.'"

"On the ship?"

"No. I think the woman," she stammered, "this woman I met at the memorial at the stadium dropped it. I think she was the inspiration for the song."

"I'm not following."

"I didn't really meet her, but—"

"Cecilia, you're not making any sense, and I have a table of people I need to get back to."

"The music was signed to Sarita from Eddie. I think it's an original."

This quieted Joan.

51

"Maybe I should stay here. Sniff around."

"Hold on. You're not on that ship? Tell me, please, you're on that ship with Pete."

Cecilia fiddled with the coil on the phone, Joan's chiding sounding an awful lot like April's. "That's what I've been trying to tell you."

"I knew you were going to fuck this up."

"Wait. I didn't plan this. I wasn't looking . . . Are you hearing me? I think I found the inspiration for a song that no one has been able to find. She was sitting at the memorial."

Cecilia pictured Joan, irritation spreading across her face at the interruption.

"I don't even want to know why you were at a memorial when you should've been on the ship."

"I'll explain—"

"Did you get her name? Is she this Sarita?"

"She said the song was written for her."

"Did you get her name? Rule one, *get a name*."

"No, but—"

"No, but," Joan mimicked Cecilia, who felt her cheeks redden.

"I can't believe you're not on that ship." And Cecilia heard the strike of a lighter as Joan lit a cigarette and puffed. "So you'll be back in the office tomorrow?"

Cecilia watched as the tiny dot that was supposed to be her vacation faded on the horizon. The tooting of the tugboats jeered at her. She saw her career, the only thing with any life left in it, hanging by a thread. "Joan, you have to let me follow this lead."

"What exactly are you asking of me, Cecilia?"

"Let me stay in Miami a few days. Let me try to figure this out."

"I'm not paying for you to shack up in a hotel feeling sorry for yourself about the relationship you just imploded."

Cecilia felt exhausted by this point. "It's not like that. You didn't see what I saw at the stadium. There's something to this. I know it."

"It's a needle in a haystack. And a needle without a name. That woman could be anywhere by now!" Joan exhaled just as a strong wind ruffled Cecilia's hair. "Stop prolonging the inevitable and get home. You detonated your relationship. Meandering around Florida won't change that."

The woman was heartless. And cruel.

Cecilia studied Eddie's signature, searching for anything that would justify staying, but then the automated voice came on the line, signaling she had one minute left on her calling card.

"Please, Joan." She hated begging. "Please trust me. I'll have the Hails piece to you when I get back. There's something here. You have to give me a chance. I promise you won't be sorry."

Joan took so long to answer that Cecilia was sure she'd hung up, so when she finally spoke, Cecilia thought she'd imagined it. "Go home, Cecilia."

CHAPTER 8

"JEREMY" BY PEARL JAM

Miami Beach
Summer 1979

Sara Friedman loved the holidays. Not because she didn't have to go to school—she loved school—or the abundance of food, the sumptuous smells of apricot chicken and matzo ball soup drifting through her mother's kitchen. It wasn't the large family that descended upon their Long Island table or the stretch of beach in Surfside, or Uncle Sy telling terrible jokes in Yiddish. Those aspects had once enthralled her, but that was before. What Sara most loved about the holidays was traveling to Miami. And seeing him.

As far back as the sixteen-year-old could remember, the Friedmans, Sara, her parents, and her three brothers, had piled onto an Eastern Air Lines flight for the three-hour trip to Miami with their extended family. And there were a lot of them. At last count, the number of cousins and siblings and grandparents tipped fifty-one, and that didn't include the first great-grandchild on the way. The multigenerational family shared a leafy block in their Glenwood Estates' gated community, where they rarely locked doors, crossing each other's thresholds with the ease of those tightly knit and closely connected.

If you happened to board the same flight as the family, you were sure to be met by a flock of rowdy children racing up and down the aisles or the boys tossing a football. Sara's cousins would discuss winter crushes and summer secrets, Duran Duran, and *Dynasty*, while the mothers rifled through oversized carry-ons filled with enough snacks to feed the entire plane. The entourage talked loudly, detailing plans, elaborate meals, and who would show up at the Atlantic, the building where they all owned condos.

Atlantic Towers overlooked the beach on Ninety-Fifth and Collins in Surfside, a modest eighteen-story building with 108 units. Its tired beige exterior matched the interior, and the friendly doormen knew them all by name. The families and an assortment of Glenwood Estates neighbors spent hours on the sand, ordered malted milkshakes at Sheldon's Drugs, and frequented the Bal Harbour Shops with F A O Schwarz and Neiman Marcus.

For the Friedmans, these trips meant afternoons on the beach, rugelach and Rascal House, Shabbat dinners, and gossiping on the sand. They were a caring, festive bunch with a deeply rooted sense of tradition. They stuck together and their family provided endless activities, marriages, and umpteen babies. Having so many relatives close by meant a listening ear at every turn, a built-in soccer team, and an accessible support group always willing to lend a hand.

Sara's maternal grandfather, Isaac, along with his brother Levi, had built a real estate dynasty and purchased the lots in Glenwood Estates, ensuring the ever-growing family a place to call home. It was the brothers' wish to have their relatives close, for the children and grandchildren to experience the many blessings that came from *mishpachah*, the family unit. There was no better friend than a sibling or cousin, no better confidant than an aunt or an uncle. Holidays were gatherings of music and laughter. Weekends were spent playing board games and bicycling in the street. For Sara, Hanukkah lights burned brighter in the presence of their many loved ones.

But this summer felt different.

That June morning at the airport, Sara couldn't shake the growing tension between her and her mother. Shira Friedman didn't understand her wayward daughter, nose in a book, bragging about the places she'd one day visit, and more recently, hanging around that Eddie Santiago. Shira preferred order in her insulated life, following the same regimented schedule week to week, structure and rules. One rule meant no fraternizing with that boy. But Sara was more like her father, Moshe, boundless and breezy, at times testing limits. Where Shira dressed modestly and was "old-fashioned" according to some of their friends, Moshe was easygoing and playful. Sara remembered the time he skipped services, claiming to be ill, when Sara and her younger brothers, Abraham and Noah, returned to find him in the basement dancing along to some of the latest disco records, no signs of being sick. This small act of defiance spoke to Sara. Which is how the bathing-suit debacle had begun.

As Sara boarded the plane, it hurt her head to think about the argument that centered on an orange bikini. Shira refused to let Sara wear it, pointing out that the thin fabric barely covered her privates, and she shouldn't draw attention to herself. Sara had rolled her eyes at the casual mention of her body parts, Shira flaunting her buttoned-up, proper self, while Sara's older brother, Elijah, laughed. Sara argued that her aunts and cousins wore bikinis. It wasn't fair that she wasn't allowed. She thought the battle was lost until her father reminded Shira of the days she had donned a two-piece, how beautiful she looked, causing Shira's face to turn a deep pink. Orange became Sara's new favorite color, the color of victory, and she couldn't wait to put the bathing suit on and jump into the ocean, feeling the salty foam against her skin.

And she couldn't wait for him to watch.

Sara studied her father as he loaded Shira's suitcase in the overhead compartment, how delicately he handled her things. Shira and Moshe had a loving marriage despite their differences. Sara couldn't be sure if it had begun all those years ago when Shira lost her sister, Naomi, but Sara was keenly aware of it now. It started with religion. Shira wanted more; Moshe needed less. To Shira, Judaism was about Torah and teachings; Moshe believed in culture and community. Shira read from her prayer book daily; Moshe preferred flipping pages on the High Holy Days.

This dichotomy confused Sara, who already struggled with where she fit. She more than once identified with her father's carefree rebellion, and like hers, Moshe Friedman's Judaism took root in the soul. She knew this every time he recited the *Shehecheyanu* blessing, every time he wrapped *tefillin*, or when they debated a challenging book or snuck out to watch *Star Wars* during a snowstorm. Religion was woven into their lives, but to Moshe and Sara, it wasn't quantified by attendance at synagogue. For them, it was about being there for one another in ways no one else could, listening, and the willingness to embrace each other's differences.

As the only daughter in the family, Sara was accustomed to her mother's watchful eye and strict set of rules, but as Sara inched closer to the age that Aunt Naomi was when she died, Shira's need for religion grew. And her overprotectiveness. It was stifling at times, hampering Sara's ability to stretch and grow. Shira worried constantly, monitoring Sara's every move, every after-school activity. And while Sara loved her large, boisterous family, baking challah at her aunt Carol's next door, playing box ball in the street with her thirty-two cousins, there were times she wanted to push through the neighborhood's gates and escape. To Eddie.

And this summer she was working toward that.

It was the long-ago conversation with her favorite teacher, Morah Emily, that unknowingly gave her the courage. Morah Emily lectured about the ordinary, but she managed to pluck out richer meanings, innovative ideas—about religion, but also about people. And culture.

And choices. Year after year, these lessons captivated Sara's inquisitive mind, but there was one that had stayed with her for some time.

The lesson about insects and their stages of growth hadn't started off interesting, but then Morah Emily introduced the butterfly. Sara was intrigued by the fluttery creatures, how they flapped through the air with a playful freedom. That day, Morah Emily went into excruciating detail about the caterpillar's metamorphosis to butterfly, how caterpillars, during the pupa stage, transformed within a protective shell called the chrysalis. Eventually, the butterfly emerged. Sara was intrigued. She raised her hand. A curious student, she wanted to better understand this phenomenon that turned a wiggly worm into something beautiful and bold. Morah Emily detailed the grim facts. "The caterpillar's body dies during the pupa stage, Sara. Then a new body takes shape."

"So it's the same soul? Just a different body?" she had asked. "What if the caterpillar is too weak to leave the cocoon?"

Morah Emily offered an appreciative smile, impressed with Sara's depth. "Look at it this way, Sara. The caterpillar's struggle to emerge from the chrysalis requires great strength." Then she cocked her head. "It's about finding that inner strength."

And that's what she had done. Over time, Sara found her courage.

Last time she was in Florida, her and Eddie's intimacy had grown. She let herself imagine a future. A future, with him, outside Glenwood Estates. This, according to Shira, was a *shanda*. A shameful betrayal.

Remaining in the neighborhood was an unspoken tradition that generations of descendants had adhered to, and the one time Sara casually mentioned her desire to live in New York City, her mother ran both hands through her brown hair, and her hazel eyes widened in disbelief. "Our family lives in Glenwood, Sara. That's just the way it is."

It had been hard for Shira. When her sister was struck by that car, her mother, Sara's grandmother, fell into a bottomless depression and was never quite the same. Shira took on the role of mother to her younger siblings, a responsibility she managed with great care and caution. Sara wasn't unsympathetic, but she was a young girl with big dreams. And though Shira rarely mentioned her sister Naomi, Sara knew that Naomi's death explained her mother's tight grip. Shira called Sara's carefree nature defiance, but Sara saw it as evolution.

Nothing said defiance, or evolution, more than Moshe recently returning home from a business trip not only having trimmed his messy brown hair and thick beard but also clothed in a form-fitting suit that accentuated his body like John Travolta's in *Saturday Night Fever*. Sara and her siblings stood in surprise at the sight of their handsome father with chiseled cheekbones and big brown eyes they'd rarely noticed. Their mother took one glance at her husband and fainted.

Moshe and Shira continued on their divergent paths, confusing the children and giving Glenwood Estates much to discuss. Words like *divorce* and *midlife crisis* were whispered through the community, and the more modernized Moshe became, the more tightly Shira clung to her safe traditions.

The evening before they were set to fly out to Miami for the summer, Sara overheard her parents bickering about what to pack. "Shira," Moshe said, "I'm the same man I've always been, except probably better looking!" Sara rolled her eyes at this. The worst thing to discuss with a woman like Shira was vanity. She didn't care about such things. She believed in minimizing the physical, connecting through the soul.

Moshe argued. "It's 1979. I want to wear proper bathing trunks on the beach—"

"Those aren't proper," Shira argued back. "A Speedo? Really, Moshe?"

Sara covered her mouth else they'd hear her laugh, but it wasn't necessary, because her mother was going on and on about how he'd changed, and how *Aba*, her father, would roll over in his grave if he saw Moshe today. Sara recognized how her mother dug in her heels. Her opinions weren't rooted in cruelty. They were in large part about holding on to the familiar. Maybe Shira didn't understand the modern world or her husband. But Sara was starting to think she didn't understand her mother.

Sara reflected on this while she patiently waited in the aisle to reach her seat. Lively chatter skipped through the air, and she glanced back at her father. He had unknowingly provided the key to a new world, but it was Eddie who had ushered her through the door. Five years before, Sara had met Eddie for the first time. She had just turned eleven, and the timing of their collision on the beach was fitting, as the Friedmans had descended upon Miami for Passover, the holiday that celebrated the Jewish people's exodus from Egypt, where they had been enslaved. Liberation. Freedom. After that, they'd met again, whether by choice or chance, through an endless stream of holidays and the sizzling summer months.

Sara likened her insulated world to that of the cocoon, a protective covering made of fine silk. Her family and their massive reach wrapped around her, providing comfort and love, but when she ran into young Eddie on the beach that blistery hot morning—he claimed she had knocked into him on purpose—the cocoon she had relied upon all those years began to weaken.

Settled in her seat, wedged between her seventeen-year-old brother, Elijah, and her friend Deborah Waxman, Sara pulled out her book. Deborah had a crush on Elijah, and she had pleaded with Sara to switch seats, but Elijah gave her the *absolutely not* look. After takeoff, Deborah finally gave up. Sara had buried her nose in her summer reading, Elie Wiesel's *Night*, when her brother peered over her shoulder.

"What the—" He tried to grab the book out of her hands, but Sara, despite her small frame, was strong.

"This isn't *Night*," he said. "Does *Ima* know you're reading this?"

Of course it wasn't *Night*. She had already read that book a dozen times. Sara remained silent. Most of the time, this tactic proved effective, and her nosy brother would back off. Deborah, though, grabbed the book and read from the page. "This is definitely not *Night*," she hollered, loud enough for the cockpit to hear. Slipping the book jacket off, Deborah exposed the spine and Sidney Sheldon's name. *"The Other Side of Midnight,"* she read aloud. Then she zeroed in on the graphic scene between Noelle and Philippe that had Sara thinking about Eddie and had Elijah ready to tattle. Her eyes widened. "Where did you get this?" Deborah was as prudish as anyone Sara knew, except when it came to Elijah.

Retrieving the book, Sara tried to reenter the scene, but the moment had passed. Instead, she dropped the novel in her straw bag and rested her head on the seat back, imagining doing to Eddie what Noelle was doing to Philippe.

This was the very thing that had been keeping her awake at night. She hadn't been able to get Eddie Santiago out of her brain. His wavy brown hair and blue eyes taunted her, crept under her covers at night. He'd invaded her studies, and she silently hoped God wouldn't punish her for the impure thoughts. But why give these feelings to her if they weren't meant to be felt? She wished she could confide in her father, but boys like Eddie were off-limits, and he would absolutely tell her mother. Instead, Sara sat in her seat counting the minutes until she'd see him again.

"You shouldn't be reading that stuff," Elijah said.

"Maybe you should be reading that stuff," she replied.

Deborah tried chiming in, but Elijah told her to butt out.

The scent of babkas and bagels wafted through the air along with the loud voices speaking over each other. The banter and playfulness knocked into Sara, but she had no desire to join. With her longing buried inside, she felt more alone than ever.

～

Much had changed in the five years since she had first met Eddie. When they had collided on the beach, he introduced himself. *Yo soy Eddie.*

And Sara, recognizing they were from different worlds, picked herself up, dusted the sand from her knees, and kept walking. After that, they frequently ran into one another—in the ocean, by the pool—Eddie with his messy brown hair, tanned skin, and big blue eyes that lingered on hers longer than they should.

"You are not very nice," he had said to her one winter day when she was seated by a cluster of rocks near the water, reading Danielle Steel's *The Promise*. She'd ripped off the paper cover, so her mother would think she was devouring Dickens.

She ignored him, flipping the pages with a zest she hoped would send him away. She was thirteen that holiday and had begun to feel the trickle effect of her father's metamorphosis, his own transition taking shape within the cocoon. After Morah Emily had completed the lesson on the subject, Sara went home and searched their *World Book Encyclopedia*, and what she read frightened her. And because the boy had made no effort to leave, she decided she'd scare him too. "Do you know what happens to a caterpillar when it's in the cocoon?"

"*Claro.*"

She wasn't sure if that meant yes or no, so she continued.

"It eats itself from the inside out."

"*Bruto.* I no believe you."

"It's true. The acid that's supposed to help it digest food ends up eating its own body."

If she thought that would make him leave, it didn't.

"That is what you read?" he asked, pointing at her book.

She laughed, and she could tell he wasn't sure if she was laughing at him or something else, and when he lowered his eyes, it tugged at her.

That afternoon, the temperature lingered in the sixties, and the birds sailed across a cloudless sky. Sara's gaze landed on her family down the beach, huddled close. They were building sandcastles and skipping along the shore, shrieking when the waves nipped their feet.

"Why do you sit here alone?" he asked.

She eyed him. "I'm not alone."

"Away from them." He nodded in their direction.

She followed his gaze to the cluster of beach chairs and colorful towels and the imaginary line forbidding others to cross. Had she purposely put distance between them? She had chosen this private spot, where the piles of jagged rocks jutted into the turquoise, the spray of salt water a surprise every time. It was where she came to read. To get lost in stories. To imagine being reckless and fiery like the women in the pages. They were glamorous and wore bright-red dresses, and men swept them off to faraway cities and did this thing to their bodies that made them quiver. Her face flushed at the thought.

She studied the boy. There was a sadness in his eyes that spoke to her.

Earlier that same year, she'd run into him in the lobby with an older man, the building's super, Mr. Santiago. When she asked Moshe what that meant, he said, "He fixes things." Mr. Santiago had a friendly smile, and he was always kind to their family. Another time, she'd watched the boy throw nickels into the pool, diving in and collecting them one by one. She'd overheard the whispers: "He's an orphan." And other times, she heard them making fun of his ears, which stuck out. If he had friends, she never saw them.

Once, he visited their condo with Mr. Santiago, who Sara had learned was his grandfather. She didn't know why Eddie didn't live with his parents, just that he and Mr. Santiago shared a small apartment on the first floor, and the elder man took care of him.

When the two had walked through the door of 7B to fix the leaky toilet, Sara watched Eddie survey the glass cabinet filled with sparkling china, the crystal menorah, the silver candlesticks, and the dozens of framed family photographs. Pausing on a picture of her parents with their four kids, Eddie's face changed. And when Mr. Santiago led him out of the condo, he wrapped an arm around Eddie's shoulders, pulling him close. Sara wondered if fixing things meant more than just things in the building.

As the years passed, Eddie Santiago and Sara Friedman formed an unlikely friendship. They'd meet at the rocks, and she'd share with him the lessons she'd learned in school—the grosser and scarier the better—and he'd recount stories about the Atlantic and its guests.

Sara liked being around Eddie. His tales made her laugh, and his accent intrigued her. He was a part of her life she kept to herself—like her yearnings. She knew her family wouldn't approve of the friendship.

When he asked her again why she was always by herself, never in the thick of her family's beach gatherings, she ignored the question. Sure, she had many relatives; it was a literal numbers game, ever present and underfoot, yet there were times in their presence when she felt overwhelmingly alone. When she was with Eddie, she felt complete.

The sand and the sky held Eddie and Sara in their own private chrysalis, and as their friendship developed, they shed their skins. Like Morah Emily's lesson on the caterpillar, Sara felt a part of herself slowly dying and another part being born. And Eddie was the furthest thing from Jewish. He wasn't even American. Young girls in her community married nice Jewish boys, and Sara Friedman was destined to marry Abel Altman, a friend since birth, their families so intertwined it was like they were already one.

But then she met Eddie. And everything turned messy. *Inner strength,* she told herself.

Sara hadn't considered marrying Eddie back then. She knew what was expected of her, the timeless tradition, preserving their religion when many before her had perished. But what Sara knew in her head challenged what she felt in her heart. And there was Abel to consider. Sweet, reliable Abel. They'd grown up together, sat in his tree house for hours at a time, swung from the tree's branches as the seasons transformed around them. She cared about Abel, but she wanted the kind of love she read about in her novels. She wanted the gut punch, the achy physical desire that transcended custom and culture.

Eddie had muddied up her feelings for Abel—something she would have to address this summer—as Eddie had become a trusted friend, someone who listened without judging. "I don't understand," he had said when the subject of Sara's mother came up.

"She's strict, Eddie. Especially with me." Then she'd list the litany of reasons, how she was the only girl, how her mother lost a sister, how Shira took her religion very seriously. More so now than ever.

"My *saba*, my grandfather Isaac, he pleaded with my mom and her siblings to maintain their faith, and before he died, she promised she would."

Eddie would nod, but she wasn't sure how much he understood.

Sara had learned to fib. Was that the same as having inner strength?

She'd tell Shira she was walking the beach or reading her books, but then she and Eddie would sprawl on their towels away from view, building their own sandcastles, and she'd confess to him how she wished they weren't labeled or put inside a box. And when he'd invite her to a movie at the Byron Carlyle on a Friday night, she wished she didn't have to tell him no.

"Friday's the Sabbath. We light candles at sundown and say prayers. Big family meal with fresh-baked challah. Then we hang out in the rec room with our cousins and play games. My uncles tell silly stories. Sometimes we go to the beach and chase each other in the sand."

"That sounds fun," Eddie had said.

It was fun. They were some of her best memories, but it didn't diminish her desire to be around him, to want to sit beside him in a darkened theater and imagine him holding her hand. And with each admission, she shed another layer, and a new one took its place.

"We can watch movies *aquí* on the beach anytime," he had suggested, unaffected by her rules. They created their own. They'd bury themselves in the sand, watching the crowds of people, making up stories better than the ones they'd see in the cinema. And when she hid her *chai* pendant under her T-shirt, after she had explained to Eddie its meaning, life, and how the Hebrew letters חי corresponded to the number eighteen, a symbol of good luck, he had lifted the chain out. "Don't ever hide who you are."

When Sara turned fifteen and her family returned to the Atlantic, she almost didn't recognize him. When she'd found him down the beach by the rocks, their castle, he towered over her, and she had to strain her neck to meet his eyes. That wasn't all. His body had changed; his once-scrawny arms rippled with toned muscles, and his chest curved. He was shirtless, and it was impossible to look away.

They had arrived for winter break, Hanukkah, the Festival of Lights, and she explained to him in detail the miracle of the menorah that had only enough oil for one night but lasted eight.

"You believe in miracles?" he had asked.

She didn't hesitate. "I do."

Finding the time to be with Eddie was tricky, but she managed to sneak out when Shira was at the beauty parlor or playing canasta. They'd walk the beach, splash each other in the water, careful not to get caught. Their friendship was a thrilling secret. *Ima* would have been terribly upset if she had known about the times they'd roamed the beach after dark, the intimate discussions they shared as the moon glistened across the water. Sara relaxed around Eddie. In Glenwood, it was as though she held in a long breath, and when she arrived in Miami, it released.

An hour into the flight, Sara peeked over at the magazine Deborah held in her hand. Donna Summer and Gloria Gaynor were on the cover, and she remembered that last trip to Miami in December, six months earlier. She and Shira had argued over *American Top 40*. Sara wanted to tune in to hear Chic's "Le Freak" knock "You Don't Bring Me Flowers" from the number-one spot. Shira said disco would numb her brain, and Sara turned to her father. "Please, *Aba*. I'm about to lose my mind. She's suffocating me!" It was the first time Sara had verbalized her feelings.

Moshe took Shira by the hand and pulled her in for a dance, twirling her like they were kids. "Shira," he had said, "remember the music we used to listen to?"

Shira's eyes flickered, but then she pulled back and switched on NPR.

Shira looked unusually sad that day, her moods erratic and difficult to anticipate. Sara stormed out of the condo, tears spilling from her eyes. It was only a song, but it felt like giving up much more. She burst through the stairwell door and ran down the seven flights of steps toward the beach and the rocks.

Out of breath, she found Eddie seated on top of the stack, waiting as though he had a sixth sense when it came to her. He hopped down, and she told him about the fight, and he listened. Then he took her face in both hands and forced her to look in his eyes.

"You want to hear music?" he plainly asked. "That is all?" His accent sounded thicker than usual.

She crossed her arms, their faces almost touching as children chased each other along the shore.

"I can't expect you to understand," she had said.

"Lo entiendo." But she knew he never could, never would. She never told him what they said about him, about his broken English and how the one-bedroom apartment meant he shared a bed with his grandfather. He would never understand their rules. The impenetrable world that no outsider could get through.

"You don't." She shook her head.

The wind picked up, so she didn't immediately hear what he was saying. But then it quieted down, and she realized he wasn't talking at all.

Eddie was singing.

CHAPTER 9

"VALERIE" BY STEVE WINWOOD

Los Angeles
September 1996

Cecilia reluctantly boarded a flight to Los Angeles, spending the interminable hours of the trip swearing to herself while crafting an apology to Pete.

At half past midnight, the cab pulled up to their duplex, but she hesitated to get out. Swinging the front door open, she found the second-floor unit dark and unforgiving, as though the wood floors and cathedral ceiling already knew what she had done. Dropping her bag at her feet, she checked the answering machine, expecting to hear his voice but heard April instead: "Welcome home, CeCe! I want every detail. Every. Single. One. I'm soooooooooooooo happy for you guys! Call me!"

The message was time-stamped at twelve o'clock Pacific time, when they would have been aboard the ship and sipping champagne on the deck. Even with the time difference, April managed to get their departure time right. How would she tell her friend that she'd royally fucked up and missed check-in? Another message played, and it was from her father: "Cecilia. I'd like to see you. I still want to talk. Tori and I would love to have you both for dinner. The kids haven't seen you in a while. It'd be nice to get together." Furious, Cecilia hit delete. The nerve. Did he and his wife even communicate? But then another message began to play, and Joan's voice sprang from the machine: "Dare I say welcome back, CeCe? Or call this exactly what it is? A major fuckup on your part? Anyway, onward. I've been thinking about this lead you mentioned, and I'm willing to play. I dipped into the archives. I once interviewed Eddie Vee early in his career. He claimed the song wasn't written for anyone in particular, but artists are bullshit liars. Maybe you're onto something. Since you weren't expected at the office this week, I'm giving you carte blanche to go ahead and dig. As a *Rolling Stone* writer. Fully credentialed." Cecilia let that sink in, her exhausted body zapped with a shot of energy. "Maybe there's poetic justice in losing the love of your life while finding the person who inspired one of the most lyrical love songs of our time."

The irony wasn't lost on her, but the two weren't mutually exclusive. She didn't believe she had to lose Pete to succeed. They would talk when he returned, and she was sure they'd work things out.

As she climbed into bed, smelling Pete's musky scent on the sheets and pillow, Guns N' Roses sang about the depressing November rain. The cruise documents mocked her from where they sat on the nightstand, and she scanned the itinerary, checking off the activities she'd already missed. Tonight they would have watched the full moon on the deck, attended the midnight dessert bar, and danced in the club to Donna Lewis and the Quad City DJs. Later, she would have put on the sexy red lingerie for him, and they'd fumble in the dark—tipsy—with the sea swishing outside their balcony. She could feel his lips on her neck, his hands moving up and down her back. She half expected him to walk through the door, to have abandoned the ship for her, but he was thousands of miles away and she was here, and there was no name for the anguish and regret that lulled her to sleep.

~

Monday morning, Cecilia arrived at the office already having decided against letting April know she was home. What April didn't know wouldn't hurt her, and the delay would give Cecilia the time she needed to figure out her next move.

The first thing she did after pouring herself a cup of hot black coffee and checking Pete's cruise itinerary was log on to her email. She wasn't sure the ship had internet access or if Pete could connect, but she sent an apology with the best intentions. Next, she typed EDDIE VEE into the search engine. Cecilia knew what she'd find. Everyone knew the story. Eddie and the band High Tide had burst onto the musical scene in 1984, their impressive blend of range and melody compared to the Who and Derek and the Dominos. And when "What You Do to Me" released that same year, it knocked Cyndi Lauper's "Time After Time" out of the *Billboard* number-one slot. And that was just in its first week.

Not only was Eddie Vee supremely talented, his vocals rich and raw, but he had that classic rock-star quality about him—a presence—akin to Springsteen and Jagger. Olive-skinned with a mess of dark hair and clear blue eyes, he made women fall to their knees when he played the first few notes. Other songs had rivaled the popularity of "What You Do to Me"—"Wonderful Tonight," "When a Man Loves a Woman," Dolly Parton's "I Will Always Love You"—but Eddie's song had that mysterious hook that kept fans listening and wondering.

Cecilia wasn't surprised by the lack of recent news. Eddie and the band had disappeared from the musical scene right after the tragedy in Miami. Their music, once worshipped and revered, became a lasting tribute to what could be lost. *In an instant.* Which happened to be the title of another one of their hit songs. A tragic foreshadowing.

Cecilia scrolled down the page, reading up on the band members. Izak was a schoolteacher in Watts, Bruno had left the country and ran adventure programs in Costa Rica, and Bob sold insurance in Pasadena.

The only one unaccounted for was Eddie. As moving and provocative as the music he left behind was, his dramatic departure from the scene was just as riveting. News reports had him fleeing his Hollywood Hills mansion and disappearing into the night, leaving behind his beloved classic Porsche 911—the first royalty-check purchase—and most of his personal belongings. The only item of value missing, according to his house manager, Francesca, was his bright-blue guitar.

Eddie had vanished into thin air, and not even his former band members or record label, both embroiled in lawsuits, knew where to find him. They had vowed to anyone who asked, under oath, that they had no idea of Eddie Vee's whereabouts. And they didn't.

Cecilia printed out every single article she could find, prepared to comb through each one, searching for some connection to this Sarita. She scanned excerpts and newspaper clippings until she landed on an old *People* magazine with in-depth coverage from that miserable day. Eddie Vee was on the cover, the shot taken just before the tumult, a sea of fans surrounding him. The headline read "Concert Turns to Nightmare."

For John Rafferty and Katherine McPherson, seeing High Tide perform in concert seemed to be the perfect way for the twenty-six-year-olds to celebrate their anniversary, listening to the songs they'd fallen in love to.

On September 28, the young couple was among the Orange Bowl's 70,000 guests listening to the iconic band best known for hits "Closing In" and "Blame It on the Sunshine," when deep into their final set, lead singer Eddie Vee struck the chords of fan favorite "What You Do to Me." What was supposed to be the final song of the evening turned into a nightmare when a crowd of fans stormed the stage and guests were pushed to the floor and trampled.

"We had no idea what was going on. One minute, Eddie was singing, and the next there was this mass hysteria. People were running for the stage, a stampede, people being stomped on," Evelyn Mars, a concert attendee, said. "People were thrown to the ground. They couldn't get up."

Five attendees—between the ages of 17 and 47—died, including both Rafferty and McPherson. More than 200 others were injured.

Cecilia continued reading, the story capturing the panic and hysteria of thousands of guests. "I thought I was going to die," said a victim who suffered two broken legs when the crowd sent him to the ground, crushing his bones. The grainy pictures showed emergency vehicles lined up along the street and the makeshift memorial set up outside the stadium. The article mentioned a looming investigation.

It was no surprise to Cecilia that Eddie Vee had vanished into thin air. One of the articles in the *Miami Herald* claimed he stopped performing as soon as he became aware of the stampede and led those closest to the stage through side exits, but his efforts, some claimed, weren't enough, and criticism of the pop star mounted. "Safety protocols should have been in place," said Miami-Dade Fire Chief Jorge Suarez. "The band should have stopped playing sooner." And another concertgoer said, "You shouldn't go to a concert and lose your life."

Cecilia imagined how the blame and culpability must have weighed on the band. The grief and guilt were enough to destroy anyone.

Moving on to a list someone had compiled of the women (and one man) who had come forward claiming the song was written for them, Cecilia spent the latter part of her morning deciphering the notes and reaching out to the most credible sources.

Jane Mangrove. Claimed she and Eddie Vee had a one-night stand in a bathroom at the Clevelander Hotel in Miami Beach, and then he proceeded to stalk her.

CJ: I'm calling about Eddie Vee.

Jane: Oh, that. No. There must've been some kind of mistake. That was a long time ago. I'm married now. Have a husband and two kids.

CJ: So you didn't have a one-night stand in the Clevelander bathroom when he professed his love for you and stalked you incessantly for months after?

Jane: (Nervously) Can we just forget about this? It was a mistake. I made a mistake. I'm happy now. Take me off your list.

Lucy Higgins, assistant to the senior VP at RCA Records. She was quoted in the *Village Voice* about the relationship that spawned the song.

Lucy: Yeah, we fucked on and off for a couple of years. Man, that one could go on for hours. I still think about him sometimes.

CJ: Have you heard from him since the accident?

Lucy: No one has. He just disappeared. What an awful tragedy. If you find him, would you let me know?

CJ: Did he ever mention a woman by the name of Sarita?

Lucy: Never heard of that one. And there were a lot of us.

CJ: And the song. Do you still think it was written about you? I have here an article quoting—

Lucy: Once I would have said yes. Not now. You know. Every one of us wanted that song to be ours. Who wouldn't? There's something special about it, and no one's ever really been able to replicate it. When it plays, people are transported. It has that effect.

Allison Whitford. Daughter of Florida Governor Whitford.

CJ: What can you tell me about Eddie Vee from the band High Tide?

Allison: I think you have me confused with my cousin. The other Alison Whitford. One *l*.

CJ: There's two of you?

Allison: Our families fought over everything. Even our names. I never dated Eddie. Alison did. The other Alison.

CJ: Do you know where I might reach her? We're doing an article on Eddie and the band.

Allison: They're still around? I thought he retired.

CJ: Something like that. Alison was quoted in *People* magazine saying Eddie wrote the song for her. Do you know anything about that?

Allison: (Laughing) Yeah. That was a dare. None of us could believe she actually went through with it.

Cecilia scratched Alison Whitford with one *l* off her list.

Brian DiPalma. Employee at US Parking Garage Services in Miami, Florida.

Brian: We met. Yeah. That's me. Make sure you got my name spelt right. That's DiPalma with a *D-i*. People always confuse me with that other guy. He spells it *D-e*.

CJ: (Hiding a laugh) You say you met at My Pi Pizza in North Miami Beach. You were with your boyfriend at the time and Eddie cornered you outside the bathroom—

Brian: Hell yeah. He was a pushy dude. But good looking. Blond with these huge brown eyes. Looked like one of those cabana boys at the Fontainebleau. Kissed me square on the lips and told me he was going to write a song about me. A year later the song came out. My man was pissed. We broke up. Didn't like him much anyway. But the song, the song was real good.

CJ: Have you heard from Eddie Vee since?

Brian: Nah. You know his type. Pretending to be someone he's not.

CJ: Let me ask you one last question, Mr. DiPalma with an *i*. When Eddie kissed you, were you sober? Meaning, you weren't drunk or on any drugs?

Brian: Of course not. I don't do that stuff. The city tests me all the time . . . Part of my probation stuff.

CJ: Thank you for your time, Mr. DiPalma.

Brian: That's all? Don't forget to spell my name right, you hear?

CJ: Got it.

She crossed Brian off the list. Eddie Vee had brown hair and blue eyes.

The list went on and on: Cathy and Kathy and Maria and Bianca and Danielle and Bunny and Natalie and Lauren and Victoria and Lourdes, until Cecilia lost track. A tiny headache formed behind her eyes. Rising from her desk and heading toward the music library, she found the shelf of High Tide CDs. Choosing the one that mattered, she returned to her desk, dropped it in the player, and hit "PLAY."

The song told the story of a couple separated by miles. Sultry and sensual, Vee's voice captured the ache in his heart, reminding her that despite the distance, he was right there. She should never be lonely. The words had a visceral effect. It sounded as though he were singing them to one single person—whoever happened to be in the room.

Cecilia got caught up in the words, like she so often did, remembering Pete telling her he loved her, missing him, when Eddie sang, "I promise you that by the time we get through . . . the world will never ever be the same."

Cecilia pressed "PAUSE" and rewound the song a few beats. A message in the previous line stopped her. Intrigued, she jotted the words on a piece of paper: "Times are getting hard, but just believe me girl someday I'll pay the bills with this guitar, we'll have it good. We'll have the life we knew we would. My word is good."

Here was the story. Cecilia felt it in her bones. Sarita was a young love, someone connected to Eddie before he became Eddie Vee of musical fame and infamy. Other reporters had dug inside his early years, but Cecilia couldn't shake the feeling that they'd missed something. She was convinced that the woman Eddie Vee wrote the song for had sat beside her at the memorial. She wasn't much older than Cecilia, which put her at about the same age as Eddie, early thirties, and while there was a possibility that the envelope wasn't hers, that someone else may have dropped it, Cecilia knew what she heard: "He wrote those words for me."

Cecilia sat back in her chair, mulling this over, when the Spice Girls blared from the overhead speakers and someone shouted to lower the volume. Amateur move, as in walked Mel B., Emma, Geri, Melanie C., and Victoria, bebopping past their cubicles, singing along to their own music. Cecilia smiled. The girls giggling about what they really, really wanted. Just another day at the office.

Returning to the Eddie files, she picked up the High Tide CD and read through the jacket copy. The cover featured a black-and-white photo of a palm tree with sunlight breaking through the leaves. Printed inside were the lyrics and acknowledgments. She skipped over the other band members' to Eddie's. After thanking his record label and manager, and before recognizing his hometown Miami fans and grandfather, he mentioned P. F. "You taught me everything I know. *Muchas gracias. Soy para siempre una marea alta.*"

"Does anyone speak Spanish?" she shouted over the music.

Jessie, one of the advertising reps who had a cubicle near Cecilia's, appeared and quickly translated. "'I am always a high tide.' Whatever that means."

High Tide. And who was P. F? A teacher? A music instructor? Cecilia turned back to her pile of articles and began another internet search for High Tide. Were there music studios or schools or instructors with the same name? Would P. F. be willing to talk about a former student? After an exhaustive search, she came up empty-handed. No High Tide or High Tides in relation to instructional music. Nor was there any current information on Eddie's grandfather, Carlos Santiago. His last known address was Atlantic Towers in Surfside, but after 1980, the man disappeared.

Frustrated, Cecilia leaned back in her chair just as Dean waltzed in with the information she had requested earlier, after the shock at finding her sipping coffee at her desk wore off. Desperate to reach Pete, and having given up on email, she had decided to send him a telegram. A telegram had a timely, romantic feel to it. She needed to be bold and daring.

Dean explained that all she needed was the name of the ship, Pete's stateroom number, and a credit card. A typed message would be delivered to his room. The magnitude of this message weighed on her, and she wondered how she could possibly come up with the right words. She thought about Eddie penning "What You Do to Me" for the mysterious Sarita. How he poured his heart into those perfect words, reached far inside himself to create impact. Eddie had struck a significant chord, and Cecilia needed to do the same.

After composing multiple drafts, Cecilia made her way to Western Union. It was a short walk, and she marveled at the temperature and blue skies, nothing like the steamy Miami heat.

She had thought about going with a song, a lyric that would capture everything she wanted to say, but that would only irritate Pete further. Besides, she needed to get to the point, as Joan often reminded her.

"I messed up. I'm sorry. I'm not next to you, but I'm with you. That's who we are, Pete. Forgive me. I promise to make it up to you. TTM."

"Ma'am," the young woman behind the counter began, after Cecilia had handed her the completed form. "You must've really messed up."

Cecilia almost laughed.

"Do you think he'll forgive you?" she asked with a look of pity.

Cecilia shrugged. She didn't know. They were stuck in a holding pattern, like two planes circling the same airspace. Landing wasn't for six days, but Cecilia hoped Pete would find a way to forgive and land in the space beside her. He had to.

Cecilia handed the woman her credit card and waited patiently while she keyed in the numbers, thinking that maybe this separation would move their relationship to another level. April said they'd grown too comfortable with one another, the way you'd pass a painting on your wall—the one you once loved, the one you just had to have—no longer noticing its beauty. Had they become those people? Maybe this separation would be good for them, give them the time to better understand what they meant to each other. Maybe they'd see that painting from a fresh perspective, in vibrant color, and remember the reasons they chose it in the first place.

The woman handed her back her card and showed her where to sign. "Are you okay?"

Cecilia said yes, but she lied. What if he really meant it when he said they were over? She couldn't lose Pete.

"When will he receive it?"

"It'll go out with our next batch, but I can't tell you exactly when it will get to his room."

Cecilia pulled out the itinerary. Monday. If she calculated correctly, he should have it tonight before he went to bed, and she banished the image of him with someone else. Tonight was the costume contest. They were supposed to go as Sonny and Cher.

Shutting out the possibilities swirling around her head, she thanked the woman and headed back to the office.

If she couldn't fix things with Pete, there was something else she could do.

She would find Eddie Vee and his muse.

CHAPTER 10

"ANNIE'S SONG" BY JOHN DENVER

Miami Beach
December 1978

If Sara Friedman were asked the precise moment her destiny fell into the hands of a boy named Eddie Santiago, she would say it was when she had fled the Atlantic Towers that December day, wanting only to listen to *American Top 40*, and Eddie sang to her instead. The temperature was mild, the breeze a whisper against her skin, and the ocean danced in a moderate chop. The waves mingled with the sand while beachgoers sat clustered together in their lounge chairs, their laughter carried in the wind. But all Sara heard was Eddie. Eddie, who could turn words into magic, spin a tune into velvet, his smooth sound unlike anything she'd ever heard before. It couldn't even compare to Chic singing about the new dance craze.

As she sat cross-legged on the sand, Eddie knelt in front of her as though he were seated on his own stage. And he belonged there. He didn't care that a few passersby turned their heads and stared, or that a handful stopped and moved in closer. Eddie was a natural, his voice soulful and transforming. The words he sang were in Spanish, and Sara didn't understand their meaning, but they silenced all her questions. His eyes held hers, as blue as the nearby ocean, like she could swim inside them. He would later tell her the song was called "El Amor," and when she asked what that meant, he put a finger to her lips. "One day. Not today."

If it had anything to do with the way her heart sped up when she was with him, or the way she wanted to be nowhere else but beside him, she already understood.

A group of her cousins walked by with some of their friends, and she ducked her head so they wouldn't spot her. But they saw Eddie, and she could read their minds, feel their pointed stares. When they passed, she glanced in the distance and saw her aunts and uncles lounging under umbrellas, sharing cocktails and cards. They were talking animatedly and seemed to be enjoying themselves.

She felt tugged in opposite directions. One path was Eddie and his beautiful voice, and the other was the gathering down the beach. Shifting her eyes toward the water, she imagined the current pulling her out to sea. What if instead of fighting it, she gave in, letting the tide pull her toward something dangerous and untamed? Her face fell, her eyes lowered, and she was unable to meet his gaze.

He stopped singing, and the small group dispersed, but the exclamations of "he's good" and "wow" swirled around.

"You are sad," he said, sitting beside her and reaching for her hand. She didn't stop him.

How she wished she could explain to him that he couldn't upset her. Only their circumstances had that power. "Your voice, Eddie. I've never heard anything like it."

He squeezed her hand tighter, and she pretended to ignore the thrill passing through each finger.

"I like to sing for you, Sara."

"You're really good," she said.

"I save money to buy a guitar. I will play for you." He motioned over her shoulder. "And for them."

Sara tensed, though she left her hand in his. She liked the way his skin felt against hers, smooth and soft with just enough heat seeping through. "You can't sing for us, Eddie."

He was confused. *"¿Por qué no?"*

"We're not like you."

He laughed. She loved his laugh. "That's a good thing, *sí?*" He leaned closer to her, his bare shoulder grazing hers. Her body came alive when he was near, she didn't know how to make it stop. She wanted Eddie to touch her. She wanted him to do more than sit beside her. But if Shira knew they were this close, she would forbid Sara to ever venture alone on the beach again, forbid her to leave the house. That's why she needed to be more careful. She couldn't bear the thought of not seeing or speaking to Eddie, and more than ever, she needed to hear his voice.

"I like that you're different," she finally said.

He let out a breath. "Why are they so . . . how do you say it in English? *Testarudos?*"

"What do you mean?"

He shook his head. *"No sé."* Then he asked, "They don't like me?"

If only it were that simple. "They don't know you, Eddie."

"We cannot be friends, Sara?"

She narrowed her eyes because she wanted to be sure his naivete was real. "They're not as open-minded as you. *Ima* has rules I'm expected to follow. She worries. I'm not safe with someone outside our world. And God forbid I should want to marry you." When she said this, she blushed.

"You wouldn't want to marry me?" He seemed hurt.

She laughed because the casual way he said it gave her a secret thrill. "*They* wouldn't want that. I told you. We have to marry Jewish."

"But you would want to marry me?"

She didn't answer because she wasn't sure if Eddie was playing with her or not.

"We like each other," he said.

She felt herself being pulled in. The way he said it—so innocently, so trustingly. She glanced in the direction of her family down the beach. "People like us can't be together, Eddie."

"You are Jewish, yes?"

She laughed.

"I am not," he said apologetically. "This is a silly rule."

"What do you believe in?" she asked.

A faraway look clouded his eyes. "I believe in nothing, if you mean," pointing up to the sky, "up there."

"You have to believe in something," she said, curious.

"When you leave . . . I believe I will see you again."

She wasn't ready to tell him how nice that made her feel. She had wondered how it had been for him to watch her family leave after each holiday, the caravan of taxis lined up on Collins Avenue, their suitcases piled on luggage carts. He'd never asked when she'd be coming back, but she'd list the holidays: Simchat Torah. Sukkot. Passover. He would smile, those words meaning nothing more than seeing her again.

He let go of her hand. "I live with *mi abuelo*, Sara. You understand?"

"Your grandfather?" She was beginning to pick up the language.

"*Sí.*" He turned to her and she could see the sun reflected in his eyes. His face was smooth and golden brown from the sun. If they had been alone, she would have touched him.

"*Mis padres . . .*" he started and stopped, drawing circles in the sand with his finger. "When I live in Argentina . . . I play *fútbol. Ocho años. Mi mamá* and *papá . . . están muertos. Por mi culpa.*" As soon as the words were out of his mouth, he realized his mistake. She knew when his emotions overtook him, he reverted to his native tongue. He tried again. "My *mamá* and *papá*, they are not here—"

"They're in Argentina," Sara said.

He breathed in and out. "*Sí y no.*"

"That doesn't make sense." She saw sadness climb inside his eyes. "Eddie? Tell me. Where are your parents?"

He locked his eyes with hers. *"Muertos."*

"Muertos?" she repeated.

"Un horrible accidente. Venían a por mí. Al entrenamiento de fútbol."

She repeated in English what little she understood. "There was an accident . . . soccer . . ."

"El carro." He used his hands to illustrate a steering wheel. "They come to pick me up." He shook his head. "They no come."

She didn't say it aloud. He couldn't either. They had died in a car accident on their way to pick him up from soccer. Sara felt his anguish, saw it across his face, and it didn't stop there. "Eddie, I'm so sorry." The weight of it was too much.

"It is because of me . . ." His voice trailed off. He swiped at his eyes, but she caught the lone tear sliding down his cheek.

She should have reached over and wiped it away, but she knew she wouldn't stop there. She would have run her fingers through his hair. Then she'd find his mouth and taste the salt from his tears. Her touch would take away his pain, take away hers.

"Eddie . . . it's not your fault. You didn't cause the accident."

"If they no come for me . . . they are here."

She shook her head vehemently. "That's not true."

"That is what you believe?" His voice rose. "You believe in the fates and . . . it does not matter. They are not here. You ask me if I believe. I do not."

"I'm so sorry, Eddie. This is terribly unfair. And that's why you have to believe in something. The world is big . . . there has to be something that matters . . . that keeps you going—"

"Tengo música," he said. And then he held her eyes so she couldn't turn away. "And I have you."

There was nothing Sara could say in response. Glancing back at her family that sat only yards away, she couldn't imagine, despite her longings, losing them. And she thought of Naomi, the aunt she never knew, and the losses that permeated their lives.

"I think *Ima* is afraid . . . afraid to lose me like she lost her sister. And that is why she holds on so tight."

"If you were mine," he said, "I would hold on too."

They were connected in a way that broke barriers. That invisible thread drew them near when they should have stood apart. Judaism had taught her to believe in miracles. How else to explain the Hanukkah candles lasting eight nights when there was only enough oil for one? And now there was Eddie. He was her miracle.

A wave slammed into the rocks, sprinkling them with water. Eddie said, "We are friends, yes?"

That was the problem. Eddie was becoming more than a friend. She didn't feel for her friends what she felt for him. Not even Abel.

"Of course we are, dummy." She felt jittery inside. "Sing me another song."

This time, he sang in English, about a brown-eyed girl. She closed her eyes and stretched out along the sand, the words and the sunlight drenching her body in heat.

~

After everyone had gone to bed, Sara grabbed a stool and snuck into the hall closet where they kept the Haggadahs and tablecloths and wrapping paper. She felt around the top shelf until she found Elijah's guitar. Hoisting it over her shoulder, she didn't expect him to miss it. He never played, and it had been collecting dust.

Making sure no one saw her, she tiptoed toward her bedroom, stuffing the guitar under her bed.

The next day, when Eddie met her at their spot, she told him she had a surprise for him and asked him to meet her there at eight o'clock that night. She couldn't risk getting caught, and eight was the magic hour when Shira spritzed Anais Anais perfume on her wrists, and

Moshe escorted her down to the club room for bingo and drinks with colorful umbrellas.

Sara smiled to herself as she took to the stairs. On the off chance she might run into her mother, she had thrown a boxy sweatshirt over her revealing tank top and extra-large sweatpants over her tiny short shorts. With the guitar strap hitched to the back of her neck, she clumsily made her way down the seven flights, counting each step in her head. There were ninety. But she already knew that.

Sara peeked out of the stairwell to be sure the coast was clear and that no one saw her sneaking off into the night. After an elderly couple turned the corner, leaving behind the stench of cigars and hair spray, Sara tiptoed through the marble lobby, past the leather chairs and couches, escaping through the double doors to the patio and pool. That's when she ran smack into Mr. Santiago, Eddie's grandfather. Mr. Santiago was dressed in his uniform, the crisp, white short-sleeved button-down with black trousers, his hair neatly combed. Sara noticed his eyes matched his grandson's.

Mr. Santiago gazed at the guitar and then at Sara. At first, she thought he wasn't going to let her pass. Oddly enough, Sara felt a kinship to Mr. Santiago, as though he could read her thoughts and she his. He seemed to say, *My grandson is everything to me. He's already endured so much pain.* And she answered, *Eddie is my friend. I'd never hurt him.* Even if Mr. Santiago's thoughts were in Spanish, they spoke the same language. He moved out of the way to let her through, and as she swallowed nervously and glanced one last time in his direction, her eyes pleaded, *Please don't tell anyone you saw me.*

Sara picked up speed as she crossed the patio and passed the locked-up cabanas. When she reached the sand, she kicked off her flip-flops and began to run. She moved as quickly as she could with a bulky guitar weighing her down, hoping to beat Eddie to their spot, hoping to surprise him. Then she'd pull off the sweatshirt and pants and throw her hair up in a long ponytail, because he had once told her that she looked *bonita* with her hair off her face. But when she approached the rocks, Eddie was already there.

CHAPTER 11

"WHAT'S THE FREQUENCY, KENNETH?"
BY R. E. M.

Los Angeles
October 1996

Eddie Vee was proving impossible to find. Every lead came up short, and if his former managers and handlers knew of his whereabouts, they remained tight-lipped, unwilling to talk. For as big and bright as his star had once shone, the man had vanished, slipped from the sky, leaving not a trace of stardust.

It was already Thursday, September rolling into October, the days sliding into one another, and Pete hadn't responded to Cecilia's telegram. Disappointment crept through her, a nagging sense of helplessness. Pete was mad. Legitimately so. And she wondered if he could find a way to see through all that anger. She tried his cell phone, and it again went to voice mail. More than anything, she liked listening to his voice on the outgoing message.

She ended the call and wondered if he thought about her when he sat on the deck, inhaling the ocean breeze. Or when the band played tunes by the pool, knowing that if she were there, she'd march toward the lead singer in the pink floral bikini that barely covered her ass and suggest her own playlist. She smiled at the thought before remembering what she'd done, how there'd be no ripping off that bathing suit later in the cabin while Dave Matthews sang about crashing into him.

She knew by the crinkled itinerary on her desk that she had missed their scuba dive in the azure waters off Grand Cayman and the hiking tour through the hills of Cozumel. They were supposed to have explored Dunn's River Falls in Ocho Rios, followed by an evening under the stars watching *When Harry Met Sally*. Normally, she could tolerate their distance and his absence, but today it was unbearably hard.

Instead, Cecilia sat in the weekly staff meeting, already surmising that her boss was in a foul mood. It didn't take much to rile Joan. She could be excitable and meticulous about most things, but some things really set her off. Like Marilyn Manson. Even though Cecilia was technically not supposed to be at the meeting, Joan had asked her to join the other writers. Attending by speakerphone in the Manhattan office were the heads of production, ad sales, and distribution, along with more writers and editor-in-chief Brett Wright.

There was no mistaking who was in charge at the magazine. Wright had managed the editorial concepts and features for the last two decades. A brash, ballsy man, his interests broke boundaries and he published edgy, intellectual pieces. Cecilia was fascinated by Wright's brazen leadership and occasional bad behavior, and she couldn't help admiring what he'd created.

"This is bullshit, Brett," Joan said, directing her voice toward the speakerphone. "We agreed Gillian Anderson was going on the January twenty-third cover. I've already promised her people—"

"Anderson was just on the cover with Duchovny—"

"That was six months ago. She deserves her own cover."

"Tell her people we'll move her to February."

All eyes landed on the speakerphone, where Brett's commanding voice had Joan out of her seat, pacing the floor. She stopped, leaned over the device, and shouted, "Absolutely not. We're starting the year with a bold woman—"

"Tori Spelling's on the December/January spread. You got what you wanted, Joan. A woman welcoming us into the new year."

"Not who I had in mind, Brett. Did we not just have this conversation? Rolston's set up the photo shoot. Lipsky's finished the article. It's a lock."

"Unlock it. Manson's the January twenty-third cover story. Anderson February sixth." But then he changed his mind. "I take that back. Anderson's the twentieth. We've got Stone Temple Pilots on the sixth."

Listening to their volley, Cecilia wondered why she was there. Was she expected to chime in on the virtues of Gillian Anderson over those of the controversial Manson? She could, but Brett Wright made her a tad nervous. And her thoughts drifted to Pete.

"Cecilia, did you hear me?" Joan said.

Cecilia's heart ticked loudly in her chest. She hadn't.

"Tell Mr. Wright what you're working on."

What the A Fuck? Cecilia wanted to strangle Joan, but she glared at her instead. She stammered and Joan watched, amused. If this was it, if this was her big moment, talking into a speakerphone with four sets of eyes trained on her, at least she was dressed in her badass leather jacket and had swiped on a fresh coat of Vamp lipstick, which gave the impression that she was a lot tougher than she felt.

"Hi," she began. "Can you hear me?"

Brett replied, "Get to it, Miss James. We haven't got all day."

"Don't be such a douche, Brett," Joan said. "This is one to watch."

Cecilia blushed, and she was glad Brett couldn't see. She sucked in her breath and got to it. "I found the muse behind 'What You Do to Me.'"

Chatter filled the room, and she inwardly beamed.

"Is this true?" Brett asked.

Joan's stare implored her to answer. Cecilia found her voice, clear and steady. "I found the lead sheet. It was signed by Eddie. The woman who dropped it was at the High Tide memorial down in Miami." You could hear a pin drop in both LA and New York.

"So you have a name?" Brett asked matter-of-factly.

Fuck. "No. But I will."

His silence felt long and prickly.

"I thought you said you found the muse. Isn't that what you said? I have Christine over here taking notes, Miss James. Would you like me to repeat what you just said? Christine, can you please read—"

"Brett, for fuck's sake," Joan barked. "Give the girl a chance. She's got a solid lead."

Cecilia offered Joan a weak smile. "I'm going to find her."

"Great, and I'm gonna find the fucking missing Raphael painting. Anyone else with other brilliant story ideas? Viable ones?"

Cecilia wouldn't let Brett intimidate her. She'd dealt with assholes her whole life, namely the one named Don. She swallowed any lingering doubts and leaned toward the speakerphone, making sure he heard her. "Mr. Wright," she began, "this is Cecilia again." She waited for him to insult her, but he refrained. "I don't expect you to trust me. Who would? But I can assure you that just as Gillian Anderson would sell more copies than Manson and Spelling, I'm going to find Eddie Vee's muse. And when I do, you're going to give me my own column."

Nobody moved. Nobody spoke. Joan sat back in her chair, victorious, and the three writers glanced at each other as a snap of energy bristled in the air.

Brett's voice swept through the room, and Cecilia sat motionless, frozen in her chair. "You get Eddie Vee's muse, Cecilia James, and the column is yours."

And Cecilia could finally breathe again.

～

With renewed momentum, Cecilia spent the remainder of the afternoon tracking down leads. When she cross-referenced multiple sources, Eddie's early years led to the same dead ends. His official biography had him living in Argentina as Eddie Santiago until he moved to Miami Beach, but she couldn't even find a yearbook picture. Dates didn't line up, and if there was one thing Cecilia knew from her years of fact-checking articles, it was the importance of a consistent timeline.

With Eddie Vee, there were many gaping holes. No parents. A mysterious grandfather who never talked to the press. After Eddie's abrupt departure from the Atlantic Towers, there were gaps, no addresses, until she located the house Eddie purchased and later fled from in Los Angeles. Celebrities were known to use pseudonyms or business entities to protect their anonymity, and the holes left barrels of questions.

On Friday, she found a promising clue. At this point, Cecilia wasn't sure what her endgame was. Was it impressing Brett enough for a column or the personal satisfaction of finding Sarita?

Digging through a microfiche archive at the local library, she accidentally came across five high schools (all along the water) with Hi-Tide, modified spelling, as their moniker. One of them was in Miami Beach, Florida.

Cecilia raced back to the office, listening to the new Weezer album on her Walkman. Checking the time in Miami, close to three in the afternoon, she slung the earphones around her neck and dialed Miami Beach High.

A woman answered on the third ring. "It's a great day at Miami Beach High, home to your favorite Hi-Tides. This is Virginia speaking, how may I help you?"

"Hi, my name is Cecilia James, and I'm a writer with *Rolling Stone* magazine." God, she loved saying that. "I was wondering who I might talk to about a former student?"

Virginia's tone lightened when she realized Cecilia wasn't a parent calling with a complaint. "*Rolling Stone*? The one they have at my beauty parlor? Is it really named after the Rolling Stones?"

When Cecilia had first accepted the job, Tori had asked the same question. And she remembered her father explaining how the magazine was a blend of inspirations, a trifecta of sorts (Cecilia suspected Tori had no idea what trifecta meant), paying homage to the band, to the Muddy Waters tune "Rollin' Stone," and to Bob Dylan's "Like a Rolling Stone." Cecilia didn't always like admitting it, but she appreciated her father's uncanny depth of music culture. He'd added how Dylan's song and the magazine's name came from the old saying "a rolling stone gathers no moss." Cecilia knew exactly what that meant. Don was nothing if not a rolling stone. The man who couldn't be satisfied with one family, he had to move on and create another.

Cecilia tucked away her disdain for her father and relayed, in brief, the magazine's connection to the band and the songs. "The Stones have already been on the cover of the magazine twenty-two times," she added.

"How interesting, Miss James. You should come speak to our students."

Cecilia said she'd love that, finally asking whether a student by the name of Eddie Vee or Eddie Santiago had attended the school.

"Oh dear, I know all the students here, and there are a lot of them. No Eddie Vee that I can think of. Santiago is pretty common. I'd have to look."

"He wouldn't be a current student. He would have graduated . . ." And Cecilia knew the exact date, having already compiled a spreadsheet. "He'd be around thirty-two today, so that puts him in high school from '79 to '82."

"Eddie Vee sounds so familiar to me, though I'm certain we never had a student by that name," Virginia said.

Cecilia stopped herself from telling the kind woman that Eddie Vee was, at one time, the most popular singer in the world. She knew that one key to good investigative reporting was letting your subject come to a revelation on their own. But could his attendance for four years have gone unnoticed? Somebody would already have put two and two together. Somebody would have recognized him.

"Oh goodness. You mean Eddie Vee the singer? If he had attended Beach High, I would've known. We all would've known. Oh my," Virginia said. "Is he in some sort of trouble?" she asked. "Again?"

Cecilia assured her he wasn't in any trouble. Quite the opposite, actually.

"I should get Dolores on the line. She knows all our former students. Maybe I'm wrong, though I don't know how that could be. Hold on a moment, Miss James." Cecilia had to hold the phone away from her ear when Virginia shouted, "DOLORRESSS."

There was a click and Cecilia listened to the school fight song when a soft, nasally voice cut into the cheer. "Hello, this is Dolores, how may I help you?"

Cecilia introduced herself and mentioned Eddie's name again.

"Oh dear, I hope Eddie Vee's okay . . . My daughters just love him . . . Just awful what happened here . . . But he didn't attend our school." A bell rang in the background, and Cecilia waited. "Once, just after the accident, we had a handful of reporters visit, thinking he had been a student. That's happened a lot with the band's name. People trying to uncover some sort of history. There are several schools with the nickname. No Eddie Vee here. No Eddie Santiago who became Eddie Vee either."

"Do you have a music teacher on staff?" Cecilia asked.

"Of course we do. We value the arts as much as the core subjects."

"How long have they been employed there?"

Dolores was no dummy. "You think maybe one of our instructors knew Eddie Vee?"

Cecilia couldn't be sure, but since this Sarita was in Miami and there was a school with the nickname Hi-Tides, it was her only link, and she was going with it. "Were there any music teachers at the school with the initials P. F.?"

"I'd love to help you out," Dolores said. "I'll pull the employment records. There's been quite a bit of turnover. I'm just packing up for the day . . . Have to get my youngest from the elementary school . . . I'll be here tomorrow to finish up some paperwork. Probably around ten in the morning. I'll check the records then."

Calculating the time difference, Cecilia thanked her. "I'll call you back. And don't worry. Eddie's not in any trouble. In fact," she added, "I think we're going to save him."

～

Cecilia didn't know which to tackle first: Pete? Or Eddie and Sarita? But since her hands were tied with Pete, and today was a day at sea, a day Cecilia hoped Pete would use to consider her apology, she turned her attention to the young couple. She wasn't the only journalist who had knocked at Miami Beach High's doors, asking about Eddie. Yet, she had a hunch that she was close. Eddie had thanked this P. F. person for teaching him everything he knew. It had to be music. Maybe this person would be willing to talk. It was worth a shot.

Feeling both hopeful and unsettled, Cecilia wished she had someone to discuss these things with. She thought about reaching out to April. It didn't feel right being home without letting her know. They'd never kept secrets from each other before, but she decided to wait, not ready for April's admonishing.

On previous nights like this, when Cecilia's mind was in a whirl and she couldn't slow it down, when Pete was off on a shoot, April was occupied with the baby, and she wanted to talk to her mother, Cecilia would head over to the Sunset Strip.

The four-lane street was noisy and colorful, just like in her childhood. Being there reminded her of the nights she'd lain across her parents' bed while Gloria and Don dressed for an evening out. Cecilia would stare up at the Sputnik ceiling light, which brightened the yellow-and-orange flowered wallpaper. The Eagles and Van Morrison played on the radio. The Byrds and Dion. Don would sing along, sing to Gloria, while she combed her long blond hair and applied fake eyelashes. And when Gloria walked out of her closet dressed in a gauzy gold dress cinched at the waist, with blue eyeshadow crowning her lids, Don scooped her off the shaggy green carpet and twirled her into the air. Cecilia could swear glitter fell from the ceiling, landing on her cheeks. They'd drag her off the bed, welcome her into their sacred circle for a dance. The smell of Charlie wafted to Cecilia's nose, and she remembered smiling so hard her face hurt.

The Charlie bottle sat in her bathroom now. She didn't dare use it, though she did take it out from time to time to breathe Gloria in.

That's what a stroll down the Strip felt like. Childhood. On the crowded street, Cecilia would sink inside the rhythm, young couples roaming the sidewalks arm in arm, singing along to whatever songs escaped the doorways of the venues and bars. Beautiful people raced by in convertibles with Guns N' Roses blaring on the radios. Noise and laughter and dreamers. The boulevard brought back those early years when music flooded her home.

Slipping on her Doc Martens and sliding into her shortest miniskirt, Cecilia grabbed her jacket and locked the door behind her. In the cab, she rolled down the window, the crisp California breeze blowing her hair as the taxi left Brentwood, crossed the 405, and wound through Bel Air and Beverly Hills before reaching the Strip.

One of the memories that always found her when she was nostalgic and alone was the time Cecilia had watched Gloria sing the Stone Poneys to Don. She held her round hairbrush like a microphone, her lips glossed in pink. She'd just cut her hair into bangs, and she'd nervously pull at the strands with the tips of her fingers. She sang "goodbye" in Linda Ronstadt's throaty voice while seductively prancing around

Don. Cecilia's father's face was etched into her memory, the dimness in his eyes, a mysterious longing. Was it vulnerability? Was he afraid the words Gloria sang were true? Cecilia had gone over the "Different Drum" lyrics dozens of times, singing them to herself, writing them out. Did Gloria believe he'd be better off without her? Had she known her destiny?

The memory dampened Cecilia's eyes, and a collage of those earlier years passed through her mind. There was her mother's gorgeous smile as she sat on Don's lap. The two of them holding hands. Later that same night, Don had slipped into Cecilia's room to tuck her into bed, and she asked what the song meant, the song that had played over and over in her mind.

"Why doesn't Mommy want a boy who loves only her?"

"It's a song, Sugar Bug."

"But she was singing it to you. You looked sad."

"I love when your mother sings to me." He kissed her nose. "It's just a song. She didn't write it."

"Your face looked sad," she said again. "Is she letting you go?"

Maybe Cecilia had known back then what was in store. Maybe the song foretold their future and prepared them for goodbye. Maybe, she thought, maybe her father knew her mother was going to leave, and it was too painful for him to bear, so he left first.

～

Hands stuffed in her pockets, Cecilia strode purposefully along the boulevard, letting the sounds and lights lead the way. She had asked the driver to drop her off at Spago, LA's hottest restaurant, so she could pop in and see who was rubbing elbows with studio heads and record producers. A slow night, so she decided to head west along the busy street, passing Tower Records (with a flip of her finger) and the Whisky a Go Go, before reaching the Roxy.

Pedro greeted her, swinging the glass door open, and Cecilia made her way toward the back of the crowded theater and up the steps to a private entryway. The exclusive nightclub, aptly named On the Rox because it was above the Roxy, was home to celebrities and musicians, where secret parties and performances converged. Everyone knew her there. At times, Cecilia thought it ironic how doors opened for her when she was at the very bottom of the magazine's totem pole, but the interns and assistants had the most clout. Their ears to the ground, they were the ones who could maneuver favors with their accessibility and willingness.

At the bar, Fig poured her regular drink—bourbon with one ice cube. He knew her well. He knew the nights when she was feeling melancholy and blue. Tonight. And he knew when to clue her in on who was there and who was expected to show up—after her second sip and never before.

Fig set the drink in front of her and waited for his cue. "Renée Zellweger's in the corner, fending off some drunk telling her he had her at hello, and I think the Pussycat Dolls might make an appearance. There's rumblings Alex Koopman's supposed to be reviewing them for *Billboard*."

The latter didn't concern Cecilia. *Rolling Stone* had a private invitation to a showcase the week before.

The dark liquid flooded her bloodstream, but it did very little to dispel her building agitation. Reaching inside her bag for a credit card, she spotted the envelope. She took the pages of sheet music out again, studying the staff and notes more carefully. She followed along with the song until she reached a line that skipped around, where the notes didn't follow the tune she'd come to know and love. Years of piano and guitar lessons meant she could read music, pick up on when something was out of place, and she stopped. On the Rox was dark, colorful lights flashing a spectrum of pink and blue on the wrinkled pages, and she squinted to be sure she was reading correctly.

She told herself it was probably nothing, but the flutter in her stomach brought forth the memory of those early years when Don regaled her with stories of music cryptography, composers dropping secret messages in songs. There was Bach with his BACH motif, Brahms, and Schumann. And there were the ciphers and musical motifs that made private messages and allowed recipients to figure them out. Some had significant meaning; others were just games musicians played with one another.

The music grew louder, and the bar filled with beautiful people. Cecilia didn't let their nearness distract her, remaining focused on the notes. She took a swig of her drink, curiosity mounting. In all her experience with reading music, she had never come across actual hidden text, yet she was sure that woven inside this well-known love song was a secret message she could not yet understand. And she knew by the shiver that slid down her neck that the recipient could be only one woman: Sarita.

CHAPTER 12

"JESSIE'S GIRL" BY RICK SPRINGFIELD

Los Angeles
October 1996

The pages burned against Cecilia's fingers, but she knew that without a key, she couldn't decode the message. And as much as it pained her to call him, she knew she had no choice. No one understood music cryptography like Don.

Cecilia fumbled in her bag for her cell phone and realized she had left it at home.

"Fig, do you have a phone back there I can use?"

She clamped her eyes shut as Fig dialed the number. It was almost eleven o'clock, but he'd be awake.

"Hello."

"Hey, Don."

"I'm sorry. Who's this?"

"It's Cecilia," she said. "Your daughter."

His voice perked up. "Cecilia. It didn't sound like you. Is everything okay? Tori said you're on a cruise . . . We weren't expecting you back for a few days."

Ah. So these two communicated after all.

She decided she didn't owe him any explanation. Same as he hadn't had the courtesy to give her one all those years ago when he left. "Do you remember those cryptology charts . . . that game we played with secret music messages?"

"Of course. The ciphers?"

"Do you still have them? Like if I needed to decipher something in a song sheet?"

"Sure, I do." He sounded pleased with himself. "Did you come across a message?"

Cecilia deliberated sharing. "I think so."

"Come by the house tomorrow and I'll show them to you."

"Can you just fax them to me?" She covered the phone with her hand. "Fig, you've got a fax machine in the back, yeah?"

Fig nodded, but Don didn't have a fax machine. "Please come, Cecilia. It would be nice to see you. I'm off. The girls have school, and we could spend some time together. Talk."

"I need to get to this tonight."

She wasn't sure why she said this. Maybe it was to avoid having to see him, but that quickly backfired when he invited her over. Right then. "I really wish you would've let me teach you to drive, CeCe, but grab a cab, and I'll cover it when you get here."

While it went against everything she'd held on to for so long, she agreed. Cecilia paid her check and thanked Fig. The Pussycat Dolls took to the stage, and Cecilia was out the door before they played their first note.

~

The ride to her father's home in the Hollywood Hills was a short one. Cecilia stared out the taxi window, watching Los Angeles unfurl around her, wondering what she'd gotten herself into.

Cecilia believed in preparation. She believed in opportunity. And she believed in the brilliant synergy when the two intersected. Every moment of her life had followed the zigzag path that began with her conception at Woodstock to the Orange Bowl, where she sat next to the woman presumably named Sarita. But how did Don fit into the puzzle?

As the cab pulled up, the headlights glared on the Mediterranean-style house shrouded in trees and vines and her father walking toward the car with a handful of cash. Before the driver had left the driveway, Don pulled her into a warm hug. "This is such a treat," he whispered into her hair. The familiar smell of Paco Rabanne brought her back to childhood, and she swallowed the memory, focusing on what she came for.

"Come inside," he said. "Everyone's asleep. Tori has a busy day tomorrow."

As if Cecilia cared.

Being around her father elicited feelings of both comfort and unease. They had an intimacy that history couldn't erase, but it didn't make up for the distance and hostility of the last thirteen years. She wasn't his little girl anymore, and at times, she questioned if she ever had been. Her feelings shifted like the tide. Let him in or let him go. Pete and April suggested ways in which to have a healthy relationship. *Take what you can get. Manage your expectations. No disappointment there.* It was always a struggle, though. She was angry. Bruised. Ready to pounce. But that night, when she entered the house and saw the framed picture of her and Don perched on the front console at the Chateau Marmont, she vowed to herself she would try.

Who was she kidding? She wanted access to his ciphers, and this was the only way.

Don led her through his perfectly decorated home, and she realized she could count on two hands how many times she'd been there. Over the course of the last several years, their visits had been minimal. When they saw each other, it was usually at a restaurant or on the rare occasions involving her half siblings—at a recital or school play.

His new place was nothing like the one he'd shared with her mother. Everything here was neat and orderly, with no signs of the warm rhythms that had swirled within the walls of his and Gloria's home.

She followed him to his office, making note of the books on the shelves, the encyclopedias she had once claimed she could read cover to cover. Photographs of Hazel and Phoebe, her half sisters, were hung on the walls along with a few of a younger, skinnier Cecilia. The office was large enough to house his piano and a sitting area where his beloved Gibson guitar sat in its stand. Songbooks were strewn along the dark-blue velvet sofa: Joni Mitchell and Simon & Garfunkel, James Taylor and Eric Clapton. His favorites. Their favorites.

"You're still teaching the classics," she said, flipping through the piles.

He smiled, and she noticed her father was as handsome as he had been a decade ago. A full head of dirty blond hair, the blue eyes looking as though he could see inside her, see what he'd missed. She turned away.

"Do you have the ciphers?" she asked.

"Come on, Cecilia. Talk to me."

A creeping sensation climbed up her legs and settled in her chest. He didn't have them. This was a trap.

"I haven't seen you in—"

She put up a hand. "Don't go there."

"It wasn't that long ago," he said apologetically.

"Almost five months," she said. "Phoebe's birthday party. The eighth of May."

"That long?" He tipped his head to the side.

"Don, do you have the charts or not?"

He waited, but when she didn't back down, he shuffled toward his desk and pulled out a drawer. Rifling through some files, he said, "There are several ciphers, but Solfa and Haydn are the most common." He dropped two pieces of paper on the desk and sat.

Studying the charts, Cecilia remembered the Solfa Cipher well. Don had gifted her with the code when she learned to read music, matching letters with a scale degree along with note length. The Haydn Cipher was for those with no musical background but who enjoyed playing the game. One only had to match the music note with a letter to form words.

Cecilia came around him and pulled out the sheet music. In this light, it was easy to spot the notes written in blue ink. Comparing both charts, she then connected each note to the code, quickly determining that the Haydn Cipher was at play:

Bal Harbour Pier. Eight.

"What do you make of it?" she asked, like she used to do when she valued his opinion. "Have you heard of Bal Harbour Pier?"

"That depends. Do you know a Sarita?"

"Maybe." She folded the music back into its envelope.

"You can't hide music from me, CeCe. I'd recognize that song anywhere. What's this about?"

She exhaled, remembering a time she would have wanted nothing more than to share with him. It was late and she was tired, but she took the seat across from him, and once she began telling the story, she couldn't stop.

"You missed the cruise?"

"Did you hear me? Eddie Vee. I think I found his muse."

He nodded, though she couldn't be sure he grasped the enormity of what she'd said. He stared at her, hands clasped together on the desk. "I heard you," he said. "And I'm concerned about you, CeCe."

Cecilia stood up. "We're not doing this now."

"You're running . . . missing the cruise . . . avoiding me . . . to chase . . . what?"

Annoyed, she reached for her bag and fled for the door. "I knew you wouldn't understand . . . you'd turn this around . . ." Then she stopped.

A tiny seed she'd kept tightly guarded slowly began to sprout, and she made her way toward him. "I'm running? Coming from you? What a joke. What a colossal A fucking joke. You . . ." And she pointed at him, unclear if it was because of the bourbon or the hour or Pete or being in her father's world that filled her with tears. She held them in, but not the insults that had been festering for years. "You left us! You! You were supposed to love us. And you went and left. With her . . ." She pointed at the closed door and all that was behind it. "And if that wasn't bad enough, I never heard from you. You just forgot—"

"That's not true, Cecilia. It wasn't like that—"

"Don't you dare say that. Don't you dare look at me and tell me it wasn't like that. I was there, and I sat on that porch waiting for you to show up. I had my suitcase packed, and I sat there for hours." She was shaking. "You didn't show up. You never showed up. You never called. You just disappeared. Do you have any idea what that did to me?"

"You don't know—"

Her voice burst through the air, cracked but strong. "Oh, I know! Don't you dare tell me I don't."

"You don't." And it happened so fast. He moved toward her, her hand shot up, and she slapped his cheek.

He didn't flinch. A red splotch formed where she'd hit him, and his eyes burrowed into hers. "Maybe I deserved that."

She wasn't a violent person, but the release of pent-up aggression felt both satisfying and horrifying. Pulling her bag tighter against her body, she tried her best to ward off the hostile feelings. "I came for the cipher and now that I have it, I'm done here."

He reached out to try to stop her. "Cecilia, let me explain. There's things you didn't understand . . . your mom . . . Aunt Denise—"

"It's too late," she said, backing away.

"Let me at least drive you home," he pleaded, rubbing his cheek with his palm.

Shit. "Just call me a cab. Please."

"I prefer you don't get into a stranger's car at this hour."

"It didn't bother you an hour ago," she said. "Or that I've been getting into cars with strangers since I was sixteen."

It wasn't a slap, but his face reddened again. "If you'd let me explain, you'd understand."

His eyes held on to hers, and though she tried to turn away, a part of her, a very sad, broken part of her, wanted to stay.

She scanned his wall of books, music playing softly in the background, and she felt an avalanche of love and aversion she couldn't fight. He followed her eyes and reached for the *B* volume of the encyclopedia and flipped through the pages. "Let me help you. Whatever it is."

Her little temper tantrum left her feeling lighter and more forgiving. With one hand on the door, she watched him search for Bal Harbour Pier.

"Most people use computers for these things," she said.

Dropping the book, he made his way over to the computer, and Cecilia considered turning around and leaving, but without transportation she was stuck. She stood there frozen before making her way to his desk. The desire to explore this lead outweighed her need to hold a grudge. He slid over to make room for her behind the monitor as he navigated his way to the online *Encyclopedia Britannica* and punched in the name. The results were scarce, but there it was, a breakwater jutting into the Atlantic Ocean from the Intracoastal Waterway connecting Sunny Isles Beach with Bal Harbour, Florida.

"Pull up a map of Miami," she instructed him.

Her father was surprisingly adept at the computer, and a blue-and-green graphic of the Florida peninsula surrounded by the Atlantic and the Gulf appeared on the screen.

"Can we move in closer?"

Colorful lines and symbols depicted highways and landmarks.

"There. Stop."

Cecilia traced the map of Bal Harbour, beginning at the pier. Then she found the Orange Bowl stadium. The high school. Atlantic Towers. They were close. Too close to be another coincidence. Eddie Vee, High Tide, P. F., and Miami were all connected. She was sure of it. This was where he met Sarita. This is where they fell in love. And fell apart.

"Is this why you missed the cruise?" Don asked.

She was just thinking how helpful he was being when the question hit her where it hurt.

"Is that what you think?"

The bigger question was if that's what Pete thought.

"Have you heard from him?"

They could bond all they wanted to over maps, but she and Pete were none of his business. Her father persisted, doing what he did best—getting under her skin.

"I'm family, Cecilia. Talk to me."

This infuriated her. "How are we family?"

"What is it you want?" he asked.

"You really don't know?"

His eyes shifted, and he pulled out the desk drawer. There was Gloria. Beautiful and blond, smiling up at them from a black-and-white photo frayed at the edges. She smiled at the camera, smiled at him. Don had relayed the story behind the picture to Cecilia a gazillion times. The photo sat on his bedside table when Cecilia was growing up. It was weeks after they had returned from Woodstock, and Gloria had just learned she was pregnant. Some nineteen-year-olds would have been terribly afraid to find out their life was about to drastically change, but not Gloria. She immediately embraced being pregnant. She loved knowing she'd be connected to Don for life, two halves becoming whole.

He wanted to mark that day for eternity. To remind her, when their baby cried all night or became a fussy teen, how much she had wanted the child. Cecilia had seen the picture so many times of Gloria long-legged in a flowery skirt. She looked so happy. But seeing her now, Cecilia felt a pang of sadness so strong it knocked the wind out of her.

Don reclined in the leather chair with Cecilia standing over him in a weird position of power, though she felt weak and small.

"I can't bring her back," he said. "I wish I could."

"You left her," Cecilia whispered. "You could've stayed."

"I couldn't stay, honey."

And before he could elaborate, she said, "I really have to go, Don."

⟳

The clock read almost 2:00 a.m. when Cecilia climbed into bed and closed her eyes. Don had driven her home, though she had made it clear she didn't feel like talking. Peter Gabriel sang on the radio about how he loved being loved, and as they passed the intersection of Wilshire and Santa Monica, she felt a bitter ache and fought back the tears. She hated him and she needed him, and since she was a part of him, she wasn't sure who she was. When she got out of the car, she didn't turn around. She just closed the door, muffling his "Goodbye," his "I love you," and let her wobbly legs carry her up the front steps. Dropping on the bed, her and Pete's bed, she was too exhausted to check the cruise itinerary.

A few hours later, when her alarm blared in her ear, she roused herself awake to call Dolores.

"Dolores, it's me again. Cecilia James from *Rolling Stone.*"

"Cecilia, I'm happy to hear from you. I looked into the music teachers for you—"

Cecilia couldn't stop herself. She interrupted. "What do you know about the Bal Harbour Pier?"

"The pier?" Dolores's tone lowered. "Oh dear, well, between us girls, that's where all the teenagers go to, well, you know . . . let's just say . . . that's where they go *to fall in love.*"

CHAPTER 13

"CAPTAIN JACK" BY BILLY JOEL

Miami Beach
December 1978

Lugging the guitar and out of breath, Sara hurried toward Eddie. She was disappointed she didn't have time to shed the bulky clothes covering her outfit. "Eddie, you're here."

"You ask me to come. Let me help you."

As he took the guitar from her hands, a strong wind blew, and when he reached out to steady her, his fingers grazed her thigh. She was relieved he couldn't see her face, that the darkness hid the blush that crept across her cheeks.

"It's for you," she said.

"Sarita." He handled the guitar, fitting it perfectly in his arms. "I cannot accept this."

"Sure, you can."

"Sarita."

"What does that mean?" she asked.

He looked up. "It means I like you."

She wanted to tell him she liked him too, and the name. "It's my brother's," she said. "He never uses it. It's been in a closet forever. He won't notice it's gone."

"I cannot take this, Sarita."

"Yes, you can."

"I get in trouble. *Pensarán que lo robé.*"

She shook her head, not understanding.

"They think I take. *O mi abuelo.*"

He had a point.

"We can paint it!" she said.

His hands ran over the smooth finish and fingered the strings, slowly familiarizing himself with the instrument. He sang a few songs in Spanish, delicately strumming the chords. She had a feeling he was telling her things he didn't know how to say in English, his eyes fixed on her. Around them, the music mingled with the breeze, and the palm trees clapped, as if they were listening too.

"*Abuelo* has a friend. I learn on his guitar. He teach music *en la escuela.*"

"Now you have your own," she said.

He shook his head. "I can't keep this, Sarita. I want to, but no good for me. Or *Abuelo.*"

"Please take it," she said. "You're so talented. You were made to play." And when she saw she wasn't getting through to him, she said, "When I listen to you, Eddie, I feel like I'm part of something big. Like the sky never ends. Do you have any idea what you do to me? What you could do to the world?"

Her words fluttered through the air, stroking his cheeks.

"You have silly dreams, Sarita. What I do to you? No. No . . . it is what you do to me."

She wanted so badly to show him that she had passions too, but taking off the ill-fitting clothes wouldn't matter. He had already seen her best parts, her vulnerability spread along the sand. He dropped the guitar beside them, and Sara listened to the waves crash into the shore, thinking about what they had just confessed, wishing they could stay like this.

Eddie fiddled with the guitar strings, and Sara asked about his studies. She thought it remarkable he was homeschooled.

"I think *Abuelo* likes *Señora Sibony*. He puts on cologne when she comes over."

This made Sara laugh.

"Doesn't it get lonely? Don't you ever want to meet other kids?"

He peered into her eyes. "You go to school. You say you are alone."

He knew her well. With him, she didn't have to explain; he read every emotion. It seemed pointless that something that came so easily could be so complicated. She knew that she could never date Eddie, but she didn't have to accept it, not when the feelings were this big. And they were young. *Aba* would love playing guitar with Eddie, and there was plenty of time for her to convince *Ima* he would never hurt her.

"You need to play music, Eddie. You need to sing. All the time. Every day. You're really good. And you can get out of here . . . go to Hollywood and be a star like Leif Garrett."

"You can come with me, Sarita."

She smiled inwardly, but she knew it wasn't possible. He would go off into the big world, and she would forever be stuck in Glenwood Estates, and their paths would never cross again.

She pulled the elastic bottoms of her sweatpants up, revealing her legs, and he reached over and placed a finger below her knee, tracing the skin down to her ankle. A spray of tiny bumps dotted her skin and she shivered. She liked the feel of his hand on her skin. When he reached her toes, he turned to her, their faces so close she could read every thought in his eyes. What she saw there scared her, but not in a way that made her want to run away. He leaned in closer, a tiny freckle at the corner of his lip appearing, and she felt his breath against her mouth.

"I want to kiss you, Sarita."

"I want you to kiss me, Eddie."

But a noise down the beach broke them apart, and they turned to look. Down by the water, Sara spotted her brother Elijah and a group of boys heading in their direction. She grabbed Eddie, and they hid behind the rocks until they'd passed, their voices muffled by the wind and surf.

"They're gone," she whispered to Eddie.

He found her eyes again, his fear staring back, and she knew at once the moment had been spoiled, a grim reminder that they were two people forbidden to be together. Had Elijah caught them kissing and told her parents, she'd be punished for life.

"I have to go," Sara said.

"I walk you back."

Eddie would never let her walk the beach at night alone, but they couldn't risk being seen.

"I'll go first," she said. "Stay behind me."

Eddie wasn't pleased. He obliged, but not before telling her she had to return the guitar.

"Your grandpa is always painting something in the building, Eddie. Paint the guitar. No one will know. It's my gift to you."

"I cannot accept."

"I'm not giving you a choice. Take it. And when you're lonely, make music."

At that, he tightened his hold on the instrument, and the sadness spread across his face. "What holiday you come back?"

"I'm not sure," she said. "I'll write to you. You can practice your English."

"It's not the same."

She knew that. But how to tell him that when she came back, their feelings would be bigger and brighter? Their world would never be the same.

CHAPTER 14

"MY SHARONA" BY THE KNACK

Los Angeles
October 1996

On Sunday, the morning Pete was scheduled to return home, Cecilia awoke bleary-eyed and stared at their itinerary. He had departed from Miami at 8:03 a.m. and was expected to land at LAX at 10:58 a.m. That was in twenty minutes.

Instead of dwelling on all she'd missed—the comedy show, dressing for the formal dinner, last-night-of-cruise sexy sex—she practiced her apology, grocery shopped for Pete's favorite foods, and went over the conversation she had had the day before with Dolores from the high school.

After filling her in on Bal Harbour Pier, Dolores gave Cecilia the name of a music teacher who had worked at Beach High from 1972 to 1982. His initials happened to be P. F.

Cecilia's heart raced when she heard this news. "Do you have contact information for this man?"

"Oh dear," Dolores had said. "We're not allowed to give that information out. I'm not even supposed to give you his name—"

"Dolores, this is really important."

"I can give him your number and have him reach out to you."

That would never work.

"Dolores, do you want to help Eddie Vee? You'd be doing him a huge favor."

Dolores hemmed and hawed, her Southern charm kicking in. She whispered into the phone, "Maybe if you drop by the office, there might just be a file left open on a certain counter, oh, but you're in California, righty?"

"Righty." But already Cecilia had considered her next move. She needed to convince Joan to let her fly back to Miami. Sarita was there. Their love story began on that beach. And a music teacher who was meaningful enough for Eddie to mention in the liner notes had to be a reliable source of information. Worst case, if this lead dead-ended, she could visit the Atlantic Towers and ask the staff about the most compelling connection to Eddie Vee, his grandfather.

From what Cecilia had gleaned from the countless articles and notes about the band, Carlos Santiago was untraceable. He'd likely changed his name and maintained a low profile on the shores of Miami Beach. The one reporter who had located him early in the investigation came up with nothing. Mr. Santiago refused to talk, going so far as denying that Eddie was his grandson. The only way to get to the bottom of the mystery woman and perhaps find Eddie's grandfather was to return to Miami.

But first, she needed to focus on Pete. The worst thing she could do, worse than not showing up on their cruise, would be to fly out of town as he walked through their door.

~

It was past twelve when a cab pulled up to the house. She peered out the window and watched as a suntanned Pete unloaded his suitcase from the trunk. She checked her reflection in the mirror one last time—an outfit she'd chosen after watching Courteney Cox on *Friends*. A pale-blue button-down, knotted at the waist, stonewashed jeans, and white Keds. Forgoing her leather jacket and Doc Martens, she aimed for a friendlier look, something that said "approachable" and "forgive me."

She heard his key in the door just as their home phone rang, and she let the answering machine pick it up. April's voice skipped through the air as Pete stepped through the door. "It's me again! I need every detail. You have to call me."

Their eyes met, and she knew at once the sun and surf hadn't quashed his anger. Pete was pissed.

She waited patiently, watching him drop his bag, his keys. Mustering the courage, she took a step in his direction.

"Don't."

"Pete."

"No, Cecilia. I can't."

He passed her on the way to the kitchen, grabbing a glass of water and guzzling it down before falling on the faded couch. As he dropped his legs on the coffee table, piled high with magazines, one slid onto the hardwood floor. The Fugees stared up at them.

"Please talk to me, Pete," she said, taking the seat beside him.

He stared straight ahead, avoiding her eyes.

"Pete?" It was a question and a statement. "You need to let me explain."

"There's nothing to explain, Cecilia. I can't do this anymore."

"This had nothing to do with work." Her voice sounded strangled. "I swear to you. I checked the itinerary. As long as I made it by four . . . and I did . . ." She stopped herself from mentioning the three o'clock boarding. "You have no idea what I went through to get there on time."

"You know what I think," he said, his legs coming off the table and landing on the floor. "I think you're completely unaware of what you do." Then he laughed, which hurt her worse than his words. "You do these things. You avoid. You cancel. There's a pattern here."

"That's not true."

"You don't see it, but somehow you always manage to disappear. To keep everyone at arm's length. Look, you knew this trip was important to me. I honestly can't believe you didn't make it on the ship."

His disappointment laced through his words, and she was desperate for him to understand.

"I tried to get a flight to meet you at the next port. Everything was sold out. I did everything I could. It was a terrible mistake."

He finally met her eyes. His mouth curved in a frown. "You have no idea what a mistake it was."

His words felt like a dagger.

"I'm sorry," she said.

"I am too."

A moment passed where she saw a hint of last week's Pete. Loving Pete. Willing Pete. But it quickly faded. She didn't know why she thought the key to fixing things involved a play-by-play from that day, but she recounted the excruciating details, losing his camera, the chance meeting with the mysterious woman.

But her explanation only drove him away. He got up from the couch and headed for their bedroom. When he reached the door, he stopped, called over his shoulder. "You should pack your things."

She was sure she hadn't heard him correctly. Pack her things? They loved each other. People who loved each other stayed together; they worked things out.

She followed behind him. "None of that made me late. I timed everything to the minute." He wasn't listening. He was pulling off his jeans and shirt. His body was trim and tan, no signs of the all-you-can-eat buffet. She imagined undressing alongside him, turning on Keith Sweat, pushing up against him in the shower.

"Please, Cecilia. I need you to go."

Worry slid through her body. "You want me to go? Where am I supposed to go? Come on, Pete. We can work through this. You're jet-lagged and not thinking clearly." Her voice sounded panicky.

"You're wrong."

He was down to his boxers, and she thought about lunging forward and just making him forgive her. Fear lodged in her throat. "Why are you doing this?"

He turned to her, chin high, confident despite being half-naked. That was Pete's way. Composed in the most vulnerable state. "I've had a lot of time to think this through. Time we should've been together, figuring out our future."

The swipe hurt, and she dared to move in closer.

"I just think it's best we part ways, Cecilia. We've had six great years, and maybe this is how it ends."

Cecilia bit her lip to tamp down the emotions clamoring to come out. Her stomach clenched, and she needed air. "You can't do this, Pete. This was a careless error. I prepared. I made a timeline! I followed it to a T."

He didn't respond.

"Do you actually think I did this on purpose?"

"I don't know what I think. But I just spent what should have been the best week of our lives alone, and even when it was difficult and upsetting, I saw things clearer than ever before."

"What's this really about?" she asked. "We've always been on the same page about our relationship."

"Maybe we're changing. Or I'm changing. You hide inside songs and lyrics, but I need reality and compromise. I need someone invested in us."

"I can give you that." She reached a hand out to touch him, but he backed away. "Please don't make a rash decision. You're mad. I get it. You have every right to be, but we love each other."

Without answering, he simply stripped down to nothing and walked toward the shower.

~

Nothing about the next twenty-four hours was pleasant for Cecilia.

When Pete exited the bathroom, smelling fresh and clean, she begged for his forgiveness. Curt and dismissive, he seemed determined to shut her out. April called again, and this time Pete answered the phone. She heard him say, "You didn't hear? She never made it on the ship." And then, "I'll let her tell you herself," before handing her the phone.

The receiver was a cold annoyance in her hands. "I can't talk, A."

"What the hell, C?" April said. "Where've you been all week?"

"Not now."

The last thing she heard was April hollering into the phone, "I knew you'd screw this up."

"What's gotten into her?" Cecilia asked.

Pete shook his head. "You wouldn't understand."

And when he told her he had to go to the office, she knew it was an excuse to get away from her—it was Sunday for God's sake—and when he left, he didn't kiss her forehead or whisper "TTM" but slipped out of the house quietly. Cecilia paced the floor, trying to figure out a way she could fix this. She told herself this would subside, that he'd eventually forgive her and come to terms with her colossal fuckup. But when he returned, as the sun began to drop from an ominous sky, he looked at her draped across the couch and said, "I'll help you pack."

She rose to meet his gaze, her voice trembling. "Where do you want me to go?"

"Stay at April's. Or your dad's."

He couldn't be serious, and the memory of slapping Don flashed through her mind.

"I need to move on with my life, Cecilia. I can't do that with you here. You need to go."

"You can't mean this." She choked on the words.

"I do. There's always going to be another story, another song you have to chase. That's just your way."

"You used to like that about me! What happened? I thought you supported my career."

"I need more, Cecilia. I need more of you. And I'm not sure you're ready for that."

He was really doing this. This wasn't some knee-jerk reaction. Pete was breaking up with her, and the shock rattled her to the core. She pleaded with her eyes, but his were calm and sure. Any sadness that may have been there had washed away, the brown flaring with conviction.

Cecilia felt blindsided. She had expected him to be angry, but she hadn't expected this. And now she was angry. Angry that he refused to hear her out, angry that he gave up so easily, angry that love turned into another disappointment.

Though she was rarely at a loss for words, Cecilia's mouth opened and closed but nothing came out. She wasn't sure her legs had the strength, but putting one foot in front of the other, she willed herself toward the closet and grabbed clothes off hangers. Her empty suitcase sat on the floor from the week before, and she threw her things in, not caring about wrinkles or order. With shaky hands, she balled up underwear and bras and T-shirts, Debbie Harry's sultry eyes reminding her of the day they had gone to the passport office, when they were on the cusp of something fresh and exciting. All that was to come now lay in a messy pile, and she pulled furiously at the zipper. When it didn't budge, she sat on the closure, pressing down with all her weight.

Adding insult to injury, Pete brought her two more pieces of luggage, and she politely thanked him, put on a brave face, and concentrated on packing the pieces of her life.

She couldn't go to April's. Her mother-in-law had just arrived, and the house was already full. She could call Joan. Or Dean. But neither option felt right.

Which left her with only one choice. And when the cab arrived to drive her away, the skies opened up, and a piece of her heart broke off, washed away in the downpour. Pete watched, expressionless. Six years dissolved in a single snap. Tears pooled in her eyes, but she clamped down on the swell of emotions. She reminded herself that she was Cecilia James. She was destined for great things. And she swallowed the hurt and decided nothing was going to stop her.

CHAPTER 15

"COME ON EILEEN" BY DEXYS MIDNIGHT RUNNERS

Miami Beach
Summer 1979

Sara's thoughts plagued her the entire flight to Florida.

They hadn't been to the Atlantic in six months, the longest stretch of time between visits. It was as though *Hashem* had been watching and knew what was about to happen, delaying the inevitable.

Normally, the family would fly in for Passover or a long weekend, but Moshe had slipped on the icy steps to their porch, requiring surgery on his knee, and then her brother Abraham was in the throes of a Bar Mitzvah year—he and his friends turning thirteen—and hell hath no fury like teenagers missing a party. It had been six months, but it felt like years since she and Eddie had parted at the beach, parted from the kiss that could have been. She thought about calling him, but how would she explain the long-distance charge on their bill? Instead, she mailed him long, detailed letters, knowing he couldn't write back, couldn't risk Shira intercepting them. She thought about him all the time, her cousins and siblings often asking her where she went, why she was always inside her head. She was with him, and as the days neared when she would see him again, she wondered if he remembered the almost kiss. And if he wanted to try again as much as she did.

Elijah and Deborah had both fallen asleep, and she'd given up on the Sidney Sheldon book that had earlier consumed her. To make matters worse, she'd spotted Abel a few rows back when she'd gone to the restroom. Most summers, the Altmans visited the Jersey Shore, but this summer, Shira and Abel's mom, Sheila, were in cahoots, their matchmaking efforts painfully obvious.

Sara's once-close friend barely waved. Abel was mad at her. Or hurt. He had cornered her in the hallway on the last day of school, asking if he'd done something wrong. "How come we never hang out anymore?" What he meant was *Why did we make out in the tree house, only for you to now ignore me?* She loved Abel. And she had gotten carried away. She was curious about his lips, his mouth, about kissing. They had been raised side by side, coordinating Purim costumes and running in and out of each other's houses, but after that experimental kiss, she had pulled away, Eddie flashing through her mind. She couldn't tell Abel it was a mistake, about her growing feelings for someone else, the forbidden attraction to a boy on the beach. This summer, she would have to be extra careful.

~

After the hour-long wait at baggage claim and confusion over who was getting into which cab, the caravan departed Miami International Airport, passing Downtown and crossing the Julia Tuttle toward Collins Avenue and the beaches. That first glimpse of the ocean at the top of the causeway always sent a thrill through Sara's body. But this time, the thrill centered on Eddie.

As they pulled up to Atlantic Towers, the excitement echoed through the lobby. Summer had arrived, and it was a race to see who would get to the water first. Sara couldn't wait to throw on her orange bikini and run out to their spot. Moshe always alerted Mr. Santiago beforehand of their arrival, so Eddie always knew when to find her.

Sara was fifteen when she last saw Eddie; sixteen had changed her. As she inspected her body in the floor-length mirror in her bedroom, she wondered if he'd notice her breasts were fuller or how she'd grown her hair longer. It was an improvement, but when she appraised herself in the mirror, all she saw was her mousy brown hair and plain face, nothing like the pretty blond, blue-eyed models on the covers of magazines. And now the bazookas! That's what Deborah had called them. Why had *Hashem* given her something so noticeable when Shira expected her to hide them away?

Turning around in the mirror, she reached for the clear gloss on her dresser to coat her full, red lips. She didn't need lipstick like the other girls, and that felt like a small win. Her mother had only begun to allow her to wear makeup—the bare minimum—and Shira rarely wore any herself. "You don't need to draw attention to your appearance," she had said when they'd walked through the cosmetics aisle at the five-and-dime. Sara was convinced her mother detested the boldness of her daughter's lips because it was something she couldn't control.

Sara's brothers ran out ahead, slamming the apartment door behind them, and her mother eyed her in the bikini, the straps tied around her neck. She gave her a long list of instructions on sunscreen, staying within twenty feet of the shore, not talking to strangers, and the kicker, being nicer to Abel.

"I'm always nice to Abel, *Ima*."

"Sheila said—"

But Sara didn't want to hear about the *shidduch*, the arranged marriage they'd put together. Once it was cute, now it was frustrating, and Shira stopped herself when she saw the look on her daughter's face.

Sara rode down the elevator and stepped outside the building, the warm air mingling with the cool air-conditioning in the doorway. Crowds of families milled around the pool area, and when she recognized familiar faces, she bowed her head, wanting to avoid small talk.

The sun was a balm, tingling her skin as she took that first step on the narrow path that led to the beach. To him.

Sara was so sure of herself, of Eddie, her steps quickened, and she hardly noticed the heat burning through her flip-flops. But when she arrived at the rocks, Eddie wasn't there. As she scanned the beach, sure she would spot him, a soft melody reached her ears. Her eyes followed the sound until they landed down the shore. It was him. Eddie. And he wasn't alone. Eddie was holding court, singing, strumming his guitar, Elijah's guitar—painted bright blue—with a gaggle of young girls huddled around.

She blinked her eyes to be sure. Yes. It was definitely Eddie. She'd recognize his voice anywhere. He was singing that song she loved where the guy dreamed of being in California. He had grown even taller, and though a large straw hat covered part of his face, she could tell he was even more handsome, his long hair tumbling down his toned shoulders. She stopped to soak him in. This beautiful boy with the velvety voice was a treat for the bikini-clad girls who swayed to his music, but no one more than Sara. She wasn't prepared for the swell of longing that hitched to her chest and squeezed. And he was enjoying himself. He always did when he sang, but today he seemed different. It was in the way he held his shoulders back and how he caught the eyes of the crowd singing along with his words.

Then someone called out, "Leif."

Leif?

He looked nothing like a Leif.

Sara inched closer. Deborah saw her out of the corner of her eye and approached. "He's so gorgeous. Be still my beating heart." Deborah was nothing if not a tad dramatic.

"You honestly don't know who that is?" Sara asked, wanting to remind her—all of them—that this was the boy they'd shunned for years. But Deborah didn't hear her; she was busy singing along as Eddie began crooning Joe Jackson's "Is She Really Going Out with Him?"

Eddie spotted Sara on the fringes of the crowd, catching her eyes in his. And because she had always been able to read him, she knew exactly what he asked. She wouldn't divulge his secret, but she was tempted to remind them who he was: the boy they had grown up alongside, the boy they had ignored all those years. But they'd find out eventually. And they'd be ashamed.

Shira and the aunts approached, curious about what was unfolding on their beach. And when they saw the young man holding the crowd's attention, they rounded up the girls, enticing them back to their lounge chairs with homemade rugelach.

The girls were ushered away, shoulders hunched, feet dragging in the sand, but Sara hung back, sneaking a last look over her shoulder at Eddie. Shira was no dummy. She watched Sara closely, noting anything that entered her daughter's orbit.

"Hard to believe that's Mr. Santiago's grandson," Shira said.

His eyes latched on to Sara's, just as a sexy Latina with feathered brown hair cozied up next to him. She wrapped an arm around his shoulder, and he turned away from Sara.

Sara's body burned, and it wasn't from the sun or her mother's scrutiny. She strode closer to Shira and dropped on a chair, cursing the day she'd met Eddie Santiago. Shira sat beside her and offered an opinion.

"I'm surprised Mr. Santiago lets his grandson perform on the beach like that. It will only lead to trouble. I heard he doesn't go to school." Then she glanced over at Sara, who was silently cursing herself, cursing him, telling herself she could atone these feelings on Yom Kippur. Her mother added, "Singing won't get him very far in life. He'd be better off getting an education."

Sara didn't bother defending Eddie's schooling. She picked up her book, bored with these conversations about the right boys and safe choices, but when she tried focusing on the pages, she couldn't follow the sentences or comprehend their meaning. Nothing could distract her from Eddie's nearness or the girls clustered around him, holding on to every note he sang.

"That's the kind of boy you girls need to stay away from," Shira said, loud enough for anyone within earshot to hear. "Boys like that are dangerous. They come with a lot of trouble. Just look at him."

Sara's cousins and Deborah swiveled their heads, none of them needing another excuse to gaze back at Eddie. They welcomed the chance, and Sara knew what they were all thinking, because she was thinking it too. Eddie was beautiful. He was shirtless, showing off his long, lean body and wild hair. He had an air of danger and passion, an edginess the girls had been warned against. Amid all the conformity and customs in their world, Eddie was carefree and unconventional—kissed by the sun—and no one could look away.

Sara knew she should pay attention to Shira's disapproval of Eddie. How easy it would be to buy into that one-dimensional, biased narrative, to shuck all her growing feelings. But she couldn't. She knew him in a way that her family didn't. She saw his kindness and inclusiveness. They'd never understand. But seeing him singing to all those girls upset her. This new version of Eddie was confusing.

The crowd grew, and so did Sara's discomfort. Had she imagined their closeness? Could the months have changed him this drastically?

Abel nervously approached, which only made things worse. They'd never been uncomfortable around each other. Their friendship had been effortless—the best kind—and she suddenly missed the safe consistency of his presence. "Do you want to go in the water?" he asked. He'd never had to ask before. Their diving into the ocean had always been instinctual. She set the book down, about to answer when she heard Shira's voice.

"What a lovely idea, Abel," Shira said, smiling up at the boy.

Abel smiled back. It was a warm smile, the kind that had comforted Sara in the past, saved her on more than a few occasions, and one she needed now.

"Sure." And when she said it, Abel's dark-brown eyes lightened. He stood up straighter, and it was as clear as the ocean's blue that Abel had grown in the last few months too.

Rising from the chair, Sara unbuttoned her shorts and pulled off her tie-dyed T-shirt. Undressing for someone other than Eddie was a letdown of epic proportions, nothing like the unveiling she had anticipated.

With Shira monitoring his reaction, Abel respectfully averted his gaze, but someone else did not. With a turn in Eddie's direction, even with a curvy woman rubbing up against him, Sara caught the fire in his eyes.

"I knew this would happen," her mother said, throwing her arms in the air. "A spectacle. See that? That boy . . . he's staring." She motioned in Eddie's direction.

Moshe caught the concern in his wife's voice. "It's okay, Shira. Nothing's going to happen to her."

To which Abel's mother chimed in, "Sara has a gorgeous figure." Which only made Shira tense up even more.

Eddie's eyes followed Sara from the textured sand to the damp, flattened beach. She could feel his stare tickling her back, grazing her skin like flames. The waves were loud and boisterous, echoing her inner turmoil. She wasn't sure what to make of this new Eddie. He had always been hers alone.

Abel drew shapes in the sand with his big toe. "Are we okay, Sara?"

"Why would you ask that?" Even though she knew the answer.

"You don't seem happy I'm here. Things are different. You seem different."

Behind him, she spotted Eddie giggling. So when a wave neared the shore, Sara skipped over it, diving into the foamy surf. Abel followed, and they swam out a few yards before standing again. The ocean had a way of lightening problems, untangling messes, and for a split second, she felt refreshed.

They waded out as far as they could, until the water reached their chests.

He playfully splashed her while his eyes kept landing on her top.

Sara dunked her head back in the water, soaking her hair. The coolness felt good against her skin, and she inhaled the salty scent, inhaled the calm.

"The anniversary's coming up," he said, a frown crossing his face. "My mom reminded me."

As soon as the words were out of his mouth, Sara remembered Naomi. She had never needed to be reminded before. No wonder her mother was on edge. She caught her pained reflection in the water, knowing she'd have to cut her mother some slack. But she couldn't forgive herself. That's what Eddie did to her. He made her careless.

When Abel saw her reaction, he apologized. "I shouldn't have brought it up."

"It's okay."

A wave came in and they floated over it, and when they grounded their feet on the ocean floor, he didn't hold back. "Look, Sara. We're not kids anymore. And I've missed you. Missed us." He stared at her with an expression she knew too well. "I really like you." He tried to catch her eyes, but she was studying the sparkling water. "I always have."

He was the sweetest boy she knew. A reel played in her head of that kiss in the tree house, how they'd once joked about getting married and living next door to Shira and Moshe, surrounded by their big families. "You know I care about you, Abel. You're my family, one of my closest friends, but maybe it's better we keep it that way." She gazed in Eddie's direction when she said it, and Abel winced, though it could've been from the splash of a wave.

Following her eyes, he joked, "You want to run off with some musician like Leif?"

"What if I did?"

"You don't mean that, Sara." He thought it was funny, reminding her of how her mother would forbid her. "You could never leave Glenwood. Your family's lived there forever, and you love having them around."

She did. And every part of her wanted to run off with Eddie.

"I think about it," she finally said. "Don't you?" His family lived just down the street from hers. "Haven't you ever wondered what it's like to live in another city? To spread your wings? Meet new people?"

"We are in another city."

"We've basically transported our neighborhood to Miami Beach."

He held his hands up, and she saw how his fingers had begun to prune. "I like having the family around. Big families are like football teams. There's a lot of players, and they argue and disagree, but they're on the same side, and they protect each other no matter the cost. Everything I need is there. Why would I leave?"

Glancing down the beach, Sara saw Eddie laughing and swinging the guitar.

"Do you ever feel sheltered? Like there's a bigger world out there?"

"She's gotten into your head," he said. "Your mom worries, Sara. Everyone knows how tough she is on you. It's because she loves you."

"It makes it hard to breathe sometimes."

A flock of seagulls squawked overhead in agreement. All the Glenwood families were close and supportive, and there were many benefits and blessings in their togetherness. She just couldn't deny that she wanted to see more of what life had to offer. She couldn't deny her feelings for Eddie.

And it would only get worse as the anniversary loomed.

They slowly walked back to the shore, and she could see Shira beaming in her chair while they talked. Abel's fingers swept through the water when he said, "I'm sorry it hasn't been easy for you, Sara, that you've been so unhappy."

He turned to her, and she studied the shape of his eyes—like almonds—and how the sun flecked the rich brown with green. "Will you think about it? About us?" he said.

Eddie's strumming floated through the air, and she heard every other note between the crashing of the waves. It took all her strength not to turn in his direction, to spread her wings like the birds above. But then her brothers raced toward them, splashing and laughing, skipping over the waves. And she glanced at her parents, seeing how her father lovingly rubbed suntan lotion on Shira's back, and it gave Sara hope. She searched Abel's eyes, wondering if she could ever be happy with him.

CHAPTER 16

"ROXANNE" BY THE POLICE

Los Angeles
October 1996

"Cecilia? Is that you?" Tori squinted through the peephole as Cecilia heard the door unlock.

No, you fool, it's someone else who bears a strong resemblance to your stepdaughter.

Tori's mouth was half-open, words stuck in her swanlike neck when she found Cecilia and her bags lined up on the front steps. Cecilia grabbed what she could, pushing past Tori, who stepped back to let her through. "Let me get your dad," she said, disappearing before Cecilia had a chance to change her mind.

Cecilia doubled back for the rest of her things, stacking them not so neatly in the foyer as footsteps approached. Light footsteps. Not the formidable kind that belonged to her father.

"CECILIA!"

The name came out all wrong, sounding more like "Suh Chee La," but there little Hazel stood in front of her in greeting. Hazel, her half sister.

"Hey, Haze," Cecilia said to the slender young girl with the clearest blue eyes she'd ever seen. "You've gotten so big!" she added, because what else does one say when they haven't seen their little sister in months? "And so pretty!"

Hazel was dressed in head-to-toe pink with a unicorn splattered across the front of her shirt. Its horn was made of pink fur. Even her toenails were painted pink.

Hazel didn't reply but flung herself into Cecilia, smelling of innocence and ice cream. Cecilia clumsily wrapped her arms around the nine-year-old girl and breathed in her long dark hair.

"Cecilia." Her father's voice rounded the corner. "What's going on?"

Dingbat must have clued him in to the pile of suitcases.

Hazel backed away, staring up at Cecilia, waiting for an answer, and when it didn't come, she answered for her, "Cecilia's moving in with us, Daddy."

Cecilia met her father's eyes, a question hitched to their pale blue. Hazel ran off to find her sister, jumping over their black-and-white furry cat, Mathilda. Cecilia hated cats.

"Cecilia, what's with the suitcases?"

There was no easing into this. "Can I stay here for a little while?"

"You're always welcome here. You know that."

She didn't, but he seemed sincere.

"Did something happen with Pete?"

Admitting they were over depressed her, so she just nodded, warding off the hurt.

"Oh honey." Don inched closer, but then Phoebe blasted into the room and wedged herself between them.

"CECILIACECILIACECILIA!" The greeting came out as one word, a chorus of cheerfulness, like Phoebe herself. If Hazel was a carbon copy of Tori—brunette and blue-eyed with pouty scarlet lips—Phoebe was Don. Golden hair laced in California sunshine, her features perfectly set on her cherubic face. The bright blue of her eyes changed like the ocean, depending on her mood.

Phoebe launched herself at Cecilia, and Hazel followed. They formed a fusion of limbs and legs and hair—so much hair—and whatever Cecilia had been feeling moments ago was stripped away by the affection. Over the girls' shoulders, Cecilia could see that Tori had returned, standing nervously by her husband. "They've missed you," she said.

Cecilia let the girls pull away first. There was nothing about them not to love, except that they were the result of her father's assholeness.

"Pete's being stubborn," she said. "He'll snap out of it. He has to."

Tori seemed genuinely upset. About the breakup or Cecilia moving in, she couldn't tell. Phoebe grabbed Cecilia's hand and tugged her toward her bedroom. "You can stay with me," she said, until Hazel grabbed the other hand. "No. My room!"

Cecilia welcomed the attention. When you've just been dumped, you'll take affection wherever it's offered, even from a nine-year-old and an eleven-year-old.

"Girls," Don said, "give us a minute to talk to your sister."

The girls didn't argue. They dropped Cecilia's hands and scurried away. Cecilia recognized that obedience. When she was growing up and Don made a request, she listened without argument.

"Come sit." He motioned toward the living room, bright and spacious with floor-to-ceiling bay windows overlooking the canyon. Tori followed, and Cecilia gave her the death stare. "Can I talk to my father alone?" she asked.

Tori shrank into herself, and a look passed between her and Don, but then she too scurried from the room.

"You really should be a little kinder to her, Cecilia."

"Now why would I do that, Don?"

"Because she's my wife. And because she cares about you girls."

"Which girls would those be, Don?"

"Don't make this difficult, Cecilia. She loves all of you."

"I'm drowning in her affection."

"You never gave her a chance."

Cecilia dropped on the cold leather couch. "Shame on me for having an opinion about the adolescent who wrecked our family. Can we just not go there? I need a place to stay and there's plenty of room here, so what's the issue?"

Don sat across from her, dressed in a golf shirt and shorts that matched the pale blue of his eyes. "We're going there," he said. "I tried to tell you this the other night. You're not a child anymore. Back then you were. And there were things between your mother and me that you would have never understood. I thought by now you might have figured it out, fact-checked the story, but maybe you don't want to know the truth."

Cecilia chuckled. "Older man bored with his wife bails for the younger model. Flees shamelessly to San Diego during his daughter's formative years. It's pretty clear-cut, Don. No further evidence required."

He stared at the floor, his lips pursed together. "If that's the version you're going with, I'm sorry to have to disappoint you." He shifted in his seat. "We'll get to that, but if I'm going to allow you to stay here, I won't have you filling the girls' heads with your stories—"

Cecilia balked at the hypocrisy. "So it's okay for you to fuck me up, but your precious love children are immune? Really, Don?"

"And I won't tolerate you disrespecting my wife."

"But it's okay for you to disrespect my mother?"

He crossed and uncrossed his legs. "I'm politely asking that we keep our issues between us. And that you don't slap me again."

Cecilia mulled this over.

"How long do you think you need to stay?" he asked.

"Does it matter?"

"Not at all. It'll be nice to have you around."

"Great. So now that we're all caught up, can I go to my room?"

"You can," he said. "When you get settled, we're going to talk. I want to know what happened with Pete. And there's something we need to discuss."

"Pete and I will be fine. Just a minor disagreement. Is that all?"

"Yes. One more thing. I did some digging. I have my own contacts in the business. Seems there's been a tale floating around that Eddie's gay. No disrespect, of course, but I don't want you barking up the wrong tree. It's a rumor, but I thought you should know."

Cecilia shook her head. "It's not true. And it doesn't make any sense."

"Since when do matters of music and the heart ever make sense?"

Cecilia stood and turned to leave, flattered to some extent that her father found her story interesting enough to snoop around, but he stopped her. "We should go to a concert together. Remember all the shows we used to go to? The Who's coming to town."

Cecilia didn't like this version of Don. He reminded her of the man she used to love, the one who wiped her tears, held her high in his arms so she could be closer to the sun. This Don made it hard to tap into the hateful venom that coursed through her veins. And all she could think about was how angry her mother would be if she knew Cecilia was softening toward him.

"I can't," she said, without drumming up a reason why. She couldn't go anywhere with him. Couldn't take any favors other than staying at his house. "I'm going to unpack," she said. "But thanks for the information."

"You know where the guest room is?"

Surprisingly, she did.

～

The girls found her in the back bedroom, unpacking her clothes, sliding T-shirts into drawers and hanging blouses in the closet. They oohed and aahed over the black leather jacket and skirt, the vintage halter dress that had once been her mother's. For every piece of clothing Cecilia hung on a hanger, the girls pulled another one off, slipping the fabrics onto their narrow bodies before tossing them on the bed. It was an entertaining fashion show, and she took the time to study them more closely. They were really beautiful girls, and not just outwardly. They were polite. Cheerful. Miss Home-Wrecker out there had to be doing something right. The proof was in front of her, as painful as it was for her to admit.

"Mommy says you work for a famous magazine," Hazel said, "and you meet famous people. Can I meet famous people?"

Cecilia dropped down on the bed, giving up on effectively unpacking. Clothes were strewn across the bed, while Hazel wore a gold lamé minidress that reached her toes and Phoebe sported Cecilia's favorite strappy sandals. "Who do you want to meet?" she asked. "Who would be the biggest star?"

The girls turned to each other for possibilities, and she envied their closeness.

Hazel cried out, "Madeline! I want to meet Madeline!"

"Madeline's not real," Phoebe replied, channeling all her big-sister knowingness into her response. "How about Mayim Bialik?"

"Yes!" Hazel squealed. "Blossom!" They gazed in Cecilia's direction and repeated the name in unison. "Mayim Bialik."

"Wait," Phoebe said, hobbling out of the room in Cecilia's sandals. When she returned, she was minus the shoes, pushing a large box along the floor. "I found this in Daddy's office."

"We're not supposed to go in there, Pheeb," Hazel said.

Cecilia was naturally curious. Carefully, she lifted the cardboard lid, welcomed by the scent of paper and print. She held the magazines up one by one, noticing they were in chronological order.

Cecilia had been employed by *Rolling Stone* for close to three years. There had to be over fifty issues stacked one on top of the other. And she noticed something else. Yellow sticky notes poked out from some of the pages. Many were the pieces Cecilia had either fact-checked or proofed. How could he have known? Were they that connected? The discovery left her puzzled and exposed.

"This is where you work?" asked Hazel.

"It is."

Hazel rummaged through the pile, pointing out pictures of Beavis and Butt-Head and Drew Barrymore.

"See all those pages of paragraphs? Someone interviews the famous people and puts them into a story for people like us to read."

"You write these stories, Cecilia?" Hazel asked, her big blue eyes fascinated.

"I will," she said. "Soon."

Phoebe jumped in, flipping through the stack, singling out people she'd seen on TV, *famous* people: Cindy Crawford, Julia Roberts, the casts of *Seinfeld* and *Friends*. "Mommy watches those shows," she said, smiling. And then she pointed at Oasis and R. E. M. and Eric Clapton and Neil Young. "Daddy plays their songs for us."

"Tell her how he's teaching us to play too," Hazel said.

"You just did, Haze."

"Where's your mommy, Cecilia?" Hazel asked.

Cecilia froze. They'd never asked about her mother before. But Phoebe had to be approaching puberty, with the hormones and wonder that came along with it, and Hazel was of the age where she understood Tori wasn't Cecilia's mother. She didn't know what Tori or Don had told them. For all she knew, they could have made up something so the girls wouldn't hear that mothers could die.

But before Cecilia could answer, Phoebe muttered something under her breath to her sister.

"Phoebe?" Cecilia asked.

"We're not supposed to talk about that," Hazel said, her eyes darting around the room nervously.

"About my mother?" Cecilia was rattled. She had a mother, and she had been beautiful and vibrant and fun. How dare they pretend she didn't exist?

"Daddy said she was sick, and she had to go." Hazel's soft voice wrapped around Cecilia's heart and squeezed.

Is that what that fucker told them? Now she was incensed. The truth was that he *made* her sick when he left. It wasn't the other way around.

"He didn't tell us, Hazel." Phoebe's voice was commanding, admonishing her younger sister. Then she turned to Cecilia. "Hazel heard them talking." She raised her voice in Hazel's direction. "When she shouldn't have been." Her eyes returned to Cecilia. "She didn't even understand what they were saying." Cecilia looked back at the little girl in the sequined, shimmery dress, wanting so badly to have someone to blame. But it wasn't her fault.

"My mom's not here anymore." She didn't think it required further explanation.

"We'll share our mommy with you," Hazel said.

And it chipped away at Cecilia's heart. She swallowed the hurt and returned to the pile of magazines strewn across the floor. The girls flipped through the pages, and she asked them, again, to pick someone they'd like to meet. And wouldn't you know, the girls chose Bill Clinton.

CHAPTER 17

"GLORIA" BY LAURA BRANIGAN

Miami Beach
Summer 1979

Sara washed up in the bathroom, eyeing her tan lines. She peered over her shoulder at the bright, blistery pink that stained her skin. This was another one of Shira's concerns about Sara wearing a two-piece—exposure to the scorching Florida sun. Her mother had warned her, but she had also warned her against boys like Eddie.

Her youngest brother popped his head in. Little Noah with his Coke-bottle glasses, his body still clinging to stubborn baby fat. "Mr. Santiago brought your book up. He said you left it on the beach."

He handed her a brown paper bag with her name on it, and when she peeked inside and saw *Sophie's Choice*, she smiled, but it wasn't hers. She held it up to her nose and inhaled, and when she did, she smelled him, smelled Eddie. Had he given the book to his grandfather to pass along to her? She carried it to the bedroom and closed the door.

Minutes later, Noah stormed in, carrying Clue, his favorite board game. Sara placed the book beneath her pillow and sat on the carpet for a game. Time slipped by, Sara rolling the dice while trying to figure out if Mr. Green killed Mr. Boddy with a wrench in the library or with a knife in the ballroom. All the while, Eddie sat on the fringes of her mind. He couldn't flirt with other girls and think a book would mend things.

It was past eight when Noah won. Mrs. Peacock had killed Mr. Boddy in the billiard room with a revolver, and Noah set off to watch television in the rec room with his older brothers and their cousins. They were trying out the brand-new VHS machine. Tonight, if the machine delivered what it promised, they would watch a recording of *The ABC Sunday Night Movie*. They all had their doubts.

Sara slid her hands under the pillow and pulled out *Sophie's Choice*. As she flipped through the pages, a folded piece of paper slipped out. She straightened and took it in her fingers.

Eddie had sent her a message. Her hands shook as she opened the lined paper.

But it wasn't just a message. It was music, with corresponding letters from the alphabet. There had to be some mistake. But then she spotted the handwritten note from Eddie, so tiny she almost missed it:

8:30. Our castle.

She knew at once what he meant, and she glanced at the clock radio beside her bed as the white numbers flipped to 8:46.

As she bounced off the bed, adrenaline shot through her. *Eddie. I'm coming. Don't leave. Wait for me.* She grabbed the clothes closest to her—jeans, sweatshirt, ugly sneakers she thought she'd thrown out last summer. She looked mismatched and frumpy, but she didn't care, not when she was about to see Eddie.

With her parents playing cards and the rest of the neighbors in the rec room, she raced for the door and to their spot, worried Eddie had already left.

And he had. When she arrived, there was no sign of him.

A lump formed in her throat. She tried swallowing it away, but worry had been weighing on her all day, anticipation turning into disappointment. She sat on one of the scraggy rocks, the ocean calm and quiet. Tiny lights flared in the distance, and she imagined being out there, surrounded by darkness, nothing to hold on to. She told herself it was better this way. There was no future for her and Eddie.

"Sarita."

His voice pulled her from her bleak thoughts, and she jumped.

"Eddie."

"I thought you weren't coming."

His English sounded different, and she felt an immediate pull.

"You were upset today," he said.

"You don't know that."

"I saw your eyes." He took her hand and led her toward the water's edge. "It's not what you think."

Sara wasn't sure what she thought. She was sure her heart beat in rhythm with his, but she couldn't shake the image of the other Eddie, the one on the beach, a much different Eddie from the one who needed no one else but her.

She pulled the paper he'd left in the book out of the pocket of her sweatshirt. "What is this?"

Eddie's eyes shifted toward the water, and the waves of his hair blew in the wind. He seemed older, no longer the lanky boy with ears that stuck out. He took the paper from her hand. "This is going to save us," he said. "We are difficult, Sarita. Our worlds don't . . . *mezcla*." And he clasped his fingers to illustrate his point.

"This you need to understand. I don't want to cause any trouble for you and your family. *Abuelo* says it's dangerous. We must pretend what we are feeling doesn't exist. Can you do that, Sarita?"

Her heart hammered in her chest.

"Those girls today . . ."

"They mean *nada*."

The tension that had knotted her up began to dissipate.

"What I feel for you . . . it is . . ." And he used his hands to illustrate, spreading them wide. "If I pretend with other girls, I am protecting you, protecting us. Your mom will never know what I feel for you." He continued. "My guitar teacher, Mr. Feinstein, he gave me this code. Through music. We can send messages in private. No one will ever know. Keep this with you always."

He then explained how to match the numbers with the music notes and showed her what her name, in music, would look like.

"How will I get the messages? Your grandfather can't bring me books every day."

He smiled, and she forgot how angry she was. She wanted to reach over and touch his lips with her fingers.

"*¿Por qué no?*" he asked. "Mr. Feinstein gives *Abuelo* books. I know you like to read. He has a daughter who reads as much as you. A book a day."

"You told him about me?"

"How could I not tell him about the beautiful girl who has my heart?"

"Do you mean that, Eddie?"

"*De verdad*, Sarita. I think of nothing but you. When you are here, I dream of doing things to you I should not, and when you are away, I count the minutes for your return. The music will connect us."

"What about *Abuelo*?"

"He is not happy. He tries to convince me this is wrong. *Él es terco.* Stubborn. But he would never betray us."

Eddie explained how he was learning to write music and songs. He carried a spiral notebook with him but instead of words, he filled it with music.

"I will message you with the code. The music I will write in black ink. My messages to you will be in blue. Don't worry about the black. Look for the blue."

Turning one of the pages, he showed her a note he'd already written. She referenced the chart and matched the notes with the appropriate letters. It took her a minute to get the hang of it, but it was worth it when she figured out the message.

Sara Friedman, will you be my girl?

CHAPTER 18

"GEORGIA ON MY MIND" BY RAY CHARLES

Miami Beach
Summer 1979

Sara couldn't believe that only hours ago she had been stewing on the beach, watching Eddie flanked by girls, and now they were sharing a secret language, one that would give them access to a private world. It wasn't ideal, lying and hiding, but there was no other way. This time, when his mouth found hers, her lingering doubts dissolved.

His lips were like silk against hers, and she couldn't get enough, letting his tongue inside. When he pulled away, she drew him in, and the kiss lasted as long as the six months they'd been apart.

When they finally separated, Sara felt certain they'd find a way to make things work. In a few years she'd be heading off to college, Columbia was her first choice, and maybe by then they wouldn't have to sneak around anymore. Maybe Shira would understand. Maybe she'd trust that Eddie would never hurt her, that he'd only make her happy.

They sat huddled close, the kiss lingering on their lips. "Why do you have to let those girls touch you?" she asked.

"No one touches me, Sarita."

"I don't like it."

"I don't like you with that boy."

"You don't have to worry about Abel."

"Do you want your *ima* to see what you do to me? It is better this way. Let them believe I am as horrible as they imagine."

She loved how he adopted the name for her mother. And she loved how he tried to protect her.

"What are you working on?" she asked.

He pulled out the notebook and showed her the songs.

"I will write you a song, Sarita. I will sing it to the world."

She didn't need him to sing to anyone but her.

"For now, you must go home. *Tus padres* will be back, and you must be there. I sent *Abuelo* because I knew they were out. The only way we can be together, Sarita, is if nobody knows, if we are *inteligentes*."

≈

Eddie and Sara eased into a routine. He'd have *Abuelo* leave books at her condo, each with a line from a song with a secret message detailing where and when to meet. They had their usual spot on the beach, away from Sara's family and prying eyes, but there were days they'd meet in Eddie's apartment. Mr. Santiago—at first leery of the relationship—had warmed up, and soon he shared his favorite Argentinean recipes with Sara, tidbits of their life back home, and what little Eddie was like. Sara cherished those days.

Sometimes, Eddie's notes just relayed how much he missed her or included a short poem to get her through the lonely nights when she lay in her bed, covered in sweat. From the outside heat or desire, she wasn't sure.

≈

One rainy afternoon, her mother had gone to a Jazzercise class, and the rest of the family went to Carvel. Sara stayed behind, nursing a headache, and Shira left a page of instructions, including the phone number of the exercise class and what to do if the headache got worse. "Maybe I should stay here," she said to Sara. But Moshe insisted she go, patting his wife's shoulder. "It's okay, Shira. She's going to be fine."

The condo was silent, and with her headache subsiding, Sara decided to go down to the rec room. When she arrived in the lobby, she found Eddie arranging flowers in the glass vase near the entryway.

He smiled when he saw her. "Just in time to see my miracle."

She eyed him curiously.

He held up the dying green, blue, and white hydrangea, their leaves saggy and wilted.

"Come with me."

She followed him into the bathroom, where he turned on the hot faucet, letting it run a few minutes. When he was sure of the temperature, he filled the empty vase with the steaming water, snipped the ends off the stems, and dropped them in.

"You're going to kill them," she said.

"Just watch."

They returned to the lobby and set the flowers back on the table.

Sara was fascinated by whatever it was Eddie was doing. She lost track of time, of being in public with him, laughing, watching the rain collect outside, and counting the seconds between the lightning and thunder. She couldn't be sure how much time had passed, but her headache disappeared, and the flowers that had only moments before been close to death had come back to life.

He pulled the fullest one from the vase and handed it to her, just as Shira walked in, catching them smiling at each other.

Sara dropped the flower on the floor and backed away while Eddie made his way over to another dying arrangement and another miracle.

"What are you doing with that boy?" Shira whisper-shouted. She closed her umbrella, linked an arm through Sara's, and led her toward the elevator.

"*Ima*, did you know you can save hydrangea by cutting their stems and dropping them in hot water?"

Shira didn't seem to care. "I thought you weren't feeling well. Did you lie to me?"

Sara didn't answer. Her mother wouldn't believe her anyway.

"Sara, I don't like you hanging around him. We don't know anything about him! What if—"

"He's nice, *Ima*. I told him about the miracle of Hanukkah, and he showed me his own miracle."

"He plays guitar on the beach! He could be dangerous. He has a tattoo!"

That Shira had spotted the heart on Eddie's ankle didn't come as a surprise to Sara, as watchful as her mother was.

"What would Abel think? Don't ruin things over—"

"Eddie. His name is Eddie. And he's my friend."

"He's not your friend, Sara. Please, stay away from him. Bad things happen . . ." And she stopped, but it was clear what she meant.

Naomi.

Aunt Naomi.

"Nothing's going to happen to me," Sara said as they exited the elevator. "Eddie would never hurt me. And I'm not like her."

Shira looked stricken. "But you are! I see it! And I can't imagine something happening to you, Sara. I wouldn't survive."

The fear in Shira's eyes enveloped Sara, and she hugged her mother. Though they'd been distant, they immediately fit, and Sara smelled the familiar scent, inhaled her childhood. Shira wept, her worry spilling out. "Everything I do is because I love you."

"I know, *Ima*."

"Please promise me you'll stay away from him."

And Sara nodded because she wanted to give her mother that promise. And when they reached the condo, she walked out to the balcony, staring at the gray skies and the murky waters. She tried to catch the rain in her outstretched palm, recognizing she had so much to lose, and yet already dreaming of what to do next.

~

Almar's Bookstore had just opened on Lincoln Road, and Sara landed herself a job. Shira argued against it, preferring that she work at the day camp. Sara would have her family close by, and most important, Abel worked there too.

"What if something happens to her?" She'd overheard her mother whisper to her father when she thought Sara was out of range. "I caught her with that boy the other day . . . Mr. Santiago's grandson. I'm scared. We know nothing about his family . . . and she's changing. She's not our same little Sarala. We're losing her, Moshe."

Moshe did his best to calm his wife's anxieties, reassuring her that Sara had a good head on her shoulders. And when that didn't work, he surprised his wife with a foot massage and bubble bath.

~

On her first few days at the bookstore, Moshe drove Sara to work and tried to talk to her about Eddie. "Your mother has a point, Sara. We don't know anything about the Santiagos. And you know it's especially hard for her this time of year. She can't help holding on to you."

Sara stared out the window at the bicyclists and couples walking hand in hand. It was best to say she understood. And she did. But the more her mother held on, the more Sara wanted Eddie.

With her job at the bookstore, her world became a touch bigger. The floor-to-ceiling shelves of colorful spines were her friends, and she quickly felt at home. Julius, the owner, fascinated her, and on her lunch breaks, she'd sit with him, listening to tales of his inspiration for the shop and the community it had created. "Miami's more than sunshine and palm trees, Sara. There are stories in the sand, tales in the sprawling beaches. And at the heart of it is a bookshop, the soul of any city. Can't you feel it?"

She did.

Sara had a robust list of favorites ranging from Judy Blume's *Forever* to Norman Mailer's *The Executioner's Song.* Julius introduced her to literary giants John le Carré and Tom Wolfe. "Not that there's anything wrong with the big, commercial names," he told her. "They're great for business. But there's a world out there that you haven't tapped into. You should always challenge yourself with a book. Pick up something outside your comfort zone."

She lowered her eyes when he said this. She had no problem venturing outside her comfort zone.

Together, they put together a shelf of employee picks, and customers raved about their selections. Sara felt great pride in being trusted and in the literary offerings she passed along, whole worlds crafted of words.

After Eddie finished his schoolwork, he'd take the bus to the bookshop and sit in the courtyard and play his guitar. Eventually, he had a following, and customers would gather around with their bags of books, sipping coffee while he played their favorite tunes.

Some of Sara's best days were spent at Almar's. While her own story was taking shape, she immersed herself in the tales that filled the shelves. She loved having Eddie nearby. She loved feeling his eyes on her, and she loved when they'd sneak off into the alley and he'd gently press her against the wall, kissing her so hard she lost her breath.

"*Ima* saw your tattoo, Eddie!"

Nestled inside the tiny heart was the letter *S*, impossible to read from afar. He held his leg out so she could rub a finger across it, and she was grateful she'd always be with him, inside his heart.

147

Shira and Moshe had raised their children to be honest and trust-worthy, but when it came to Eddie, Sara was powerless. When Julius handed over her schedule for the week, she saw nothing wrong with making her own modifications, adding extra days so she could escape with Eddie.

"He's working you hard," Shira commented when she scanned the schedule.

"It's not work," Sara said. "I love it."

Her mother tilted her head for a closer look. Love meant many different things, and Sara's face flushed.

She should have known at some point that she'd be caught. That her mother would be suspicious of the place where her daughter spent so much time, the place that was stalling a romance with Abel Altman. She shouldn't have been surprised when Shira appeared and caught Sara and Eddie sitting in the alley sharing a cigarette, his arm resting casually around her shoulder.

Shira's face drained of color. She couldn't speak. She clutched at her chest, backing away as though a few steps would make it less real that her daughter was cavorting with . . . she couldn't bring herself to say it, but it shone in the whites of her eyes.

"How could you? We trusted you!"

To make matters worse, today was the anniversary of the day they had lost Naomi.

Shira's reaction was a collision of fear and grief. Sara wasn't being heartless—she felt her mother's sadness deeply—but she was tired of being punished for Naomi's decisions. She sat quietly as Shira drove her home in the brown station wagon, clutching the steering wheel until her knuckles turned white. Only one thought spiraled through Sara's mind. As soon as she got to college, she was never coming back.

The punishment was almost as bad as her parents' stony expressions. They sat in the living room, across from each other on the leather couches, and despite Sara's pleading arguments, her mother made it perfectly clear she was to quit her job at the bookstore, and she was forbidden from socializing with Eddie Santiago.

"He's my friend!" Sara cried out. "You can't do that!"

"That's not a friend, Sara. A friend doesn't coerce you to smoke cigarettes in a dangerous alley. What's next? Marijuana?"

"He didn't force me."

"Moshe," Shira pleaded, "tell her she needs to use better judgment. Tell her she can't take these kinds of risks."

"You're just mad because he isn't Jewish," Sara argued.

Shira clenched her fist in the air. "That boy is not the answer, Sara!"

"*Aba?*" Sara looked to her father. "Tell her! Tell her she can't do this! Eddie's kind. And he's thoughtful. He listens to me. We have dreams!"

Moshe averted his eyes. "Smoking is a terrible habit to get yourself into, Sara."

She appraised her parents. Her teachers and rabbi had always taught her to be accepting, to practice open-mindedness, because Jews, more than any other people, had already been persecuted and discriminated against. There wasn't a family in Glenwood who didn't have a relative who had perished in the Holocaust. They were trained regularly to practice tolerance and inclusivity. So, she wondered, how was treating Eddie this way acceptable? Wasn't that a similar form of prejudice?

"I don't know how you stand it," she shouted at her mother. "This hypocrisy, this cloak of moral virtue. I care about Eddie. And he cares about me. What if I don't want the same kind of life you've chosen? What if I want something else?" She had never raised her voice to her mother before, not like this, and her father placed an arm around Shira's shoulder, drawing her close, while he demanded that Sara show some respect.

She glared at him. "You defend her! And look at you. You want different things too!"

"You think I don't know what they say about us?" Shira said. "Your father and I are different, but we are unified, our foundation is the same.

We may be growing in other ways, and I might be fighting like hell to keep my family safe, but we share something that at sixteen you are way too young to understand. We want what's best for our children."

"What is that?" Sara pleaded. "What is it you want for me?"

"I want you to make good choices."

"I'm a proud Jewish woman, *Ima*. I always will be. No matter what. My religion is here in my heart. The people I choose to have in my life aren't meant to denounce you or our faith. I promise you, I promise, no matter where my path leads, I'll always honor our family and our history. I know this is difficult to hear, but I don't want secrets between us." She stared at her hands when she said, "I love him."

Shira stood up, staring out the window with her back to her husband and Sara. "Do you know what happens when you love the wrong person, Sara? Love alone is not enough. It can be very dangerous if you don't choose the right person and very beautiful when you do. Aunt Naomi thought she knew what was best for her. Do you see how stepping out of the neighborhood cost her everything?"

Sara wasn't sure she was expected to answer, and dredging up that day wouldn't do any of them any good. When Shira spoke again, her voice was measured and resolute. "You are forbidden to see that boy. For the remainder of the summer, you'll work at the camp with your brothers and your cousins. If I catch you with him again, you'll attend a community college—"

"You can't do that!" Sara's voice cracked.

"Yes, I can," Shira said.

"I hate you," Sara screamed. "How could you? How could you do this to me?" Shaking, she stormed out of the room, slamming the door so hard a picture fell to the floor and cracked. Sara didn't care. Everything was broken anyway.

CHAPTER 19

"April Come She Will" by Simon & Garfunkel

Los Angeles and Miami
October 1996

Cecilia was back in her cubicle, thumbing through final drafts of an upcoming issue. The cover photo showed a wide-eyed Dennis Rodman with his unusually long tongue climbing down the page. The visual made her queasy, but the nausea could very well be from the conversation she had with Pete earlier that morning. She had been leaving him another rambling message on his answering machine when he picked up and asked her to please stop calling. Could she even call that a conversation?

"That's one hell of a cover." Joan appeared, glancing over Cecilia's shoulder at Rodman's outrageous tongue. "I have good news. Brett's agreed to let you go back to Miami. Here's your ticket." She tossed the envelope on Cecilia's desk.

Cecilia shot up to thank her, but Joan stuck her hand out to prevent an overt display of affection. Was Cecilia going to hug Joan? She sat back down.

"You better nail this story," Joan said.

Cecilia stared up at her boss. "I intend to."

Cecilia looked forward to telling Don she'd be leaving town. In the few days she'd been staying with him and the girls, he had been attentive in a way that puzzled her, and it made her long for the closeness they had once shared. That first night she had slept in the guest bedroom, she was tormented by his music filtering from the office. She tried stuffing a towel under the door to block out the sounds, but the same song kept playing over and over in a continuous loop. Finally, she sat by the doorjamb and copied the words in her notebook.

Cecilia recognized the ballad. Patty Loveless had released "You Don't Even Know Who I Am" the year before, and it was nominated for two Grammys. Fans expected the song to be a wife's one-sided version of her marriage, but after the first verse, the words shifted to the husband's perspective. Neither of them knew each other at all.

Drowning out the song, Cecilia had picked up her cell phone and punched in April's number. "Where the hell have you been?" her friend had asked, shouting into the phone.

"Quiet or you'll wake the cutest boy in LA."

Cecilia heard a door shut and the sound of April fumbling with the phone. "For fuck's sake, CeCe, how did you miss that boat?" It was a rhetorical question because April didn't wait for a response. "Please tell me you and Pete worked things out."

"You and Pete worked things out."

"Not funny. Did you? Work things out?"

Cecilia shared everything with April, though telling the story was almost as unbearable as living it.

"Yeah, you blew it," April said.

"Thank you for the vote of confidence."

"Pete loves you. You love him. There's got to be a way to fix this."

She could have reminded April that love wasn't always enough, but she knew it wasn't the time for quoting from song lyrics.

"You really don't know?" April said.

"Know what?"

April had hesitated. "He didn't tell you?"

Cecilia didn't like the tone of her friend's voice.

"I shouldn't—"

"Spill," Cecilia said.

"I shouldn't be telling you this, but maybe you'll understand." She hesitated. "Pete was going to propose to you."

The phone fell out of Cecilia's hand and landed in her lap. Had she heard her correctly? Picking up the device, she heard April say, "Cecilia. Are you there?"

Pete. Her Pete. He was going to propose. "I'm here." Her voice was shaky.

"I shouldn't have said anything."

"That's why your message . . . You said you were happy for us. I misunderstood. I thought you were just happy we had this romantic getaway—"

"He even asked Don for permission. Everyone knew. Joan too. I'm sure the bottles of champagne we had sent to your cabin were well received."

Cecilia felt sick. That's why all the pitying looks. The idea of Pete picking out a ring, loving her enough to want to make it forever, and then carrying the ring with him onto the boat filled her with a surprising joy, but it also wrecked her. Hadn't she considered the possibility, even if she refused to believe it? Pete's response wasn't an overreaction, it was entirely warranted. Missing that boat was far worse than she had thought.

"I'm at Don's," Cecilia finally said, unable to process this news.

"Like, at his house? Why on earth would you go there?"

Cecilia described Pete's return, how he asked her to move out and refused her apology. Now it all made sense. No wonder he wouldn't take any of her calls. "He must have been devastated when I didn't show up. I'm such an idiot."

"I shouldn't have told you."

"No. I needed to know."

Pete loved her. Pete was going to propose.

April waited before asking about Don. "How's it working out over there?"

She'd been there only a few hours, but she answered, her voice strained. "We're not *Party of Five*."

"But Don's?" April asked. "You hate Don and Tori."

She did. But during a crisis, some feelings were best ignored.

After they said goodbye, Cecilia had dialed Pete again, but he didn't pick up, nor did he respond to the pleading message she left on the answering machine. So she had slept fitfully while Patty Loveless swept in and out of her room.

~

Today she sat staring at a really long tongue, wondering if Pete was right. If there would always be another story. Another song. She had a ticket on her desk. An opportunity she had dreamed about. Fate was taking over and moving her in a direction she was powerless to control.

In the days leading up to Cecilia's trip, conflicting emotions plagued her. The painful sadness surrounding the botched proposal coupled with Pete's refusal to talk collided with the tiny crumbs that were becoming a story. Cecilia vacillated between reaching out to Pete and letting go. And then there was the situation at home.

Most mornings, Cecilia hid in her room until Tori and the girls left for school, and as soon as they were out the door, she escaped to the kitchen. A few times Tori knocked to let her know breakfast was ready, but Cecilia feigned sleep or pretended to be showering. When she finally took a seat at the breakfast table, she nibbled on the fresh fruit

Tori left on her plate and the generous servings of pancakes and eggs. *Is the bitch trying to make me fat?* Yet with every bite of delicious food, she swallowed the guilt, knowing her mother could be watching, and she bit back the appreciation for a home-cooked meal, savoring the flavor but never the warm gesture.

Don typically left the house before anyone woke up. He drove Downtown for his classes at USC, returning in the afternoons for private tutoring sessions. Tori picked the girls up from school after what Cecilia assumed were long lunches and shopping excursions with her bimbo girlfriends. One afternoon, Tori asked if Cecilia would like to join her to pick up the girls.

"Why would I do that?"

Cecilia had to admit that Tori had surprised her in the short time she'd been staying there. She never flinched at Cecilia's biting tone, and she never bit back. In fact, she was pretty even-keeled. Cecilia chalked it up to missing brain cells. But that afternoon, Cecilia had taken the day off to nurse a hangover from the listening party she'd gone to the night before. Eminem had released his debut studio album, *Infinite*, and she and her coworkers had consumed infinitely too many cocktails.

So when Tori found Cecilia under a blanket, watching *General Hospital*, and invited her to pick up the girls, Cecilia figured it was the best way to avoid dialing Pete again. A ride with her giggly and innocent sisters might free her from the heaviness in her head.

Tori made mindless small talk as they turned on Sunset and passed the rolling hills and stunning homes. She droned on and on about the girls' upcoming recital and the cushy academy they attended, but Cecilia was thinking about her mother. She was thinking about how irritated Gloria would be if she saw them together. Tori was being nice, but could she be trusted? Cecilia assumed there had to be an angle.

She thought about how her father used to pick her up from school. Every day. He'd park, never waiting in the carpool line, and he'd lean against the car, waiting for Cecilia to run out. He'd always have something in his hand. She'd squeal, choosing the right fist first. Sometimes it was a piece of her favorite candy. Other times it was earrings he'd picked up from the drugstore. Cecilia wondered if she'd always chosen right, how come everything had gone so wrong.

"Does my dad ever pick up the girls?" she asked.

"He's usually tutoring," Tori said.

Cecilia studied her. She had both hands on the wheel, opening and closing her fingers as though she was afraid of what would come next. She had dressed in a light-blue sweater that accentuated her slim figure. If Cecilia didn't dislike her so immensely, she might have said she looked pretty.

She felt a small satisfaction knowing her dad had never missed picking her up, even when he was teaching, and there was no better time to rub it in. "Don always picked me up from school."

Tori focused on the light in front of her as it changed from green to yellow. She stepped on the gas, and Cecilia lurched backward just as the light turned red.

"Are you trying to kill us?" Cecilia asked, her head against the headrest.

Tori made sure to stop at the next yellow light, her mane of bronze hair blowing in the breeze as she turned in Cecilia's direction. Straight-faced, she said, "I would never hurt you, Cecilia. I know you don't understand that, not yet anyway, but it's true. I'd never hurt you . . . or your father."

Cecilia noted that she didn't mention Gloria.

"I'm okay with you hating me. I am. I know you blame me for your parents' divorce and ruining your family." She stopped, hesitant. "You should really talk to your father. He's been wanting to tell you . . . You should ask him what happened. You might not like what you hear. It won't fit into your idea of me and us, but it may explain some of it. Like why your father picked you up from school every day."

"What the fuck is that supposed to mean, Tori?"

"He loves you, Cecilia. More than anything."

"He has a really fucked-up way of showing it, and if you don't see that yourself then you're even more of a monster than I thought you were."

Tori didn't respond, but Cecilia's assault must have pricked Tori's skin, painting it red. Tori turned the wheel and pulled into the school driveway, and the conversation came to a halt.

A knot in Cecilia's stomach twisted, aggravated by Tori's silence. The girls exited the building, and only when Cecilia saw them skipping down the steps did she relax. When they spotted her in the car, they started running, and the school patrol whistled for them to slow down. "They love you too," Tori said, breaking the quiet just as the door swung open and the girls flung themselves into the back seat. "Cecilia! Cecilia!" they shouted, smelling of pencils and lunch boxes. "You drive! Mommy's the slowest of the slow."

"Cecilia doesn't drive," Tori said.

"Why don't you drive?" asked Hazel.

"Yeah, why don't you drive?" Phoebe said. "I can't wait to drive!"

For a reason she couldn't explain, Cecilia glanced at Tori, but Tori had already moved on to the next subject, asking the girls about their day.

Cecilia sat back in her seat, half listening to the girls recount a story about the frog that got out of the aquarium and hopped around the classroom and how Mrs. Melrose colored her hair pink. Cecilia was distracted, a thought clawing at her mind that she couldn't quite put a finger on. *Why don't I drive?* Shockingly, it wasn't something she had dissected, for someone who made overthinking an Olympic sport. And when she thought about it now, she honestly couldn't come up with a reason for choosing not to learn. She made a note to herself to ask April about it. April remembered everything. Unlike Cecilia, she never drank or smoked, so her memories were crystal clear.

∼

The night before her trip to Miami, Cecilia sat on the patio, puffing on a joint and taking in the scenery. Her father found her there and plopped beside her, a little too close for Cecilia's comfort.

"I'd prefer if you didn't smoke in the house."

"We're not in the house."

"I don't want that stuff around the girls."

Don wanted to talk, and Cecilia wasn't ready. She stared out at the magnificent view of the city below, puffing harder, hoping he'd get the hint. It was the hour between day and night, when cars crammed the freeways, people either coming or going. Cecilia felt stuck in between. Ever since she had gone with Tori to pick up the girls, she'd been wondering why she didn't drive. April was no help. She was in the midst of a simultaneous work and Arthur crisis, and it never came up again.

The sound of the sliding glass door startled Don, and he grabbed the joint from Cecilia's hand and tossed it down the ravine.

"Let's hope you didn't just start the biggest fire in the history of Los Angeles," Cecilia said.

"Let's hope the girls don't ask what that smell is."

One by one they climbed into his lap.

Watching them in his arms, Cecilia remembered being their age and feeling like there was no safer place in the world than on Don's lap. And then the feeling passed, something sinister took its place, and she closed her eyes for a better look but came up blank.

"I'm going to pack," she said, standing up and heading toward the house.

As she folded her clothes in her suitcase and prepared for bed, her thoughts drifted to the girls. The irony wasn't lost on her. She found a great source of comfort in being around Hazel and Phoebe. It was easy to dislike them from afar, as an outsider looking in, but when she was in their presence and they climbed into her bed and begged to hear stories about the famous faces that adorned her magazine covers, they were difficult to resist, their laughter one of the best tunes Cecilia had ever heard. They were her blood; they shared features and those faint freckles. She would stop smoking pot in the house.

∾

When Cecilia arrived in Miami the next day, the exhaustion of the last few weeks kicked in, and she crashed onto the pillowy softness of the hotel bed. Bright and early the next morning, she taxied over to Miami Beach High, where Dolores, as promised, had left a file on the counter after they introduced themselves and exchanged pleasantries.

Cecilia wasted no time dialing "P. F.," who she had learned was a man named Phil Feinstein. She explained who she was and how she'd like to meet and discuss Eddie Vee. Disinterested, the man was about to hang up, but Cecilia pleaded with him to hear her out. "I want to help him." And then she boldly added, "I think I can save him." She didn't know this at all, actually, but she went with it, and he eventually agreed to meet.

She spent the rest of the day flipping through her file on Eddie and the mysterious Sarita. She read and reread the *Rolling Stone* article published right after the fateful accident, searching for more clues, but found nothing. Eddie Vee had disappeared and taken with him all his secrets. Just before she closed her eyes for the night, she buried her head in the *Miami New Times*, catching up on the local music scene. She was pleased to find a nice piece on the Hails. She considered stopping by the venue where they were performing, but she remembered what had happened last time, and she couldn't afford any mishaps.

CHAPTER 20

"DESIRÉE" BY NEIL DIAMOND

Miami Beach
October 1996

Cecilia entered Rascal House at seven o'clock the next morning, feeling energized. As planned, Phil Feinstein waited for her at the last table on the left. When she approached, he stood up, basketball-player tall, once having played for the Hi-Tides. He had pale-brown eyes and a cap of short white hair.

"Thanks for meeting me," Cecilia said.

"I'm not here for you, Miss James. I'm here for Eddie."

That got Cecilia's attention.

A waiter took their order, dropping fresh pickles on their table. "Just coffee for me," said Cecilia. Mr. Feinstein ordered one too.

"Do you mind if I tape us?" She didn't let on that she was still a novice at interviewing, and she had to be sure to capture every single word.

His forehead creased, and he shifted in his seat before reluctantly agreeing. Cecilia removed the black recorder from her bag. She double-checked to be sure the tape she'd inserted an hour before was still there and hit the red button to record.

CJ: This is Cecilia James at Rascal House in Miami, Florida. Today's date is October 14, and the time is 7:09 a.m. With me is Mr. Phil Feinstein, a former music teacher at Miami Beach High School. Mr. Feinstein, you worked at the school from 1972 to 1982?

Phil: Yes. And call me Phil.

CJ: Phil, while there, did you come across a student by the name of Eddie Vee?

Phil: (Pause.) At the school, no. (Pause.) But I privately tutored a music student during that time. He went by the name Eddie Santiago.

CJ: Eddie Santiago changed his name to Eddie Vee when he joined the band High Tide. Can you confirm this is the same Eddie?

Phil: Yes. They are the same.

CJ: How did you come to meet Eddie Santiago?

Phil: (Exhales.) Let me start off by saying that I don't have any idea where Eddie disappeared to. I'm not about to divulge any secrets that the press doesn't already know. The family doesn't deserve that. They've already been through too much.

Cecilia already liked this Phil Feinstein. She admired anyone willing to take an interview while remaining loyal to the subject. It took balls and a hell of a lot of class. But she would have to break him.

CJ: I'm trying to find Eddie, but not for the reasons you think.

Phil: Eddie's a good kid. His grandfather too. Honest, upstanding, hardworking people. Eddie never got over his parents' accident. It broke him in a way that could never be fixed. And then the stadium tragedy. It's no surprise he disappeared. I'm guessing it became too much for him. How does anyone recover from all that?

CJ: Does the name Sarita mean anything to you?

Cecilia studied him closely as the waiter brought their coffee.

Phil: If you've lived in Miami as long as I have, sure. Sarita is the endearing Spanish twist on Sara.

Sara. She should have known.

CJ: Had Eddie dated anyone named Sara?

Phil: There were tons of girls in and out of Eddie's life. Have you listened to that boy play? Eddie never tied himself down to one woman. His heart was just too big for that.

CJ: Then how do you explain "What You Do to Me?"

Phil: Is that what this is about? Are reporters still trying to solve the mystery woman behind that song?

CJ: That song was written for someone.

Phil: You think so? (Pause.) You strike me as someone who believes every song is written for someone. Am I right? (Long pause.) Music's not always that specific. Songs are merely broad representations of experiences.

Artists have a way of taking the emotion—not the person—and putting it into words. And the words are universal.

CJ: That's a simplified way of putting it, but I respectfully disagree. I think music is inspired specifically by personal pain or joy. And I think what Eddie wrote was deeply personal.

Phil: I need to use the restroom.

Cecilia pressed "STOP" on the recorder and sipped her coffee while watching as Phil made his way to the restroom. She couldn't shake the feeling that he knew more than he was letting on, that he was holding back. When he returned to the table, relief kicked in.

"Thanks again for doing this, Mr. Feinstein . . . Phil. You ready?"

"Ready."

CJ: You were obviously very special to Eddie. He thanked you in the album notes.

Phil: You're the only one who figured it out. (Long pause.) The boy was a natural. (Pause.) I knew it the first day I heard him sing. His grandfather . . . this is where we first met . . . we had a weekly breakfast that lasted for years . . . but the morning he brought little Eddie in . . . we went back to my apartment, and I handed him my guitar . . . I'll never forget my wife's face when he played. The rest is history.

Cecilia handed Phil a napkin and waited while he dabbed at his eyes.

Phil: (Blows his nose.) Eddie was a remarkable musician.

CJ: You obviously had an impact on him. I believe you also taught him this.

Cecilia handed Mr. Feinstein the Haydn Cipher.

Phil: I haven't seen one of these in a long time. (Laughter.) Yes, Eddie and I had quite a bit of fun sending each other messages through our music.

CJ: I'd like to show you something.

Cecilia slipped the original sheet music to "What You Do to Me" in front of Phil. He took a look, and when he reached the last page, he let out a deep sigh.

Phil: How did you get this?

CJ: Imagine that song was written for you. Imagine after all these years you were walking around with the words in your pocket, at the bottom of a pocketbook or briefcase—

Phil: I'm not following.

CJ: What if I told you I recently saw Sarita? That she's been holding on to these pages. And what if I told you that she still loves Eddie Santiago?

Phil: I know nothing about this.

CJ: Just tell me where to find Eddie. Or his grandfather. Maybe knowing Sarita still loves him will help him heal.

Phil stood up, his chair scraping the floor.

Phil: I thought you were different. You're just like the rest of them. Out for your own good. These are people's lives you're playing with.

CJ: Please don't go, Phil. I only want to help. You should have seen her. She loves him. Maybe she can get through to him.

Phil: Goodbye, Miss James.

CJ: I'm staying at the Sheraton . . . in Bal Harbour . . . if you change your mind.

She stopped the tape.

~

Cecilia lingered after Phil Feinstein's departure, sipping lukewarm coffee and nibbling on a sour green pickle. The combination was lethal to her stomach. She knew she had gotten to Phil, but she didn't know how much. Her cell phone rang, likely Joan following up on the interview, but when she saw the number, she was surprised. It was Pete.

"We should talk," he said.

"I've been wanting to talk," she said.

"Can you have dinner tonight?"

Regret surged through her body. "I'm in Miami."

He took a minute to process this. "Already?" The displeasure was hard to miss.

Cecilia found her voice. "I told you about this lead. It's work."

He exhaled loudly.

"What do you expect me to do? I've called you a dozen times and you've ignored me."

"When will you be back?"

"In a few days."

He waited. "Okay, we'll talk then."

She squeezed the phone close to her ear. "I'd like that."

The call gave her hope. Maybe there was still a chance they could salvage the relationship after all.

∾

Back at the hotel, Cecilia could hear her cell phone ringing in her bag as she fumbled with her key card. She raced inside and pulled it out. It was Don calling to ask her about the interview. Plopping on the bed, she was careful not to divulge too much. She was still being cautious with him, and what she really wanted was to ask if he had any insight into why she didn't drive.

The mystery perplexed her. In the cab ride over to the hotel, she had watched the driver at the wheel, wondering about this decision. But she knew the answer. She had been sixteen. Gloria had just died. Of course, Cecilia wasn't thinking about getting a driver's license. She was thinking about how to survive without her mother. Although that didn't explain the years that followed.

Don must have noticed the way she drifted away from their conversation, because after a moment of silence, he said, "Whatever it is, Sugar Bug, it's going to work itself out."

It was the name he'd called her when she was a lot younger, the name that made her feel loved. She thanked him, not sure what to do with the feelings it elicited. "I have to go," she said. And she ended the call a little abruptly, immediately regretting it.

Restless, she headed downstairs, working her way through the throngs of guests, and exited the hotel doors leading to the pool and beach. She needed to clear her head, stretch her legs. The Sheraton Bal Harbour was nestled on a ritzy street stacked with luxury high-rises. Once a playground for Frank Sinatra and his Rat Pack, the property sat on one of the most desirable parcels of sand and surf. The view spanned for miles, and the mild temperature carried her the short distance to the pier.

The air bristled with energy. Turquoise water slapped the jutting rocks, and waves jostled the boats as they slipped in and out of the inlet. But the real draw was the expanse of sparkling blue ocean laid out around her. She knew it was impossible, but she thought she could feel Eddie and Sarita there. She felt their love story rippling like the water, imagined them holding hands and laughing. But it was only the waves crashing into the pier.

When she returned to the hotel, Cecilia asked the woman behind the front desk if they had a business office where she could use a computer. She needed to do another search on Eddie's grandfather. And when she told the woman her name and room number, the woman mentioned Cecilia had a visitor and pointed over Cecilia's shoulder.

She scanned the lobby. "I wasn't expecting anyone. Did they give a name?"

The woman checked her computer. "Santiago. Carlos Santiago."

CHAPTER 21

"DANIEL" BY ELTON JOHN

Miami Beach
October 1996

Cecilia studied the man seated on the lobby's lavish sofa. Joan had once described a hunch as a feeling lodged in the gut, like a kernel of hope, spreading a tingly warmth through your veins. That was the sensation Cecilia felt looking at Carlos Santiago.

Quickly, she raced up to her room, threw her tape recorder into her bag, and made sure she had her notepad and pens too. With one last look in the mirror, she swiped a bold red on her lips and checked for any pickle left in her teeth.

"Go get 'em, girl," she said to her reflection.

As she rode down the elevator, sunscreen and chlorine filled her nose, but Cecilia smelled only the sweetness of success. Crossing the lobby, she appraised the older gentleman who was dressed in a pressed white shirt and black trousers. He stood out against the sofa's bright-yellow velvet and the menagerie of vibrant beach attire and colorful totes. He stared down at the floor and didn't look up until Cecilia stood right over him.

"Cecilia James?"

"That's me."

He got to his feet, a thin, small man with a firm grip. "I'm Carlos Santiago—"

"I know who you are."

"Can we talk?"

The accent was thick, but his English was perfect. The leathery skin on his face spoke of years in the sun, each crease another hard-won battle. He didn't wait for Cecilia to answer. Instead, he led her through the glass doors to the busy pool area, choosing a quiet spot in the shade.

"You people ask a lot of questions about my grandson. They want to know where he is. They want to sink their teeth and claws into him. Hurt him."

"I wouldn't do that."

"Phil warned me you were using the girl as your angle. That you had some sheet music. Tell me why you're really here."

A waiter approached, asking if they'd like anything. Carlos ordered water, and Cecilia ordered an iced tea. She thought about her answer. She also thought about reaching for her tape recorder or the pen and paper, but something in Carlos Santiago's eyes stopped her. She knew better than to let her emotions cloud the story. It was best to remain at arm's length from a subject. Personal feelings were a distraction, they compromised objectivity, but that something in Carlos Santiago's blue eyes had her believing they were on the same side.

She opened her bag and rested the envelope on the table. She remembered the sadness in Sarita's voice at the memorial. *He wrote those words for me.*

"Go on," she said to Mr. Santiago. "Open it."

He didn't immediately move. They sat facing each other in a tense waiting game while an afternoon breeze flitted in and out. Cecilia wished she had her sunglasses to shield her eyes, not from the glaring sun but from Carlos's imposing stare.

"Whatever's in here isn't going to change anything. I won't let anyone hurt my grandson." He only then reached for the envelope, holding it up as though he could see inside. When he finally retrieved the papers, Cecilia was sure it would change everything.

The pages rustled in the wind, and Carlos secured them with his hand.

"I told Phil this was just another reporter trying to scam us."

She hadn't missed the flicker in his eyes. It was there, though he tried to hide it.

"You know exactly what this is."

"Have you any idea how many stories and leads I've been privy to that are completely fabricated? I'm not as naive as I'm made out to be."

"No disrespect, Mr. Santiago. I don't think you're naive at all." She smiled at him. "I actually know how smart you are. You've protected your grandson for this long. And her."

"She has nothing to do with this."

"I think you're wise to be cautious. There are bad people out there who will take advantage of you. I'm not one of them."

He raised an eyebrow.

The waiter arrived with their drinks, but neither of them moved.

"Instead of trying to prove that's Eddie's original music, let me tell you why I'm here."

"I know why you're here. And using the girl to get to him just to exploit that terrible day is shameful."

"I want to do a story on her. On them," Cecilia said.

He dropped the papers on the table and pounded on them with his fist.

"You think we haven't been approached about this before? There's a reason no one's been able to figure it out. It's nobody's business."

Cecilia wouldn't let him deter her. She held his eyes in hers long enough to see the sadness. And the conviction. He studied the pages, and when he reached the end, he froze on what was clearly his grandson's handwriting.

Tread lightly, she told herself. "I saw her." She waited a beat before continuing.

"Every girl thinks they're the one," he replied, tossing the sheets in her direction, one floating off the table onto the deck. Cecilia bent down at the same time as Carlos, and their hands met. He pleaded with her. "Please leave them alone."

She gathered the pages and stuffed them back in the envelope and into her bag.

"Why is this so important to you?" he asked.

It should have been obvious to her: this larger-than-life story about a boy and a girl and a song. But then there was her own thrumming need to make sense of lyrics and words, to arrange and rearrange them so everything made sense. If she understood what pulled Eddie and Sarita apart, she could piece them back together. Piece her and Pete back together. Or her parents. And that's when she realized the story was secondary for her. Because she had done what she told herself not to do, what Joan had *demanded* she not do: she had become emotionally involved. And the article could expose two people who might not want their story told. Three, if she counted this kind man.

"I saw her. I think I saw her. I was at the Orange Bowl covering a story on a band, and to make a long story short, I came across the memorial for that awful day, and she was sitting there."

"Sarita's in Miami?"

"I'm guessing it was her. That's where you come in."

He seemed intrigued, less perturbed.

"From what I could tell, she was upset. We talked for a few minutes. And she left with another woman, but when they pulled away, I noticed the envelope under the bench where she'd been sitting."

"It could've been anyone's envelope. How do you know it's hers?"

"Because I know."

"Did she tell you her name?"

"She didn't have to."

He leaned back in the chair.

"She was talking to this woman on the way to their car. I heard them." Cecilia took a lengthy sip of her drink, knowing this was the moment she would hook Carlos Santiago.

"The other woman told her she needed to let this go . . . to let him go . . . and I heard her . . . I heard her response."

Carlos Santiago was rapt, his eyes unblinking.

"She said, 'I'll never let him go. He wrote those words for me.'"

Speechless. She had rendered the man speechless.

"Help me find them," she said.

Carlos faced the ocean behind her, a weary surrender in his gaze.

"I promise you I won't hurt him."

He straightened and stood up. "I have to get back to work."

And Cecilia begged him, pleaded. "Please, Mr. Santiago."

"You said you work for *Rolling Stone*?" he asked.

"I do."

"Give me your number," he said.

Cecilia was so close she could taste it, but she scribbled her number down, anticipating his call.

"I'll be in touch, Miss James."

CHAPTER 22

"CRACKLIN' ROSIE" BY NEIL DIAMOND

Miami Beach
Summer 1979

After the fiasco at Almar's and the unpleasant aftermath, it became impossible for Sara and Eddie to be together. When Sara wasn't working at the day camp, Shira kept a close eye on her whereabouts, while Eddie made music and entertained crowds on the beach.

On the weekends, Sara watched him from behind the covers of the latest bestsellers, growing restless. And because Abel had always been a trusted companion, and because aligning herself with him made Shira less suspicious, she gravitated to their old friendship. Besides, she liked Abel. He was a stabilizer, a comfort, and if she couldn't be with Eddie, she enjoyed their walks on the beach or frolicking with the others on the sandbar. Eddie was always in the back of her mind, but Abel managed to convince her to join their friends after work for Cozzoli's Pizza or to ride the train at the 163rd Street mall. Their pack filled the Byron Carlyle Theater and took over the arcade at Fun Fair, sipping Shirley Temples at the Red Coach. Sara enjoyed herself, she always did, but she yearned to be with Eddie, and when they passed on the beach, she loathed having to pretend he didn't exist.

Shira watched from the sidelines, gossiping with Abel's mom under their umbrellas about the *shidduch* unfolding before their eyes, and a smile found its way to Shira's face. The fine lines relaxed, and she resumed her card games, loosened her hold. Eddie did his part without even trying. The young girls continued to worship him, elbowing each other to catch his eye, each one believing that he was singing just for her. And he let them believe it.

A collective sigh could be felt across the beach, and it wasn't the waves releasing along the shore.

Then the shooting at Dadeland Mall occurred. It was broad daylight when two men, the "Cocaine Cowboys," opened fire in the popular mall, exposing Miami's dark, dangerous side. The Friedman clan had been at the mall the week before, and Sara read the *I told you so* in her mother's eyes. The incident frazzled Shira and the aunts and uncles. The kids were told to stay close to Surfside, and Sara felt hands around her neck begin to squeeze.

Sara gained no pleasure from betraying her mother, but what she felt for Eddie was too big to contain. On the nights her parents went out or played cards, she resumed sneaking out to visit Eddie at their spot. Using the chart he had given her, they sent secret messages. He could no longer risk leaving notes in books, so instead, they found a spot high on a shelf in the rec room. By then, they could have just left handwritten notes, but they found a thrill in their secret language that intensified the exchanges.

The cluster of rocks down the beach provided privacy, and Eddie would pluck his guitar while the moon crossed the sky. His music reached inside her and held on tight. Every song felt as though it were created for her, and a fluttering spread through her chest. Tears formed, but she wasn't sad. Eddie had found her soul.

Other times they'd sit in the Santiagos' apartment while *Abuelo* prepared spinach empanadas and plantains. They'd talk for hours about their childhoods or lay out their futures. "When I start at Columbia, you should come to New York and play your music," Sara said.

He'd smile at her as though she had the world figured out, but they both knew she didn't.

"I can't leave *Abuelo*, you know that."

Sara admired his loyalty. She understood that Eddie was all the older man had, and it wouldn't be right for Eddie to start a life somewhere without him. But she dreamed of leaving her nest with Eddie beside her. She wanted him to have the same dream.

Then he'd kiss her. And the logistics of a future didn't matter because they had that, and it was enough.

Sara's duplicity continued, made more complicated by Abel's growing feelings. She could tell by the way he looked at her, the way he blushed in her presence, and she cared about him more than any other boy in the neighborhood. Their friendship had resumed its former pace, and Sara enjoyed the companionship. Their conversations were laced with commonalities and comforts, and though he didn't push her, she knew he wanted more. And maybe if Eddie weren't always in her head, she might have explored the feelings further, let those stolen childhood kisses with Abel turn into more. Eddie was real, though, and when he'd kiss her neck, goosebumps trailed down her skin, and when he'd roll on top of her on the hot sand, she wished he'd never stop.

Deborah badgered Sara daily about Abel. "He's gorgeous, Sara! Almost as hot as Leif!" That her friend never suspected her biggest secret was both reassuring and alarming. Maybe it was because Elijah had finally taken notice of Deborah that made her, victorious in her catch, oblivious. It wasn't always easy for people to see what was laid out directly in front of them.

"I can't believe that's Mr. Santiago's kid," Abel had said one afternoon. He had caught her staring at Eddie while he sang to a group of fans.

"Hmm." Sara had trained herself not to respond.

"I wish you'd look at me like that," he'd teased, though there wasn't any humor in it.

She caught Abel's beautiful brown eyes, and for a fleeting second, she felt something tap inside her. It was her childhood, a safety net catching her in one glance.

And Eddie saw it too. "They want you to be with him," he said as they went for a walk near the end of the summer. "Do you want to be with him, Sarita?"

"He's my friend, Eddie. You and I are going to be together."

But she wasn't thinking rationally. She thought it was as simple as graduating from high school, enrolling in Columbia, and Eddie joining her. She imagined him making music in the city and fans falling in love with him as she had. And somehow, it would work. Somehow, she'd convince her parents it was okay. She just wasn't sure how.

"I love you, Sarita."

She loved him too, and she told him. All the way up to the sky and beyond the moon.

"You are made of stars, Eddie."

∼

Summer had drawn to a close, and saying goodbye was imminent. On the day before Sara and her family were scheduled to return to Long Island, the air was thick with heat. Eddie seemed off. Distant. Their goodbyes had become harder, but this one felt especially painful. As Sara talked endlessly about New York, Eddie wrestled with leaving his grandfather and joining her. They discussed part-time jobs—waiter, handyman—while he performed in local bars. "It won't be long before you get a record deal," Sara promised.

~

When Sara found the envelope tucked up on their shelf that last day, its contents were different. It wasn't just a short note. There were pages of sheet music, the kind that Eddie pored over when they sat on the beach, humming, jotting down lyrics. The few times he'd shared them with her, she'd felt a switch inside, a desire she didn't fully understand.

It was music. A song. The date across the top read June 28, 1979.

She didn't understand the melody, but as she read the lyrics, her entire body came alive.

He wrote of New York City, of the two of them thousands of miles apart. And he called her pretty. "Times Square can't shine as bright as you."

He told her not to worry about the distance, that he was right there if she got lonely.

And she did what he asked, closed her eyes, feeling him all around her.

"What you do to me," he wrote. Repeating it so she understood how much. And the tears pooled in her eyes. Because he then promised to take care of her, giving her the life they'd always imagined. The words blurred. "If every simple song I wrote to you would take your breath away I'd write it all, even more in love with me you'd fall, we'd have it all."

Sara felt the words in her bones, heard his voice singing in her ear, a tune she did not yet know. But it didn't matter, not when she'd never read anything more beautiful in her life. And when she reached the end, she sobbed. "I can promise you that by the time we get through the world will never ever be the same. This one's for you."

He had written the song for her, and at the very bottom, on the last page, he'd signed it: *For Sarita. I love you. Eddie.*

Her hands shook, unable to fully process what she'd just read. Their love was bigger than anything she'd ever known. And that's when she spotted the secret message. She'd almost missed it, but there it was in blue ink. "What you do to me," written right above it. Digging in her back pocket, she took out the folded chart and matched the notes to the letters.

Bal Harbour Pier. Eight.

The pier meant only one thing. She'd heard rumblings on the beach, couples strolling the pathway toward the romantic spot. It was where feelings turned to passion, and the thought sent a rush of blood to her cheeks. Not even Shira's warnings or Moshe's trusting face could stop her. They didn't deserve this, but Sara wasn't thinking logically. She stuffed the papers back in the envelope and returned to the condo to prepare.

That night, the family had planned to watch *Grease* in the rec room. Everybody was going. It was the last night of the summer, and they brought in pizzas and Carvel Flying Saucers. While there, Sara made sure to dote on her younger brothers while comparing tan lines with her cousins as they discussed school resuming. Deborah and Elijah were sitting close together, and her parents were opening a bottle of wine.

When the lights went out, Sara positioned herself by the exit, and when Olivia Newton-John and John Travolta rolled in the sand, she slipped out the door. Passing through the lobby and out toward the pool and beach, she already felt her parents' disappointment. This would kill them.

But her love for Eddie was too strong. She couldn't stop herself.

Sara didn't walk to the pier. She ran. She ran as fast as her sneakered feet would carry her, and when she saw Eddie standing there, remnants of sun glistening across the purple sky as it made its way west, she knew when that same sun rose tomorrow, she'd be a butterfly sailing through the air.

CHAPTER 23

"HEY JUDE" BY THE BEATLES

Los Angeles
October 1996

Cecilia sat at the kitchen counter, watching Tori, Hazel, and Phoebe in the backyard. It was the weekend, and they were splayed across a foamy lounge chair, dressed in tiaras, having a tea party. Cecilia held her cell phone to her ear, listening to Joan. Joan, who was royally pissed that she didn't get anything out of Carlos Santiago. Joan, who was beginning to doubt Cecilia's capabilities.

"He trusts me," Cecilia said. "He'll come around."

"Whatever you say, Cecilia. Just don't make me regret this decision."

"I told you, I've got it covered."

She didn't, but success began with visualizing one's goals.

Before Joan hung up, Cecilia reminded her she was off duty tonight. "I'm seeing Pete," she said, reflecting on her delight when he had called and invited her to dinner. "I need to be attentive to him and inaccessible to you."

"Good," her boss said. "Getting laid will be good for you."

Cecilia smiled, craving sex with Pete more than she ever had. She set the phone down on the counter and returned to the scene outside.

Tori held her teacup to her lips and laughed at something funny with the girls, while a stab of envy hit Cecilia. She snapped up an apple from the overflowing fruit bowl and bit into it, conjuring up memories of her own mother. She missed Gloria an ungodly amount, but for the life of her, she couldn't explain why she was unable to unearth singular moments like the one she witnessed now. Instead, she flashed to Don and Gloria circling around their living room in a seductive dance. Gloria twirling in a long, silky dress, the golden shimmer matching her wavy hair.

Cecilia acknowledged that Tori was a decent mother. The proof was in her girls. They were sweet and well mannered, and Cecilia felt a soft spot in her heart beginning to grow. Hating Tori and Don was something separate, and the girls had nothing to do with that. They were merely innocent bystanders.

Cecilia cracked the sliding glass door open just enough to tell them she was leaving. Don had specifically asked her to be mindful of their rules. They were entitled to know when she was heading out and where she was going, and he expected her to nudge him awake when she came home. This overly protective behavior felt off to Cecilia. At twenty-six she was hardly a child, but Don insisted. "Under my roof you're always my little girl."

These paternal gestures were beginning to warm the cold, empty parts of Cecilia and spread unexpectedly. Though she didn't like to admit it, in the short time she'd been staying with Don, she hardly recognized the man she'd pegged as an asshole. He seemed genuinely interested in her job, and when she'd let her guard down, they'd shared some riveting debates on trending songs and the future of music in the digital age. When they sat around the dining room table, Don engaged everyone in conversation, singling them out individually with personal questions. Afterward, he helped Tori with the dishes and then escaped upstairs to play music with the girls, just as he had done with Cecilia.

It was as though the man she had imagined in her head, the man who had destroyed their family, didn't exist. But then she'd remember all the birthdays she'd waited for him to show up, and all the times she'd sat by the phone waiting for his call, only to be buried in the cloud of endless disappointment.

"Don't wait up for me," Cecilia shouted to the girls, tossing the half-eaten apple in the trash.

Hazel and Phoebe squealed, bouncing off the cushion and beelining in her direction.

"You look pretty, CeCe," Hazel said.

"Where you going?" asked Phoebe.

"I'm going to see Pete. Wish me luck."

"Is he your boyfriend?" Hazel asked.

"He was. And I'm going to try to win him back."

"Is he like a prize?" Hazel asked.

Cecilia smiled inwardly. He was.

"How do you win boyfriends back?" Phoebe asked.

Tori approached, stunning in a black tank top and linen shorts that showed off her gorgeous figure. "Girls, let Cecilia go so she's not late."

Cecilia glanced in Tori's direction. "They're actually making me less nervous."

"Why are you nervous, Cecilia?" Hazel asked.

Tori intercepted. "They'll go on for hours. You'll never get out of here."

"It's fine." Cecilia waved a hand and turned to Hazel. "Because I really like Pete, and I messed up. I made a big mistake, and he's been super angry. Tonight, we're going to talk about it, and I'm going to apologize."

The girls stared up at Cecilia, the afternoon sun emphasizing their delicate features.

"Kind of like you and Daddy?" Phoebe said.

Cecilia was taken aback.

"You're always mad," Phoebe continued. "Did he do something wrong?"

Cecilia met Tori's eyes.

"I love Don," she said.

"Then why don't you call him Daddy?" Phoebe probed.

"Come on, girls," Tori said, opening the door to pass through. "Let's let Cecilia go and fix things. Then she can come home and tell us all about it. Who wants to bake cookies?"

The girls squealed again, and Hazel jumped up excitedly. "Cookies!"

"Go wash up," Tori said, "and bring your stuff inside."

The girls ran off in different directions, and Tori appraised Cecilia. "You okay?"

Cecilia shrugged.

Tori took a seat at the island. "When I first met your father, he wanted nothing to do with me. He loved your mother so much. He was broken up about her."

Cecilia was ready to pounce, to point out that Tori's story omitted the part where she threw herself at Don and broke up their family. But she refrained, too anxious about seeing Pete for a confrontation.

"I left it alone," Tori said, "although I felt something with him I'd never felt before."

Cecilia held herself back from cracking a joke about how at Tori's age there couldn't have been many other contenders but the boys in junior high.

"One day he called. He had moved out, and he asked if I'd go for a drive. He picked me up, and I asked where we were going. He had no idea, only that he wanted to move. So I sat in the passenger seat as we wound up Sunset, hitting the Pacific Coast Highway, and we drove for miles, only stopping to watch the sunset. I don't think I said a word. I just listened to him. He talked about your mom, and he talked about you. He loved you both so much.

"I really liked him, but I was pretty sure there was no room in his life for me. And he was hardly ready. We drove back down to Santa Monica, and he took me for a few whirls on the Ferris wheel. The city was lit up by then. Like magic. And I remember he held my hand the whole time, and I thought, *This is nice. If this is all we are, that's okay. This is enough.*"

Cecilia was rapt, but when she glanced at her watch, Tori's face dropped. "Now I'm the one holding you up. I'm sorry. Isn't it time for Pete to be here?"

"No, go on," Cecilia said, always addicted to a good love story. "Finish. He'll call when he gets here."

"When we got back on earth, your father asked me what it was I wanted. We were standing in front of the burger shack, and I thought he meant something to eat. He made me nervous, and I couldn't imagine eating, but I told him a snow cone. He laughed, and I was afraid I'd said something stupid.

"Then he corrected himself. He said, 'I meant what do you *want*. What keeps you awake at night? What do you want more than anything?'"

Hazel and Phoebe returned, opening and closing cabinets and drawers, plopping flour and sugar on the countertop. "She said, 'You,'" said Phoebe.

Tori rolled her eyes. "They've heard this story before."

Hazel said, "Mommy says that her mommy always told her that if she ever wanted something she had to ask for it."

And Phoebe finished. "She told him she wanted him."

Cecilia didn't know what to make of this, but she didn't have time to dwell on it. Her cell phone rang, and she saw Pete's number on the screen. "He's here." She grabbed her bag off a nearby chair. "I've gotta go."

"I'm not sharing this to upset you, Cecilia. No one will ever take the place of your mother."

"I know that."

"I'm telling you because it's important." Tori looked as though she might actually care. "When you want something in life, it's okay to ask for it. You'll never know what's possible without asking."

Cecilia's body crackled with a strange energy. Sure, she didn't want to hear how Tori sank her claws into her father, but this story felt very different from the script she'd been reading all these years.

She tried to block out the unease lodged inside. "Thanks," she said, *for falling in love with my dad, for stealing him from my mother, for being . . . kind.*

"Tell him how you feel," Tori said.

Cecilia nodded. "Got it."

And the girls sang in unison, "Cecilia and Peter down by the schoolyard!"

This actually got a laugh out of her.

~

Pete stood waiting when Cecilia stepped out the front door, the bright sun hitting her eyes. She blinked. *Pete's here.* She walked casually toward the car, aware that he followed her every step before opening the door. She hopped in, and they set off down Laurel Canyon. "You look nice," he said. And she was happy he noticed the effort she'd put into their reunion—soft-pink lipstick and a long, flowy T-shirt dress.

Cecilia studied his profile as they traveled toward Sunset. "You look nice too." And he did. His hair was cut short, shorter than usual, revealing the smooth skin on the back of his neck. She wanted to reach over and touch him, but she waited, Tori's words echoing as LA unwound around them.

"Where are we going?" she asked.

"I thought we'd go to Shutters."

Shutters Hotel was for special occasions. At first, they could only afford lunch at the restaurant, 1 Pico, but eventually they'd begun celebrating birthdays and anniversaries with dinner. They hadn't been there in a while, and maybe he remembered the last time, how they'd shared scallops and corn with shishito peppers, then walked over to the pier and played carnival games and munched on cotton candy. Afterward, they'd dipped their sugared fingers into the salty water, lazing on the beach and watching the waves crash into the shore. It was touristy, not glamorous, only neon and laughter. That night they had talked for hours, curled close together, stopping only to touch hands. And lips.

Staring out the car window, she couldn't help but wonder if Tori's story had traveled the universe into Pete's waiting ears.

As they made their way toward Santa Monica, Smashing Pumpkins' "1979" ended and the first few notes of No Doubt's "Don't Speak" played. Gwen Stefani's emotionally charged plea about an inevitable breakup was not what Cecilia needed to hear. She reached for the radio dial and snapped it off.

"I'm not letting go, Pete. I don't want you to, either."

"Lyrics can't save us anymore, Cecilia."

"I'm not giving up. How's that for original?"

He didn't reply, making the right turn into Shutters.

The lobby bustled with guests, and while Cecilia thrived on celebrity sightings, today she paid careful attention to Pete. Only Pete. His indifference vibrated across the table. His face was drawn, his brown eyes pensive. When the waiter appeared, Pete ordered two tequilas and their favorite appetizers. She offered another apology while they took turns picking at the breadbasket. He didn't toss the apology back, but he didn't accept it either.

Cecilia couldn't get a read on him, and the awkward silence made her jumpy. She gulped down her tequila too fast, and when the waiter dropped off the crispy wrapped squash and focaccia with burrata, the two of them sat and stared, their old reliable favorite failing to ease the tension. There was a wall between them she couldn't get through, the safe subjects like photography and music no longer dependable. At last, he asked about her father.

She filled him in on Tori's niceties, how the girls were sweet and fun to be around, before mentioning Don. "That man's an anomaly."

He listened, letting her continue.

"It's like he's the old Don, the Don of my childhood. It's weird."

"Maybe you were wrong about him," he said, fiddling with the lime in his tequila.

"Come on, Pete. You were there. You saw my constant disappointment."

"I also saw your resistance when he reached out. You didn't make it easy." He brought the drink up to his lips and swigged as though salvation were at the bottom of the glass. "There's always another side to the story."

The way he said it felt like a betrayal.

"Cecilia," he finally said, as the waiter delivered their main courses.

"Pete. Whatever you're about to say, I need to say something first."

He leaned back in his chair, the lamb chops waiting.

"I should've been on the boat. I should've allowed for a margin of error. I didn't. I miscalculated and that's not like me. You didn't deserve that. But you have to know that not showing up is very different from not loving you—"

He leaned forward, hair falling in front of his eyes. She wanted to touch it. "Do you remember what you used to say to me when your father upset you?"

When she didn't answer, he repeated the question.

"Okay," she said. "You have a point."

"I believe you quoted a song. Something about loving someone means showing up."

"No. It was actually about someone holding on to someone who only offers pain." U2 said it way better in "One," but Pete wouldn't appreciate the reference.

The waiter approached, noticing that neither of them had touched their food, asking if everything was okay.

Cecilia politely assured him that everything was fine.

When the man scampered away, she found her kind, patient voice. "You can't compare me to my father. I'm nothing like him."

"Aren't you? You always have a toe out the door." He stopped, apparently changing his mind. "Actually, it's more like a foot. But it doesn't matter anymore."

Cecilia was torn between feeling miffed and misunderstood, and Tori's words came to mind.

"I love you, Pete. I don't want to lose you."

Interestingly, he chose now to start cutting into his food.

"Is this about the proposal?" she cautiously asked. "I would have said yes."

"Look," he said, ignoring her. "There's something I have to tell you."

His beautiful brown eyes were fixed on hers, and she braced herself for something close to a seven on the Richter scale. She crossed her legs tighter, held on to the table. Pete was going to tell her he met someone. On the ship. He didn't want to work things out, and he didn't want to accept her apology.

"I've been offered a job."

She slowly let out her breath and composed herself. "That's great," she said. "*LA Times*? *TIME* magazine?"

"Not exactly." He slowly set down the fork. "It's overseas."

She cocked her head, believing she misunderstood.

"They want me to shoot what's happening over in Afghanistan. For *National Geographic*."

"That's amazing, Pete. You've always wanted this!" But it came out stilted as she did her best to disguise the well of sadness forming in her throat. This meant he was leaving, traveling thousands of miles away.

She raised her glass to her lips, sorry she hadn't ordered another round. She could have used the boost, but when she turned it on, she really turned it on. "Look at you going after your dreams. Making shit happen."

"There's more. When *LIFE* caught wind of the offer, they promoted me. I have to make a decision."

Cecilia sat with this. Pete. Pete moving across the planet. Or Pete in Los Angeles. The answer came out too quickly. "*National Geographic*'s been your lifelong dream."

"I know." And he caught her eyes.

"You have to go! How can you turn down an opportunity like that?"

"It's far away," he said. "I'm not sure when I'll be back."

Every fiber of her being screamed for him to stay. "You can't turn down *National Geographic*, Pete."

He waited, raising a napkin to his lips, in an interminable silence that had the power to break them. "Are you sure?"

She wriggled in her seat. "It's all you've ever wanted, Pete. You have to go."

He didn't seem convinced, waiting for her to say something else, and when she didn't, he tapped his fingers along the table. "I love working for *LIFE*. But you're right. I should take it. This is the time to do it, nothing holding me back."

She should have fought him. She should have told him exactly how she felt—broken—at the idea of his leaving. She should have asked him to stay, like Tori suggested. Instead, she played this game. Because it felt familiar being left. Despair bubbled in her chest as he rattled off the details. If he accepted the offer, he was only days away from flying out. How could she steal his happiness after everything that had happened? This was what he'd wanted forever.

"I'm really happy for you," she lied, pushing her uneaten food away and flagging down the waiter. Pete followed, offering up his unfinished chops, finishing off his drink, and staring into her eyes.

His gaze pulled at her, sadness mixed with regret.

"I think you're making the right decision." And because she was exhausted from her lies, she added, "You probably could've told me over the phone. You didn't have to splurge on the fancy, half-eaten meal."

"I thought I owed it to you to tell you in person, Cecilia. It was important for me to see you. Get your opinion."

She eked out a smile. "Here it is. My happy face!"

"Don't do that."

"I'm not doing anything. I'm fucking thrilled for you, Pete. Things are looking up for the two of us. We work hard. We deserve it."

Pete's expression was unreadable as he paid the check and she followed him out of the restaurant. The car ride was a quiet one, and instead of taking her back to Don's he parked in front of their old building and shut off the engine.

Without looking at her, he said, "Spend the night with me."

Of course she'd imagined this was how the night would end, Pete's body on top of hers, Pete inside her again. But the circumstances had changed, and this could be the last time.

HAnd her answer didn't really matter, because soon they were both out of the car, entering their old house, drawing on a long line of memories, and she wished he wasn't leaving, and she wished love could fix everything. They reached their old bedroom, and she shimmied the dress down her hips and flung her shoes off. He stood watching. Watching her unhook her bra, watching her slide her underwear down her legs.

He made no move to get undressed, and she worried he planned on some overdue payback. But she couldn't have been more wrong. His desire was all over his face.

He stepped closer, her body naked against his jeans and thin sweater. He ran his hand through her hair. At first delicately and then harder, and he tilted her head back, his lips brushing her neck. Her fingers fumbled with his zipper, and she wrestled with his shirt. Then he lifted her up and dropped her on the bed.

She pressed "PLAY" on his CD player, and Bruce Springsteen sprang from the speakers. Pete wasn't always predictable, but Bruce was his rabbi. They weren't in a car like Bruce described, but Pete on top of her felt like they were, and the windows were down, the wind rolling back their hair. By the time Bruce crooned about a last chance, Cecilia felt a dampness in her eyes, and Pete was inside her.

She didn't know which was more beautiful—the song or what they were doing. The music grabbed hold of her, the sounds lodging beneath her skin. The empty, broken parts of her filled up, and she let herself be carried away.

Closing her eyes, she channeled every one of her senses. She felt Pete. She smelled his clean skin. She heard the sounds of their bodies in sync. She held on to this minute. The hour. The day. Because he had to leave. And things in Afghanistan were dangerous. This was why he'd brought her here.

They danced in a perfect, familiar rhythm. Pete's lips brushed her hair and cheeks. He tasted the salt of her tears.

"I love you, Pete."

"I love you too, CeCe. I'll always love you. TTM."

And she wished she could tell him to stay, beg him not to leave. But she couldn't. Not when he'd always supported her career. Not when he had this opportunity. This was what he'd always wanted to do, needed to do. She couldn't hold him back. And there was something else. If she asked him to stay, what if he said no? What if he chose to leave? She just couldn't bear that sort of rejection again.

He rolled off her and held her tight.

He whispered the words, or maybe it was Bruce, about his love and his heart and his soul. And Cecilia held on to the bittersweet taste of their goodbye and to him. The song cushioned the sadness, a melancholy bliss that would have to bridge miles. Bruce asked her not to cry, but it was Pete who wiped her eyes.

And they stayed like that for hours, and she told him she'd be there waiting when he returned, and he said he didn't expect her to wait. And when his phone rang, he untangled himself from her, and she wondered if she'd ever feel that complete again, while she heard him say, "She's fine. She's with me."

And she loved the sound of it. *She's with me.*

And she didn't know whether she should laugh or cry at Don checking up on her, so she smiled.

"I want to go with you to the airport. We can share a cab." And by curling around her he gave her his answer, and they stayed like that, Cecilia imagining, maybe, he'd do a short stint and they'd pick up where they left off. But that all changed when her cell phone on the floor began to ring, with a number she didn't recognize.

"Hello."

"Miss James?"

She recognized the voice at once. Straightening, she held the phone close to her ear.

"Eddie, my grandson. He's in Bisbee, Arizona."

"Mr. Santiago, thank you."

"I trust you, Cecilia. I trust you won't hurt him. Tell him about Sarita. Maybe she can get through to him."

"I'll get there as soon as I can. Tomorrow. You can trust me, Mr. Santiago."

And the spell had broken. Pete sank into the pillows.

CHAPTER 24

"DARLING NIKKI" BY PRINCE

Bisbee, Arizona
October 1996

Two days later, Cecilia touched down in Tucson, Arizona, met by a driver who took her the ninety miles to Bisbee. Bisbee was like no other town she'd visited before. Described as an old mining village frequented by hippies and artists, the area was constructed on a hill, where steep stairways connected streets or led to the middle of someone's backyard barbecue.

Downtown Bisbee consisted of a single road lined by historic buildings and storefronts. Colorful murals covered the brick walls of nearby bars, the general store, and the post office, all set against a mountainous terrain. She could see how Bisbee would be the ideal hideaway for a dejected, regretful artist to live anonymously.

With little to go on other than knowing Eddie lived here, Cecilia checked into the Bisbee Inn. Erected in 1904, the hotel, as Mary-Ann behind the counter explained, was a training center for the Peace Corps, and before that, lodging for the miners. "We've been a hotel since

1983!" She said this with a vigor that matched her freckled complexion and flaming-red hair.

She leaned closer to Cecilia. "You may have heard we've had some paranormal activity here. I don't want you to hear it from anyone else, so I'm doing the honorable thing by sharing it with you."

"I'd prefer ignorance."

"It's nothing to get your panties in a twist. We've had guests say they've seen a cowboy in room 11. Abigail lives in room 12. People swear they smell her lavender perfume. You're in 23. We hear Millie the cat lingers around there."

"How about a room minus the paranormal activity?"

"Where's the fun in that?"

Cecilia muttered under her breath. Of course, she was stuck with a cat.

~

Besides the occasional sound of a drill and a potential ghost at any turn, the hotel had charm, a mix of period pieces, lavish rugs against hardwood floors, and antique furnishings. Room 23 was on the second floor, with walls covered in golden toile wallpaper and a musty quilt on the bed that Mary-Ann said had been hand sewn. Cecilia dropped her carry-on atop the worn leather bench at the foot of the bed and began to unpack.

Hopping on the bed, she was met with a pang of regret. When she and Pete used to check into hotels, as soon as they'd dropped their bags, they'd pounce on the bed. Today, she found it depressing to be in this quaint little town, knowing she might never tumble on a mattress with him again.

She'd been trying not to think about their last night together. Their bodies had fit so perfectly it was ridiculous that was goodbye. She suppressed the urge to call him, to tell him to choose *LIFE*, but she knew what *National Geographic* meant for him, and she refused to hold him back.

"It's better we say goodbye now," he had said after she offered to accompany him to the airport, not bothering to ask about the call from Mr. Santiago. But he knew. He knew exactly what the conversation meant. He did them both a favor, and when he dropped her back at Don's house later that night, they squeezed each other's hands.

"These were some of the best years of my life, Cecilia James."

"We'll have more," she said, "when you get back."

And he held her face one last time, kissed her, and he was gone.

∼

Staring up at the ceiling, she shook the thoughts of Pete away and decided to go for a walk around town. Mary-Ann stopped her on the porch. "I can show you around! You're lucky it's Thursday. Most of the stores are closed earlier in the week. There's the Mining Museum or the Queen Mine Tour. I can get you in for free. I've got connections." And she winked. Maybe it wasn't a bad idea to have the excitable girl provide the backstory; perhaps she'd take Cecilia to a secret spot where she could find Eddie Vee.

"Bisbee isn't known for much," Mary-Ann said as they strolled down Ok Street. Mary-Ann didn't really walk. She skipped, and it was an effort for Cecilia to keep up. "We were a big mining town, and you know what that means."

"I don't, actually."

"Lots of booze and gambling and chaos. The unions and the mine owners were always at it."

A car shot by, spraying dust in the air, and Cecilia fanned the plume from her face. Unfazed, Mary-Ann inhaled, and it only made her perkier. "When the mines shut down, our little town became a hot spot for artists and musicians. I mean, look at this view," she said, fanning out her fingers at the majestic mountains framing the storefronts.

They stopped in front of a collection of murals: a collage of faces, Elvis, and a hula dancer showing off her midriff. Someone had spray-painted on a wall, *Let's Be Better Humans*. Cecilia had a sense that Eddie was near. As the townspeople swept by, Cecilia studied their faces, searched their eyes.

"Is there a bar in town?" Cecilia asked. "Perhaps one with live music?"

Mary-Ann winked. "So that's what you've got on your mind. We've got a bar the likes of the best."

"Is it open?" Cecilia checked her watch, which read four twenty-five.

Mary-Ann shimmied up to Cecilia and bumped her with her narrow hip. "You about ready for the happiest hour of the day, Cecilia James?"

She hooked her arm into Cecilia's and tugged her down the street.

Entering St. Elmo Bar on Brewery Avenue was like stepping onto the set of *St. Elmo's Fire*, the movie. When Cecilia's eyes adjusted to the darkness, she narrowed in on a wall with highway signs and junk parts that made for interesting art. Inhaling the stench of beer, cigarettes, and Pine-Sol, she focused on the back of the room, where there was a mike setup surrounded by round tables and chairs. Two men sat at the bar while a hefty, tattooed bartender smiled at Mary-Ann.

"Whatever my friend here wants, Billy. She came all the way from the city of angels."

"That right?" Billy said, sharing a big-toothed grin with Cecilia. "What brings you this way?"

It was a question any bartender would ask a customer, but it was hard to miss the probing look in his eyes. Cecilia understood how people in small towns protected their own, and if there was a celebrity among them, someone in need of privacy and confidentiality, they'd aggressively conceal their identity.

"Trying to cure this writer's block." It wasn't entirely false. She was crafting a story.

"Everyone's writing a book. You hear that, Jack?" he said to the man seated beside Cecilia. "You two can start a book club."

"First, I gotta write the book," Jack said. He turned his cowboy hat and thick mustache to Cecilia. "How far along are you?"

Cecilia ordered a beer. "I'm close to the end. It's a mystery," she said.

Cecilia spotted a small chalkboard beside the rows of bottles, where someone with perfect penmanship had written in colorful chalk the names of the artists performing that weekend. No one Cecilia recognized, but she was intrigued.

Jack noticed where Cecilia's eyes had shifted. "You into music?"

She hesitated. "It's all right. Sometimes I listen while I write."

"Then you'll like Carlos Atiras. Most of our visitors do."

Carlos. "What's he like?"

"You'll soon find out." He motioned toward the door. "That's him."

Cecilia didn't immediately turn. She needed to play this out without drawing obvious attention. Billy set the beer in front of her. She felt a nip in the air, a cool breeze that tickled her skin. She waited. And when she finally caught a glimpse, she let out a stiff breath. He was not Eddie Vee.

The man strutting through the bar carrying a guitar case had long, dark hair that brushed the middle of his back. His scraggly beard hid most of his face, and Cecilia sensed poor hygiene by its greasy shine. She turned away.

"He has that effect on women," Jack said. "Nobody wants to get close. But then he sings."

Cecilia took a closer look, remembering the fresh-faced, youthful boy who had captivated the world with his beautiful blue eyes. This man wore dark sunglasses that hid much of his face. Cecilia wanted it to be Eddie, but that would have been too easy. Besides, the Eddie Vee she and the world knew was half this man's size. Carlos Atiras looked like he had eaten Eddie Vee for breakfast. No, the two men were not the same.

Cecilia watched, discouraged, as Carlos Atiras walked toward the stage. He wore faded jeans and a black leather jacket with an array of necklaces dangling from his neck. Whoever he was, the man was a mess. She peered back at the chalkboard. Tomorrow's lineup was Dixie Rose. Then Rylee Dylan.

Carlos Atiras swung his guitar from its case and took a seat on the barstool at the center of the stage. The bar began to fill up with hippies and artsy types. Mary-Ann threaded her arm through Cecilia's again, a strange chumminess that made her feel both uncomfortable and less alone. "Let's find a seat."

She really didn't want to sit through amateur night in Bisbee. She wanted to poke around, ask questions, find Eddie, but she knew she had to be patient, fit in, build trust. She scanned the room, though it was hard to make out anyone's features in the near darkness. Carlos Atiras strummed his guitar while guests pulled their seats closer.

At once the room quieted, and Carlos welcomed the crowd. His accent was thick, straight out of the old West. Cecilia closed her eyes and tried to identify the voice, but she couldn't match the sound. This voice was older, and she reminded herself Eddie would be older too.

Carlos played the first few notes of Pearl Jam's "Black" and the bar roared. The voice was familiar, but not. It was rich, heavy, as though the man singing the words had a weight bearing down on his chest. If she closed her eyes, she could almost convince herself this was Eddie Vee, but when she opened her eyes, it was impossible. He cradled the guitar, his hands plucking the chords like it was his lover. It was an odd-looking guitar, not your typical wood finish. This one appeared to have been hand-painted bright blue.

CHAPTER 25

"MANDY" BY BARRY MANILOW

Miami Beach
Summer 1979

When Sara reached the pier at eight o'clock, Eddie whisked her up, twirling her in the air. And when her feet touched the pavement, his face was close enough for her to feel his breath, smell the minty scent. She stared into the blue of his eyes.

"That song, Eddie."

"It's for you, Sarita."

She didn't think it was possible to fall any harder for him, but she was.

He walked her along the water, where the Intracoastal Waterway met the wide ocean, to a secluded spot hidden by hedges and a canopy of trees. In its center, a blanket lay on the grass.

"What's that for?" she asked, pointing at a lantern.

"So I can see you," he said.

She moved in closer and kissed him, the words getting lost between their lips. He kissed her back, his fingers sliding through her hair, pulling her closer so his tongue explored her mouth. But it wasn't enough. It had never been enough. His hands slid down her shoulders until they found her hands, and they dropped onto the blanket and away from the world.

"Sing it for me," she said.

He didn't have the guitar, but it didn't matter. His voice, the words, they captured the very best parts. When the song ended, she lay in his arms, and she knew what she wanted. She wasn't sure Eddie would agree. Eddie was respectful and protective. But this was all she thought about. The feelings had been building for years. Besides, Eddie was already inside her.

So when they kissed and Eddie cupped a breast in his hand, she let her hands move up and down his body. And soon she was unbuttoning his shirt, her fingers tugging at the waist of his jeans. "Eddie." It came out a whisper. "I don't want to stop."

"Sarita."

"Please," she said, shimmying her shorts down her legs.

"We can't. It's too dangerous."

"We have to."

"I don't want to hurt you."

"You could never hurt me."

And she kissed him.

And Eddie gave in, taking in all her secret parts. He kissed her shoulders, her breasts, her inner thighs. And it still wasn't enough. And when he slipped on top of her and entered her, she felt pain mixed with something else. Something that had her body completely alive. They moved together, and she couldn't understand how they hadn't done this sooner.

"I'm right here," he whispered in her ear. "Close your eyes. Listen to my voice."

She did what he asked, memorizing every inch of his body. When she left tomorrow, she would have this part of him. And he would have hers.

Afterward, he wrapped the blanket around her, their legs tangled together. The sky was inky black, a spray of stars poking through. She could hear the waves crash into the pier as his fingers tickled her skin.

"Where have you gone off to?" he asked.

She hesitated. "How we can stay like this forever."

He held her close, and she pressed against him, but then he sat up and reached for his jeans, taking something out of his pocket.

"This is for you, Sarita."

She took the cloth bracelet and read the words stitched in the fabric, *Be bold, be brave*, as he fastened it around her wrist.

"Maybe New York could work," he said. "After you're settled at school. *Abuelo* too. He's good at his job, and—"

She threw her arms around him and kissed him.

"What about your parents, Sarita?"

She smiled so hard her cheeks hurt. "We have time to worry about that. We'll figure it out. Just like you said in your song."

She felt his body tense. "I don't want to be the reason for difficulty in your life, Sarita."

"That's impossible. You're the best thing that's ever happened to me. I'll talk to *Aba*. He's far more rational than *Ima*. He'll understand."

"You can't tell them," he said, leading her back down on the blanket. "They'll punish you. I don't want that for you. Or *Abuelo*. Let's talk to *Abuelo* first."

Sara curled into him, the dilemma resting between them.

"Let's not make any decisions tonight," he said.

She agreed, only because Eddie was coming to New York. It didn't matter when or how, as long as he was there. She moved closer, resting her head on his chest. "Tell me what our life's going to look like, Eddie. Can you see it?"

He traced her eyes with his fingertips, then her lips. "We have a house on the ocean to watch the sunrise. *Tres niños*."

"Four," she said.

"We will make *Abuelo*'s fried yuca and *Ima*'s matzo ball soup, and we'll dance around the kitchen to Leif Garrett while the kids make fun of us. After we read them your stories and they go to sleep, I will take you to bed and do naughty things to you."

She laughed. "Like what you just did?"

"Much naughtier."

A warm thrill shot through her body.

"I will build you a shelf for all your books and a desk for you to write your own. It will be a story about two people. Two people from *muy diferentes* worlds who have a happy ending."

Sara interrupted. "I'll follow you to clubs where you'll sing to a crowded room. Standing room only. The girls will throw themselves at you, and I'll tell them you're mine. And when you become a star, I'll whisper in your ear, *I told you so*."

"I could become a Bar Mitzvah," he said. "I could change my religion . . . maybe that would make *Ima* happy."

"I don't want you to change who you are."

"I will do anything to make you happy, Sarita."

"I'm already happy, Eddie."

"I want to make you the happiest woman in the world."

She smiled because she already was. They would be together. They just needed time to figure it out.

"Tell me more about our life," she said, turning onto her back, feeling the pull of the moon.

"I will write music for you. I will sing to you and our babies. I can even write something for your brothers. They would like that."

"They like you," she said. "They don't admit it, but I see them watching. They move along to your music, mouthing the words. They all do. If they could only get past the other stuff."

"It is important to your *familia*, Sarita."

"I can't believe how accepting you are."

"They are part of you."

"You're going to be a famous musician, Eddie. Your life is going to change too."

"I am happy if I am with you. And *Abuelo*."

"You're talented. You have to do something with that talent."

"I am not like you, Sarita. I'll sing on the streets. As long as you are there."

"If we're really going to be together, Eddie, we have to think about these things."

"I don't want to think tonight," he said. "I just want to be with you, Sarita. I want to hold you like this, so I never forget."

"You'll never forget." She looked at her watch and knew it was time to go. "The movie will be over soon."

"Will I see you before you leave tomorrow?" he asked.

"Of course," she said. "I'm going to pick up bagels for the flight home. Meet me outside the deli at eight."

CHAPTER 26

"MAGGIE MAY" BY ROD STEWART

Bisbee, Arizona
October 1996

"He came here about five years ago," Mary-Ann whispered in Cecilia's ear. "Said he was just passing through but never left. No one knows much about him. He keeps to himself. No fuss. He just comes here and plays and drives the town wild, then disappears to his room."

"Where's that?" Cecilia asked.

"Oh, I can't tell you that," Mary-Ann said with a laugh. "You could be some crazy stalker!"

Cecilia didn't join in her laugh. Instead, she focused on Carlos Atiras as he followed up "Black" with Jeff Buckley's "Hallelujah" and Frampton's "Baby, I Love Your Way." He was good. He sounded a lot like Eddie, but she couldn't be sure. She needed a closer look. After a round of applause from the packed house, he set the guitar down and made his way toward the saloon-style doors, disappearing down a corridor. Mary-Ann had been swallowed by the crowd, chatting it up with locals, which gave Cecilia the chance to slip away.

Squeezing through the bar, she pushed past the swinging doors in search of Mr. Atiras. A line had formed outside the door with the sign that read "Cowgirls," and she made her way to another one with a sign that read "Private: Staff Only." When the door suddenly opened, she was face-to-face with the man who had just graced the stage, and he had removed his sunglasses. His eyes were so blue. A deep, gorgeous blue. Cecilia couldn't believe it. There was no doubt. The person staring back at her was Eddie Vee.

"The bathroom's over there." He pointed.

Every nerve in her body screamed Eddie Vee, and she had to make her move. "I was actually looking for you."

He tried to scoot past her, but she stopped him. "I know who you are."

"Okay, now can you get out of my way?"

Cecilia didn't budge.

"Please," he added.

"I'm not leaving until we talk."

"Whatever it is you're selling, I'm not interested."

"I think you are. I think you will be."

They were caught in a deadlock stare when Mary-Ann materialized in the corridor. "Cecilia! Let's get back to the bar," she said, tugging on Cecilia's elbow.

The distraction gave Eddie the opening to squirm past, pushing through the doors so hard they swung wildly.

Cecilia chased after him, but it was too late. He'd already reached the stage, hitched his guitar strap around his shoulder, and grabbed the mike.

Cecilia wasn't discouraged. If anything, his reaction only confirmed what she already knew. Carlos Atiras was Eddie Vee. It was there in his eyes; it was there in the painful glare. And it was wedged in that brilliant voice. She had no problem waiting until he wrapped up the next set. She had all night.

CHAPTER 27

"FERNANDO" BY ABBA

Miami Beach
Summer 1979

When Sara snuck inside the Atlantic's doors, she was someone else, and there was no going back to who she had been before. She buried her secret where no one could see and held on to the dream that she and Eddie would live out the life they had imagined.

He had followed her back to the building like he'd always done, a few feet behind, watching her step inside. Then, she knew, he would wait a few minutes to be sure no one had spotted them before disappearing through the double doors. She wondered what he thought about while he waited. Was he playing it over in his mind, how perfectly their bodies fit? How her hips pressed against his?

She stopped in the lobby restroom to clean up, taking her time to stare at her reflection in the mirror, rub the bracelet and its words, certain she could see Eddie's hands imprinted on her skin. She straightened her hair and brushed the sand from her clothes, and when satisfied, she entered the rec room. Only, the movie was over.

She told herself it was okay, she could have been in the restroom when the film ended, and she climbed the stairs two steps at a time. When she entered the condo, her father had poured himself a drink, and she wondered if he could tell just by looking at her what she'd done. She pulled her shirt tighter against her chest while he swallowed the drink in one swig. Noah and Abraham stormed in, chattering about a commotion on the beach. Sara couldn't see the red-and-blue lights swirling below, but she could hear sirens sounding off in the distance.

"Where's *Ima*?" the boys asked.

"She's at one of the aunt's," her father said, pouring himself another drink.

Floating on her imaginary cloud, Sara rebuffed her brothers' requests to play another game of Clue. She wanted to get to her room so she could close the door and relive every detail, capture every feeling, and jot them down in her diary. Tomorrow they would head home, and she wanted to remember everything about that night.

Sleep didn't come easily. In fact, it hardly came at all. Sara tossed and turned, imagining the sheets wrapped around her waist were Eddie's hands and the pillow cradling her head was his chest. She couldn't bear another goodbye. At some point, Shira cracked open the door, knelt beside her bed, and whispered a prayer, grazing Sara's forehead with her lips. Shira performed this routine with all her children before going to bed herself. And it was only then that Sara fell into a deeper sleep.

When she finally rose in the morning, she rubbed at her eyes and looked out the window at the sheer blue ocean. A few early risers were already setting up chairs by the pool, and she thought about how much she would miss the Atlantic. And how she would never forget what happened here. She may have lost something, but she found something too.

Throwing on clothes, she jammed her feet inside her sneakers and headed to the bathroom to wash her face and brush her teeth. All the while, she thought about seeing Eddie again.

Sara found her mother at the dining room table with her prayer book, mouthing the words. She planted a kiss on the top of her head, but *Ima* didn't seem to notice, lost in her morning ritual. "I'm going to get the bagels," she said, and her mother nodded, not looking up.

The blue sky spanned for miles, a clearness that matched the ocean. The temperature had eased up over the last few days, but it was the usual hot and humid. Normally, the humidity clung to her, thick and confining, but today she felt light and free. Sara set out for the short walk to the deli, cars coming to life on Collins Avenue. She stopped at the crosswalk, staring up at the towering palm trees, their branches waving as she passed. She thought to herself, *Remember this moment.*

Continuing her stroll, Sara passed Sheldon's Drugs when she spotted Eddie.

She squinted, unsure, but it was him, albeit a disheveled version. He stood waiting in the alley by the drugstore, wearing the same clothes he had worn the night before. He pressed his finger to his beautiful red lips to shush her, motioning with his other hand to come close.

"This isn't where we're supposed to meet," she said, moving in to kiss his lips.

"I can't meet you, Sara." He backed away.

There was something broken in his face; his eyes had lost their glow.

"Eddie, what's wrong?"

Eddie trembled. He motioned for her to sit. There was a rusty bench beside the building, cigarette butts littering the ground. They sat close, their shoulders touching, and instead of feeling the residual bliss of last night, Sara felt a faint chill.

"Last night . . . Sara—"

She rested her head on his shoulder. "I haven't stopped thinking about it, Eddie."

He pulled away. Enough for her to notice. "It was a mistake."

"Come on, Eddie." She swatted him. "Don't be ridiculous. It was the best night of my life. Our lives."

He stared at the ground. "I'm serious. *Muy en serio.* We shouldn't have."

She straightened, a tiny seed of dread planted in her stomach.

"It's okay," she said. "What we did . . . I wanted it to happen. I'm almost seventeen! You don't have to protect me."

"I shouldn't have let it happen."

She couldn't believe what she was hearing. She stood up. "I won't let you do this," she said. "You're like the worst book. What's next? You're going to tell me you're no good for me? That you'll only end up hurting me?" Sara laughed at the absurdity, crossing her arms close to her chest. "No. It's not true. You're lying."

He eyed her cautiously, a cold, lifeless stare.

"We're going back to Argentina. Me. *Abuelo.* I won't be here the next time you come."

Her voice cracked. "Why would you do that?"

"We have to go back." He tried, but he couldn't look her in the eye.

"You can't do that," she stammered. "We made promises . . . you said . . . you said you loved me . . . you said you were going to make me breakfast . . . and we were going to read and sing to our children . . . how can you leave?"

Her legs felt weak, and the warm air pressed against her. She sat back down beside him, dropping her head in her hands, the tears spilling out. He dabbed at his eyes too.

"We are happy today, but how long? This is not real, Sarita. You can't see it, but these things that make us different . . . they will get bigger. And we will end up hating each other."

"That's stupid, Eddie. I could never hate you. I love you. We love each other."

She reached for his hand, tears blotting her face, but he pulled it away. "Please don't cry, Sarita. It will only make it harder."

She shook her head, furious. Argentina was thousands of miles away. They'd never see each other. How could he do this?

"Can't you talk to *Abuelo*? You can still meet me in New York. We can have that life. Don't you want that?" She could barely breathe. "It's another hurdle, Eddie. Another test. We can do it. Be bold and brave. Aren't we worth fighting for?"

"I was foolish. I should have never—"

The words bit into her. "Stop it," she said. "I know when you're lying. I've known you for too long. Why are you doing this?"

He was resolute, holding back. He stood. "I don't love you like that."

"Stop it, Eddie."

"There have been other girls." He refused to say the words to her face, and Sara hated him, knowing he didn't mean a word.

"You should be with someone like Abel. He will give you the life you need. The life you deserve."

She felt herself beginning to crumble, his lingering touch starting to fade. "You wrote that song for me. How could you do this?"

"I am a musician," he said, turning to walk away. "That is what we do."

Sara begged him to stop, to talk to her, and in a fit of rage, she ripped off the bracelet he'd given her only hours before and threw it at him. "You're a liar. And a fake. And a phony." But he disappeared around the corner without looking back.

∾

The next few hours were a blur. In slow motion, as though she inhabited someone else's body, Sara walked back to the condo with the brown paper bag stuffed with bagels from the deli, almost tripping over two little girls playing hopscotch on the sidewalk. The air felt sticky and sweat dripped down her back. Each step fueled a growing fury.

Entering the condo, she found her mother busying herself with packing. *Ima* barely looked up, so she didn't see the heartbreak on Sara's face. That was fine, because if her mother knew all that had transpired, this would be her moment of triumph, the moment of gloating satisfaction. Sara stared at her mother, wondering how it was possible to be physically close to someone, related by blood, and unable to see what was beneath the skin. Shouldn't *Ima* instinctively be able to detect these things, to read between the lines? Sara didn't know if she was happy that her mother was clueless or just plain sad.

But nothing compared to the hole in her heart, what Eddie had just done to her. Closing her bedroom door behind her, she fell on her bed and buried her face in the pillow.

CHAPTER 28

"MARY JANE'S LAST DANCE" BY TOM PETTY AND THE HEARTBREAKERS

Bisbee, Arizona
October 1996

Cecilia remained seated in the St. Elmo Bar long after Mary-Ann left and Billy the bartender called the last round. Carlos Atiras, a.k.a. Eddie Vee, grabbed his leather jacket and dropped the blue guitar inside the red-velvet-lined case when Cecilia approached.

"Lady, I told you I'm not interested."

"Hear me out." Her heart beat wildly in her chest. "Can we go somewhere and talk?"

"The only place I'm going is outta here and away from you."

His accent threw her. Eddie Vee was from Argentina, but she detected no hint of an accent other than a thick Southern drawl.

"I have something you might be interested in."

He gathered his guitar and squeezed by her. "Trust me. I'm not."

She followed him to the door, refusing to let him go without telling him about the woman at the memorial and the envelope she'd left behind.

"Please stop," she begged, blocking the entrance.

"Please get out of my way," he said, brushing past her, his red-rimmed eyes dull and empty.

"I can't," she said, skipping along beside him, a cool mist making her shiver. "Carlos Atiras. You almost fooled me, spelling her name backward." She waited until she was sure she had his attention. "I saw her."

He refused to slow down. "I have no idea what you're talking about, lady."

"I saw her," she said. "I saw Sarita."

He quickened his pace, and Cecilia tried to keep up, but he was fast. He led her on a chase up steep, narrow steps as the space between them lengthened. When she reached the top, she looked right and left, but he was gone. She called out, "Eddie! Carlos!"

But as he had managed to vanish all those years ago, he'd figured out a way to disappear again.

~

That night, Cecilia couldn't fall asleep. What if she'd scared him off? What if he skipped town again? She refused to give up. Not yet. Not when she was so close. Her mind returned to Pete. She wanted to hear his voice before he left town, so she dialed his cell phone number. But it went straight to voice mail. Had he left early, maybe already on a flight overseas?

Eventually, she fell into a shallow sleep, dreaming she was a little girl riding in her parents' Buick Estate station wagon. Gloria was at the wheel, and Cecilia sat beside her in the passenger seat. "We're an American Band" played on the radio, and Gloria, unbuckled as was the custom back then, swayed to the melody, one hand on the wheel, another dangling a cigarette out the open window. Cecilia hung out the opposite window, the wind blowing her hair, the breeze whipping her cheeks.

One minute they were driving down the Pacific Coast Highway, the sun lighting up the ocean, Gloria mouthing the words to Grand Funk Railroad, and the next, somebody had flicked a switch—everything fading to black. That's when Cecilia woke up.

Drenched in sweat, she shot upright, the dream feeling all too familiar. Disoriented, she reached for her phone beside her bed.

Don picked up on the first ring.

"CeCe, is that you?"

"Was I in a car accident?" Her words felt broken and choppy.

"What's this about?"

"With Mom?" Her voice rose. "I just had a weird dream. But it didn't feel like a dream. It felt real."

"Cecilia." Using her full name wasn't a good sign. "We should talk about this when you get home."

"Just tell me, Don."

"Not over the phone, honey. There's a lot we need to discuss. I prefer to have the conversation face-to-face."

Her patience began to wear thin. "It's a simple question, Don. Was I ever in a car accident? In the station wagon? With Mom?"

Interminable silence, then his response came out a whisper: "Yes."

"Is that why I never wanted to learn to drive? Did I get hurt?"

"I prefer we talk about this when you get home."

Cecilia hung up as this revelation sank in, but minutes later, unable to stop herself, she punched his number again. She gripped the phone so tightly her fingers turned white. "Please tell me what happened that day."

CHAPTER 29

"ALISON" BY ELVIS COSTELLO

Miami Beach and New York
1979–1982

Packed and heartbroken, Sara exited her room with swollen eyes and a throbbing headache. She watched her mother clear out the fridge, dumping condiments and milk and cheese into the garbage can. The tears pressed against her eyelids when she imagined never seeing Eddie again, but she couldn't let her mother know she'd won. Somehow it was her fault. Somehow, she'd made good on that deathbed promise to *Saba*, forbidding outsiders into their lives, ensuring Sara only dated Jewish boys.

When her father entered the room, Sara was so angry, she gave in to the urge to punish them. "I don't love Abel. And I'll never love him the way you want me to, so you can stop throwing us together."

"Did you two have a fight?" Moshe asked.

"He's my friend," Sara said. "That's all. Tell Sheila Altman to back off."

"I'm sure you'll work things out," her mother said. "I have faith in you two."

"And I'm never going back to Glenwood after Columbia. You can't cage me there forever."

"Then we won't send you to Columbia," her mother said matter-of-factly.

And with what little strength she had left, Sara carried her suitcase toward the door, each step compounding her grief. "I'll be downstairs."

~

On the flight home, Sara kept to herself, and she didn't even try to read a book. Every so often, she snuck the sheet music out of the envelope and read the words, his words. Then she closed her eyes, rested her head on the seat back, and thought of Eddie holding her, kissing her lips. She had memorized every detail of their night together, how it hurt until it didn't, how she'd never feel that way again. No. Eddie wouldn't do this to her. But he had. And she would never understand.

Once home, Sara sent dozens of letters to the Atlantic and made numerous unanswered calls to Eddie's apartment. For days, she didn't leave the house, her heart irrevocably broken. It was as though Eddie had disappeared into thin air, leaving her to question if what they had was real. When she finally reached the Atlantic front desk, they told her that Eddie and his grandfather had left for good, and they had left no forwarding address.

Eddie was gone, home to Argentina, and the realization sank in. They would never live together in that home that backed up to the beach with their four children. They would never see each other again.

Stricken with grief, Sara went through the motions of life in Glenwood Estates. At least that world was comfortable and safe. There were few surprises, and she wouldn't run the risk of getting hurt. One of the many benefits of having a large extended family was that there was always a celebration, an activity to participate in, or some compelling drama that occupied her time. When her family gathered around the table for a festive meal or met on the street for a game of running bases, she daydreamed about Eddie. She imagined he'd find her and confess he'd made a mistake, tell her he was sorry, and beg for her forgiveness. There wasn't a day she didn't wake up feeling the pang of his absence or open her eyes to his memory. The books she read could no longer satisfy her, and she ran his name across her tongue to see if it still fit.

School started, and Sara immersed herself in her studies and kept to herself. Abel was worried. She could see the question in his eyes, but he didn't have to know about the life she secretly mourned. She could never deliver that blow. "I was worried you'd found someone else," he said to her over a Shabbat dinner when she forced a smile. He had grown more handsome and more determined to win her over, and in her misery, she felt herself being pulled in his direction, drawn to him like a comfortable blanket.

Their time together was always easy. His kind eyes and reassuring presence made her feel safe. Shira relaxed somewhat, watching Abel open the car door for her. "Seat belts!" she hollered. Abel always had a flower waiting for her on her seat. She'd bring it to her nose, inhaling the sweet scent. She caught herself staring at his profile while he drove, noticing the changes, and that one night they stayed up late watching *Somewhere in Time*, his hand found hers and squeezed.

And on that first trip back to Miami without Eddie, Sara closed the chapter, but unlike the novels she'd read, there was no satisfying conclusion, only an abrupt, ambiguous ending with things left unsaid, things left to smolder beneath the surface. Sara filed that part of her life away, and she chased waves and built different kinds of sandcastles. It wasn't long before she closed her eyes and the images of Eddie were grainy and dull. Until one day, he was a faraway dream.

In seemingly no time, Sara was accepted to Columbia University and bid her family goodbye.

≈

Despite being in New York City and living in the on-campus housing, Sara's relationship with Shira began to change. As Sara matured and had more time and distance to reflect, she saw how Shira was tougher on her, how the rules didn't apply to her brothers, so when it came time for vacations or holidays, Sara made excuses not to go home—an exam, a paper—and she'd walk the big, bright city, mesmerized by the crowds and culture. As she watched the commuters pass in the streets and the couples entangled at outdoor cafés, she imagined all the stories she would one day tell.

At the beginning of Sara's sophomore year at Columbia, Morah Emily's words ran through her head, reminding her that she was like the caterpillar. Only it wasn't her body that had died, taking a new shape. It was her heart. She decided she would never love someone the way she had loved Eddie Santiago. That kind of love was dangerous and not entirely real. But there was another kind of love, the kind that was growing between her and Abel. He had visited her from the University of Pennsylvania, handsome as ever. Her roommates fawned over him and his sexy, thick hair. "He looks an awful lot like John F. Kennedy Jr.," they said. She began to look forward to his weekend visits. They attended theater and enjoyed long walks in the park. There was always a story about Glenwood: who was dating whom, who had gotten into trouble. And they'd laugh, enjoying the long line of history they shared. With Abel, the conversations were pleasant, their time together safe. And over dinner and a bottle of wine, he told her he loved her, that he'd make her the happiest woman in the world. It was a promise she'd heard once before, but this time, it was different. She knew she could trust Abel.

So when Abel Altman dropped to his knees and proposed, Sara said yes, and she let go of Eddie Santiago.

Until she heard him on the radio, singing the song he had written for her.

CHAPTER 30

"ME AND BOBBY MCGEE" BY JANIS JOPLIN

Bisbee, Arizona
October 1996

Just as Don James started to explain to Cecilia what happened in the car that day, she heard a loud knock at the door, and she jumped. Mary-Ann had told her no fewer than seventeen times how safe Bisbee was. Still, she set the phone down so her father could listen in as she threw a sweatshirt on and cautiously opened the door.

She heard Don shouting, "Cecilia? Is everything okay?"

But she didn't respond, because when she opened the door, there stood Eddie Vee.

She doubled back to the phone and told a worried Don she'd call him later. "Everything's fine," she said, "but this conversation isn't over. You owe me answers." And she hung up.

~

Eddie stood in the hallway, leaning against the faded wallpaper, reeking of alcohol and cigarettes. His face was hidden beneath a dark-gray hoodie, but it was him.

"So it's not just me. You charm everyone. Who'd you say you are again?"

"Cecilia James."

"How do you know Sarita?" he asked.

Cecilia leaned against the doorjamb, careful not to scare him away. "I was in Miami. At the Orange Bowl. There's a memorial there." She held on to his gaze. "She was sitting next to me. Wait." She turned and found the envelope inside her bag, handing it to Eddie. "She dropped this."

Minutes ticked by as he just stared at the envelope.

"Why are you doing this?" he asked. "Who are you working for?"

She was too ashamed to say *Rolling Stone*.

"Leave her alone. Leave me alone. Can you do us that one favor?"

She wasn't sure she could.

"I loved someone. I loved him so much I let him go because I was afraid we'd only end up hurting each other." The picture taken during the LA riots flashed in her mind. "I never thought I could live up to the image of us. Now he's gone overseas, putting himself in danger, and I may never see him again."

"You're tugging at my heartstrings," he said dryly.

"What happened between the two of you?"

"You're a reporter. I knew it. First one to find me, so I'll give you credit for that."

She took some small pleasure in the feat and confessed she worked for *Rolling Stone*. More interesting was that Carlos Santiago hadn't warned him of her arrival.

"They've been after me for years," he said. "But you don't seem to want to hear about that day."

"I want to hear about her. About the song. That same guy . . . the one I told you about . . . he told me he loved me for the first time to your song."

"I hear that a lot. Or it's some girl who lost her virginity."

"You touched a lot of people, made them long for something. It isn't just the words, it's hard to explain."

He eyed her wearily. "You don't have to."

"You still love her."

"Saint Cecilia. Patron saint of music and musicians."

Cecilia offered a shaky smile. "Just parents with an affinity for Simon & Garfunkel."

"You hear heavenly music in your heart, like her, don't you?" he asked.

"Maybe."

He stepped away from the wall, about to leave. "Solving this riddle won't change anything. It won't make you happy."

"It might make you happy." She couldn't let him go. "And Sarita."

"I doubt Sara Friedman has thought about me since 1979."

Cecilia latched on to the name so she wouldn't forget. "What if I told you you're wrong?"

"I'd tell you this little matchmaking exercise will only disappoint you. She's married to Abel Altman. That was always the plan."

The words stumbled out. "She still loves you."

He backed away, like the words were a kick to the stomach. "I knew this was a mistake."

"Talk to me, Eddie."

He closed his eyes, hands coming over his face.

"I've gotta go."

And he slipped away as quickly as he had arrived.

∼

Shaken by Eddie's appearance, Cecilia composed herself long enough to jot down Sara's last name and then called her father back. The call went to voice mail, though, so she'd have to wait to finish the conversation. She tossed and turned in the creaking bed, her mind whirling with Eddie Vee and Pete and the dream that had her feeling as though she'd just woken up from a much deeper sleep. She'd been in an accident. With Gloria.

The next morning, motorcycles roared outside her window, nudging her from a restless sleep. She wondered if she dreamed Eddie's visit, dreamed about riding with her mother. What happened that day, and why couldn't she remember any of it? More concerning was why her father hadn't told her about it. Thoughts crowded her mind, vying for attention, but she needed to find Eddie Vee.

Cornering Mary-Ann in the pocket-sized foyer, she tried to wrestle out of her the whereabouts of Mr. Atiras, perhaps an address, but the young woman was stubborn.

"Stick around for his show next Thursday."

But Cecilia didn't have time to stick around. She had to get home for Don's birthday. The next twenty-four hours were crucial.

~

A determined Cecilia entered the St. Elmo Bar for the second night in a row. The venue wasn't as crowded as the previous night, though she recognized some familiar faces. Dixie Rose climbed onto the stage and guests scattered, settling in their seats. If Eddie was trying to maintain his distance, he wasn't doing a very good job. Cecilia spotted him at the end of the bar beneath his hoodie.

Cecilia slid onto the empty stool beside him while he pretended not to notice. This Eddie was far worse than the Eddie she'd met yesterday. With four empty beers on the bar, he brought the fifth to his lips. The smell of alcohol wafted off his body, the foul stench of sweat. She bet he hadn't been home, hadn't changed out of yesterday's clothes. The man was a grubby mess.

"You're doing a masterful job avoiding me," Cecilia said.

"Am I?" He swigged the beer. "Hey, Billy, get this one a drink, will ya?"

"I'm all right," she said.

"You might change your mind."

"Why's that?"

"Because we're going to talk."

~

Cecilia followed Eddie to an empty table in a quiet corner away from the stage. When he sat, his hood slid down, revealing unkempt, greasy hair. "You've really changed," she said.

"That was the point."

"This is a little drastic."

He stared at his hands, not at Cecilia. "After the accident, I took a shower . . . something so basic . . . I couldn't wash it off. The grime from that day stuck to me. No matter how hard I tried to scrub it away."

"It was an unfortunate accident."

"Yeah," he answered. "That's what I hear."

The waitress stopped by, and Eddie ordered another drink.

Cecilia appraised him. Though only thirty-three, he appeared older, haunted in a way that aged him.

"You shouldn't drink so much."

"A reporter and a shrink." He took another swig. "It numbs the pain, Cecilia James. Haven't you ever just not wanted to feel?"

More times than she would admit, but not to him, and there was a lot they needed to uncover. "Do you mind if we do this the right way?"

"Meaning?"

"I need to run a proper interview."

"What for?"

What she wanted to do with the interview and what Joan wanted to do with it were two different things. "I promised my boss I found the woman behind the song," she said. "Our readers have been waiting for this for years. Everyone has, but—"

"You just want to play Cupid."

"Maybe."

"Who's playing Cupid for you?" he asked.

Letting the comment slide, she pulled the recorder out of her bag. Was this a story about a man broken by a tragic mistake? A love story? The lines blurred, but she would work every angle she could. Before he could stop her, she said, "I'm going to ask a series of questions, and I want you to answer whatever you're most comfortable with. That work?"

He didn't answer, and Cecilia expected him to get up and walk out, but he stayed, holding her eyes so all she saw was his pain.

"This is Cecilia James at St. Elmo Bar in Bisbee, Arizona, joined by Eddie Vee," she said into the machine. "The date is October 25th and it's 6:00 p.m."

"Does that make a difference?" he asked, and Cecilia liked his sarcasm.

"I'm new to this. Let me have my moment."

He smiled.

"Before we start, tell me why you changed your mind. Why have you agreed to talk to me?"

"I didn't really agree. You're just kind of pushy." He swigged the beer, but then he gave her the answer she was waiting for. "You said she still loves me."

Cecilia sat with this, her mind marinating the possibility, and then she began.

CJ: How've you been, Eddie? The world's been wondering about you.

Eddie: (Laughs.) I think the world was happy to see me disappear.

CJ: What happened at the Orange Bowl was tragic. Do you want to tell us about it?

Eddie: You go right in.

CJ: You never spoke about it. No one's ever heard your side of the story. You must have something to say.

Eddie: (Muffled voices. Dixie Rose singing "Girl, You'll Be a Woman Soon.") It might be easier to talk about her. (Pause.) Just hard to think about her without thinking about that day.

CJ: It's your story, Eddie. Tell whichever version you want.

Eddie set the beer on the table and played with the chains around his neck.

Eddie: Being in Miami that day, so close to our history, I felt off. She was everywhere, and I was distracted. I decided that after the show I'd go find her, tell her I loved her. (Sighs.) The rest . . . you know.

CJ: You still loved her?

Eddie: She's hard to let go.

CJ: If you're able, tell us in your own words what happened next.

Eddie: (Pauses.) We had a sold-out crowd. It's always that way in my hometown. It was good to be back. They love when I play that song. It's theirs, not mine. They just wait for it. But the words felt different that night. And someone thought it would be a good idea to rush the stage, and like that (snaps his fingers), the stadium broke out into complete chaos. I tried to help. It was just . . . pandemonium.

Most people don't understand what it's like to be on a stage with thousands of adoring fans clamoring for you, to be center stage, the focus of everyone's attention. But having those same people witness your darkest moment and having to relive it over and over on the news for days and weeks—the blame, the accusations. It was living hell. If I thought finding Sara would've helped, I would've gone to her, but nothing could've helped. When you're singing the song you wrote for your only love and something that horrible happens, you believe it's a sign. She'd be better off without me.

CJ: That sounds painful. I'm sorry.

Eddie: Yeah. Everybody's sorry. If only sorry erased what happened. People died that day.

CJ: A terrible tragedy, Eddie, but I have to ask, you were quoted in an earlier interview that the song wasn't written for anyone in particular, but you just admitted . . . the song was for her.

Eddie: (Shakes head.)

CJ: Which one is it?

Eddie: I thought I was protecting her. Can you erase that?

CJ: So you escaped here to Bisbee, Arizona—

Eddie: And that? Can you leave that out too?

CJ: So you moved away and got a job singing covers at a bar.

Eddie: You're pretty good at this, Miss James.

She was beginning to like him more.

CJ: When are you going to stop running, Eddie?

Eddie: Waitress, another beer, please.

CJ: You don't need it, Eddie. You're doing fine.

Eddie: I don't feel fine.

CJ: Tell us about living a life in anonymity. Giving up your career.

Eddie: We caused one of the worst tragedies in musical history. No one thinks they're going to go to a concert and die. None of us intended for that to happen. I had to disappear.

CJ: Physically, you've disappeared. But someone like you, with the musical legacy you've left behind, you're never really gone.

Eddie: Poetic.

CJ: Several news outlets said by running away and refusing interviews you admitted culpability.

Eddie: News outlets. What a joke. When those same outlets needed to boost their ratings, they couldn't get enough of me. There's no loyalty. They watched me fall, applauding the entire time. See, what no one understood is how it affected us. How we watched people suffering.

How helpless we felt. How a song that our fans loved was now a reminder of so much ugliness. We'd always be *those* guys.

CJ: Izak. Bruno. Bob. Do you keep in touch with any of them?

Eddie: I broke ties with that life.

CJ: And her. Tell us about her. Tell us why she's been a secret for so long.

Eddie: (Long pause.)

CJ: Eddie?

Eddie: Give me a minute. (Shifts in his seat, drinks his beer.) We were eleven. We met on Miami Beach . . . literally on the beach. Girl ran smack into me. She says I ran into her. I didn't speak a lick of English back then. We could barely communicate, but she intrigued me. Fiery and temperamental. We call women like that *mujer luchadora*. I was living with *Abuelo*. My parents died years before in Argentina. Sara and her very large family had a condo in the building where *Abuelo* worked. They came for holidays. The summer.

Sara's family's Jewish. I'm not. Her mother was strict. Boys like me were off-limits. She worried. It was all about keeping her daughter safe. Outsiders weren't welcome. But we became friends, meeting at secret spots on the beach, communicating as best as we could. Funny. We didn't really need any language to get to know each other. And then music connected us, the universal language.

Every year, we got closer and closer. By the time we were teenagers, we were more than friends.

CJ: Was that why you never named the person the song was about? Because her family objected?

Eddie: Her parents would have disowned her. I loved her too much.

CJ: That's quite a romantic gesture. The two of you holding on to that larger-than-life secret.

Eddie: I guess you can say that. We didn't have to share it with anyone. It was ours alone. She pushed me to become a musician. She gave me her brother's guitar . . . We painted it bright blue so he wouldn't recognize it. The first time I strummed the chords, it felt like it had always belonged to me.

CJ: How did you come to write "What You Do to Me"?

Eddie: We were sixteen. She was planning to go to Columbia. University. Hadn't even applied, but Sara would make it happen. I worried about leaving *Abuelo*, but Sara . . . she can be headstrong. My music teacher thought New York was a good idea for my career.

CJ: Phil Feinstein?

Eddie: You got to him?

CJ: He's proud of you.

Eddie: Man, he taught me everything. I wish I could properly thank him.

CJ: You already did. He watched your star rise. That gave him tremendous pride. And you could tell he really appreciated the acknowledgment in your album notes.

Eddie: (Pause.) Thank you. (Pause.) I wasn't sure anyone ever read those things.

CJ: And the song?

Eddie: (Pause). Music's all the words we're afraid to say out loud. So we create lyrics. And the tune carries it where it needs to go. I must've written a thousand songs for Sara. She made it easy. She was the best song. The only song.

CJ: Tell us about "What You Do To Me."

Eddie: I knew I had to win her over . . . Sara . . . I knew it had to be a song about a long-distance relationship. It had to be authentic, from my heart. A simple and straightforward melody. Uncomplicated. She needed patience and trust—assurances that we could work. And that I was willing to do whatever I could to give her the life she deserved.

CJ: What happened?

Eddie: (Pause.) There's just some forces you can't fight. You can't win. She went to Columbia. I went to LA. We broke up. It was for the best.

CJ: Sounds abrupt.

Eddie: (Eyes fall to the floor.) It would have never worked. You know that. I would have never fit in her world.

Cecilia disagreed. Theirs was the kind of relationship that would have endured.

CJ: You said you planned to find her after the show. What made you decide to do that?

Eddie: I don't know. Age. Wisdom. I'm sure you can come up with some cheesy cliché. I missed her. I made a mistake letting her go.

CJ: The good old *what if?*

Eddie: Maybe. But what does it matter? We all know how it ended.

CJ: And when you hear the song on the radio?

Eddie: Most stations stopped playing it right after the accident, but you know how it is. People forget. When I hear it now, it's not mine anymore.

CJ: And in all this time, you've never crossed paths? Never tried to find her again? Or vice versa?

Eddie: Her parents wanted her to marry Abel. I think it was a pact made at birth. I'm sure she's running around Long Island with a bunch of *niños*, writing her stories, nose in a book. It's better this way. Her family is very close. I didn't want to make things difficult for her. Everything happened as it should.

The woman Cecilia met wasn't happy. Neither was he.

CJ: You never saw her again? In Miami?

Eddie: We moved. (Pauses.) Like I said, it would've never worked. Sara needed to be with her family. We weren't right for each other.

CJ: And your grandfather?

Eddie: *Abuelo* and I keep in touch. I don't see him as often as I'd like. He's always worried about the press following him. All of it . . . it's just very sad.

Cecilia turned the recorder off, and the two sat quietly as Eddie finished another beer.

"You've gotta get your shit together, Eddie."

"I drink too much. I smoke too much. What does it matter? I've already lost everything."

He dropped his head down, and Cecilia felt an overwhelming urge to touch him, to offer some comfort.

"It wasn't your fault. You didn't cause the accident."

"Try telling that to the people who lost loved ones. The ones permanently scarred or damaged. It's me they see up there on that stage."

Cecilia had no quick comeback, and they listened as Dixie Rose sang Tracy Chapman's song about reasons.

"You should find her," she said. "I'll help you."

Eddie dug inside his back pocket. He tried to hide it, but she spotted it at once.

"Don't take that," she said as he popped a yellow pill in his mouth. Cecilia had seen enough drugs in her business to recognize a Valium.

"Give me one good reason why I shouldn't." Then he laughed at his joke and swallowed the pill down.

"Because you're going to wind up dead," she said.

"That's the thing, Cecilia James. I already am."

CHAPTER 31

"BETH" BY KISS

New York
1984–1985

The first time Sara heard "What You Do to Me" on the radio, she was with two classmates at Tom's restaurant. It was her junior year at Columbia, and she was working toward a degree in English language and literature. She and Abel were set to marry upon graduation, and they saw each other throughout the school year when he would ride the train into the city from Philadelphia. They had just said goodbye when the song made its appearance.

Z100 was playing on the radio, the on-air DJs discussing the singer who wrote the hit song—and Sara was struggling to find the right word for a paper she had been writing. Her thoughts had drifted to their cheerful voices when she heard the name Eddie Vee. The name meant nothing to her. But then the first notes of the song began, and Sara, who had just brought her coffee to her lips, felt the cup slip from her hand, making a loud clanking sound as it hit the table. The coffee seeped through her paper, staining it a dark-caramel color, and Violet and Arden jumped up as the cup rolled in their direction, soiling everything in its path. Sara sat motionless.

"Sara!" Violet shouted.

But she couldn't move. She was rooted to her seat, stuck on Eddie's voice. Eddie Santiago. Eddie Vee. It didn't matter. It was Eddie. Eddie was on the radio. And the DJs said he was a star.

The girls gathered napkins and blotted the stain. "He has this effect on people," Arden said.

Eddie sang in her ear. *Don't cry,* she told herself, twisting the modest diamond on her finger. *Don't think. Just breathe.*

"What's wrong with you, Sara?" Violet asked.

She held back. "Sorry. Shaky hands." If she went with the truth, they would never believe her.

"Can you imagine being the person he wrote this for?" Arden said dreamily.

Sara found her voice. "Who is he?"

They stared at her, eyebrows raised. "You're kidding, right?" Violet said.

Since Eddie, Sara had given up a lot of things, actually surrendered. One of them was music.

"Don't tell me you don't know who Eddie Vee is," Arden said.

She didn't know him at all.

"He's only, like, the most famous singer. And superhot. Didn't you see him in this month's *Cosmopolitan*?"

She hadn't.

"I heard he's dating that Fabiana girl," Violet said. "She was Italy's Miss Teen when she was thirteen."

"How do you know all this?" Arden asked with a laugh. "Someone's a little obsessed."

Violet and Arden blathered about Eddie as though they were his personal friends, while his voice filled the small café. Sara focused on every word, every note, remembering that night they had made love.

Eddie's voice was so close, like he was in the chair beside her, sing-ing in her ear, his breath against her cheek. When the song ended, she couldn't concentrate on schoolwork. Instead, she wrestled with the painful feelings she thought she'd put to rest. She was thrilled for Eddie's success, but she also felt deeply betrayed.

I should reach out to him. The thought slipped through her head, fleeting and fast.

No. She couldn't. It had been years. He had been adamant when he broke things off. He said they could never be together. That he had never loved her. And how would she even find him? He was a famous musician, inaccessible, and he had girls falling all over him. He could have anyone he chose. He wouldn't want her. He would have forgotten her by now.

Abruptly standing up from the table, Sara gathered her books and papers and stuffed them in her backpack. "I have to go," she said, hid-ing her eyes as she made her way out of the crowded café toward her drugstore. Ducking in, she beelined for the magazine rack. She'd always skipped past these shelves, but there he was. Eddie. On every cover. *Teen Beat. Tiger Beat. People.*

She gathered copies, plus the *Rolling Stone* with his name across the front, and carried the stack to the register, where Mrs. Schneiderman knew her by name.

"Sara!" she said in her thick accent. "What is this you are reading?"

She and Mrs. Schneiderman often chatted about the latest literary bestsellers. They both had just devoured Marguerite Duras's *The Lover.*

Sara smiled nervously. "Book research," she said, referring to the novel that she had told no one about other than Mrs. Schneiderman. The novel that had many words but no story. A long, shameful love letter to her past.

"I am intrigued," Mrs. Schneiderman said. "I will need to read this book of yours."

"One day," Sara said.

Mrs. Schneiderman dropped the magazines into a brown paper bag and swung a fist in the air. "Strong female protagonists, Sara."

"I know," she said, hurrying Mrs. Schneiderman along so she could take Eddie home.

It was only five short blocks to her building, and Sara moved quickly, flinging herself through the glass door and climbing the steps to the roof, where she could be alone with him.

There were dozens of articles and pictures: Eddie strumming a guitar in front of a packed Louisiana crowd. Eddie with his arm linked through Fabiana's, strolling through LAX. Eddie dressed in black leather pants that showed off his body and made Sara gasp.

Reading on, Sara learned that Eddie had emerged on the music scene with his first single, "Blame It on the Sunshine." In that time, the band, High Tide, had blown up because of their talent and boyishly handsome good looks. Sara had never heard the song, and she didn't recognize the trio by his side. But it didn't matter because she was busy studying Eddie's face for a glimpse of the boy she used to know. His skin was a golden brown, and his blue eyes smoldered, finding hers and holding on. Eddie was still the most beautiful boy she'd ever seen.

This new song, according to one article, promised to elevate the band to another level. There was speculation of Grammy nominations, a European tour in addition to the American tour. Sara sat back in the rocker, staring out at the Manhattan skyline and the Twin Towers off in the distance. Honking from the street below reached her ears, but all she could hear was Eddie singing. Eddie Santiago.

Sara devoured the articles, soaking Eddie in, one word at a time. Eddie with Chelsea Noble at a club in Hollywood. Eddie at home with his Siberian husky, Pancho. She read the words aloud: "The infectious laugh. The generous smile. Eddie Vee is talented and timeless, a star in the making." *Teen Beat* featured a centerfold pullout of Eddie shirtless, the shot capturing his tanned, muscular body from the waist up. He was so close. Her fingers brushed his face and chest. She held the picture up and peered into his eyes. *Can you see me?*

"Oh, Eddie."

She folded the pages, reaching for the *Rolling Stone* magazine, and flipped to the article with his name. The piece was written by a woman named Joan Kadushin, and Sara wondered if Joan was pretty. If he flirted with her too.

Chasing the thought out of her head, she began to read:

> Unless you've been living under a rock, you've heard the name Eddie Vee flitting through music's golden circles, first with "Blame It on the Sunshine" and "Closing In" and now the poetic-sounding "What You Do to Me." The Argentine has taken the charts by storm. His soulful acoustics and blend of rich tempo and range have made him an industry favorite, with a staggering number of potential Grammy nominations.
>
> We caught up with Eddie and the band after their recent Palladium gig, the one that had the industry abuzz.
>
> **Joan:** Eddie, you've become quite the household name rather quickly. And yet, you're only twenty-one years old. How does it feel to be center stage?
>
> **Eddie:** You talk very fast! (Laughter.) My English, it's better than it was, but forgive me if . . . It's great! I do what I love. I am happy for the people who wish to hear me sing.

Joan: Your bio says you hail from Argentina. Tell us a little about that.

Eddie: I come to the US when I am eight. My parents . . . they were in a terrible accident. I come to live with *mi abuelo*. He raised me.

Joan: You always wanted to be a musician?

Eddie: I always wanted to sing. I had no idea it would become . . . this. A friend gave me a guitar. You've seen it. It's bright blue. *Azul.* Since that day, I am not alive without music.

Joan: The world wants to know about "What You Do to Me." Someone did something to you . . . maybe still does something to you. Do you want to tell us about her?

Eddie: (Silence. Pause.)

Joan: Did you write the song for someone specific?

Eddie: (Laughs.) She is not real. She is . . . what do you call . . . the imagination? None of us have *una novia*, one girlfriend. In life, I think we have many loves. We are enjoying, how do you say it, being young?

Joan: So, there's no woman out there listening to that song, knowing it's about her?

Eddie: No. *Nada.* I wish there was.

Sara read on, aware of a few things: she had been living under a rock, Eddie Santiago never moved back to Argentina, and he quite possibly never loved her at all.

From that day forward, Sara paid close attention. She didn't have to seek him out; Eddie was everywhere. He was on Casey Kasem's *American Top 40*; he was in Sam Goody, a full-length display of Eddie and the band, the blue guitar—her brother's guitar—in his hands. The song played everywhere she went—in her favorite coffee shop, in Central Park on a Sunday afternoon, booming from the portable radios everyone seemed to be carrying around. Sara bought the cassette tape, playing it over and over so many times that it got tangled in the cassette player's wheels, forcing her to purchase a second copy. She was ashamed of how fixated she'd become. She thought she had let this part of her life go.

Abel noticed the shift in Sara's temperament. Ordinarily agreeable, she'd become withdrawn. When he asked, she said it was nothing, blaming it on classes and a few all-nighters. But they were different all-nighters from the ones he might have imagined. Eddie infiltrated her dreams, Eddie kept her awake at all hours, Eddie sang in her ear the song he had written for her.

She'd overheard dozens of conversations of women and teenagers who wondered aloud about the girl—who she was, where she might live. The public knew Eddie didn't have a steady girlfriend. He was linked to many women, their pictures appearing in the gossip rags, always half-naked, whether on a beach in Mexico or at a club in Manhattan. Sara would study their posture, the way he'd gaze into their eyes. He looked happy, but Sara thought he'd been happy before. And she had been wrong.

After a few soul-crushing months of obsessive daydreaming, Sara had no choice but to step outside the fantasy and back into her own life. Her wedding was set for after graduation, and Eddie would sail across the sky with his adoring fans, and she'd watch his star shine from a distance. She was happy with Abel. She loved him and the ease of their life. They laughed and their lovemaking was tender and satisfying. Shira was happy. They had a big house in Glenwood Estates waiting for them, close to her brothers, and she would write her stories there. It was all planned out.

And when she graduated from Columbia summa cum laude, she married Abel Altman.

And if she thought it was difficult being in a world with Eddie's voice singing in her ear, it wasn't any easier being married to Abel.

CHAPTER 32

"ROSANNA" BY TOTO

Los Angeles
October 1996

Cecilia spent the plane ride home thinking about Eddie Vee. The accident had left a dark stain on his once bright life, the ripple effect spanning wide. Though his voice thrived, the rest of him was lifeless. And because Cecilia had blown her own relationship, she was trying to fix theirs—Eddie and Sara's. Jotting down notes from the interview, Cecilia listened to his words through the headphones, piecing together what happened to these two lovers, and a question gnawed at her. Why would Eddie write such a profound song about someone he loved so much, only to give up without a fight? Something had to have transpired. Something big. Because what else could have pulled these two lovers apart?

～

Back home, before she had even unpacked her bags, Phoebe, Hazel, and Mathilda the cat appeared in her room.

"You're here!" Phoebe shouted.

The girls flung themselves at her, while Mathilda curled her furred body around Cecilia's legs. Cecilia was struck by how happy she was to see them. The wall she'd erected to keep them out had crumbled.

Tonight was the surprise party, and Don was at work. He thought he and Tori had plans to meet friends for dinner while Cecilia babysat the girls. Cecilia would have to put on her best smile and save her questions about the accident for later.

The girls, wearing matching party dresses, hopped on the bed and peppered Cecilia with questions. They hadn't seen her in a few days, and they were curious.

"Did you win him back?" Hazel asked. "The prize?"

Cecilia liked that she remembered, and she wished she had better news to share. "Pete and I are done," she said, and the words felt miserable coming off her tongue. "He's moved far away."

"I'm sorry, CeCe. You must have done something really bad."

"I'm sorry too, Hazel Bee. Now help me pick out something to wear tonight. And then we can do our makeup together."

"Mommy doesn't let us wear makeup," Phoebe said.

"It's a special occasion," Cecilia said. "We'll do just a little."

The girls chose a dress for Cecilia that most resembled the ones they were wearing. White and gold, and not Cecilia's first choice, but she played along. She applied a thin dusting of blush on their cheeks and a muted shadow on their eyes, paying special attention to their delicate features. She saw so much of herself in them. And a flash shot through her head. Of Gloria. It moved so quickly she could barely catch it: Gloria at the bathroom sink, her head lowered, body swaying to music that wasn't playing. Cecilia gently rubbing her mother's back until Don appeared, whisking Gloria off her feet and whirling her in the air. Something about it wasn't right.

"I like this color," Phoebe said, holding up the brightest red lipstick in Cecilia's drawer.

"How about something a little more subtle?"

"What does that mean?"

"Less upsetting to your mother."

They agreed on a soft, sheer pink, and the girls resembled little angels. Their smiles sent the confusing images of Gloria away, and Cecilia began to unwind.

A knock at the bedroom door turned all their heads.

"Mommy got you something for the party," Hazel said. "Wanna see?"

Tori entered the room carrying a small box with a white satin bow. She didn't greet Cecilia but simply offered the gift.

"It's not my birthday."

"I know," Tori said, looking more beautiful than Cecilia cared to admit in a tailored cream jacket with black leather pants and a black turtleneck. The look said classic and sophisticated.

"I've been waiting to give you this, Cecilia. But it seems there's never a right time—"

"Open it! Open it!" the girls squealed, clapping their hands together.

"Girls," Tori said, "do you mind giving us a minute?"

Pouting, the girls turned to leave the room.

A song about living in a world of fools swept down the hallway.

"My mother loved this song," Cecilia casually mentioned. "She loved the Bee Gees."

Tori's eyes lowered. "I'm sorry," she said. "I'll turn it off."

This made Cecilia feel like a colossal bitch. "It's fine."

Her stepmother gestured at the gift, a hopefulness in her eyes. "Open it."

Cecilia tugged on the bow, unable to guess what was inside, and terribly uncomfortable with the attention of her enemy. Only, Tori didn't feel like an enemy. She hadn't been an enemy since Cecilia had arrived. In fact, she'd been nothing but nice. But it still made Cecilia sick inside that her mother wasn't here. She felt as if she were cheating on her with the woman who had betrayed them.

Inside the box was a smaller box. Velvet. And Cecilia opened it to find a pair of earrings. And they weren't just any earrings. They were gold hoops, her mother's favorite. She knew this because they had the tiny letters *C* and *D* engraved on them, for Cecilia and Don. They were the hoops that had defined Cecilia's childhood—wisps of Gloria's blond hair swirling around the shiny gold. Her mother wore them every single day. She slept in them, but sometime before her death she lost them, leaving her devastated. On seeing the earrings for the first time in years, Cecilia's eyes welled up, but she refused to let Tori see her cry. And she held the earrings in her hand, running her fingers over the initials until the sadness turned to something else, something rooted far inside.

"Why do you have these?" Her eyes narrowed. "Did you . . . did you take these from my mother?" Then a sickening thought occurred to her. "Did he *give* these to you?"

Tori stepped back as Cecilia's words crashed into her. Their eyes locked and Cecilia thought she saw a flash of sympathy, pity.

"This isn't funny, Tori. These earrings . . . my mother was a mess over them. We all were. Don and I looked everywhere for them. Now they suddenly appear?"

Tori's voice came out a whisper. "I know the earrings were missing. And I had nothing to do with that. Neither did your father."

"Why should I believe you?"

"It's the truth." Her voice picked up, calm and deferential. "The important thing is that we found them . . . I found them . . . and I know how much your mother means to you, and I wanted you to have them."

"You wanted me to have them? You think you're doing me some favor by giving me what's mine?"

Tori flinched, shrinking into herself. Then she abruptly straightened her jacket with both hands, wiping away the imaginary creases.

"We should go," she said. "Take the earrings or not. They're yours. Someday you'll understand."

~

Cecilia entered Il Cielo on edge. For the girls' sake, she smiled. Don's favorite music played, "Lay Lady Lay" and "Have I Told You Lately," but Cecilia remained fixated on the earrings. She hadn't yet put them on; instead she'd shoved them in her leather clutch, which she now gripped tightly.

Cecilia helped herself to a glass of merlot at the bar and scanned the room. She recognized hardly any of the guests, which amplified her edginess. Don and Gloria had had tons of friends. Beautiful couples flocked to their house for loud parties with dinner and dancing. Sometimes April would sleep over, and she and Cecilia would sneak out of her bedroom and watch the grown-ups making out, drinking fancy colored drinks, and swimming naked in the pool. And sometimes, Cecilia would fall asleep in their bed, waking up to her parents bookending her, snoring, the smells of alcohol and cigarettes and perfume drifting off their skin.

Tonight, those fun friends were nowhere to be found. In their place was a cast of stuffy, uptight couples with names like George and Phyllis and Theodore and Clementine. They were sophisticated people, conservatively dressed, holding proper drinks, and carrying on proper conversations. Cecilia was perplexed.

At precisely eight, Don strolled through the door, astonished as the crowd shouted a chorus of "Surprise." When he spotted Cecilia beside Tori and the girls, his smile widened, and she thought he was going to sweep Phoebe and Hazel and Tori into a hug, but he cast his arms wide to include her, pulling them all close. Cecilia smelled his fresh-scented aftershave and felt the tickle of his stubble. And she momentarily let herself fit inside this unfamiliar world, Phoebe's strawberry shampoo mixing with Tori's sandalwood perfume, and Hazel's giggle shooting through the air.

As soon as the party was underway, guests noshed on bacon-wrapped dates and spinach phyllo rolls, danced to seventies throwbacks, and made amusing toasts. Cecilia filled and refilled her wine, numbing herself. When the waiters rolled out Don's cake, Cecilia, Tori, and the girls stood by his side. The cake was a vinyl record doused in sprinkles that read, "You're not getting older, you're getting better." As the candles were lit one by one, Cecilia began to sweat, and it wasn't from the flames warming her face.

Approaching the bar, she wondered if Gloria could see the change in her. Was Gloria watching from somewhere above and angry? She opened her bag and stared at the earrings. The bartender poured her another drink, and at some point, her father appeared, cautioning her to slow down.

Cecilia chuckled.

His eyes held on to hers a second too long. "C, I'm serious."

Cecilia turned away from him and his disapproving look. Drunk and defiant, she tilted her head back and swigged the remainder.

"Cecilia, please don't," he said. "You're making a mistake."

Every long-hidden emotion brewing beneath the surface bubbled over.

"No, Don," she said, banging the glass down so hard it shattered on the marble bar, drawing a handful of eyes. With a bloodied finger, she pointed at him. "You made the mistake. And so did Tori. Thinking she could take what wasn't hers."

Don grabbed her by the arm and led her through the crowd of curious guests until they were outside, cars shooting past them on Burton Way.

"Get away from me," she said, slurring her words. "How could you give Tori Mom's earrings? She loved those earrings. They belonged to the three of us!"

"Cecilia, this isn't the time or the place."

"Don't tell me about time and place when you failed at both."

"I've tried, but you haven't given me a chance to explain."

"What? How you abandoned us? Abandoned her?" A thin line of blood ran down her wrist. "All you've ever done is let me down . . . and you let that woman, that bitch, ruin our family . . ." She stopped to catch her breath. "How do you sleep at night, knowing you killed my mother? You're a monster."

His steely glare startled Cecilia into temporary sobriety, and he backed away, outrage painting his face. "I'd never hurt your mother, Cecilia. I'd never hurt you. Sober up and get your shit together. You're behaving like a child. You want to know the truth? About the accident? About your mother and Aunt Denise? Because I'm not sure you're ready."

Cecilia gazed at the city lights, feeling nauseous.

"I've never wanted to tell you any of this. I've never wanted to tarnish the image you've had of your mother all these years, but you've given me no choice." He waited before continuing. "Cecilia, your mother, she was such a bright light . . . I loved her so much. You loved her so much. Your memories of her are so innocent and so pure. But there was so much about her you didn't know."

"What the A fuck are you getting at, Don? Everything was fine in our lives until you decided to leave her for that child. We were happy." Her voice cracked. "You went and ruined everything."

"Your mother was troubled."

Cecilia felt dizzy, and the ground rolled beneath her. "I knew it. I knew you'd do this. I knew you'd turn it around and blame it on her. That you'd find some way to ruin her in death as you did in life." She crossed her arms close to her chest, unconcerned with the blood staining her silky dress. "You did this. You ruined everything."

The nausea climbed up her throat, and she was powerless to stop it. She hated him for disparaging her mother like this, for ruining her memory, for turning things around to assuage his own guilt. He talked around her, trying to convince her of something that made little sense, but she couldn't make out the words. Or she refused to. And when she couldn't hold it back any longer, she vomited all over her father's shirt.

CHAPTER 33

"ELEANOR RIGBY" BY THE BEATLES

Los Angeles
October 1996

Tori stepped out of the restaurant just in time to witness Cecilia cover her father's shirt in vomit. Springing into action, she slipped an arm around her and motioned to Don. "I'll get her home."

Cecilia flung her away. "I'm not going anywhere with you." She wiped her mouth with the back of her hand, while Tori went back inside, returning with a stack of "You're Better, Not Older" napkins. Patting Don's shirt down, Tori repeated, "I'll take her home and pick up a clean shirt."

"I told you I'm not going anywhere with you."

This time, Tori's patience hit its limit. "I don't care if I have to throw you over my shoulder, Cecilia. You're getting in that car."

Cecilia glanced at her father. "I told you she's a bitch."

Hazel and Phoebe pushed through the door.

"Girls, back inside," Tori said. Then she caught Cecilia's eyes. "I won't have your sisters subjected to this. Let's go."

Cecilia gave in and slumped inside Tori's Volvo. They drove in silence, except for Cecilia's occasional belches as she rested her spinning head against the window. When they reached the house, Cecilia ran through the front door, barely making it to the guest bathroom and the porcelain bowl.

Tori joined her, kneeling on the floor and holding Cecilia's hair back. "Let it out. You'll feel much better."

Cecilia was light-headed and nauseous. Her head hurt, and she wanted to cry. She also wanted to tell Tori to leave her alone, but her stepmother's comforting hand across her back actually felt nice.

"What's going on with you?" Tori asked.

Cecilia closed her eyes, unable to speak.

"Your dad worries about you," she said, handing Cecilia a fresh towel. "He has good reason."

"I'm not an alcoholic. Shows how little you know about addiction."

Cecilia couldn't will herself to get up, so Tori took a seat beside her, making no effort to leave.

"Do you have any idea what I do for a living, Cecilia?"

If she weren't so sick, she might have come up with a snarky response.

"I work at a wellness center," Tori said. "We specialize in all types of issues, mental health, alcohol and drug addiction. But you wouldn't know that because you've already made your assumptions about me, pegged me as the enemy." She paused. "Let me guess. 'My stepmother's a brainless brat who spends her days on a treadmill or shopping, followed by long lunches at the club.' Am I close?"

Cecilia wouldn't give her the satisfaction of saying yes.

"I was in school getting my master's to be a counselor while managing Tower Records. That's how I paid for most of my schooling. That and my student loans. But you didn't know any of this."

Cecilia shrugged, her throat raw and achy. "Tower Records. Be still my heart."

Tori shook her head. "That's not where I met your father." She inhaled and ran a hand through her brown waves. "I met your father at the clinic. I was volunteering. Your mother was a patient."

"You're crazy, Tori. And a liar."

"I wish I was. I wish it was all a lie."

Cecilia mustered the strength to get off the floor and pushed past Tori. She headed toward her bedroom, though Tori was close behind, the click-clack of her heels coming closer. "Cecilia, he's been trying to talk to you . . . to tell you . . ."

"You think I wouldn't have known if my mother . . . if she had to go to some clinic? I lived with her. I knew everything about her."

"The accident, Cecilia."

That got her attention. "What about it?"

"You ended up in the ICU for three days. She almost—"

"Don't say it," Cecilia said, putting up her hand. She couldn't breathe. Frightening images shot through her head. It couldn't be real. It couldn't be true. "I would know. I knew her best. She was the happiest woman . . . she was always smiling . . . singing . . . laughing. Go back to the party, Tori."

"I'm worried about you, Cecilia." There was no denying the kindness in her blue eyes. "You can hate me all you want, but I'm not the enemy."

Cecilia straightened so she could meet Tori's eyes. "My mother's not the enemy either. Please. Just go." She shooed Tori away, making sure to lock the door behind her. Then she crashed on the bed and sobbed.

Memories flooded back, old, familiar ones. But they felt different. As she pored over the grainy film running through her head, her senses heightened. The distinct scent that had permeated the house was her mother's perfume, but it could have been another strong, golden liquid. And Gloria dancing . . . her slow-motion swaying . . . no. It couldn't be. She shook the images away, jumped off the bed, and made her way to the kitchen. She had a blaring headache and desperately needed water. Waiting for her on the counter was a note from Tori.

Take two of these, drink this, and nibble on these. You'll feel a lot better.

Beside the note sat a can of ginger ale, a bottle of ibuprofen, and a small bag of pretzels.

Glinda, she thought. *The Good Witch.*

Following Tori's directions, she poured the ginger ale over a cup of ice, swallowed the pills, and shoved the pretzels in her mouth. She felt famished and angry and confused, and all she could do was collapse on the couch.

～

Hours later, she woke to the sound of the front door swinging open and the girls chattering. Somewhat sober, she saw the events of the night unspool before her eyes. Throwing up on her father, her awful behavior, the accusations Tori had made about her mother. A tall figure entered the living room and Cecilia sat up, curling herself farther inside a blanket.

"How are you feeling?" Don asked, taking the seat beside her.

Remorse spread through her body. Despite the spectacle she'd caused, he still managed to care.

"Is it true?" she asked. "About Mom? And the accident?"

He leaned back on the cushions, crossing his arms behind his head. "I've been trying to tell you."

Her eyes brimmed with tears. "How's that even possible? What happened to me? Why don't I remember?"

"You had a concussion. They kept you in the ICU in an induced coma to keep the swelling down. When you woke up, you didn't remember any of it. You lost a chunk of days."

"So you thought it best not to tell me."

"We were so young. You were so young."

"How old was I?"

His arms fell to his sides when he said, "Four."

Cecilia sat with this. Her head felt heavy, and the hurt had nothing to do with alcohol.

"She had a problem? A real problem?"

He nodded.

"I would've known. I would've sensed something."

"You were a child, Cecilia. To you, she was light and laughter. Every day was a holiday. But the truth is, your mother drank too much, and I tried for years to slow her down. She saved her worst parts for when we were alone. She kept that from you, and I sure as hell kept it from you too."

Cecilia wrestled with this disturbing turn of events. Everything she'd once believed was a lie. He was rewriting the past, and she couldn't accept that her mother climbing into the window display at Macy's and posing with the mannequin or sharing ice cream for breakfast was anything more than Gloria's fun-filled, daring personality.

Her head throbbed, her brain overloaded with information, and she had to be up for work in a few hours. She rose from the couch. "You left me with her." This realization tugged at an already open wound. "You didn't care if I got in the car with her again." And just as she was about to leave the room, she turned. "What kind of person does that?"

∿

The following morning, Cecilia left for work while the house slept. She had already decided she had to move out. Though she didn't like having to leave Phoebe and Hazel, she couldn't stay there any longer. She'd made her decision.

She punched in April's number on her phone. "Of course you can stay. Monster-in-law flew off on her broom this morning. What happened?"

"Gloria had a drinking problem. Did you know that?"

April was silent, which could have meant anything. Cecilia told her she'd fill her in, basking in the relief of getting out of Don's house.

Hungover as she was, the glaring office lights made her wince. The bustle that had once invigorated her made her headache worse. If she could live out her childhood in make-believe, if she had the ability to block out days of her life, then surely she could shut out the noise and concentrate on finding Sara Friedman Altman. Sipping several cups of coffee, she used the early morning hours to research and track leads. When Joan approached, she didn't look pleased.

"Someone had a rough night. What's the latest on the Eddie Vee story?"

"I'm making progress."

"And Sara?"

She liked how they were on a first-name basis with the woman.

As if on cue, Jay-Z waltzed through the office, followed by a posse from his Roc-A-Fella Records label. The interns halted their game of ping-pong, and one of them queued up "Can't Knock the Hustle." Music blared and Jay-Z shot his wide-toothed grin, kissing Joan on both cheeks and shaking Cecilia's stiff hand as he passed her desk. Staffers pranced around to the musician's rich voice. A whiff of marijuana filled the air, and Cecilia took in the scene—the kind that made her feel vibrant and alive, lucky to have this job, except today she didn't feel a thing.

"You didn't answer me." Joan turned her attention back to Cecilia.

Cecilia had already forgotten the question.

"Sara?" Joan repeated.

"Right." Cecilia reached for a pad of paper on her desk and flipped pages. There were seven Sara Altmans with matching criteria from the Tri-State area to Florida. Cecilia had already dead-ended with the first three, awaited return calls from the next three, and was about to call the last. This Sara Altman resided on Pine Tree Drive in Miami Beach.

A minor fib wouldn't hurt anybody. "I have a call with her in an hour."

"Good, because there's something you should know." Joan cocked her eye, her green blouse emphasizing her dewy complexion. "I heard from a pretty reliable source that we're about to get scooped by *TMI*."

"*TMI?*" *TMI* was a competitor . . . or attempting to be.

"Someone over there's been tipped off to your investigation," she said, "because they're claiming they've found the inspiration for the song."

"That's impossible." Cecilia sucked in a nervous breath, wishing she had another coffee. "They're lying."

"Don't be so sure. You need to move on this. We can't risk being one-upped."

"It's bullshit, Joan. Eddie hasn't talked to anyone. Neither has Sara."

Joan eyed Cecilia skeptically. "Can you verify that?"

"*TMI's* bluffing." She said this with all the conviction she could muster.

Joan tapped her high-heeled pump on the floor. "I wouldn't wait an hour, Cecilia. Get Sara on the phone now."

Cecilia grabbed the receiver of her desk phone and dialed the last number on her list. She wasn't in the business of home-wrecking, but she had to know the story behind Sara and Eddie and what broke these two apart. Joan had disappeared when a woman answered on the third ring. There was a casualness in her greeting, as though she couldn't be bothered, a nonchalance that should have put Cecilia at ease but had the opposite effect.

"Sara Altman?"

"Who's calling?"

"My name's Cecilia James—"

"Can you please take us off your list?"

Before Sara could hang up, Cecilia blurted out, "I'm calling about Eddie. Eddie Vee."

"Eddie who?"

"Eddie Vee."

"I don't know any Eddie Vee," she said.

"Maybe you know him as Eddie Santiago."

Silence. "You have the wrong number."

"I think we met." Cecilia spoke urgently. "At the Orange Bowl. You were with your dog. The High Tide memorial. I was going on about making it to the cruise ship on time, how my boyfriend was going to be pissed." She hadn't hung up, so Cecilia kept talking. "It was the anniversary. You were upset. I offered you a tissue, and I never did make it. My boyfriend dumped me."

"I think you have me confused with someone else, Miss James. I'm hanging up now."

Cecilia's voice rose. "Sara, wait . . . please. You dropped something that day. An envelope. I picked it up. I have it."

Sara said nothing.

"It's yours, right? It was on the ground when you got up to leave."

"I don't know what you're talking about, and I really need to go."

Cecilia wasn't giving up. "You know what I found, Sara."

When Sara didn't respond, Cecilia drove the point home. "I have the sheet music to 'What You Do to Me.' I heard you," she quickly added, rushing out the words before Sara hung up. "I heard you when you were walking away with that woman. And she told you to forget him, but you argued. You said, 'He wrote those words for me.'"

And the line went dead.

Cecilia hit redial, but Sara didn't answer, and an answering machine picked up. She heard a voice she assumed was Abel Altman's. He sounded kind. Cecilia left a message. Knowing Sara was likely standing over the machine, she used cryptic words in case Abel was nearby. "Sara, I know this is difficult. I want to return to you what's yours. The envelope . . . and . . . well, I found something else. Here's my number. Please call me back."

Most of the staff had followed Jay-Z into the studio, and Cecilia sat at her desk, breathing deeply. She distracted herself from waiting on Sara by flipping the pages of the magazine's latest issue with R. E. M. on the cover. She told herself she should have pushed harder; she should have been more aggressive. So when her phone rang, she was prepared, but it was only Joan.

"My office. Now."

Cecilia sped down the carpeted hall, mouthing the words to "Feelin' It," which blasted from the studio. As she burst through the door, Cecilia spotted the day's trades in Joan's hands. Before Cecilia had a chance to sit, Joan shoved a paper in front of her—the pages open to Charley's Chatter column.

Everyone read Charley's column. A local writer, she captured whatever celebrity gossip happened to be floating around LA, and she was rarely off the mark. Joan's annoyed expression forced Cecilia to sit.

Cecilia read aloud: "George Clooney spotted with French law student Celine Balitran."

"Try again," Joan said.

Cecilia had already seen the line at the bottom, Eddie Vee's name in black, bold letters. This was too much. First *TMI*. Now Charley. Tension knotted in Cecilia's neck, and she was too annoyed to read the words aloud.

Seems that someone's let the kitty cat out of the bag, a.k.a. the biggest musical mystery in modern times. Friends, you heard it here first: the muse behind the love song that captured the country, the vixen who's left us wondering what if? Are they or aren't they? "What You Do to Me's" paramour is about to be outed . . . wait for it.

"She's wrong," Cecilia said. "They're all wrong. Whoever they think they're outing, it's not Sara Altman."

"We need to break this story before somebody else does. Get Sara talking fast. I want her on the cover of the next issue."

"We can't do that," Cecilia said.

"Why in hell not?"

"There are reasons they've kept their story private."

Joan put a hand to her ear. "What is that I'm hearing, Cecilia? Is that the sound of getting too close to a subject? Am I hearing you've compromised your objectivity?"

Whatever it was, she felt the need to protect Eddie and Sara.

"This story's about to launch your career. You're finally going to have the chance to show Brett and the big dogs in New York your West Coast muscle. You're not getting soft on me, are you?"

Cecilia tightened her fingers into fists while Charley and her big pearly smile peered up from the crinkled newspaper.

"Cecilia, if you can't exploit this story, I'll hand it to somebody else. Someone more seasoned and willing."

"Joan, I know what I'm doing. I'm going to break the story. They've got the wrong person." Then she found her inner bravado. "I promise you the utter satisfaction of watching Charley and *TMI* retract their stories."

"Atta girl," Joan said, sliding back in her chair. "You're sure about this?" Her green eyes dug into Cecilia's.

"I've never been more sure about anything in my life."

A knock at the door interrupted, and Dean popped his head in. "Cecilia, your stepmother's on the phone. She said it's important. Do you want me to put the call through?"

Joan nodded, and Cecilia was already up on her feet to take the phone from Joan's outstretched hand. She wasn't in the mood for Tori's crap, but that changed when she heard her stepmother's voice. "Cecilia, you need to get to the hospital. Your father's had a heart attack."

Cecilia froze, unable to process what she'd just heard. Tori repeated it, and an icy chill slithered down Cecilia's spine. Her voice trembled when she told Tori she'd be right there. Before she hung up, she had to ask, "Is he . . . is he going to make it?"

"I don't know." Cecilia could barely hear Tori. "Please hurry."

Handing the phone to Joan, Cecilia felt queasy, and she grabbed the desk to steady herself. All her festering feelings—the anger, the blame—leaked out, replaced by memories of Don racing around their house with stars in his eyes, Don singing to her before bed.

Joan offered to drive her to Cedars-Sinai, and Cecilia nodded, wondering what would happen if Don died. "Let me get my bag," Cecilia said.

Walking through the dimly lit hallway felt much like stepping through a foggy music video. The video was soundless, and her legs moved in slow, pitiful motion. She blocked out her fight with Don and the horrible things she'd said, and when she reached her desk, her phone rang.

Cecilia picked up fast, expecting it to be Tori again, but the feathery voice on the other end was somebody else.

"We should talk," Sara Altman said.

Cecilia's voice wobbled. "Sara . . . now's not a good time . . ."

"Oh. Okay." And then, "I thought this might be a mistake."

"No. It's not a mistake. I have a family emergency. Can we talk later?"

Sara hesitated. "Oh. Of course. I hope everything's okay."

Cecilia's words were tied to the lump in her throat. She didn't know what to say. "I'll call you later. And thank you, Sara. I know this is hard . . ."

"It's okay." Her voice fell. "Go to your family."

Family. The realization hit her hard. Don was all she had left.

"I'll call you as soon as I can."

CHAPTER 34

"BRANDY (YOU'RE A FINE GIRL)" BY
LOOKING GLASS

New York and Miami Beach
1985–1991

Sara married Abel on a gorgeous spring day at their Long Island synagogue, surrounded by her parents and their extended family and
friends. By then, Deborah and Elijah had celebrated their second anniversary and were expecting their first child, and Abraham and Noah
were ensconced in their community, happy to date and befriend the
Jewish girls at their private day school. Shira's delight rippled through
the synagogue.

Abel was a kind man, a gentle lover, and their union brought comfort to Sara. When Shira had sat her down the day before the wedding
to have "the talk," her innocence was on full display, and Sara felt a
gnawing guilt for that and for a distant memory that crept inside. Eddie
on the beach atop her. Eddie's body, long and lithe, his musky, salty
scent filling her nose. Sara averted her gaze, unable to make eye contact
when her mother led her to her bedroom and brought out the box of
silky lingerie.

Sara understood the rhythms of the body. How yearning grabbed hold, heightening every sense. As Shira held up the white lace panties and matching top, discussing with a straight face the anatomy and its alluring sensations, Sara held in a laugh. Her mother had no idea where her mind had gone, and so she smiled and nodded, oohed and aahed at the appropriate times, holding in her secrets.

An easy, agreeable life began, and if Abel suspected there was someone else, that something had transpired between her and Eddie, he never made an accusation. A dependable friendship took root beneath the towering red oaks lining their driveway, and for a time, it buoyed the fragile relationship.

~

The first sign of a crack in the couple's facade arrived in their second year of marriage. Up until then, the union was pleasant and comfortable, consistent and reliable. Sara and Abel treated each other with a well-meaning politeness, and they were supportive partners. Abel marveled at the way Sara lost herself in books, reading funny passages out loud, the two of them laughing until their bellies ached. He bragged to anyone who would listen that his wife was going to be a famous author, and she waved him off, though she secretly clung to the idea. Sheila, Abel's mom, visited often, and they entertained the larger family regularly. There was no shortage of questions regarding children—the family was still as loud as ever—as Glenwood saw an uptick in baby carriages and bassinets, cousins flaunting their baby bumps and offspring. Sara wasn't in a rush. They were young, and she wanted a career, and Abel supported the decision. They'd foregone protection, adopting the *if it happened, it happened* attitude, and Sara wondered if this ease was the way real relationships worked. A safe predictability that didn't threaten the status quo.

The smooth, effortless marriage continued until the day Sara stopped in front of the avocados in the supermarket, squeezing them for ripeness. That's when Eddie's latest single filled the air. He had crept inside her dreams a few days before, and the excitement she felt had frightened her. She wasn't sure what it meant. But now, as she listened to Eddie's words, his voice filled a place in Sara she had forgotten was there. That day she went home and began to write different kinds of stories. Eddie's music had reawakened something in her, and she longed for something bigger. Something that moved her heart, tipped every scale. She wrote ferociously at all hours, magic and mystery crowding the pages, tapping into her deepest passions. What was missing in her marriage, she captured on the page, stories of lust and recklessness, her body alive like it hadn't been for years. She missed it. She craved it. She couldn't stop.

Abel noticed the shift and the inordinate amount of time she spent writing in her notebooks, but it didn't stop him from broaching the subject of starting a family. "A little girl," he said, "who looks like you." And the string that Eddie had plucked was stilled, as Sara considered all the goals she had yet to reach. When Abel found a way to cozy up to her while she worked, she shooed him away, caught up in the rhythm of her stories. He complained that she didn't make him a priority. "They" weren't a priority, and as the idea of having a child began to simmer, a dangerous signal traveled through Sara. She wasn't quite sure what it meant, but it filled her with fear and apprehension. And when she watched him sleep, her sweet Abel, the guilt and emptiness plagued her. And the voice telling her *no*.

Word spread through Glenwood that their marriage was strained, the fissure attributed to their inability to conceive. But the rift was deeper than that and had begun long before. The crack was hidden in the early foundation of two people marrying for the wrong reasons.

So when Abel, Sara, and their families traveled to Florida for the High Holidays, Sara felt the friction and tension about to boil over.

Perhaps it was being back at the Atlantic and Eddie Santiago's taunting memory that had Abel on edge. Or perhaps it was Sara's devotion to her writing, or merely the heat, but one afternoon, when Abel found her on the balcony, he was furious.

Sara lay across a lounger, overlooking the ocean, sipping an iced tea. The portable radio played a song about someone wanting to make love to someone, and Sara was thinking about the chapter she'd just written, the star-crossed lovers stealing away, taking off in a convertible down Collins Avenue, their hair whipping in the wind. When they reached the secluded resort on the beach, they barely made it through the door before he tugged at her shirt, ripping the buttons off her blouse, kissing the nape of her neck. He dropped her on the bed, his lips trailing up her thigh until she cried out.

Abel hurtled toward her, holding the notebook.

"What is this, Sara?" His cheeks were bright red, his brown eyes filled with hurt.

Startled, she sat up, reaching for the pages, and he yanked them back.

"Who are you writing about? I don't understand. Who is this?"

"It's my book, Abel." Sara tried to explain. "It's a story."

Abel moved in closer, his voice wavering. "These are the things you write about?"

There was no sense arguing with him when he was this upset. She understood it had hurt Abel to read his wife's story about seduction and passion with someone else.

"It's fiction, Abel," she said.

He shook the pages in her face. "I don't understand. Is this what you want?" He rubbed his temple. "How is it I don't know this side of you? How come you have never shared this with me?"

"It's not real, Abel."

"How can you write about such things? What would people think of us?"

Sara felt something inside her breaking. She had a right to creative expression. He couldn't snuff it out. And she watched, powerless, as he proceeded to tear the pages out of the binder, pages she had spent months perfecting, and rip them into tiny pieces. The bits scattered in the breeze and down the beach.

"You can't do this," she hissed.

Sara felt a rush of rage. It was the same rage she had felt growing up when Shira exerted control over her. And once she tapped into that emotion, a torrent of repressed emotions surfaced. All the parts of herself she had denied by maintaining the peace. She didn't like his mother being in their kitchen every morning. She missed living in the city, meeting her writer friends on the weekends. She wasn't ready to have a baby. But more than anything, she hated that she ached for the passion in her stories. She loved him, but it wasn't enough. It had never been enough.

She raised her head to meet his eyes, his pain on full display.

A few scraps of paper blew across the balcony, but she withheld the anger, sucked in her breath, because she'd write another. And another. No one would stop her. And she asked herself if this was love. And if this was the reason they hadn't been able to conceive. Because maybe, she thought, maybe they weren't meant to be joined for life.

She felt sorry for him. For them. Her eyes watered, and she turned toward the ocean.

Seemingly realizing what he had done, he dropped what was left of the notebook on the end table and cowered before her. He put a hand on her shoulder, but she shrank away. "I'm sorry. I didn't mean that," he said. His face fell in his hands, and he may have been crying. "I just love you so much . . . and we . . . I don't feel like I know you. Not like that."

She kept her eyes fixed on the swimmers below jumping over waves.

"It's embarrassing for me, Sara. You have no idea. To see your love for someone else. Imagining you with him."

He didn't say the name, but she knew. Abel knew. He had known all along. And he had kept it to himself. And he married her anyway. He was a good man. A loving man. But the larger picture became clear. And a question arose: How could she be with a man who accepted half of what she could give? What kind of life was that for either one of them?

And though she wasn't proud that she had hurt him, this revelation confirmed what Sara already knew. They had love, and respect, and even a form of happiness. But he didn't understand who she was, because she had hidden her true self, never revealing the driving spirit that made her restless, in need of more. She had been living a lie, never giving Abel a chance.

Could she stay married to him when their passions and desires didn't align? It would go against everything her family valued and cherished, but maybe the next chapter of her story was to leave.

CHAPTER 35

"ME AND JULIO DOWN BY THE SCHOOLYARD" BY PAUL SIMON

Los Angeles
October 1996

An uneasiness descended on the car as Joan shuttled Cecilia down Santa Monica Boulevard toward Cedars-Sinai. When they reached the hospital entrance, Joan told her to forget about Sara and Eddie. "Focus on your dad."

"I've got to call her."

"You will." Then she squeezed Cecilia's shoulder before shoving her out of the car. "Go on."

Around her, the hospital bustled with activity. Cecilia hated hospitals. A disinterested man in green scrubs pointed her toward the ER, and when she entered the waiting room, Tori stood talking with a doctor, hands on her hips. The doctor towered over Tori, but Cecilia had never seen Tori look more intimidating.

Inching closer, Cecilia heard the persistence in her voice. "I need an update. I need to know if my husband's going to make it."

"We're doing all we can, Mrs. James. They found an arrhythmia, and they're working on him."

"What about his brain function? They were doing CPR on him for a while."

The man responded thoughtfully, "We'll know a lot more in the next twenty-four hours."

Cecilia's anxiety rose, and when Tori spotted her, she opened her arms wide to let Cecilia in. "Oh, honey, I'm so sorry," Tori said.

Cecilia found a comfort in Tori's embrace that she had missed, and tears welled up in her eyes.

"He's going to be okay," Tori assured her. "He has to be."

Cecilia backed up, gazing at her stepmother. It was hard to believe it had been only a few short hours ago that Tori had been holding her hair off her face while she puked.

"What happened?" Cecilia asked.

Tori linked her arm through Cecilia's and led her toward a less crowded corner of the waiting area where her father's briefcase sat. "I had just returned from driving the girls to school, and he said he wasn't feeling great. He had some heartburn, hadn't slept well. He'd been upset about your fight, not really up to talking—"

"This isn't my fault." It came out half question, half assertion, and she felt a twinge at saying it out loud.

"No. Of course not . . ." Tori's voice trailed off as though there was more. She sat, and Cecilia took the seat beside her, pulling her cardigan tighter. "He had planned to stop by your office on the way in. He wanted to finish your conversation, and I thought it was important he did. I saw him get into his car with his briefcase, but then a few minutes later he was back. He unbuttoned his shirt and started complaining of tightness in his chest. And the sweat. I knew he was having a heart attack.

"I called an ambulance and followed it to the ER. Thank God we were close." She began crying. "I didn't know if he was going to make it."

Tori's entire body shook, and tears stained her face. Cecilia reached for her hand and squeezed. "Thank you, Cecilia. Thank you for coming. I don't have anybody but you and Don and the girls. They're so young."

"I'm here," Cecilia whispered. "Whatever you need."

They locked eyes, and Cecilia had never noticed how beautiful and blue Tori's were. Soulful.

"I don't know what I'd do without him," Tori said, wiping her nose with a tissue.

"Don't think like that," Cecilia said, gathering all her strength. "This is Don we're talking about. He's tough." The words rolled off her tongue. "And he loves you. He'll fight for you."

Tori turned in Cecilia's direction. "He loves you too." Then she reached inside Don's briefcase and handed her a stack of letters held together in a rubber band.

"What is this?"

"I drove his car. The briefcase was there. And I found these inside. I'm guessing he had planned to give them to you today."

Cecilia shuffled through the stack, recognizing her father's neat handwriting on dozens of envelopes addressed to her, Cecilia Caroline James.

"I don't know if your father's going to have a chance to tell you everything. It's not my place . . . it's his story . . . but . . ." Tori's voice lowered with her eyes. "You just need to take these."

"Whatever it is," Cecilia said, trying to sound confident, "he's going to tell me himself."

Tori inhaled the certainty. And so did Cecilia. But she was baffled by the stack of letters postmarked from years ago. Why hadn't she received them?

"They're dated so you can see how far back they go," Tori said.

Cecilia pulled the top envelope out from beneath the rubber band. It was a letter from 1983.

Cecilia,

I know you're mad. I'd be too.

I promise you there will come a time when you understand.

Until then, I'm writing to let you know how much I love you. Mom is angry right now. She'll come around. That's what happens with her. You need to know something. My leaving your mother had nothing to do with my love for you. You're my sweet Cecilia Caroline. You are stardust in the sky, the perfect melody, every time.

One of our favorites is playing on the radio, "Fantasy" by Earth, Wind & Fire. Do you remember the day we danced in the backyard and you wore that wreath in your hair and twirled barefoot in your new dress? We were so happy. I hope the music travels across the sky and finds you. Because I'm with you even though I'm not under the same roof, and I will fight for you. I am fighting for you. Remember what I told you about the wreath? It means victory.

I'll see you soon, Sugar Bug. When you count the stars, I'll be counting with you.

Daddy

Cecilia didn't understand. How come she never got the letter? This was her father, the man she had worshipped all those years. This was the Don she used to know. Where had the letter been all this time? Desperate to understand, she flipped through the stack, trying to make sense of it all.

Just then a nurse came up to them, and they both jumped up. "How is he?" Tori said.

"The doctor asked me to come out and give you an update." Her tone was flat. "They found a blocked artery, and they're working on opening it right now. His heart rhythm's normal, and they have him sedated. The ventilator's helping him breathe."

"How long until he's out?" Tori asked. "Do they know—"

"We'll know more in the next twenty-four hours, Mrs. James." And before she turned to leave, she added, "We're doing everything we can. Your husband's in very good hands."

They sat back down, and Cecilia squeezed Tori's hand again. "It's going to be okay."

Tori mustered a flimsy smile and squeezed back.

When the waiting turned excruciating, Cecilia wandered down the hallway, searching for a distraction and a quiet spot to call Sara Altman. Using her cell phone, she punched in the number, hoping Sara's husband wasn't home, while she blocked out images of her father lying in the operating room and the stack of letters she'd just stuffed in her bag.

When she heard the busy signal, Cecilia ended the call.

She squeezed her eyes shut, wishing Pete were here. The deeper she was pulled inside Sara and Eddie's story, the more she wondered how she might have done things differently. Now Pete was miles and time zones away, and it was too late. She'd do anything to hear his voice, have him sitting beside her, reassuring her that everything would be okay.

She should have fought harder, but this was her way, doubting love. When you've been broken, it's hard to trust. And even harder to let someone in. She decided to write him tonight. She'd nail this Sara and Eddie story and fly overseas to meet him. She'd tell him what she should have told him weeks ago: to take the job with *LIFE* so they could have theirs together.

Pleased with herself and her plan, Cecilia punched in Sara's number again. This time the call rang through.

"Sara. It's Cecilia James."

Sara took a moment to respond. "Hi." And then, "I hope everything's okay."

"My dad. He's in the hospital."

"I'm sorry. I hope it's nothing serious."

"Me too. But look, I'm sorry to intrude. I know how hard this must be."

"No, Miss James, I don't think you do."

"Then tell me."

She paused. "I can't. I can't do that to Eddie."

"I'm not sure I'm following."

"He'd never forgive himself." She waited a beat. "I don't know. I thought I could do this. Maybe I can't."

"Look, I know my working for *Rolling Stone* concerns you, but that song . . . my boyfriend, Pete—"

"I thought you two broke up."

"We did. But the first time he told me he loved me, 'What You Do to Me' was playing. It's hard to hear it and not think about him. And not miss him. So I have to wonder how it makes you feel. When you hear it playing on the radio, what's it like to know someone wrote those words for you?"

Sara didn't make a sound.

"You have to know how it's touched people, Sara."

"That's what I've heard," she said. "But I try not to think about it."

Cecilia felt Sara's sadness. "Whatever happened between you two, it sounds painful. And I'm sorry."

Growing impatient, Sara asked, "What is it you want, Miss James?"

"I want to tell your story. Don't you want to claim what's yours?"

"I'll never let anyone have that much power over me again. Not anymore."

"It would be your story."

"That's what you don't get. Sometimes I wish it wasn't."

Cecilia empathized, hyperaware that she was overly invested, Sara and Eddie's story touching on every single one of her own losses.

"What was it like?" Cecilia asked, easing into it. "When he first sang you the song?"

Sara sighed. "I don't know," she said. "I never thought it would become as big as it has. It was ours. That same night, we discussed a future. He gave me a bracelet. It said *Be bold, be brave.* And then the very next day, he ended things . . . said we could never be together." Her voice softened when she added, "He said he didn't love me, that he and *Abuelo* were moving to Argentina. It was shocking. And I was forced to shut him out. And the song. And I did, but the feelings always found their way back in."

Cecilia was surprised. "He broke up with you the next day?"

"Yes."

Silence filled the phone line.

"We went back to Long Island, and I tried reaching him. I called their apartment, wrote letters, but they had moved. I had no way of finding him."

"I'm sorry. That sounds horrible. And abrupt."

"It made me question the song, question Eddie. I saw the way women threw themselves at him. In Miami, his way of keeping our relationship a secret was to play into those flirtations so no one would suspect he was tied to me. Now I wonder if I was wrong. If the one being played was me."

"You can't write a song like that without having big feelings."

"I'm a writer, Miss James. So are you. You know how easy it is to make things up."

"Yes, but you can't make up feelings like that."

Sara quieted. "Maybe." And then, "I'll never know."

"You could."

"No. That was a long time ago, and a lot's changed."

Cecilia felt a door closing, so she shifted the conversation to Abel.

"We grew up together," Sara said. "Our families have always been close. Our parents wanted us to marry from a very young age, but I was with Eddie, whatever that means. Was it even real if he was a secret? Abel was that stable force in my life . . . and when I graduated from Columbia, we made it official.

"Abel's a good man. I may have set us up to fail. I was never fully present in the marriage."

Cecilia caught the disappointment in her voice. "Are you happy, Sara?"

"What does that even mean?" Sara asked. "Isn't it just some fleeting emotion we're all trying to chase? A wise teacher once told me that the goal isn't to be happy all the time. It's better to experience a range of emotions, especially the difficult ones. He said that's how we learn, how we grow. I think he said, 'Sunshine all the time makes a desert.'"

Cecilia loved the idea that happiness was part of something bigger, and not only the means to an end. "My ex, Pete, he moved overseas to cover the war in Afghanistan, and I worry about him. I worry I may never see him again. Or have the chance to tell him I love him. That I should have told him to stay. But I wanted him to be happy. Maybe he needed something else."

"You think we'd both be happier if we fought harder?"

"Maybe."

Neither one spoke for a moment. Then Cecilia said, "I saw him." Sara didn't immediately answer, so Cecilia repeated herself. "I saw Eddie."

Sara took her time answering. "How is he?"

"Do you want the truth?"

"I'm not sure."

"He's terrible. Close your eyes and imagine the Eddie you once knew. He's not that boy anymore."

"I don't have to close my eyes," Sara said. "Where is he?"

"He's living in a small town. You'd hardly recognize him. Full beard. Long hair. He goes by a different name and sings covers at the local bar. He's let himself go, but he never let go of his music."

"None of that surprises me," Sara finally said.

"The accident changed him."

"It changed a lot of us."

"Eddie feels responsible," Cecilia said. "It's been his undoing."

Sara filled her in on Eddie's childhood. How he blamed himself for his parents' deaths. "That tragedy at the stadium had to have brought up all those feelings again."

Cecilia decided to take a risk. "I'd love to meet you, Sara. Face-to-face. We can do a proper interview. I can give you back what belongs to you, do justice to your story."

"That's not a good idea."

Cecilia understood. Sara was a married woman.

"The story's over," Sara said. "Leave it where it belongs. In the past."

"I want to. But you and I both know that neither of our stories is finished."

CHAPTER 36

"LAYLA" BY ERIC CLAPTON

Miami
Fall 1991

After that afternoon on the balcony in Miami, the tension between Abel and Sara rippled. Every time she sat at her desk to write, she could feel the air around them crackle. There was no subtle shift. Abel became outwardly suspicious and insecure. They argued about her getting a master's degree in creative writing; he thought her focus should be on children. She wanted to vacation in the mountains; he only wanted to travel to their Miami condo. When he asked her pointedly what she wanted, she avoided his eyes because what she wanted, he couldn't give her.

She thought about talking to Shira, being honest about her unhappiness, but she knew her mother would never understand. She'd tell her that marriage was a series of ups and downs and compromises. Marriage ebbed and marriage flowed; it was mostly friendship. But Sara wanted more than a friend. She wanted passion, that feeling that stopped her breath, and a partner who shared her vision.

Glenwood was too small. She wasn't turning her back on her parents and their traditions and kindnesses. She loved them. And she still loved Abel, but it wasn't romantic love. She had to tell him. She had already sacrificed too much, and she refused to waste another minute dwelling in regret.

And on a stifling, humid day, fate intervened with Sara's restlessness.

It was Sukkot, and they were in Florida for the holiday when Sara flipped through the *Miami Herald*. It was there she spotted an advertisement for an upcoming concert at the Orange Bowl. High Tide was coming to town. Eddie Santiago was coming home.

Sara gave herself a minute to remember the last time she'd seen him, how heartbroken she'd been, how he'd told her he'd never loved her. She closed her eyes, reliving the awful memory. This was no coincidence. This was the sign she needed. After the holiday she'd tell Abel she couldn't be with him. Then she'd be free, and she wouldn't have to rely on her stories to fill her up. In the meantime, she needed to see Eddie.

The show was only a few days away, and Sara immediately picked up the phone and dialed the number for Ticketmaster. After thirty minutes on hold, she reached a sales agent and enquired about a ticket.

"I need the very best seat. Whatever is closest to the stage."

"You're a little late for that. The best seats are long gone."

"Please. Just one."

The sales agent drawled in a Southern accent, "A single seat may be a little easier to find, but it could cost you a couple hundred dollars."

Sara didn't care about the cost.

"Here's one," the agent said. "Seventh row. Center stage. That's the best I've got."

"I'll take it."

"Mastercard or Visa?"

Sara blocked out the image of Abel seeing the charge on their monthly statement.

~

The morning of the concert, a light drizzle glossed Miami Beach. It was Saturday, the Sabbath, and when she had lit the candles beside her mother and aunts the night before, a wave of doubt had crept in. The flames burned brighter than usual, as though they felt her breaking away, so they lured her in. Unable to sleep, she tossed and turned, thinking about the ritual and the beautiful connection to her family, but then she'd imagine Eddie and his bright light. Eddie telling her to be brave and bold. She was conflicted, though she convinced herself leaving Abel and going to see Eddie were two separate decisions. She had to leave Abel, tell him their marriage wasn't working, had never worked. And seeing Eddie was something else. She was curious about him after all these years, and he would never spot her in the crowd, so what harm would it cause to go to his concert?

Sara could barely contain herself through the morning services, the ticket burning a hole in her pocket. And afterward, as she and Abel walked toward the Atlantic, they discussed dinner in the sukkah on the beach, followed by cocktails with the family at the Fontainebleau.

The famed, glitzy hotel meant a late night, and Sara would simply tell Abel she wasn't feeling well. Then she'd go up to the condo, change her clothes, and take a cab to the stadium. She knew how these nights went, and Abel wouldn't be home before midnight. With each step, her doubts about what she was doing disappeared. It was as though *Hashem* had given her permission.

The day dragged on, and Sara searched her closet, looking for something special to wear. Even though she kept telling herself there wasn't a chance she and Eddie would meet face-to-face, that he'd never see her, let alone single her out, she imagined a scenario where he would. And that evening, as she sat beneath the sukkah beside her brothers and sister-in-law, parents, and aunts and uncles, she took it all in. She watched her cousins laughing and telling jokes. She watched the new babies eye the lulav with wonder. She felt an overwhelming, deep love for her family. But when the group set off to the Fontainebleau, Sara hung back. Abel wrapped an arm around her, and she told him her lie. "I'm going to go up to bed."

And she gave him a gentle kiss before walking away.

CHAPTER 37

"RUNAROUND SUE" BY DION DIMUCCI

Los Angeles and Miami
October 1996

Standing in the hospital hallway, Cecilia pressed Sara to continue the conversation. But Sara had said enough, and she asked Cecilia for her father's name so she could include him in the *misheberach*, the prayer for the sick, and encouraged Cecilia to move on with her life—as she had. Cecilia offered the name, but she couldn't shake her disappointment.

Love shouldn't be so complicated. But if that were the case, she'd be with Pete right now. Instead, she had let him go. But what if Sara and Eddie were different?

Cecilia found Tori in the waiting room, hunched over, praying into her hands. Cecilia sat beside her, wrapping an arm around her shoulder. At first Tori resisted, but then she released into Cecilia and sobbed.

"It's going to be okay," Cecilia assured her, though she had no way of knowing for sure.

"What if it's not? What if . . ." And she stopped herself from saying the rest.

"He's Don." And Cecilia felt the ache growing in her throat. "He's not leaving us."

She wasn't sure where her faith came from. Maybe from the letters he'd written that she'd never received. Or the childhood she'd remembered, with him, when he encouraged her to toughen up, to keep going.

Tori got up and paced the floor while Cecilia wrestled with the countless thoughts and questions flooding her mind. She reached inside her bag and pulled out her spiral notebook, jotting down the various pieces she had to string together.

Sara. Returning her music. Making some sense of Don's letters. Finding a way to get Sara and Eddie together for an interview. Going to see Pete. Bringing him home?

The doctor poked his head in the waiting room just as Tori completed another lap. When she saw him, she rushed to his side.

"Your husband's out of the procedure. Everything went well. We put a stent in one of the main arteries supplying blood to the heart, and we have him on a ventilator, sedated. We'll wake him in the morning to see how he is neurologically."

"Can we see him?" Tori asked.

"As soon as he gets to the ICU."

After an excruciating wait, they were able to visit him one at a time. Tori went first while Cecilia thumbed through the stack of letters. She found one from her fourteenth birthday where he included the lyrics to "That's How Strong My Love Is." He told her how he'd come to the house to surprise her that day, but her mother had changed the locks.

She found another that he had written when Cecilia had broken her arm roller-skating. She remembered that day. Her mother had taken her to Roller Palace, said she'd meet her inside. And it was fun, until Cecilia fell, and though she picked herself up, she remembered searching for her mother, but she couldn't find her in the stands. April's mom tended to her instead.

She settled back in the chair, wondering how she'd been so wrong. The childhood she'd thought she had was very different from reality. What if something happened to her father and she never learned the entire truth?

When Tori returned, Cecilia jumped up to meet her.

"How is he?"

"Sleeping."

"Any news?"

Tori raised her eyes to meet Cecilia's. "We won't know until tomorrow."

Cecilia scurried down the hall and pushed through the door. When she saw her father, she did a double take. The bed swallowed him, and his tanned skin looked translucent. The ventilator covered his nose and mouth, and his hair lay flattened against his head.

"Don," she whispered. And when he didn't open his eyes, she said, "Daddy." And saying the word, the way she used to say it when she was a small child, filled her with tears.

"Why didn't you tell me?" she cried. "You should've told me!"

She squeezed her father's hand.

He couldn't die. He couldn't leave her again. She needed answers. She needed understanding. He had to wake up. She sat with him a few minutes, watching the machine breathe life into him.

"Don, you listen to me, and you listen to me good. You said you were going to fight for me. You have to fight. You can't break your promise. Not this one. It's too big. Please." And she squeezed his hand again, stood, and dropped a kiss on his forehead.

"Come back to us. We have to count the stars."

~

That night, the girls stayed at the neighbor's house, and Cecilia and Tori huddled close together on the couch. They talked about Don. They talked about Gloria. They talked about secrets.

"I was at the center when your dad first brought Gloria in. I was young—"

"That's actually funny," Cecilia said with a laugh.

Tori laughed too. "I was in training. They seemed so happy and in love. She wore those earrings with such pride . . . and she was a bit of a firecracker, your mom. She fought Don, fought the staff's help. She didn't believe she had a problem. People usually don't. She visited on and off. A day or two here and there. But she never really committed to doing the work. I think she came because Don forced her. Usually, she'd doze through her appointments and sessions. This went on and on for some time. Your dad and I would talk sometimes. It was always professional. He never crossed a line."

"How did you end up with the earrings?"

Tori drew her knees into her chest. "This might be difficult for you to hear."

"Try me."

"Before she died, she checked in for a short stint. She said she was ready to do the work. And she tried, but then she fell off track and left. Weeks went by, and that's when she passed away. About a year ago, one of our employees was charged with providing prescription drugs to our guests. The police found her earrings in his trove of goods, patients paying him for access. His side gig. You know where I'm going with this."

"She gave the earrings away in exchange for . . ."

Tori just nodded her head, letting the realization sink in.

Cecilia said, "How is it possible I didn't see it? Or did I, and I just buried it? All that anger for Don leaving . . . it was misplaced. I misunderstood."

"I hope you two can talk this through when he wakes up."

"He still left me with a drunk, Tori."

"That's a conversation you need to have with him. But he was around more than you know. He was the one who asked Daphne to move in. They were always in contact. And your aunt Denise. I'll let him tell you about her. But you loved being with your mom. And while you may not remember, he saw you when Gloria was feeling generous. I know it wasn't enough for either one of you. But by then you were your mother's daughter. He couldn't break through. You'd refuse to see him, and you'd cancel on him. You didn't want him in your life."

Cecilia listened, trying to make sense of it all. Was that love she'd felt being with her mom or was it something else?

"I'm glad you're here now," Tori said. "I'm sorry we have to go through this, but I'm glad we're doing it together. I just need him back."

"He'll come back," Cecilia said. "I'm going to make sure of it."

That night, she read through all the letters. There were pictures he'd taken while Cecilia and her friends played box ball in the street, notes expressing his love. There were articles about music and musicians he'd pulled from magazines, letters conveying his disappointment when Cecilia canceled a sleepover or skipped a planned dinner. He was ever present and watching. He wasn't the horrible person she had conjured him up to be.

He wasn't perfect.

But he wasn't evil.

He was like everyone.

Imperfect.

But he loved her. He had always loved her.

～

The next morning, she and Tori drove the short distance to the hospital. Rain tapped on the car windows, and Cecilia worried it was an ominous sign, like somebody crying. Her heart pounded—she was sure she could hear Tori's too—as they clung to the hope that Don would be okay. And when they met the doctor, the news was positive. They'd removed the ventilator, and Don, although weak and tired, was breathing on his own with normal brain function.

Cecilia entered his room, he smiled at her, and the life returned to his pale skin.

She released her tangled-up worry and sat in the seat beside him. "You scared us."

"I'll be fine," he whispered, the monitors beeping and blinking. "Just a little damage to the artery . . . I'll be good to go with some cholesterol medicine."

"Finally acting your age," Cecilia said. "Are you in pain?"

"It's not so bad."

Tears filled Cecilia's eyes. "I'm glad you're okay."

He reached for her hand. "We should talk."

"You should rest."

He shook his head and took a sip of water. "You saved my life, Cecilia."

"I did no such thing."

"I should've been on my way to work. But I delayed, planning to visit you first. I would've been on the highway. If I hadn't made it to the hospital sooner—"

"Tori saved you. Not me."

"You both saved me." He pointed at his briefcase. "There's something in there for you. I had intended on giving them to you yesterday, but I was sidetracked."

"Tori gave them to me."

"Oh. Good. That's good."

"We can talk about all that when you're out of here," Cecilia said.

"I'm sorry I worried you girls."

"I wasn't ready to lose you." And she meant it.

"There's a lot we should discuss," he said.

"I got some of the CliffsNotes."

"I'll be home in a few days."

"And we'll talk," Cecilia said.

"We'll talk."

~

Cecilia didn't rest much that night, because Phoebe and Hazel decided to have a sleepover in her bed while Tori spent the night at the hospital. She wasn't complaining. They smelled nice, and their bodies, snuggled close to hers, made up for some of Pete's absence. She liked the way they freely expressed themselves, shared whatever was on their minds—and there was a lot. When you're deeply loved, it's easy to give it in return. She could have done without the karate kicks to her stomach, but she liked how they reminded her that they were there, and she liked that they were there.

That next morning, when she got to her desk, Joan was waiting. Cecilia filled her in on Don and asked the million-dollar question, "Can you get me back to Miami?"

"I thought you'd never ask," Joan said, handing Cecilia the latest trades. "This would've been heartless and cruel to drop on you sooner."

"That never bothered you before."

Cecilia browsed the articles where both Charley's Chatter and *TMI* outed Brian DiPalma as Eddie Vee's lover.

"This just got so much more interesting," Cecilia said.

"Yes," Joan said. "So here's what we're going to do. We're going to get you to Miami so we can prove these suckers wrong."

~

In the few hours she had before the flight to Miami, Cecilia tracked down the international fax number for where Pete was staying. It was time for a bold move, and she started a letter.

Pete,

I'm heading back to Miami. I found the inspiration behind the song. It was Sara, the woman I met at the memorial that day, the day I missed the boat. About that. We're so much more than that one single day. Just like there's so much more to the song and the story behind it.

But first, my dad. He's not the person I thought he was. Neither was Gloria. I know. It's confusing. I'm trying to make sense of it myself. Don's in the hospital. He had a heart attack, pretty much scared the shit out of all of us. He's going to be okay, but there were a few minutes where it was touch and go, when I had to face some pretty startling truths.

Which is to say, I was wrong about him. About all of it. Gloria was an alcoholic, Pete. All the glitter and gold . . . it was an illusion. She was an illusion. When I was four, she took me for a drive, drunk, and we got into a horrible accident. I was hospitalized with a concussion. It's the reason I don't drive, though I don't have a clear memory from that day.

There's a lot more that I'm still processing, but here's what you need to know. What I learned from this. I didn't mean to be this way. I didn't mean to be hostile or have one foot out the door. I believed something that was told to me, and it took on a life of its own. I doubted myself, then doubted you. It made me distrustful and foolish.

You were the one solid presence in my life.

But I thought if my own father found me unlovable, you'd deem me unlovable too.

And you'd leave. Just like him.

So I did it first.

And that's not an excuse.

I should have begged you to stay. Or figured out a way to go with you. But I didn't. Because I didn't want to get in the way of your career, and that was stupid. I should have proved to you I would do anything to stay together. To make it work. But I thought if I asked, you'd say no. And I couldn't bear the rejection. So much like his. So I let you go, I let you leave. And I was wrong.

I'm going to make it up to you. I know how to fix this. Just say you forgive me, because I'm not giving up on us.

TTM,

Cecilia

~

On the plane to Miami, long-buried memories crowded Cecilia's mind, flashes that didn't seem to make much sense. Don singing to her before bed while Gloria slipped in and out, hard to pin down. Gloria's loud laughter. The dreamy shadows in her eyes.

The illusion of her childhood had been shattered. But in the broken glass, she found shards of light and meaning, and though the pieces would never fit perfectly together, they would find a way to meet.

~

Cecilia had an address for Abel and Sara Altman, but she didn't want to show up unannounced, so when she arrived at the hotel, she punched in Sara's number. When it went to the answering machine, she quickly hung up.

She repeatedly pressed redial between reading through her notes and pacing the floor until finally, a woman answered.

"Sara. It's Cecilia James."

When Sara didn't respond, Cecilia asked if she was alone. If it was okay to talk.

"It's fine," Sara said.

"I'm in Miami. Can we meet somewhere and talk?"

"I told you not to come."

"I want to return what belongs to you."

"You came cross-country to deliver some old sheet music?"

"You know it's more than that," Cecilia said.

Sara hesitated. "You really don't know?" she asked.

"What?" Cecilia asked.

"When you saw me at the Orange Bowl?"

Cecilia was confused, having no idea what Sara was getting at.

Sara exhaled. "Just leave the envelope in the mailbox."

Cecilia felt for the woman. It had to be difficult with her husband. Not many men would want to be reminded of the music and stardom of an ex-boyfriend.

"I thought we could talk a bit more. About Eddie."

"I'm done talking about Eddie." Then her tone changed. "Please just leave it in the mailbox, Miss James. You'd be doing all of us a favor."

Undaunted, Cecilia hopped in a cab and rattled off the Altmans' address. They traveled across canals and past magnificent waterfront homes. The views were beautiful, the water like glass.

Eventually they pulled up to a modest, well-kept house on a leafy residential street. Flowers edged the path leading to the front door, and a row of perfectly trimmed hedges lined the sidewalk.

Cecilia could have dropped the envelope in Sara's mailbox, but she hadn't flown cross-country to give up that easily. While she respected

Sara, she had a job to do. To tell a story. Her first story. The one she lost Pete for. She had to make it worth her while. She told the driver to wait.

No one answered when she knocked on the door, though she knew Sara was inside. They'd just hung up, and there was a car in the driveway. Knocking harder, she peered through the window. The home was still and quiet, and she turned around, her eyes following the path leading to the sidewalk and the bright-red mailbox by the hedges. Retracing her steps, Cecilia was reluctant to drop off the envelope without talking to Sara first, but she had to. The music was Sara's.

When the metal door on the mailbox clanged shut, Cecilia gazed over her shoulder. Let down, she walked back to the taxi and asked the driver to wait a few minutes. When there was still no sign of Sara, they pulled away, and when they approached the intersection, Cecilia turned and spotted a figure walking toward the mailbox.

"Wait," she instructed the driver.

Cecilia watched. It was Sara, and she appeared to be holding a long stick. But then she lost her balance and tripped, falling to the ground.

"I'm sorry," Cecilia said to the driver. "Can we go back?"

Cecilia strode up the walkway to where Sara sat on the ground, patting the pavement around her.

"Sara, it's Cecilia." And she went to pick up the stick, but Sara screamed at her to go away. "Are you okay?" she asked. She placed a hand on Sara's arm and helped her to her feet. Then she handed her the stick, which wasn't an ordinary stick at all.

"I told you not to come!" Sara yelled.

And like a puzzle, the pieces came together. That afternoon at the memorial with the dog. Sara's dark sunglasses. How Cecilia offered her a tissue, and she didn't accept. She didn't accept because she couldn't see it.

The stick was a white cane.

Sara Friedman was blind.

CHAPTER 38

"RHIANNON" BY FLEETWOOD MAC

Miami Orange Bowl
September 28, 1991

Sara stood in front of the mirror, closely examining herself. The green tank top was the vibrant shade of the palm trees lining Collins Avenue, and the denim shorts she chose accentuated her trim legs. She pulled her long brown hair back in a ponytail, dusted her cheeks with blush, and dabbed clear gloss on her lips. Turning her head from side to side, she caught a flash of her hoop earrings in the mirror, the gold reflecting in her dark eyes.

Abel's kiss lingered on her mouth, and the emptiness made her want to cry. It brought her decision to a head, and her fingers shook while lacing her sneakers. On the way to the stadium, she stared out the taxi window, trying to calm her nerves. Eddie's song came on the radio, and when the DJ mentioned he was in town, she thought about everything she'd say to him if given the chance.

When Sara entered the packed stadium, the opening act had just finished their set. It took her no time to find her seat in the seventh row, directly in front of the stage. Glancing around at the crowd—mostly young girls—she noticed how they waited expectantly. They had all come to see Eddie. To them, he was a star, unreachable. To her, he was stardust buried in her heart.

The murmurs of "Eddie" and "High Tide" echoed through the stadium, and Sara pitied the up-and-coming band that was trying to make a name for itself. They were good, but they weren't Eddie.

The roar of the fans shook the stadium. They stomped on the fiberglass bleachers, chanting "High Tide" until, one by one, the band members appeared. Bob, Bruno, Izak, and the star of the show, Eddie.

Eddie Santiago. He was right there in front of her. It was hard to look away. She noticed how the steel-gray T-shirt hugged his chest and the way his hands held the bright-blue guitar she had given him all those years ago. When his fingers curled around the neck, she felt them on her skin.

Eddie's broad smile greeted the crowd, and they welcomed him home with cheers and screams. He began with a song Sara had sung along to dozens of times. His voice had transformed into something richer and more nuanced than when she had last heard him sing, the eve of their goodbye. She surveyed the swells of people watching him in awe, the girls holding up poster boards with the words "Marry Me, Eddie Vee." She planned to make her way closer to the stage. She'd smile up at him, and once he saw her, he'd invite her backstage. And if that didn't work, she'd borrow a poster board and write her own message: "Eddie, it's me, Sarita."

Goosebumps trailed up and down her skin at the thought of their reunion.

She was so close.

The woman beside Sara said to her friend, "What must it be like to bed that man? He's the hottest guy on earth." To which her friend replied, "I bed him every night when I'm with Barney." And they laughed so hard, Sara almost laughed too.

The stadium roared, the crowd chanting, "What You Do to Me." They snapped their lighters and waved the flames in the air until Eddie shouted, "Is this what you all came here for?" And the woman beside Sara screamed back, "We came here for you, Eddie." That's when Eddie began strumming on her brother's guitar, and Sara shivered as he sang the first words. The crowd around her stilled. Perhaps they all imagined the famous lyrics were written for them. They imagined being loved like that. By him.

He cradled the microphone in his hands, and she remembered those hands on her face. Remembered her name on his lips. "I'm right here if you get lonely," he sang. "Close your eyes. Listen to my voice."

His words sank inside her, and that was all she needed. She would tell him. She would tell him she couldn't live without him, that she didn't care about being from different worlds or what she'd have to give up. She missed him. With every fiber of her being. And she loved him. And the way he sang their song, she knew he loved her too.

When he sang the last words, "what you do to me," he looked in her direction. He couldn't see the crowd past the bright stage lights, but she thought she saw a look of recognition flicker across his face.

She smiled back.

It was going to be okay.

Then she heard a loud rumbling noise. Screams. People running toward the stage. And everything went black.

CHAPTER 39

"BAD, BAD LEROY BROWN" BY JIM CROCE

Miami Beach
October 1996

Sara and Cecilia sat huddled together at the kitchen table with Elliot, Sara's service dog.

"At the memorial," Cecilia said, "I didn't think twice about the dog. Or your glasses. Not even when you walked to the car."

"He wasn't wearing his harness that day," Sara said weakly.

"I'm so sorry, Sara," Cecilia said.

"Me too." She sipped her tea.

"What happened?"

Sara set down her cup. "I was there that day."

Cecilia waited.

"At the concert. I went to surprise him." She laughed, though there was nothing funny about it.

Cecilia dropped back in her seat. Sara was there. Sara was at the concert. She was one of the injured. "Sara. I don't know what to say."

"There's nothing to say."

Cecilia's compassion steered her in a different direction. Joan would be pissed. "You don't have to tell me. I had no idea."

"It's okay. You made the trip out here. That was a lot of effort."

"It was important for me to return the music to you."

"I was an idiot," Sara said. "I actually thought I'd go backstage, or he'd pluck me out of the crowd, and that long-ago feeling would fix everything. Abel and I were never the right fit. We loved each other. We still do. But we didn't really know each other, not in the ways we needed. I had to find Eddie. I had to know what happened between us."

"But you never got that chance."

Sara's head dropped. "No. The crowd stormed the stage. I fell and hit my head. 'A traumatic brain injury,'" she said, holding up air quotes. "You know the rest."

"Eddie never knew you were there."

"It would kill him to know what happened to me," Sara said. "He already blamed himself for what happened to his parents."

Sara brought the tea to her lips, then set the cup down. Her eyes moved in Cecilia's direction. "How is he?"

"Not good."

A garbage truck rumbled loudly down the street, and they used the interruption to collect their thoughts. "I'm sure he blames himself for what happened at the concert," Sara said.

"You know him better than anyone."

"I guess. I thought I knew him."

Cecilia reached for her bag and pulled out the tape recorder. "I have a tape," she said. "From when we spoke." She placed the device on the table.

"Eddie's in here?" Sara's fingers searched the table. "I don't know if I can do this."

"You should. He still loves you."

A tear slid down Sara's cheek.

"We were so young and naive. I was a girl who never really knew where she belonged," she said, "so when I met Eddie, he validated those feelings. I was raised in this giant family, but it was full of contradictions. I say that because there are a lot of us, but we were sheltered in our little world. There's, like, seventy-five of us from grandparents to grandbabies, and we all lived on the same block in the same community. Don't misunderstand me, it was the greatest way to grow up, having built-in best friends, but I wanted more. I imagined traveling, living in New York City.

"We were raised Jewish—my mom stricter than my dad—but it went beyond religion. I had an aunt who died at sixteen, my mother's sister. She fell for a Catholic boy, and when she snuck out of the house one night to meet him, she was hit by a car and killed. My grandmother never recovered, and it changed my mom. Because I was her only daughter, she was superprotective of me. It was a constant battle about clothes and friends and choices. To my mother, we had to stay within the neighborhood. Outsiders were dangerous."

"It sounds like she thought letting you grow up . . . letting go . . . wasn't safe," Cecilia said.

"I had to break away. Not just for Eddie. I needed my mom to let go so I could be free, to breathe. But that didn't mean I wanted to lose her love or my family.

"Abel and I were never meant to be more than friends. I tried turning platonic love into romantic love, and what a surprise, it failed. Then he got ahold of my stories, and when he read about this side of me he didn't know, it played into all his insecurities. I think the stories shed a light on what was missing in our marriage. We couldn't pretend any longer. Then it was a domino effect. We argued about everything. Kids. Traveling. Our home."

"But you stayed."

Sara shifted in her seat, and Elliot raised his head, sensing her movements.

"By the time I got to that stadium, my decision was made. I was caught up in a nostalgic moment. I was leaving Abel. My not-so-well-thought-out plan was to move to New York, get a graduate degree. And who knows where Eddie fit in. I had some foolish notion that we'd open our hearts to one another, reconcile our unfinished business. I would deal with my mother's disappointment . . . the family . . . whatever repercussions."

Sara's eyes filled with tears. "When I was with Eddie, it felt like anything was possible. That's the feeling I'd missed. The feeling I'd suppressed all those years." She stopped, and she smiled. "I may be blind, but I see it all so clearly now. And even back then, Eddie and I were able to see beyond the barriers we faced."

"What's it like?" Cecilia asked. "What's it like to lose something so precious?"

Sara clasped her fingers together and rested her chin on her hands. "Eddie or my eyesight?"

"I guess both."

"I was so angry when it happened. One minute I was watching Eddie, imagining our life together, and the next I woke up in a hospital."

"Your parents . . . Abel . . . ?"

"The hospital called them. Luckily for me, I was out of it, so I didn't hear their reactions. I'm sure there was shock and disbelief, but they figured out why I was at a High Tide concert. That Eddie Vee was Eddie Santiago. And when the doctors shared the prognosis, when we heard the word *blind*, that became the focus. My family did what they'd always done, rallied around me, took care of everything."

"How'd you keep your name out of the papers?"

"Have you not heard of Shira Friedman?" She laughed.

"And Abel?"

"Look, he knew why I'd gone to the concert. And he knew that I lied. He never said a word. Neither did my mother. No one did. We rented this house to be near Bascom Palmer, the eye institute. Abel did his best. It didn't take long for him to become the loving boy I'd grown up with, but I didn't like depending on him, on anyone, and I was stuck.

"I found, as the days literally blurred into one another, that I wasn't mad at Eddie or the fans who stampeded the stage. I was angry at myself . . . for marrying for the wrong reasons. And do you have any idea how unbearable a marriage becomes when you have to rely upon that person to do everything for you?"

Cecilia didn't know how to answer that.

"I spent the first year in a dark fog, questioning God, questioning my faith. Was this my punishment for wanting something more? Managing daily tasks was a challenge. I'd trip and fall, knock into things, bruise myself. It was humbling and humiliating. How was it possible that I'd never get to see another sunset, never watch myself grow older in a mirror?

"I had no choice but to accept my circumstances. What was the alternative? I thought about that bracelet Eddie had given me, and I held on to the message. Eventually, I stopped feeling sorry for myself, got Elliot, became entirely . . . mostly . . . self-sufficient, and I left him."

"Wait. You and Abel—"

"We're divorced. He lives in New York."

"But your answering machine . . . the car in the driveway."

"That's him. I never changed it. It's safer to have a man's voice on the machine. And the car's Eleanor's. She lives with me, helps me around the house with cooking and cleaning. She's next door visiting with the neighbor who just had twins."

"Why didn't you mention the divorce?"

"I guess it kept me from delving into all this."

"What about Shira? How did she handle it?"

"It was bad. It got ugly for a few years. She wanted me back in Glenwood with the family, especially in my condition, but Miami had become my home. She didn't understand me. I didn't understand her.

I never intended to disrespect my mother, or Abel. But I know I've disappointed them. I've had to learn to accept Shira the way she is. And if I wanted her to accept my choices, I had to accept hers. We've had a few honest moments. We've apologized to each other, had some mother-daughter crying fests. My father . . . he passed away last year." Sara swiped at her eyes. "It's not always easy missing my siblings and family gatherings, but we do our best to make it work. And when they come to Florida, it's like old times, and my nieces and nephews love spending time with their Auntie Sara."

"And Abel?"

"Interestingly, he remarried quickly. Already has a bunch of kids. He called me one day when he heard the song. He came right out and asked if it was about me. He's the only person I ever admitted it to; that's how deeply our history binds us. And he understood. And we became friends again. We should have never married in the first place."

Sara inched closer to Cecilia's side of the table and raised a palm to Cecilia's face. "Is this okay?" She gently stroked Cecilia's cheek, outlined her chin and nose. "You're pretty."

A blush crept up the back of Cecilia's neck.

"I know what you're thinking. Don't feel sorry for me. You think there are five senses, but there are more. I lost one, a big one, but I gained clarity and intuition. I experience things with my other senses that some never do." She barely stopped to take a breath. "I'm happier than I've ever been. Eleanor's here, and she's family. And I got a master's at the University of Miami, and I work part time at Almar's. My recommendations are reader favorites. When I'm not working, I dictate my stories into a recorder, and they're transcribed. One of my manuscripts is on submission as we speak."

"You're incredible."

"So don't feel sorry for me. I don't. Not anymore. I felt sorry for myself when I was half living in a loveless marriage. And even though I'm completely blind in my left eye, I see shadows and some color in the right. Maybe someday I'll see again. I'm hopeful." She paused. "You know what that means? It means I have faith. It's in here." She pointed at her chest. "Faith is seeing the light through the darkness. I'll be okay with whatever *Hashem* has planned for me."

"What about Eddie?" Cecilia asked.

"What about him?"

"His song . . . your stories. How does this one end?"

Sara sat back in the chair. "I can't answer that for you."

"But you still love each other." There was urgency in Cecilia's tone. "Let me write this story."

"You can't write the story," Sara replied. "Not the whole story."

"The fans deserve to know."

"That his music blinded me? No one wants to hear that, Miss James. Especially him."

"You need to call me Cecilia."

"Is that what your friends call you?"

Cecilia smiled, and she knew that now was the best time to hit "PLAY" on the recorder. One press of a button and Eddie would be there in the room with them.

"You're really making me do this." Sara closed her eyes as Eddie's sultry voice sprang from the recorder. He recounted the story of how they met. Of how they became friends before they were lovers. How he ached for her when she returned to Long Island, so he wrote music for her.

When they reached the part about the breakup, Sara looked surprised at the way he described it, as though he'd gotten the details wrong. She fumbled for the recorder, visibly upset. "Turn it off. Please." Elliot bounced to his feet and nuzzled her thigh with his damp nose.

"You love him," Cecilia reminded her. "Go to him."

"I can't. What happened at the stadium was a sign. To stay away. He can't see me like this. He'd take responsibility, and I don't want that for him." She stroked the dog's head. "You can tell the story, the story of Eddie and me on the beach, but leave it where it ended all those years ago. We parted. We went our separate ways. That's the only way nobody will get hurt. Please, Cecilia."

"If I write the whole story, if I give it the justice it deserves, I think you'll change your mind."

Sara was resolute when she said, "I'm not going to change my mind."

CHAPTER 40

"JOLENE" BY DOLLY PARTON

Los Angeles
November 1996

Forty-eight hours later, the first of November, Cecilia sat in her cubicle listening to Joan berate her, blasting her for getting too close to the story. The article was perfect. Moving. Evocative. But she was having second thoughts about pulling the trigger on exposing Sara's secret. She wanted to leave that part out.

"You need to tell the whole story. That's what we do here. Not a portion. Not the pick-and-choose parts. The entire story."

"I can't," Cecilia argued.

"Wrong answer." Joan puffed madly on her cigarette, her green eyes trained on Cecilia. "I should've known you'd go amateur on me. For fuck's sake, Cecilia, this is it. This is the piece that's going to catapult you to the next level. You've been itching and scratching for this for years!"

"I know," Cecilia said, and she knew she shouldn't admit this to Joan, but she couldn't help herself. "The truth will destroy Eddie Vee."

"And what about your career? Do you care at all about that?"

Cecilia wasn't sure. This thing with her father . . . with Pete . . . she wasn't sure what she wanted anymore. She wanted Eddie and Sara back together. If she could fix them, give them their happy ending, maybe she'd get hers. But she knew it wasn't that simple, and she was mad at herself for getting personally involved.

"Cecilia? Are you in there?"

Cecilia nodded, but she wasn't. She was miles away on a ship with Pete, at a bar in Bisbee, Arizona, with Sara and Eddie. And when she gazed upward, she saw her mother sprinkling her with gold glitter. But it wasn't glitter. It was Joan flicking water at her from the cup on her desk.

"The whole story or no story," Joan said. "Take your pick."

Cecilia was too exhausted to think.

She had flown to LA on an early morning flight so she could be at work by eleven. She spent those hours on the plane perfecting the piece, making the tough call to leave in Sara's condition. The next issue closed in three days, which meant she had three days to change her mind. For Sara to change her mind.

Dean popped his head in, waving a piece of paper in the air. "Fax from sexy boyfriend." He smiled, which made Cecilia smile too.

Joan snatched the fax and held it up. "Are you two back together?"

"Difficult when we're thousands of miles apart."

"Phone sex," Joan said. "Works actual wonders."

Cecilia snagged the page from Joan's hand and stuffed it in her back pocket.

"I need to think this through, Joan."

"Phone sex or the Eddie-Sara story?" Then Joan laughed as she walked away. "You're on the clock. Shit or get off the pot."

Cecilia didn't like waffling, but she felt the pressure from both ends. She wanted nothing more than to break this story, but it would have far-reaching repercussions. She picked up the phone and dialed Sara's number. Just as the answering machine picked up, Sara said, "Hello."

"I'm not sure what to do with your story," Cecilia said.

Sara sounded out of breath. "I can't talk right now, Cecilia. I want to, but I've got somewhere to be. I'll call you when I can."

The clock ticked, and Cecilia felt unsettled.

She pulled the fax out of her pocket. Pete's perfect handwriting. Three perfect words.

I forgive you.

CHAPTER 41

"MICKEY" BY TONI BASIL

Bisbee, Arizona
November 1996

It didn't take Sara long to find him.

Cecilia had mentioned Bisbee, Arizona, at the beginning of Eddie's taped interview. She also mentioned a bar. She wished she didn't know his whereabouts, but knowing was knowing, and she couldn't shake the feeling that she had to see him. Abel had called that night to check on her, and when she told him about Cecilia James, he asked her one question: "Do you love him?"

"Yes."

"Then you need to go to him."

The next day, she booked a flight, and Eleanor joined, refusing to let Sara take the journey alone. After they'd settled into their hotel, Eleanor ushered Sara through the door of the St. Elmo Bar. She did a quick sweep of the dimly lit room, searching for Eddie, before warning Sara to be careful. "I'll be at the hotel if you need anything."

Sara assured Eleanor she'd be fine, they hugged, and Eleanor whispered in her ear, "You're fierce and strong, Sara. Don't you ever forget that."

Elliot guided her toward the bar and an empty seat, and there he dropped by her feet. Sara ordered a shot of tequila and anxiously waited to feel Eddie's presence. When she heard the clatter of the glass landing on the counter, she picked it up and pressed it to her lips, swallowing it down in one quick swig. The warm liquid flooded her bloodstream, easing her nerves.

The last time she had planned to surprise Eddie, she had been a different person. Today she didn't think about what she was wearing or how to style her hair, though she hid her eyes behind tortoiseshell sunglasses. And while she couldn't see her surroundings, she could sense the camaraderie among the bar patrons, the warm, amiable way in which they laughed and mingled. There was something peaceful and cozy about Bisbee, so she wasn't entirely surprised that Eddie had landed here. The Lovin' Spoonful played on the jukebox, and she wondered if Eddie was listening. Did he hear the lyrics asking if they believed in magic?

She had come to Bisbee because she needed to know. She needed to know why he broke things off. And she needed to assure him that it didn't matter. She still loved him. And she believed he just might love her too.

The bartender enlisted her in small talk. "What brings you to these parts?"

"I came to find an old friend."

"Anyone I can help you with?" he asked.

She shook her head at the same time she felt someone approach. She had a sensation of warm, familiar heat. "It's really you," the voice said, drawing closer. "I told you Times Square couldn't shine as bright as you." The man behind the bar laughed. "Come up with a better line than that, Carlos."

Carlos. She inhaled an old, familiar scent mingled with something new and foreign. He hovered, and she dared not turn in his direction. But she felt him. Every inch of her recognized Eddie.

"She told you where to find me."

"Sort of."

He touched her hand, and she jumped. "Look at me," he said.

She couldn't. There'd be nothing but a hazy shadow. But her other senses were keenly aware. She felt his energy pulsing against hers.

"Please look at me," he said again.

"I can't."

In their physical proximity, she felt as though they'd never parted, and the sheer power of her feelings terrified her. That and what Eddie's reaction would be when he learned the truth.

She stood up. And when she did, the dog at her feet stood too.

"Eres tan hermosa," he said, and she felt his fingers near her face, but she was quick, her hand shooting up.

"You can't stop me from looking at you," he said.

That wasn't what she was doing. Her palm found his chin and spread along his face. She felt the changes in him, the fullness of his cheeks, the sadness he'd been dwelling in. She brushed his beard, stroked the skin near his forehead. The lines told his story.

"You're still so beautiful," he said. "Take off your glasses so I can see you."

She stumbled to find the right words. "I can't see you."

"Yes, you can," he said. "You're here—"

"No," she said, dropping her head, wanting to put off this conversation. She quickly changed the subject. "Sing me a song, Eddie. Tell me another story."

"I don't need to go up there. We can get out of here . . . We can be alone and talk."

Sara pretended not to hear. She wanted to keep the truth from him a little longer. "Just sing me the song," she pleaded. He moved closer.

"Sarita," he said, leaning in and brushing her ear with his lips. Hearing the name he'd given her all those years ago weakened her, brought forth a trail of memories. He continued to press, reaching for her hand, his smooth skin warm and familiar. "See what you do to me? *Ven conmigo.*"

The shouts of the impatient crowd surrounded them. They begged him to play. "CARlos! CARlos!"

"Stay for the set?" he asked.

She said she would. "But sing the song, Eddie."

"I can't sing that song, Sarita. I'm not that man anymore."

"Maybe you are," she whispered.

Elliot guided her toward an empty seat at a round table. She wasn't surprised Eddie hadn't picked up on her condition, since people tended not to see what they didn't want to see. Tonight she had put Elliot's harness on, announcing her condition, but the bar was probably dark, and Eddie likely didn't notice. She was sure he was so startled to find her there that he didn't consider anything else.

The room was noisy, and Sara smelled cigarettes and barbecued chicken. A strong whiff of beer. The loud sounds clamored in her ears, but all she wanted was to hear Eddie. Eventually he greeted the crowd with a little more twang than when they'd spoken earlier. Someone whistled. Someone else hollered his name.

Time stood still as Eddie strummed the first notes on the guitar. It wasn't their song. It was Steve Winwood's "While You See a Chance," and she wondered if he'd chosen it to deliver a message.

His voice had grown deeper, and he was still so talented. She felt a pang of envy for all the women who had come after her.

Upon finishing the set, he found her at the table. She couldn't keep up the charade much longer.

"Eddie, there's something you need to know."

"There's something I have to say first."

And soon his fingers laced through hers, and she could barely breathe, touching him again.

"Sarita. *Tu madre.*"

She could tell by the wobble in his voice that he was nervous, that whatever he was about to say was important.

"Your mother," he said again, this time in English.

His fingers tightened around hers.

"She saw us that night."

The thrill of her hand in his turned into a quiet terror spiking through her entire body. She stiffly asked him to go on.

"She waited until you were back in the building, and then she came after me. She was screaming . . . yelling . . . she told me to stay away from you. I told her that wasn't possible. I told her we loved each other. She was furious."

Sara bowed her head. "Just say it. What did she do?"

"She had *Abuelo* arrested."

Sara froze, and when she tried to speak, no words came out. She thought she might be sick, and her hand came over her mouth. When she finally found her voice, she asked, "For what?"

"*Abuelo* had a key to your apartment. He was there that day, working on something, I don't know what, but she accused him of stealing some jewelry. Earrings, I think. It was easy for her to blame him."

A seething anger spread through Sara's veins. The police cars that night. The commotion on the beach. Her mother, so scared, so afraid to lose her, had cruelly interfered. This was far worse than Sara had imagined, and her throat burned with tears. "How could she?" Her mother had selfishly twisted their fate in her hands.

"They didn't find any earrings in his possession, but she already knew they wouldn't. She even bailed him out, but not without another threat. She mentioned friends in high places who could force him out of the country if I didn't end things with you. Stay out of your life forever."

"She threatened to have you deported? Could she do that?"

He didn't answer. He didn't have to. And the silence stretched as Collective Soul played on the jukebox. She had no way of knowing that

Eddie, in that instant, had finally noticed the dog by her feet and the bright-red harness with the telling letters. She was busy wondering how Shira could possibly do such a hateful thing to Carlos, someone who had been nothing but kind to them, a loyal, hardworking man. But she already knew the answer. Shira would have done anything to preserve her family, to keep the outsiders out.

So when Eddie asked her again to take off her glasses, she had no idea that he knew her secret, and she shook her head and kept talking. "Is that why you moved? Was he fired?"

"Please, Sara. I need you to take off your glasses." Something in his tone had changed.

"No. I need you to tell me what happened with Carlos."

Color Me Badd's "The Earth, the Sun, the Rain" played, and the mood of the crowded bar transformed, or maybe it was their table.

"*Abuelo* was fired," he said. "And I knew what I had to do. We had to break up. I had to let you go. And I knew you would fight me, so I told you we were leaving for Argentina, because a part of me believed we were going to be sent back. And you were so stubborn, you couldn't accept that, so I lied. I lied about not loving you."

She had always known he had lied, but what did it matter when he was gone? And what should have made her feel better only made her feel worse. "Where'd you go? I called . . . I sent letters."

"Mr. Feinstein arranged for us to stay with him. He convinced *Abuelo* not to move back to Argentina, and he helped him find another job and pushed me toward music. We found a place to live. We changed our names. And I hated every second of it, but I learned to live without you. I couldn't let *Abuelo* suffer for our mistake."

Disbelief coated her words. "We loved each other."

"I learned to live without you. I didn't say I was good at it. *Abuelo* gave me everything, Sarita. Without him . . ." His voice cracked. And she felt her love for him growing even stronger.

"There had to have been a way," she said. "There had to have been a way for us."

"I didn't think I had a choice. I was a kid, and your mother . . . I couldn't lose *Abuelo*—"

"So you lost me instead."

The words of the song landed between them, and he sang along, about gazing into her eyes and seeing the beauty God had created.

And before she could stop him, he took the glasses from her face. "I want to look you in the eyes when I tell you how sorry I am for what I did, Sarita. But you can't see me, can you? That's what you meant before. You didn't mean you can't be my girl. You meant you can't see me."

Her body slackened, and he pulled his chair around so they could touch. His arm came around her shoulders, and she felt Eddie on every inch of her skin. Exhaling, she released all the secrets, the sadness spilling out, and he pulled her close, whispering in her hair. "Tell me."

"I don't know how."

"Just say it."

"I can't see you."

"What happened?"

Her voice trembled. "When you broke things off with me, Abel was there. I was in too much pain to think clearly. And with Abel it was easy. I loved him. It was a different kind of love. And I cared about him. You took a big part of me."

"I'm sorry."

"I thought I could be happy, Eddie. And I was writing, channeling all those . . . feelings . . . into beautiful stories." She paused. "Abel didn't like my stories. I think he thought they were all about you. Maybe they were. There was so much passion and *life* in them. They shed light on our differences. Our distance was magnified. We fought constantly over it."

"That must have been hard."

She shook her head. "Nothing was harder than losing you. But I knew I had to leave. I didn't love him. Not the way I wanted to, not the way a wife should, and I was slowly dying." She hesitated. "And then I saw that you were performing at the Orange Bowl."

She dropped her head, and in that second, he knew.

"Oh my God. Sara."

"I was in the seventh row, close to the stage, when they started running toward you. I was pushed to the ground. My head hit the bleacher, and I lost consciousness."

The air around them shifted, and she went for his hand, but it was gone.

"I thought I was going to surprise you . . ." Her voice trailed off. "I don't know what I thought. I had some crazy idea you'd spot me, and we'd have some sort of reunion. That you'd explain what happened, and I'd tell you I still loved you, have always loved you . . ."

"Sara, I did this to you."

She heard the shock in his voice and felt him back away. She imagined tears filling his eyes, like the ones that fell for his parents, for the people lost at the stadium that day. "You didn't do this to me. No one did this to me. It was a horrible accident. And I didn't want you to know, I didn't want you to carry the burden, but now—"

"How come I didn't know? The injured were listed in all the papers and all the lawsuits." And before she could answer, he figured it out. "Your family. They knew I'd find you."

She nodded, and Eddie was silent, and she felt him slipping away.

"I can see when I'm with you," she said. "Like when we were kids. Do you remember? How we saw things no one else could? We've always been bound inside."

Eddie took his time responding, and it tore at her heart.

"That night," he said. "After the show. I was planning to find you. But then . . . my life fell apart . . . and now . . . I can't believe I did this to you . . ." His voice trailed off, and Sara heard his chair scrape against the floor. The crowd began chanting his name. He had to return to the stage.

"Go," she said. "But come back."

She felt him rise from his seat, and she heard how pleased the crowd sounded when he stepped on the stage. He fumbled with the microphone, and the room waited in silence. He was taking longer than he should, and she wondered if he had left, walked out, the truth too much of a burden. But then she heard the guitar. The first few notes. And Carlos, Eddie Vee, began playing the song that had captivated a generation and ruined his career. And the small crowd went wild.

The girls next to Sara exclaimed, "Holy shit. He sounds just like the guy from High Tide. What was his name?"

Sara whispered, "Eddie Vee" to herself.

"That can't be," another one said. "He doesn't look anything like him."

But it was Eddie. Her Eddie. And they were on the beach, and he was kissing her hair, her mouth, her neck, and she knew by the way he sang the song that he still loved her and they would figure out a way to move on. They would finally be together again.

The crowd screamed and clapped, unsure of what they'd just heard, and he continued to play another thirty minutes of covers that could never compare to "What You Do to Me." When the set ended, she waited for the applause to die down and for Eddie to make his way over to her table. She sat patiently. Voices once loud and shrill turned soft and timorous. Sara felt the space around her opening up, sensed that the crowd had fled. She reached for Elliot, patting him on the head. She thought about what her mother had done and how at one time she might have picked up the phone to confront her, but they'd just had the High Holidays, and Sara relied heavily on forgiveness. Shira was in poor health. Maybe they'd have the conversation one day, maybe not, but what would it change? She didn't need to condemn her mother, especially now that she was here with Eddie.

Time stretched, and the bartender finally approached. "Lady, we're about to close up."

And the shock that he hadn't returned paralyzed her, snatched her breath. He couldn't do this to her again. He couldn't walk away. But he had. She bit back the tears, the familiar ache. Seeing her like this must have wrecked him further. Elliot buried his face in her lap, and as she struggled to her feet, all she could think about was losing Eddie a second time.

CHAPTER 42

"BUDDY HOLLY" BY WEEZER

Los Angeles
November 1996

Three words, but they brought so much satisfaction. Pete forgave her. Cecilia held on to them as she entered her father's house, immediately sensing the change in the air. As she dropped her bag on the floor, Mathilda wound around her legs, and she bent down to scratch her behind her ears.

"Is that you, Cecilia?" came a voice from the kitchen. "Your father's in his room."

The house was quiet but for Mathilda's purring and the faint sounds of the girls playing in the backyard. She was excited to see them.

When she reached the bedroom, she found Don asleep, the *Rolling Stone* with Tupac Shakur on the cover fanned out across his chest.

She sat next to him and whispered, "Daddy."

Don's eyes fluttered open. "Cecilia."

He offered her his hand, and she took it in hers.

"I'm glad you're here," he said, squeezing her fingers.

"I'm glad you're here too," she said.

"Tori said you flew back to Miami. Did you get what you needed?"

"You mean did I nail the story? Uncover what no other investigative reporter could?"

He smiled, his blue eyes extra clear.

"You're damn right I did."

They sat like that, just like they used to do when she was younger, and Cecilia could feel his pride without his uttering a word. She wanted them to stay like that—not speaking, not discussing all that went wrong, but she knew they couldn't.

"I know Tori filled you in," he said, "but we should talk about your mother."

Cecilia felt the familiar feelings swirl around her stomach, the anger that she had used to protect herself no longer a shield.

"There were things you didn't see. Unfortunate things."

The wound inside Cecilia widened as he detailed what no child should have to hear about her mother.

"Maybe I should've told you when you got older, but you worshipped her. I didn't want to take that from you."

"We were happy," Cecilia said. "I thought all those bright, shiny memories were because of us. Like there was magic under our roof."

"That magic had a name," he said, holding her eyes in his so she couldn't break away. "Your mother was sick, Cecilia. She liked to drink. A lot. Those bright lights you saw . . . the magic in our house . . . was alcohol."

Somehow, hearing it from Don made it more real than hearing it from Tori.

"That's why you always tucked me into bed, why it was always you and me at the beach, jumping over waves . . ." she said.

He finished for her, recalling the times he'd held her hand when they walked past the house with the mean dog, Izzy, in the driveway, and how they'd always sit through two or three movies on a Sunday afternoon. It was because Gloria was either drunk or hungover. And that's why it hurt so much when he left.

Once her father started telling her the story, he couldn't stop. How at first it was a glass of wine, a vodka, and then it turned into two or three, until he completely lost count. He reminded her how Gloria was always the life of the party, the one who woke her up in the middle of the night and let her dance with them under the flashing lights.

"She was fun and lively, until she wasn't. When she drank, her moods changed, and sometimes she got mean. I'd beg her to slow down, to get help, and she refused. But she was beautiful. That blond hair and gorgeous smile."

Cecilia caught the glint in his eyes.

"She saved the ugliness for me. She saved it for when we were alone. That carefree side of her was mostly chardonnay."

Cecilia hated white wine.

"I loved her so much—you loved her so much—I covered up for her, refusing to let you see that side. And she was tough. I threatened to leave, take you with me, and she'd threaten to hurt herself, take you away. I would never let anybody hurt you."

"The accident," Cecilia said. "She was drunk?"

"Gloria snorted a line of cocaine and swooshed it down with a bottle of vodka. Then she took you for a joyride."

The description made her wince. In her memory, Gloria had seemed so happy that day, riding down the highway, watching the ocean slip by. Cecilia had been happy too. She was with her beautiful mother, and they were singing at the top of their lungs while the sun kissed their cheeks.

Shaking the memory away, she tucked her hair behind her ears.

"I don't understand. She didn't get arrested? A DUI?"

"You two were driving down the coast, and she said she needed to take a bathroom break, so she veered into the hills, somewhere near Malibu. I think she must have gotten lost, and that's when she crashed into a tree. No one was around. When she saw you lying there, unconscious, she ran to find a pay phone and call me. I found you there. We took you to the hospital—"

"Didn't they wonder what happened to me?"

He stared down, unable to meet her eyes.

"You didn't tell them."

"We said you fell at the playground. Banged your head."

"What happened to the car?"

He looked up. "Does it really matter?"

Cecilia sat with this, neither of them talking. Her memory of the day was different from this. She had seen what she wanted to see.

"It's why I don't drive."

"You never had any desire. I figured the accident had something to do with it."

After a few minutes of silence, she began again. "Tori told me how you met. You two are full of surprises."

"I never cheated on your mother, CeCe. I left her. Never you. I had to save myself. I couldn't be in an abusive marriage."

This struck a dangerous chord in her. "Why didn't you think to save me? You left me to live with an alcoholic."

"I thought I was doing what was best for you. I thought taking you away from the mother you worshipped would hurt you worse. I trusted Daphne. She would've never let anything happen to you."

"Daphne wasn't my parent."

"I begged you to come live with us. You refused. You only wanted to be with Gloria. You threw tantrums, demanding to stay with her. What was I supposed to do?" He stopped to take a breath. "I didn't want to hurt you more than you'd already been hurt. I felt like such a failure, and I didn't want you to hate me more than you already did. I thought somehow I was protecting you.

"Your mother never drove again. She didn't have a car. And Daphne hid the keys to hers. Over and over she promised to sober up. I believed her. She tried so hard and there were glimpses of the old Gloria, but then it became too much for her. She overdosed."

Cecilia jerked her head. "That's not what happened. Mom had a—"

"Cecilia, your mother died of a lethal combination of pills and alcohol. I have the coroner's report to prove it."

Her entire body went limp.

"You told me she died of an aneurysm."

"How could I tell you the truth?"

Everything about her mother had been a lie. She couldn't sit with it, so she got up, legs shaky and weak, and stared out the window. "You had me believing she was this . . . this ethereal being." She turned back to him. "And I hated you. I hated you with every fiber of my being. If . . . if you had told me—"

"What would that have done? You loved her so much. I didn't want to take that from you. I could handle your mother's ridicule and scorn. But the only way I could've proved myself to you, shown you I was there—had always been there—was by sharing the truth, and that would've broken your heart. I couldn't tell you all the ugly things she had done. I couldn't do that. I loved your mother too. A hell of a lot. We had some great memories together. And we had you."

"I just don't understand why you didn't try harder."

He lowered his head. "I was wrong. I didn't make the best decisions. And I regret it. But at the time it seemed like I had no choice. I loved you so much I wanted to protect you. And I thought the best way I could do that was by letting you stay with her. Every day I worried about you. And every day I wondered if I'd done the right thing."

"You were right," she whispered, nearing the bed. "I'd already formed my opinion about you. I probably would've rejected you, but I wish you'd tried to change my mind."

She was barraged with old memories. The nights she refused to sleep over at his house. The awkward dinners when she'd barely speak. She was happier with Gloria.

He patted the space beside him, and she sat. "Daphne kept a good eye on you. She kept me informed about everything going on in that house. And that stack of letters. I made sure you knew how much I loved you. I had no idea your mother wasn't sharing them with you. Right after Aunt Denise died, we received the box in the mail. She had continued the nonsense your mother started. All that time, I thought you were reading them and just avoiding me."

Cecilia stared at the floor, anywhere but at him. "What about the last . . . what was it . . . ten years, Don?"

"It was eight. It's been eight years."

"Denise wasn't intercepting letters then."

"You're right, Cecilia. I was wrong. And I'm sorry."

She had to admit his apology lessened the anger she'd been carrying. But there was no disputing how her mother had had a role in this. How her trusted ally had orchestrated things so that Cecilia closed her father out. Even if he had tried, which he had on a few unremarkable occasions, she had lost interest. And she felt cheated and robbed.

"We missed out on a lot."

His eyes brimmed with tears. "She told you terrible things about me, and you were young and impressionable. Of course you believed her. You have to know there wasn't a day I didn't think about you. Not a single day. And I maintained my parental responsibilities, not because I had to, because I wanted to. CSU. Rent. Insurance. You were always my daughter."

How could Gloria have done this to her? To them? She sat back on the bed, angry and confused.

He reached over to touch her hand, but she wasn't yet ready to forgive.

Her entire childhood had just turned upside down. She was mad at Gloria and mad at him. And yet, a part of her loved Gloria. She was her mother. And she missed her terribly, and she wished she were here so they could talk this through.

The room began to spin. Her history, unraveling, was no longer hers.

They sat like that for a few minutes until he broke the silence. "I've loved having you here with us, Cecilia."

"Please. I'm not easy to have around."

"You're tough. I'll give you that. But you're loyal. And bighearted. And I appreciate the way you are with the girls. I see how much you care about them."

She looked up. "I love them. They were never the problem." She chose her words carefully. "But you have to understand how that little girl in me wanted her dad, and when she believed he abandoned her for a new family, it hurt."

"I understand."

"I read all the letters." Her voice lowered. "They made me really sad."

He squeezed her hand, and this time she let him. "Me too. Tori said you deserved to know the truth, no matter the fallout."

"She didn't deserve my anger either." And then she had to ask, "Remember that song . . . ?" And before he could name the title, she flashed back to the day. Stone Poneys. Linda Ronstadt. "She sang to you that she didn't want a boy who loved only her."

"Let's not go down that road, Cecilia."

The name Jack flitted through Cecilia's mind. Don and Gloria were arguing after the song ended. Cecilia had paid attention.

"She was with this Jack person?"

"Your mother was a passionate woman."

She dropped her head and thought about all the time she'd spent being disappointed in Don and idolizing Gloria and realized how wrong she had been.

And as if reading her mind, Don became her dad again. Passing along the lessons she needed to hear. Caring. "We both stand to learn a lot by seeing the people around us with clear eyes. None of us should be put on a pedestal. Every one of us is conflicted, limited, or ugly in some way. But that doesn't mean there isn't a lot of good. It's possible to be many things at once. It's called being human."

"Are you asking for my forgiveness?"

"I'm not talking about me. I'm talking about your mom. She was troubled, but she loved you deeply. Her imperfections made her one of the most beautiful women I know."

Cecilia wasn't sure she could forgive her mother. "She kept you away from me. She didn't let me read your letters. She *cheated* on you. And then made it appear as though *you* cheated on *her*. How can you be so forgiving?"

"Because you're here. And it's been the best few weeks I've had in a long time. Minus a heart attack. And I'm watching you come into yourself. Watching you succeed at a career you were meant for. You have to forgive—both of us—because if you don't, you're never going to completely heal. You're never going to let somebody love you. And you're never going to be able to love someone back. Completely. Take the best of your parents and you'll always find a way to fly."

Her throat felt dry, and she thought about Pete's three words: "I forgive you." She said quietly, "I just need some time to digest this."

"Take all the time you want. I'm not going anywhere."

CHAPTER 43

"867-5309/JENNY" BY TOMMY TUTONE

Bisbee, Arizona
November 1996

Once outside the empty bar, Sara gasped for air, wondering how she'd been so wrong about Eddie. She needed to move, to get out of there. Fast. Elliot guided her down the uneven sidewalk until he stopped, barking at something.

"Who's there?" Sara called out.

"It's me," Eddie said.

She was angry but relieved. "You left me in there. You can't leave a blind woman in an unfamiliar place."

"You've always been tough, Sara Friedman." His voice was hoarse when he continued. "But how do you expect me to feel, knowing I did this to you?"

The question was suspended in the cool air, and before she could answer, he threaded his arm through hers. She didn't fight him. She let him lead her down the street, Elliot in tow. The breeze picked up, the air became fresher, and the noises of the street faded behind them.

"There's a step coming up," Eddie said. "I mean, it's in front of us, and you need to step down." Then they were on a gravel road, the rocks crunching beneath their feet. It turned into a dirt road that climbed upward. Sara lost her footing a few times on the spotty patches of grass, but he held her steady.

A brisk wind blew around them, and she felt as though she was on the edge of a cliff, that if she took one more step, she could fly.

"Where are we?" she asked.

"This is where I come when I want to be close to you." He helped her to the ground, guiding her with his hands. "Will he run away?" he asked about Elliot.

"He'll never leave my side," she answered.

"I should've been more loyal," he said.

"Look what you did for *Abuelo*."

"That cost me everything. I shouldn't have had to choose."

"I understand you doing what you did."

"You shouldn't," he said.

"Of course I should. I love you."

She waited the excruciating seconds for his reply. "I'm afraid I don't deserve your love."

She tossed her head back as though she could see the sky. "Don't say stupid things. Just tell me what it looks like."

"This is so difficult, Sara."

"It doesn't have to be. Go on. Tell me."

"Bisbee's an old mining town—"

"I know that already. I did my research."

She could tell by his silence that he was confused, so she filled him in on learning braille. "I learned Spanish when I needed to, remember? And our codes. You do what you have to do. Tell me what it looks like. Why you picked here."

He sighed. "For starters, it's quiet. I'm away from the noise. Girls throwing themselves at me."

He laughed, which made Sara laugh too.

"That's a joke," he said. "I've let myself go."

She didn't care what Eddie looked like.

"The elevation here is just over five thousand feet. We're surrounded by hills and steep mountain ranges. Remember when we used to go to the rooftop of the Atlantic? With the city lights in one direction and the ocean in another? The world stretched out around us. That's how it looks now."

She liked that he used their past to orient her.

"But the sky, Sarita. It's . . . I wish you could see it."

"Is it anything like the sky when we used to walk the beach?" She remembered it so well. An inky canvas with a spray of stars.

"Almost as beautiful," he said.

"I see it," she said. "I feel it."

She longed to be on the beach, backed up against his chest, with his legs wrapped around her waist. And he must have wanted it too, because his arms came around her, the same way they'd watched sunsets and waves crashing onto the shore from their castle. She collapsed against him, holding on to the moment. His beard tickled her face, and he began to sing a song. Something she hadn't heard before.

"Half of my heart. The whole to my part . . . you make me who I want to be. You're all that matters to me."

"Did you write this?"

"You were always my muse," he said. And he continued, singing in her ear. "Let me whisper these words. You're my sun and moon. You're the air I breathe, and my heart's your home. You'll never be alone . . . we are made of stars. I'll love you from afar. No matter where you are."

"Eddie, you have to write your own songs again."

"Music's always hurt the people I love, Sara."

"You're wrong. Your music has power. It heals and it will heal you. And I'll be there. You won't be alone."

"I'm not sure that's the life I want anymore."

They talked about the victims, those who had perished that day, and Sara tried to help him understand that he had punished himself enough. It was time to forgive himself.

"What about you?" he asked.

"I'm okay, Eddie."

"You're not, Sarita."

"I'm here. I'm alive. And Abel and I are divorced."

Either Eddie didn't hear her, or Eddie was in shock. He waited a beat to answer. Sara imagined the two of them staying in Bisbee. She would write books with happy endings; he would write songs. They'd be safe from the cruelty of the world, living life in their untouchable cocoon. They needed to move on from the past. They needed to let go of all that had been taken from them and grab hold of what was still possible.

"I used to see you," he said, "in my dreams. In my head. When we got the contract with the record label, we had some big-shot attorney, and before I signed on the dotted line, I asked him if your mother had the power to deport Carlos. He said because *Abuelo* wasn't legal he would always be at risk. But he promised me he'd do anything in his power to stop her if it came to that.

"Then the accident happened. I blamed myself for those innocent people who died. I tried to do the noble thing, paying for funerals and sending money, and not just the money required by all the lawsuits. I didn't need the money anymore. My life was over.

"And I had hurt you so much. I knew how much. And the accident was my punishment. I thought, *I ruined her and now I'm ruined.* And now hearing about your eyes. Your beautiful eyes."

"They're still the same."

"You know what I mean. I don't deserve you. I never did. That was always our problem. But you know something, Sarita, I was already ruined. The day we said goodbye, I was never the same. The record deal, the money, the women, nothing could lessen the pain of losing you."

"It didn't have to be that way." She corrected herself. "It *doesn't* have to be that way. You're not blaming me for my mother's actions, and I'm not blaming you for what happened that day. That's because what matters is in here." She pointed at her chest. "When I'm with you, everything is bright. I see your face. I see us on the beach. And there's no darkness. I feel you, and that is enough."

Sara bit back a tear, unsure if she was getting through to him, but then she felt his hand curl around hers, and he turned her around, and she could feel his face coming close. First, his lips brushed her right eye, then the left. She imagined he tasted the salt.

"I'm sorry I left you at the bar. Hearing what I did to you . . . I wanted to erase it . . . not be the reminder of what you'd lost. I was ready to leave. My suitcase was out . . . dumping my clothes in there . . . and I found . . ."

He took her by the hands and lifted her up so she stood in front of him.

"I meant it when I told you I was going to New York after the Miami show."

He was so close, their noses practically touched. Sara felt invincible. Unafraid. Eddie would catch her.

"I made a mistake, and I needed to fix it. Apologize. Win you back. And then . . . you know . . . everything went to shit, and I knew there'd be no way to fix what happened." He paused. "I found something when I was packing my bag. I don't remember it making it to Bisbee, but it appeared. Funny how these things happen."

She felt him back up and he placed her hand on his closed fist. She slowly pulled at each finger until his palm spread open. Her entire body was alive, and she felt his outstretched palm. And she could feel the cloth, the texture, the raised letters. It was the bracelet she'd thrown at him all those years ago. *Be bold, be brave.*

"Had I made it to New York, I was going to ask you if you'd consider being my girl," he said.

Sara's broken eyes filled with tears. He took the bracelet and placed it around her wrist. In her mind she saw the words. She saw his brilliant blue eyes just as she had the night he had given it to her. She saw how much he loved her. How he'd never stopped.

She smiled. "You have no idea what you do to me. What you've always done to me."

"Now she's stealing my lines."

He inched closer, his mouth close to hers. "I know we need some time to get to know each other again. So think about it."

Their lips were about to touch when Sara stopped. "You want me to consider being your girl?"

"I do."

She'd waited too long to find Eddie again to waste any more time. "Then you have to promise me you'll consider writing music again. And giving me that house on the beach. And those four kids."

Eddie was silent, but Elliot must have sensed something big and let out a yelp.

"If I'm going to be bold and brave, so are you," she said.

Eddie took her hand and kissed each one of her fingers, slowly, deliberately. Then he dropped to one knee, and even though she couldn't see him, she felt him in every inch of her body. "Sara Friedman, you are the miracle. Will you marry me?"

They were kids on the beach holding hands with an ocean spread out before them. A blanket of stars scattered across the sky. And she slid down to meet him and kissed him, giving him her answer.

CHAPTER 44

"ANGIE" BY THE ROLLING STONES

Los Angeles
November 1996

Cecilia had only a few short hours to get back to Joan on the piece. In the morning, she would have to make a decision: the full story or no story. The deadline weighed on her, cutting into their family dinner and game of Monopoly.

Cecilia returned to her room full and satisfied, and not just because Tori had whipped up a serious lasagna with cheesy garlic bread. Feeling at peace, she took out the stack of letters and began to read through them again, savoring them with a newfound understanding.

It had to have been difficult for Don to receive no responses from her. And when they spent those rare occasions together, it had to kill him when she was distant and cold, only wanting to return home to her beloved mother.

As she thought about all they'd missed out on, she listened to Oasis sing about living forever, and she felt grateful to have been given more time. And then her cell phone rang. At first, she was thrilled at the idea of it being Pete, but it wasn't Pete. It was Sara. And Eddie.

They were giggling. Cecilia could feel their smiles through the phone, and she sat up straighter. "You're in Bisbee!"

"I am. And we would've never called so late, but we wanted to give you the green light."

"You followed your heart."

"I was bold and brave." Sara corrected her.

Cecilia cradled the phone, feeling every bit of their joy across the miles.

"Tell the world our story," Sara said. "All of it. Every word. We don't know how to thank you."

"I didn't do anything. You wrote this story. You brought it to life."

"Without you, we would've never found each other again."

"I think you might have," Cecilia said, feeling a lump form in her throat. "I'm happy for you both. Thanks for letting me know."

Sara filled her in on the rest of the story, how Shira had intervened, threatened Carlos. It was a story that only one of the best writers could have written, and Cecilia's heart swelled at their happiness.

"One more thing," Sara said. "You have to go to Pete. You have to go after what you want. Promise me you'll do that?"

Cecilia smiled, and when they hung up, she felt triumphant. Sara and Eddie made it real, proving that love wins, and love songs do come true.

Tori poked her head in the doorway, offering her a carton of Häagen-Dazs chocolate chocolate-chip ice cream and a spoon. "Good news?"

"The best," Cecilia said, patting the seat beside her on the bed. "I found the muse behind 'What You Do to Me,' and she and Eddie Vee are reconciling as we speak."

"That's fabulous, CeCe."

"Thank you." Then, "I don't deserve this, Tori."

"Sure you do. Everyone deserves ice cream."

But she didn't mean the ice cream.

"I had it all wrong. And I'm sorry. You didn't deserve my cruelty, and I hope you can forgive me."

Tori swiped at her eye. "You had what was given to you. That's not your fault."

"I'd feel better if you accepted. The apology."

Tori wrapped an arm around Cecilia. "I accept. I'll always accept."

They sat beside each other, and Cecilia relished the warm feelings.

"I don't want to make another mistake. I don't want to misjudge. I want to ask for what I want." She took a spoonful. "And I'm going to need your help."

~

Cecilia and Tori worked until the wee hours locating Cecilia's passport, finding a last-minute plane ticket that Tori insisted on paying for, and crafting a letter to Pete with her flight information that Tori would fax from her office (Cecilia no longer rolling her eyes at this). Satisfied with their efforts, Cecilia revised the article, adding Shira's interference, taking it out, then putting it back in again. But then she thought about the purpose of the piece, and she edited the breakup so Shira wouldn't be crucified by readers and went with the *I'm doing you a favor by letting you go* version. Only then did Cecilia sleep peacefully through those last hours of night.

Early the next morning, charged and ready, Cecilia eyed her suitcase, the building excitement nothing like how she'd felt before leaving for the cruise. She barely touched her breakfast and then got into the car with Tori, the girls, and an insistent pajama-clad Don. First they drove her to the office, where she planned to leave the completed piece on Joan's desk, not trusting email. To her surprise Joan was there, and when Cecilia handed it over, Joan beamed with a pride that almost made Cecilia weep.

"What's with the suitcase?" Joan asked.

Cecilia told her the plan, and she waited for a snarky remark, but Joan had softened. Somewhat. "Bring that boy home, Cecilia. You're going to need him after breaking this Eddie and Sara story wide open." And Cecilia waited ever so patiently for Joan to read the pages, and when Joan finally glanced up at her, expressionless, Cecilia had a flash of panic.

"This is excellent," Joan said. "This right here . . . Cecilia . . . I just might hug you."

And she did. Joan hugged her as though she couldn't let go. A warm rush washed over Cecilia, and she said her goodbye.

Back inside Tori's Volvo, the girls talked a mile a minute, asking questions about Pete, reminding her to *win him back.*

And when they reached the airport, Tori helped her with her suitcase, and the girls hugged her hard. When she leaned through the car window to say goodbye to her father, she told him she loved him. "All the good and all the bad." And he smiled, dropping a small bag inside her purse. "It's a little something for Pete. And for you. Make sure he gets it."

"I will."

Cecilia sailed through security and sat at the gate.

Once she'd made the decision to go, she had no doubt in her mind. Reconciling what had happened with her own parents and their marriage gave her clarity. And hearing from Sara and Eddie gave her the push, while crafting the perfect article gave her the confidence.

Pulling out the copy she planned to share with Pete, she read it one more time, relishing the accomplishment. At the end, Cecilia described the allure behind the love song.

> In my interview with Eddie Vee, he talked plainly of the girl who captured his heart. "She was the girl I couldn't have. My one true love. And there was only one way for me to tell her." I told him he had captured a feeling that all of us wanted

to be privy to. "What You Do to Me" will forever be about a momentous love, a question mark about what could be, and a deep dive inside a story we wish would never end. For all the romantics who may be wondering, Eddie alerted me that he proposed to Sara Friedman, and I just received word that she said yes.

The plane ride was long, and not even her favorite playlist could lessen Cecilia's impatience, but when she spotted Pete outside the terminal, waiting for her, tanned and smiling and delighted to see her, she felt complete in a way she never had before. He picked her up and twirled her in the air, and then he kissed her.

"I've missed you," he said.

"Not as much as I've missed you."

And that night, after they'd made love, Cecilia told Pete everything she couldn't say before. How the night of their dinner at Shutters she was too afraid to tell him that she really wanted him to choose the opportunity at *LIFE*. Never the war. But she was afraid of holding him back, afraid he'd say no. And she told him about the letters from Don and how it felt to learn he'd loved her all along, when she'd doubted that was possible.

"I read the letters in the hospital when I thought my dad was going to die. They opened my heart. Opened *me*. And I thought about something happening to you and never having the chance to tell you. Life is way too short, Pete. Sorry. Clichés sometimes fit. Fate twisted my past and the stars didn't always align, but I won't let that happen to us."

She took a breath, anxious to finish the rest, the most important part, the piece her father helped her understand, about forgiveness and letting someone in. "So if you haven't figured it out, I'm hoping you'll spend the rest of your life with me."

He smiled as though he had been waiting for this.

"Are you sure about that?" he asked.

"I'm positive."

"Did you bring me my gift? From your dad and Tori?"

Cecilia was confused, but her body felt electric. She smiled, her eyes dancing with his. She reached inside her purse and handed Pete the bag, watching him untie it with his nimble fingers.

"Now, you're sure?" he said. "About forever?"

And suddenly she knew. And she grinned, a big, silly grin because she wanted it to happen. His fingers disappeared inside the bag and pulled out a ring.

"When you moved out, I gave this to your dad." He seemed pleased with himself.

"Why would you do that?"

"I knew you'd come to your senses. I waited. As patiently as I possibly could. I knew it had to be your decision."

"You were all in on this?"

"All of us. Don. Tori. April. Joan. And Hazel and Phoebe. They said it would be the best way to win you back."

Cecilia covered his mouth with hers, and they didn't part, but Pete managed to slip the ring on her finger, and he may have asked her to marry him, and she may have said yes as the moon smiled down on them, and he whispered, "I'll find you in every lifetime, Cecilia James. TTM."

CHAPTER 45

"SARA SMILE" BY HALL & OATES

New York
2023

Cecilia stands at the podium, nervousness crawling up her spine. She doesn't normally get nervous. But seeing this man at the back of the room who so closely resembles her lover makes her quake inside. It's been a long time since they've seen each other. She never stopped loving him, and she resists his pull, all the memories and feelings flooding back.

Cecilia focuses on her speech. About music. About chances, choices, and risks. About acknowledging what's right in front of you. And fighting for it. She mentions some of the songs featured in her column over the years and their relevant backstories. "Jack & Diane." "Maggie May." "Danny's Song." And of course she mentions the couple who became the impetus for the column. She mentions them by name. She's formed a close relationship with the pair, godmother to their four grown children. She also asks the members of the Grammy Award–winning band the Hails to stand at their seats so she can properly acknowledge them. "Andre," she says, "when we met, you invited me to a showcase for your band the following day. You said, and I'll quote you, 'Tomorrow just might change your life.' And it did. In some good ways, and some not so good. I think that's the thing about life. About relationships. About music. We never know what we're going to get, but if we find a way to turn it into something that matters, we win."

When her speech comes to a close, she thanks her father and Tori, Hazel, Phoebe, and their spouses and kids, and, of course, Penelope. April and Arthur are the first to stand, clapping. Cecilia lets the applause embrace her, fill her with courage, and she heads to the outdoor patio where he waits. He looks the same as he did all those years ago. His smile is extra wide. Their reunion is bittersweet as Pete whispers in her ear, "I'll always love you, Cecilia Caroline James." And she lets him in. All in. Knowing that she can trust love, trust him. Cecilia couldn't always see him before, but she's able to see him now. Clearer than ever. She tells him she loves him too. That she will always love him. That she is who she is because of that love. The door swings open, and Penelope heads in Cecilia's direction with Sara and Eddie's youngest, nineteen-year-old Ilan. He looks just like Eddie, his yarmulke resting on his dark locks. When they're close, Cecilia overhears Ilan asking Penelope why her mother's talking to herself. "Is she crying?"

Penelope whispers, "She always does this at these things. She talks to my dad."

EPILOGUE

After their reunion in 1996, Cecilia flew home, and Pete made plans to return to the States, to *LIFE*. The turn of events was symbolic, as less than six weeks after her return, the doctor confirmed what she had suspected. New life had hitched itself inside her, and a pregnancy test confirmed the news. Cecilia was having Pete's child. Tori went with her to the appointment, and they wrapped their arms around each other and cried. And laughed. And cried some more. But not more than when Cecilia greeted Pete at the airport and they hugged, their creation pressed between them.

Cecilia and Pete had four great years. She, writing her famed column, mining hidden stories, and he, photographing for *LIFE*, up until the final 2000 cover. Penelope was a delight of a baby with her head of dark curls and matching eyes, and Don, Tori, and the girls doted on her, babysitting whenever they could. Their life was happy and full. Music filled every crevice, and Pete documented every baby step with his camera.

After *LIFE*, Pete was quickly scooped up by *TIME*. Which should have meant more but unfortunately became less. Cecilia begged him not to go. "It won't be long," he said, and Penelope plopped on his lap.

"Stay with me, Daddy." But he kissed her soft cheeks, kissed Cecilia's lips, and flew out to Afghanistan a second time for a story. The kind that kept him awake at night. The kind that would boost his career. Cecilia couldn't hold him back. She loved him too much.

A few weeks after he left, she woke up in a cold sweat, an ominous ache inside her chest. She went to Penelope's room, curling up beside her, soaking in her daughter's fresh scent. And the next day, after several attempts to reach Pete went unanswered, his boss confirmed what Cecilia already knew. Pete was gone. He'd been killed when insurgents overran their base. That same day, Penelope had gone to the mailbox to retrieve the mail—it had become her favorite activity—and she was thrilled to find a letter from her dad to give to her mom.

CeCe and P,

I miss you girls. Twenty-two days until we're eating ice-cream cones and dancing to Mommy's favorite songs. I hope you're behaving. I mean you, CeCe. P, make sure Mommy isn't working too hard, that she's serving you vegetables at dinner and not just In-N-Out Burger. Remind her about the sunsets on our deck. Take it all in. You have no idea how much worse it can be. Trust me. I know.

Tonight, I sat outside staring up at the sky and there were a million stars. It reminded me of you girls, of home, and this is the part you can stop reading out loud, Cecilia. Tell Penelope I'll be right back.

Hi. I've been thinking about us, and I think we should have another baby. P needs a little brother or sister. I need more of you running around my house. So what do you think?

Now you can read aloud again.

P, did you know your mom speaks in lyrics? I didn't understand it when we first dated, but I do now. My girl speaks in song, capturing feelings too big to explain. There was a song playing last night as we drove through the mountains to a new camp. I didn't have a way to write the words down, but he was singing to a woman. Her name was Cecilia. I'll try to remember, but it's for the two of you: No matter where life takes you girls, and I know it will be great places, don't be scared. Look up. And I'll be the star in every single sky.

TTM,
Daddy

AUTHOR'S NOTE

While there are real-world people and places featured throughout the novel, I have taken the liberty of using creative license to merge fact and fiction. You'll find places where I've changed locations and/or dates to create the story I wanted to tell. For example, *Rolling Stone* does not have a Century City office, the Hails did not come on the music scene in the nineties, and places like Almar's Bookstore have been moved in either time or location. One of the things I most enjoy about writing fiction is integrating imaginary worlds with real-life moments, providing a place where readers can suspend their disbelief and travel to magical places.

Music has a similar effect. When I was much younger, I didn't always have the right words for what I felt. Sometimes the emotions were too big, and the only way I could sort them out was through a song. With tunes and lyrics, I finally felt heard and understood. So to write a book combining both these mediums has been a dream come true.

Like many of you, I fell in love with "Hey There Delilah" by the Plain White T's when I first heard it on the radio back in 2006. Like Cecilia, I had to know the story behind the lyrics. Every description of the soulful song in the novel is real. I felt every word when Tom Higgenson sang. The haunting rhythm was laced with longing and nostalgia. When we learned how Tom met the real Delilah at a bar in

Chicago, promising to write her a song even though she had a boyfriend, it sparked a lot of conversation. "Hey There Delilah" wasn't based on a real-life fairy tale, but we can all agree that it remains a beautiful love song.

So what if there was another story behind the song? What if, as a writer, I could reimagine the names, the dates, the players, and fate, giving readers the fairy tale? That became the basis for *What You Do to Me* and the tale of this star-crossed couple. Eddie Vee did not write this magical song. It was all Tom. Tom Higgenson and the Plain White T's. And for anyone who has had a connection to a song, believed in its words, or found their own interpretation, this story is for you.

Like "Delilah," the song title at the beginning of each chapter includes a name. I've always believed that the songwriter was inspired by someone, real or imaginary, so much so that it inspired music. Those chapter titles are the reminders of those individuals who impacted a life enough to write about it.

I write books about people and places and experiences. Songwriters write music about the same. They write about love and friendship and loss and pain. They write of sunshine and forgiveness. We are all writers sharing our feelings with the world. We are storytellers.

ACKNOWLEDGMENTS

Thank you to my editor Danielle Marshall for believing in me and this book. Your unwavering support and enthusiasm kept me going, and I am grateful for that and for you.

Jane Dystel, may this be the first of many successful books together.

Thank you to Jodi Warshaw, Tiffany Yates Martin, Jen Bentham, and the team of copyeditors and proofreaders who make me wish I had paid more attention in English class. And to Gabriella Dumpit for always taking care of our Lake Union family.

Doug Cohn, when the idea to showcase "Hey There Delilah" came up, I knew you'd find a way to make it happen. And you did. I owe you well beyond any thank-you or acknowledgment.

Tom Higgenson, the Plain White T's, and Warner Chappell's Carianne Marshall, Johnny Navas, and Michael Worden, there would be no story without you. I imagined a happy ending for the "Hey There Delilah" song, and you trusted me to deliver. Thank you for the gift of this magical song. Tom, I'm working on that album. Wink.

This novel required additional assistance, research, and fact-checking, and I am indebted to those who offered their generous time and insights: Jodi Peckman, Dr. Ron Berger, Dr. Richard Berger, Lynne Kolodny, Monique Chera, Amy Gelb, Amy Berger, Andy Okun, Bettina and Jerry Hollo, Leah Aaronson and Joe Powell, Joelle Berger, and Ken Komisar.

Lisa Petrillo, I'm touched to be able to share the gift of the Hails. For more on this talented band, please visit www.thehailsofficial.com.

Izzy Goihman. When I asked, you wrote a song, and I'm so happy we found a place to highlight your gift. Cliff Whitakker. When we weren't sure "Delilah" was going to pan out, we had to bring in a singer-songwriter—the pinch hitter. Because of your incredible talent, you nailed the song. Readers can find you and your music at ffm.bio/cliffwhitakker.

Dr. David Leeman. Somehow, I flubbed your name in the acknowledgments for *When We Let Go*, so here is my apology and sincere gratitude for the medical advice.

Thank you Ann-Marie Nieves for your PR prowess, Heather Wheeler-Sadlemire for the promotional tutorials, and M. J. Rose for the valuable guidance, without which this book probably wouldn't exist. Lauren Margolin and Jamie Rosenblit, thank you for the best book recommendations and for being two of my favorite people. Zibby Owens, Renee Weingarten, and Suzy Leopold, I appreciate your friendship and support. Liz Fenton, your advice and guidance were invaluable.

Thank you to the booksellers, bookstagrammers, influencers, reviewers, podcasters, and bloggers who have recommended my books or invited me into their worlds. I appreciate all that you do. Readers, I wouldn't be here without you. I cherish every text, post, email, review, and connection. Thank you for making my dream come true.

The author world is a large, generous community, and there are so many whom I admire and consider friends. I wish I could list every single one of you, but inevitably I'll leave someone out, which for someone like me would be devasting. You all deserve the praise. So thank you to every one of you.

I couldn't have survived the last year without the constant support, advice, and friendship of Merle Saferstein, Camille Di Maio, Samantha Woodruff, Lisa Barr, Allison Winn Scotch, and Andrea Katz. Thank you for always providing the hard truths along with your great wisdom. To my friends, especially Barbara, Stephanie, Mindy, Liz, Erika, Wendy, Jill, Joni, and Diane, thank you for understanding "I'll call you when I break." Arleen, thank you for trying to be at every single event.

To the RB5, Randi, Rob, and Ron, you are my siblings, but you're also my best friends, the team that raised me in so many ways. The closeness we share gets me through the toughest times, and I just know that Ruthie B is paying close attention, and she's smiling.

To my Berger-Weinstein family, thank you for always supporting me, being there, showing up, and providing the love, laughs, and encouragement. Special shout-out to David Weinstein, who regularly shares his support as though my work is more important than that of a renowned pediatric endocrinologist who cured a disease.

Bear, Jordan, and Brandon. It's not always easy being the lone woman in a house of blue, but you have shown me your sensitive pink sides, and I am grateful every single day to share this colorful world with you. Every story I write is a love letter to you—proof that love exists. Never doubt that you're deserving of it. Be bold. Be brave.

BOOK CLUB DISCUSSION

1. What song brings you back to childhood? A favorite memory? A first love?
2. Have you ever googled the meaning behind a song? Did the answer meet your expectations, or were you totally off? Share the song.
3. Name a song title that would be your current theme song.
4. In your family, was it important for you to marry within your religion? What about your children? Do you expect them to marry someone of the same faith? Why?
5. If you could run off with a musician, who would it be?
6. What was your first concert? Did anything special happen there?
7. Have you ever subscribed to *Rolling Stone* magazine? Do you still read magazines? Which are your favorites?
8. There's a lot about perspective, being able to see things clearly, and things not being what they seem in the novel. How did Cecilia and Sara both deal with these circumstances?
9. What are your thoughts on Don leaving Cecilia with Gloria? Do you believe he was young and thought he was

doing his best? Or do you think he was being selfish and shortsighted?

10. Have you ever experienced any form of discrimination or prejudice in your life? How did you handle it?

11. Why do you think Cecilia had such loyalty to her mother? And was it loyalty? Or was it fear? How did that affect her relationship with Don?

12. Shira influenced Sara and Eddie's relationship in unforgivable ways. How do you feel about Sara's decision to forgive? To just let it go?

13. Eddie struggled with leaving his grandfather, while Sara had a wanderlust she couldn't tame. Whom did you relate to in their approaches to family?

14. Some parents are stricter than others for whatever the circumstances. Which do you think is the most effective approach? How were you raised? Your children?

15. Is there a location where you and your family travel for holidays? Is it an annual trip? What's so special about it?

16. In the novel, the characters have to "lose" things to find themselves. Do you feel that is an effective character arc? How did we see Cecilia and Sara grow from this?

ABOUT THE AUTHOR

Photo © 2018 Hester Esquenazi

Rochelle B. Weinstein is the *USA Today* and Amazon bestselling author of seven women's fiction novels, including *When We Let Go, This Is Not How It Ends,* and *Somebody's Daughter.* A former entertainment industry executive, she splits her time between sunny South Florida and the mountains of North Carolina. As Miami's NBC *6 in the Mix* monthly book contributor, Rochelle is on the hunt for the next great read while she teaches publishing workshops at Nova Southeastern University. She loves hiking, beach walks, her two dogs, and finding the world's best nachos. She is currently working on her eighth novel. Please visit her at www.rochelleweinstein.com.